A KISS TO REMEMBER

Jason rose. Instead of helping her, he had added to her pain. He turned and saw her slumped on the couch, softly crying, and he knew he couldn't leave her. In four steps he reached her side. He gathered her into his arms.

"I know . . . I understand." Her tears wet his shirt. He murmured in her ear, not words, but sounds he hoped were comforting. Her curls brushed his lips. Her hair smelled of coconut and brought visions of tropical isles, sunlight, and her body glistening with oil.

"I'm sorry. I didn't mean . . ." She looked up. Her green eyes glistened.

He continued stroking, feeling the silky material of her caftan against his palms. He bent his head. His lips found hers and the light kiss he had meant to offer, the friendly gift of sympathy, exploded like a forest fire burning away everything except a desire to claim, to possess and to be possessed.

"Maggie, Maggie," he murmured. He slid his hands up her arms and cupped her face. "Beautiful."

THE BEST MEDICINE

JANET LANE WALTERS

ZEBRA BOOKS
KENSINGTON PUBLISHING CORP.

ZEBRA BOOKS are published by

Kensington Publishing Corp.
475 Park Avenue South
New York, NY 10016

First Printing: July, 1993

Printed in the United States of America

To Jane Toombs, who issued a challenge I couldn't resist. To Kathy and Renee, who kept me on track. And to Denny, Keith, Scott, Sharon, Veronica, and Ashley, who have lived and suffered with me.

One

Maggie Carr pulled the last nursing textbook from the box and placed the thick volume on the unit that covered one wall in the living room of her new condominium. Hoping to erase the dull, aching throb in her head, she massaged her temples with her fingertips. All week, doubts and second thoughts had swarmed around her like mosquitoes. Had she made the right choice? A year ago, returning to nursing had seemed the perfect way to support herself. Today, after two semesters at college to complete her B.S. in nursing and a month's refresher course, she still felt unsure of her skills.

A cold blast from the air conditioner raised gooseflesh on her arms. Beads of moisture condensed on the sliding doors leading to the balcony. Another humid July night.

She retreated to the doorway into the hall. Her

nose wrinkled. The smell of newly purchased and as yet unused possessions filled the air. Very little belonged to the years of her marriage except two spool vases filled with red plastic flowers and a pair of plaster handprints made years ago by the twins.

The mantel clock chimed. Maggie braced her hands against the door frame and counted. "Ten, eleven, twelve. Happy birthday." Her long sigh carried the wish that her fifty-second would be less traumatic than her fifty-first, the day her illusions had been shattered.

As she turned toward the kitchen, the phone rang. Her heart pounded. Beneath the weight of memories, her shoulder muscles knotted. Last year at this time, a phone call had roused her from sleep. "Mrs. Carr, Officer Greene, State Police. Could you come to the emergency room at West Shore Hospital? Your husband has been involved in an accident."

The words she had held inside for a year exploded in a shrill scream nearly as loud as the phone. "And he wasn't alone." Slowly, the memory receded.

With shaky steps she crossed the living room and reached for the phone. Twenty-nine years of marriage had ended with the realization that the whispers she had dismissed as jealous gossip were true. She sucked in a breath and lifted the receiver. "Hello."

The twins shouted their greetings in unison. Maggie sank down on the gray couch and felt a laser burn a tunnel through the ice she had packed around her emotions. There would always be a path to her heart for Ellen and Morgan.

"Thank you." Happiness colored her voice. "How did you manage this call?" The how of the triple phone hookup eluded her. Ellen was a first-year resident in Baltimore and Morgan was in Santa Fe, taking part in an opera workshop program.

"Mother, haven't you heard of three way? There are even conference calls for large groups." Ellen giggled. "Did your year in college keep you isolated from the latest in technology?"

"Just what belongs to the ordinary world," said Maggie. "I've been busy learning about respirators that have replaced iron lungs and computerized intravenous monitors that calculate drops instead of having to count."

Morgan laughed, and for a moment the deep sound held echoes of his father's laughter. Maggie's hand tightened around the receiver.

"Do you really think my sister could exist without the latest advance in phone technology? If they ever come up with phone transplants, she'll be the first in line."

"And tenors will be replaced by electronic voices that don't forget the words or miss the notes."

"Enough," said Maggie. "Before the pair of you start acting like two-year-olds, tell me what you've been doing." She sighed. "I miss you both."

For the next fifteen minutes the twins alternated bits of news about their lives. Maggie ran her fingers along the soft velvet of the couch and found the action soothing.

"How are you celebrating your birthday?" asked Morgan.

"Settling into the condo, having lunch with Laura, and battling an acute case of anxiety."

Ellen chuckled. "Shelve it. You'll do fine."

"I've been away from nursing too long."

"It's like riding a bike," said Morgan. "As we say, break a leg. Love you."

"Visit soon."

"I'll try."

"Me, too," said Ellen. "Just pretend your patients are your kids and you'll do fine. 'Bye."

For several minutes Maggie leaned against the back of the couch and visualized her children. Both had her russet hair and their father's blue-gray eyes. Gregarious Morgan charmed everyone, and quiet Ellen brought joy to those who knew her well. Maggie's sandal dropped from her right foot. She slid it back on, rose, and headed for the kitchen, where she unpacked dishes, glasses, pots, and pans and placed them on shelves lined with a pink and gray paper that matched the walls.

One month of days at Hudson General Hospital, she thought. Four weeks before she found refuge on the night shift. Sometimes the need to hide in darkness grew until her body ached.

The clock struck two before she reached the bedroom. For another hour she lay on the queen-size bed, fighting anger, rejecting shame, and trying to chase away an acute sense of guilt. Her hands clutched the sheets. Would she ever be able to grieve for the twenty-nine years lived as a lie?

A band of sunlight slid across Maggie's face. She rolled on her side and stared at the clock.

How had she managed to sleep until quarter to eleven? Laura was due soon and lunch still had to be prepared. Maggie grabbed her robe and padded across the teal carpet to the bathroom. Ten minutes later she finger-combed her wet curls and pulled on a dark green skort and a pale green knit shirt. She slipped her feet into her favorite sandals.

As she hurried to the kitchen, she thought about the last time she had seen Laura and how they had disagreed about the decision to remain in Hudsonville after the refresher course ended instead of returning to Long Island.

"Why stay? Because you've lived here for thirty years. Your friends are here."

11

What friends, she had wanted to shout. After George's death, the ones who had called and expressed the deepest sympathy had been the ones who over the years had dripped poisonous gossip about him. Why didn't Laura understand the need to be away from places filled with memories of George and the people who knew of her shame?

Maggie stood at the kitchen counter, waiting for the flurry of memories to dissipate. Selling the house, returning to school, and moving to Hudsonville hadn't erased the emotions she had carried for a year. The scene in the emergency room holding area—George on one stretcher and the young blond nurse on another—was planted in her memory with roots too deeply embedded to be pulled out.

She pressed the heels of her hands against her eyes. After forcing her breathing into the relaxation pattern learned in yoga class after the twins' birth, she felt the acute edge of her memories ebb. The clock struck eleven. Laura's coming, she thought. She assembled the ingredients for chicken salad with tarragon dressing and recalled Friday's conversation with her friend. "I'd like to see you Sunday, but—"

"I'll be there in time for lunch," Laura had said.

"It's a two-hour drive each way," she had protested.

"Don't argue. We haven't missed a birthday

12

lunch in years. You shouldn't be alone, and I'm sure you haven't made droves of friends yet."

Laura had been on target. Until yesterday, when Maggie moved into the condo, she had lived in a cramped studio apartment near Hudson College. The other women in the refresher program had been married, had families, and had lived in Hudsonville long enough to be part of the community.

Maggie cut chicken into chunks, minced celery, green peppers, and pecans. She tossed the ingredients with the tarragon dressing and added green grapes. When the doorbell rang, she had just put a pan of water on the burner.

"Laura." She hugged her friend. Laura's graying hair, cut short, feathered around her face. Maggie smiled. While she got a perm to curl her hair, Laura's hair treatments straightened hers. Keen brown eyes studied Maggie closely.

"Happy birthday." The petite black woman stepped back and nodded. "You win. The move was right for you. I swear, you've lost ten pounds in the last five weeks."

"All flattery is gratefully accepted." Maggie stepped aside to let her friend enter the foyer.

Laura handed Maggie two boxes. "Cannoli for dessert and a present." She walked to the living room doorway. "Nice. Have you ever considered interior decorating as an alternate career choice?"

Maggie laughed. "Are you reading minds

13

again? All week I've been fighting a desire to be anything other than a nurse."

Laura moved to the fireplace and stooped to stroke the small, jewel-tone Persian rug. The ruby and cobalt hues glowed against the pewter-gray carpet. "It's real silk."

"My final indulgence. Took the last penny of George's money." Maggie smiled. Laura's presence had sent gloomy thoughts scurrying into dark corners. Their friendship had been born the same night as the twins when Dr. Laura Richards had stepped in for the obstetrician who had been late.

"You've spent every cent?"

Maggie pursed her lips. "After paying his debts, there wasn't much left."

"But the house?"

"Had a large equity loan. Don't fret. Nurses' salaries have vastly improved since the last time I worked. I'm not going to starve."

"Open your present."

"Come to the kitchen while I put the finishing touches on lunch. Would you believe I overslept?"

"Good. You could do that for a month."

"And be late my first day of work?" Maggie put the cannoli in the refrigerator and dropped angel hair pasta in the boiling water. She poured two glasses of white wine. "Here's to a better year."

"And a brilliant new career." Laura touched her

glass to Maggie's. "Would you open your present?"

Maggie tore the paper from the box and pulled out a Sprague Rappaport style stethoscope. "Thanks. It's great, but don't you think I'll be accused of impersonating a doctor?"

"I got tired of that purple plastic thing you sported all last year. Instead of looking like Barbie plays nurse, you'll look professional."

"I'm not a blonde."

"You have a pair of similar attributes."

Maggie put her glass on the table. "Laura, I'm scared."

Laura's hand covered Maggie's. "You'll do fine. Just remember that buried beneath the fear is the terrific nurse I've heard stories about."

With an angry sputter the pasta water boiled over. Maggie turned to Laura. "Let's hope this isn't an omen." She turned off the fire, drained the pasta, and tossed it with olive oil. "I'm glad you came. I've missed you."

"And I you. Let's eat. Then I want a tour and a walk around town. On my way in, I saw some interesting antique shops." She tugged at the bottom of her yellow shorts. "What are your neighbors like?"

"I haven't met any yet."

"No men?"

"Or women, children, cats, or dogs." Maggie shook her head. "First let me learn to be myself."

15

"You've never been anything else."

Maggie served the salad and pasta. "I'll have to think about that." She wasn't sure who she was today or who she had been for the past year. Most days, she saw herself as an introspective woman afraid to reach for laughter or for life. She swallowed. Tomorrow she had to believe she was a nurse.

The next morning Maggie stood in front of the full-length mirror that hung on the bathroom door. She draped the stethoscope Laura had given her around her neck, hooking the bell between the earpieces. Would she ever present a picture of confidence and competence like the young nurses who had led the series of classroom lectures at Hudson College? She stared at her watch and willed the hands to move. Since four A.M., she had been awake, and she had been dressed since five-fifteen.

Anxiety kept her adrenaline at a near-panic level. She turned from the mirror and walked to the four-poster, canopied and draped with teal batiste. Six uniforms covered the bright floral bedspread. She had tried on her entire uniform wardrobe before deciding to wear a white scrub dress.

With a sigh she headed to the kitchen. After scraping an untouched egg into the garbage, she sat at the oval oak table and finished the cup of now-cold coffee. The piece of toast she had forced herself to eat lay in an undigested mass in her stomach.

Six-thirty finally arrived. Maggie drove along the nearly deserted streets of downtown Hudsonville. At six-forty she followed a line of cars into the employees' parking lot.

For several minutes she sat in the car and considered running like a mouse from a stalking cat. She practiced every relaxation technique she knew until the panic reached a manageable level. Then she trailed a group of nurses to the center section of the red brick hospital.

The automatic doors next to the emergency room entrance opened. Maggie entered. The blend of familiar odors that spoke of hospital gave her a sense of homecoming. In a brisk rhythm her new white oxfords tapped on the beige tile floor. She joined a group of women, many of them younger than her children, and waited for the elevator. Thirty years ago she would have been in the center of the group, sharing a dozen bits of gossip she had heard.

The elevator doors opened on two and three. Maggie inhaled and uncoiled her hands. On four she followed a strikingly attractive black nurse into the corridor leading to orthopedics.

The young woman smiled. "You're new. Private duty or agency hire?"

17

"Neither. A refresher assigned to Four Orthopedics."

"Am I ever glad to meet you. We need all the bodies we can get. I'm Charlene Rodgers."

"Maggie Morgan." With a quick intake of breath, Maggie realized she had used the name on the license she had renewed dutifully every year. She shook her head. "It's Carr. I've flipped and returned to the past."

"Glad to meet you, Maggie whoever." As Charlene reached for the door, a multitude of tiny braids swayed and white beads at the ends clicked against each other. "Locker room on the right. Lounge on the left. Purses are kept at the desk. There's always a pot of coffee and one of hot water for tea, plus a refrigerator for our lunches. Cafeteria food's the pits."

"Some things never change." As she watched Charlene's dancing braids, Maggie's tension ebbed an inch.

"Sorry to hear that. I always thought Hudson General held the patent on inedible food." Charlene grinned. "Bet the patients' complaints haven't changed either. Help yourself to coffee. I'll see if April's here and send her back. No sense of you getting trampled in the mob scene at the desk."

Maggie crossed to the credenza and poured a cup of coffee she didn't want. She sat at the rectangular table with her back to the window. Panic

18

surged with such force that if she had been standing, she would have staggered.

What was she doing here? The ghost of the nurse she had been had vanished long ago. Marriage, children, and betrayal had changed her. With an effort she straightened. Today she was a nurse. Though her skills were tarnished, with practice they would shine again. She smiled. No one at Hudson General needed to know how badly she had been hurt by the exposure of George's affair with a younger woman.

The click of the door caused her to look up. A tall, cool blonde walked toward the table. "I'm April Grayson and you must be Mrs. Carr."

"It's Ms." Maggie rubbed the callous caused by years of wearing a broad wedding band. A year ago, in the hospital holding area, she had removed the ring and discarded the title.

April Grayson moved with a dancer's sway. Maggie sighed. Years of yoga had kept her body trim, but never in her lifetime would she move with such inborn grace. Her hands tightened. She stared at the floor. Could she work with this nurse who reminded her of the young woman who had died with George?

"We'll get acquainted first," said April. "It's a zoo at the desk with everyone fighting about who counts narcotics and who gets first report."

Maggie lifted the coffee cup. "No patients today?"

"Or the rest of the week. We're scheduled for unit orientation, videos on orthopedic care, a trip to physical therapy, and a score of other interesting expeditions. Nervous?"

"A little . . . no, a lot. It's been so long." When April tilted her chair so the front legs were in the air, Maggie resisted the urge to scold.

"How long? Fifteen years?"

Maggie's laughter sputtered like a newly opened air-filled water line. "Twenty-eight, unless you count my clinical experience the past year while I finished my B.S. One semester of home care and one in the hospital."

"With one patient and a pre- and post-conference that took half the day."

"You've got the picture. One day they let me have two patients."

"Both ambulatory, of course."

Maggie shook her head. "It was a snowy day and only half the clinical group arrived."

They shared a moment of laughter, their voices blending to form a bond. April's chair thudded to the floor. "My spiel begins. Four ortho is a thirty-bed unit with five R.N.s on days, three on evenings, and two on nights with two nursing assistants on each shift." As she spoke, they walked down the hall past several patient rooms. "We'll take a look at one of the rooms and the special equipment later."

April opened the door of the nurses' station, a

triangular area enclosed by clear Plexiglas walls. Long desks divided at intervals by drawers lined two and a half sides of the enclosure. A medication room, divided from the main area by the same clear material, filled one end of the triangle.

"Fondly called the fish bowl," said April. "Takes time to get used to your techniques being on display." She stopped beside the unit clerk. "Helen, this is Margaret Carr, soon to be on nights."

Maggie nodded to the dark-haired woman. She waved at Charlene.

"Hey, Maggie," called the black woman. "These are Bev and Peggy." She indicated a tall and a short woman dressed in rumpled uniforms. "You'll be working with them."

April spewed a string of names and pointed to the nurses gathered for report. Maggie shook her head. Would she ever get the names straight?

The blond nurse grinned. "If you don't remember, just ask. We're a pretty decent group." She headed to the door. "You'll meet Lorraine Phillips, our nurse manager, later. She's in a meeting with the D.O.N."

Maggie translated the new terminology into more familiar terms. Nurse manager meant head nurse and D.O.N., director of nursing.

"We practice total patient care. That means you'll be assigned to a group of patients who will be yours until they go home or you take a vacation."

"Sounds good for continuity of care," said Maggie.

After a whirlwind tour they returned to a nearly deserted nurses' station. "Helen, do you want to show Maggie the phone system and the patient call system?" asked April.

"You do it. I have enough filing to fill half the morning." Helen's fat curls bounced as she reached for a stack of charts.

April explained the phone system. Maggie thought of how easily Ellen could solve the problem of hook switch. Before Maggie completely mastered the system, April moved to the patient call board.

Maggie looked into the hall. A doctor strode toward the station. As he drew nearer, she saw his chestnut hair was touched with gray. His lean, rugged face teased her memories. Convinced she didn't know anyone in Hudsonville, she frowned.

"Miss Grayson, sorry to interrupt your fun and games, but Mrs. Schultz needs help with her breakfast. She's been waiting ten minutes."

His deep voice and clear blue eyes reminded Maggie of a younger man from some moment of her past. She knew him and yet she didn't. On several occasions he had been part of the group of nurses, interns, and residents gathered in the West Shore Hospital cafeteria for late supper. She had listened to him talk about a doctor's responsibility toward patients and they had worked together on the men's medical ward, but they hadn't become friends. George had held the core of her attention in those days. *What was Jason Knight doing in Hudsonville?*

April laughed. "You know Mrs. Schultz. She always wants something fifteen minutes ago."

"And it's your job to keep her comfortable." He scowled. "Patient care comes before gossip."

April's smile and her body language telegraphed her interest in the doctor. "Though I'm not her nurse today, I'm on my way. Dr. Knight, this is Margaret Carr. She's here for the clinical part of the refresher program. She'll be starting nights next month." She winked at Maggie. "Keep the doctor entertained until I return."

Maggie looked at the floor. When she looked up, she saw Jason Knight staring after April. Maggie released her held breath. He was much too interested in the younger nurse to notice her. The observation disappointed her. Jason Knight had changed. Why had he grown more like George?

"Pleased to meet you, Margaret Carr."

His smile said welcome and hinted at more. Her cheeks burned. She gripped the edge of the desk. When she had chosen the refresher course at Hudson College, she hadn't considered how to act if she met someone from the past. Did he know about George? Would he remember her?

Jason moved to the desk and dropped several

23

charts in the order basket. Maggie felt uncomfortable. Why hadn't she followed April?

He walked toward her. "Have you lived in Hudsonville long?"

"Five weeks."

His smile raised her blood pressure at least ten points. "Good. I was afraid we had met and I'd forgotten you. This is a nice town."

Relief swamped Maggie. He didn't know; he hadn't remembered. A perverse part of her wished he had. "I'm finding that out."

He lifted his medical bag from the desk. "I'm sure I'll see you around. Tell April I'm sorry I yelled." He strode away.

For several seconds she wished he had recalled Maggie Morgan. She swallowed. What was she thinking about? If he remembered her, he would ask about George and learn things she wanted to forget. She slumped in a chair at the desk.

April dashed into the station. "Darn, he's gone." She sighed. "Jason Knight can put his shoes under my bed anytime."

The younger nurse's statement confirmed Maggie's opinion. Did all middle-aged men believe rejuvenation occurred with younger women? "I suppose he has a girl on every unit?"

April's stunned look made Maggie smile. "Worse luck," said the younger woman. "He used to date several of the nurses, but he hasn't been seeing anyone special for the past year. We just drool. Do you have anything against dreams?"

Maggie shook her head. "Not unless the dream poses as reality."

"No chance of that. Besides, I'm getting married next year." She raised an eyebrow. "Jason Knight never noticed the under-thirty crowd. Still, these days the only time he pays attention to a nurse is when she's done something wrong. It's a shame, because he's not only nice, he's eligible."

April's words brought a sense of relief so strong, Maggie thought she would faint. She made a face. Now who's reaching for a dream? With my luck, the dream would quickly become a nightmare.

"Back to orientation," said April. "This is the patient call system."

Before Maggie mastered another piece of technology, the station door opened. April's lips thinned.

"April honey, you're as beautiful as ever." The doctor draped an arm around the young nurse's shoulders. "I'd like to change Mr. Patton's dressing."

His ebony hair fell into such perfect lines that Maggie wondered if he wore a toupee. She frowned. April's spine had stiffened and her clenched fists hung rigidly against her sides. Is the man dense, wondered Maggie. Why doesn't he sense April's dislike?

He turned to Maggie. Leering dark eyes appraised her. "Well now, you must be new. I'm sure I couldn't have forgotten you."

Maggie shifted her weight from foot to foot. His hand slid down April's back. For a moment his fingers rested on her hip. Then he stepped toward Maggie.

"Dr. Giancardi, Ms. Carr," said April.

Perfect teeth gleamed between parted full lips. "Ms. Divorced? Widowed? Do you have a first name? I quite prefer the new informality." He grasped a hand Maggie hadn't offered and bent his head to read her name pin. The odor of his aftershave made her cough. She tasted a bitter sweetness. "Margaret. Irish, I presume. It's the red hair."

April rushed away. Maggie felt as though she had been abandoned. How dare this man treat her like an object? Had George come on this strongly with the nurses? She drew her hand away and stepped back.

April appeared in the doorway. "Let's go. You're interrupting orientation."

"Rank has privileges."

Maggie joined the younger woman, leaving Dr. Giancardi to follow a half dozen steps behind. Her lips were clamped as tightly as her mentor's.

One bed in the semiprivate room was empty. Mr. Patton lay in the window bed. Maggie's fingers itched for a razor to shave the several days' growth of white whiskers from his sunken cheeks.

April pulled the curtain around the bed. "Mr. Patton, Dr. Giancardi's here to change your dressing."

The elderly man opened his eyes. "Mornin', Doctor."

Dr. Giancardi waved aside the sterile gloves April had opened. Without warning the patient, he pulled out the hemovac used to drain excess blood from the surgical site. Mr. Patton grasped Maggie's hand tight enough to cause pain. The doctor ripped off the dressing and probed the suture line with his fingers. "Looks good. You'll be out of here soon." As he spoke, he backed to the door. "See you tomorrow."

Mr. Patton's mouth opened and closed like a feeding fish. "But . . . but . . ."

"I'll try to answer your questions." April pulled on the gloves and cleaned the dried blood from around the suture line and the hemovac site.

"Where am I goin' to go from here? I cain't go back to the hotel."

"I'll have the discharge planning nurse come to see you tomorrow morning. Don't worry, you won't be discharged until there's a bed somewhere for you." When they left the room, April steered Maggie toward the lounge. "You look like you're going to burst."

Maggie contained her anger until the lounge door snapped shut. "I'm amazed that man has any patients. He treats the nurses like sluts and patients like animals."

April nodded. "Mr. Patton's a social service case. Just wait until you see the Barber with a paying customer. He exudes oily charm."

"The barber?"

"As in barber surgeon, medieval variety."

"He didn't wear gloves and he didn't wash his hands before pawing the incision."

"He never does. Has the highest rate of nosocomial infections in the hospital and the nurses get blamed most of the time."

Maggie stared at the younger nurse. "Then we'd better document this carefully. What would he have done if we hadn't been in the station?"

"Pulled the hemovac, removed the dressing, and left the wound exposed until one of us discovered it."

Maggie shook her head. "Someone should bell him so we have fair warning when he approaches."

April laughed. "I like your sense of preservation, but you'll soon learn it's a no-win situation. Let's chart the dressing change and continue orientation. Welcome to Hudson General. You've seen our best and our worst."

Jason Knight emerged from the hospital into the bright July sunlight. He blinked away the im-

28

age of Maggie Carr that had flashed in his thoughts at irregular intervals since they had been introduced. Her somber expression had seemed hauntingly familiar and had brought aching loneliness rushing from beneath the overlay he had constructed over his emotions. He paused at the top of the steps. What would his life have been like if he had married someone like her instead of a woman fifteen years younger than himself? Janine, the flower child, had been a beautiful woman on the surface but an infant inside.

He shook his head as a vision of Margaret Carr reappeared. Auburn hair, a trim body, and a face marked with lines of laughter and sadness shouldn't cause his imagination to run wild. At this moment, he felt fifty-five going on fifteen and ready for the kind of infatuation that consumed hours in idle fantasy. Was it her age that had sent his thoughts in such an unexpected direction? To him, her age was a plus. In recent years the nurses at Hudson General had seemed to be growing younger.

As he walked down the steps, he thought about his marriage. He had wanted a family and a quiet life. Janine hadn't. Parties, alcohol, and pot had twisted her into someone different from his expectations. He had no real idea of why she had left, though once his friends and neighbors knew she wasn't returning, stories of other men had surfaced.

The night he had returned home to find that she had left and taken their two-year-old daughter hadn't seemed different from other times when she had flitted off to visit her parents. He had called and learned the Larsons were on vacation. For two weeks he had expected a call or an appearance by his wife with a story of some resort where she had a marvelous time, better than anything this stuffy town offered.

The news of her parents' death in a car crash had both raised and smashed his hopes. Janine and Beth hadn't been with them. Then Reno divorce papers had arrived. He had hired a detective. Two months later he had joined the detective at a commune in California, but his wife and daughter weren't there or, it seemed, anywhere.

The month had been August. Another August loomed. Would he spend his vacation as he did every year, this time armed with a picture of his daughter aged by technology into a stranger? Would he spend a month searching phone books for Janine's name and the faces of teenage girls, hoping to find Beth and wondering what she knew about him?

He gulped a ragged breath and pushed these thoughts away. Today, for some reason, loneliness festered. Somewhere, he had lost the ability to make personal commitments. Since Janine, his relationships with women had asked for nothing and given little.

In his imagination, Margaret Carr smiled and he reached for the lure. He shook his head. Why did this woman bring the shadow of a dream long vanished?

A car horn blared. He jumped back and waited for the light to change. Only a fool wasted time in fantasies. He had made such a mess of his marriage that to try again would be like jumping into the middle of a sandstorm.

Two

As she followed April down the hall past the patient rooms, Maggie suppressed a groan. The last eight hours of working as the blond nurse's shadow had left her completely exhausted. Each ligament and every muscle screamed about the abuse she had forced them to endure. April had darted from task to task, explaining her system of setting priorities and demonstrating the special treatments required by several of the orthopedic patients, until Maggie's head ached as much as her body.

She rounded the corner from four orthopedics into the central hall. Stopping abruptly, she stepped to the right and barely avoided a collision with Jason Knight. The spicy aroma of his aftershave invaded her lungs. Her heart rate sped. Unable to take another step, she pressed a hand against the wall.

Summer-blue eyes appraised her; his forehead wrinkled into a frown. Though she tried, she couldn't pull her gaze from his face. She swallowed. Was this to be the moment of recognition?

"Sorry." He flashed a smile.

Maggie felt a desire to touch his face, the cleft in his chin, his lips, to take some action instead of engaging in a staring match and suffering an inane inability to speak. She cleared her throat. "My fault." The words emerged in a husky whisper that carried traces of an insane desire to step into his arms. What's wrong with me, she wondered. I'm too old for fairy tales and too burned to indulge in fantasies. She edged past him and hurried to catch up with April.

What was Jason Knight doing in the hospital this afternoon? For a week she had carefully studied his routine. Every morning between seven-fifteen and eight o'clock, he arrived to make rounds. She had planned to use this regularity as a way of avoiding a chance encounter at a patient's bedside that might remind him of similar meetings from the past they shared.

April leaned against the elevator door to keep it open. "Just think, if we'd been a few seconds earlier, there would have been an interesting collision. You have all the luck. Wish it had been me."

"So do I."

The blond nurse laughed. "What's wrong with you? He's up for grabs and he's definitely interested in you. If you watched the way his expression changes every time he sees you, you'd know what I mean."

Maggie closed her mouth. If she told April she had known Jason Knight years before, the younger nurse would ask questions until she learned more than Maggie wanted to tell. "I'm not interested. He's all yours."

"I'm too young and I'm taken." In an exaggerated gesture April put the back of her hand against her forehead. "It's a shame, because unlike most of the gentlemen we call doctors, he's not into thinking he's a catalyst to set every woman's hormones raging."

Maggie closed her eyes to hide the flash of anger April's comment had drawn to the surface. Had George felt that way, and had his actions lowered his reputation in the eyes of some of the nurses?

"Some nurses are eager to accept anything that's offered." The words emerged in a harsh whisper. April's curiosity-filled glance made Maggie wish she had kept the comment to herself.

"I agree a hundred percent," said April. "I also think they're fools for thinking they'll win

34

more than some nights between the sheets. Wives always have the inside track."

Do they, wondered Maggie. How hard would she have fought if she had known George was seeing another woman? For several years, closing her ears to the rumors she had heard had seemed easier than learning the truth.

The elevator doors opened on the first floor. April waited in the hall for Maggie. They hurried to the exit. The outside air smelled like mildew and felt like a laundry room. Exhaustion seeped through Maggie's veins. Her brisk pace faltered until she lagged several yards behind the younger woman.

Her thoughts drifted to the condo and the peach and off-white bathroom. A hot bath, she thought, and visualized steaming water misting the glass tub enclosure. For an instant she smelled the lavender bath salts she intended to pour in generous measure into the water. A lengthy soak held a promise of relief from the needles jabbing nerve endings throughout her body and the burning sensations in her feet caused by trying to maintain April's effortless pace. What would she do when instead of being April's shadow she had the entire six-patient assignment?

A wave of inadequacy threatened to wash away her confidence. She'd never be able to organize and set priorities the way her preceptor did. Years earlier she could have, but she had been lulled by comfort and financial dependency. She straightened, knowing she would never again allow herself to fall into the trap of being someone else's dependent.

"Are you all right?"

April's low, melodic voice interrupted Maggie's dive into a lake of pity. "Just feeling my age." She massaged her temples.

"Sure hope I look like you in twenty years."

"And I hope you don't feel like I do in thirty."

April shook her head. "I know you insist you're over fifty, but so is my mom. She moves at half your pace and she's thirty pounds overweight. I'm headed in the same direction. Let me have your diet so I can start it before I end up like her."

Maggie laughed. The way April moved, she didn't see any chance of that happening. "There's no diet. You've seen the way I eat. Exercise is the secret. I spend half an hour most days doing yoga and on the weekends I walk three miles a day."

"Exercise. Are you sure? I'd die. Unless Steve comes over and we go dancing or swimming, I curl up with a book or tapes of my soaps." She made a face. "Guess I'll end up fat."

Maggie smiled. "It's your body." She paused beside her bright blue sedan. "See you tomorrow."

"Right on. It's your big day. You get one patient. Do you have a choice?"

"Mr. Patton. Since last Monday, I've been itching to shave him."

"Why? Could be he wants to grow a beard."

"Maybe he can't see well enough to shave himself. Haven't you noticed the way he squints. I bet he wears glasses."

"Could be, but there's nothing about glasses in the admission assessment."

"Could be no one asked him if he wears them." Maggie shook her head at the way she had fallen into April's speech pattern. "Any idea why he's spiking a temp?"

"Guess."

"I'm glad we documented the dressing change." After unlocking the car, Maggie eased into the driver's seat. Though her joints didn't creak, she knew it was a matter of time before they did, especially if she had to move at April's pace for the rest of the month. Three weeks minus one day, she thought. Would nights be any easier? Fewer nurses meant more patients in each district. Before pulling out of the parking space, she waited until the vapor dried from the windshield.

Fifteen minutes later she pulled into the parking lot behind her condo. She slumped in the seat and gathered the energy to leave the car and face another dose of the steamy afternoon heat.

As she strolled down the slight grade to the commons in the center of the four five-unit buildings of cluster A, her body felt as limp as her uniform. The silence shocked her. Though she wasn't surprised to find the heat had kept the afternoon gathering of laughing, shouting children and their gossiping mothers indoors, she missed the usual birdsong.

She reached the commons and noticed a woman wearing a shapeless blue dress trudging along the walk ahead of her. When Maggie drew closer, she realized the woman was a girl. The girl sank down on one of the tree-shaded benches. Her shoulders hunched. With her knees drawn against the bench, and her head bent, she presented a picture of dejection. A runaway, thought Maggie.

She paused. The years of mothering her children and those of her friends nearly caused her to sit beside the girl and offer a sympathetic ear. Slowly, Maggie passed the bench. A year and a few weeks ago she would have stopped, but these days her own problems demanded her complete attention. As she opened the door of her unit and dragged an aching body upstairs, she wondered how long she would remain emotionally in limbo.

The cool air dried the film of perspiration from her skin. Though she wanted to curl in the softness of the velvet couch and seek the oblivion of sleep, she strolled to the bathroom and filled the tub. After stripping, she slid into the lavender-scented water and sighed with pleasure as muscles unknotted and ligaments relaxed.

Maggie closed her eyes. Jason Knight's face appeared. His eyes appraised her. She blinked, grabbed the soap, and pushed away an aching need for someone to listen to her fears. Not him, she thought. He's up for grabs, but not by me.

At seven P.M., Jason leaned his elbows on the oak desk in his office and read the note he had just written on the chart of the last patient of a long day. He rolled his shoulders to ease the ache between them. After signing his name, he stared at the framed licenses on the wall across from his desk.

The day had been longer than he had planned because of the unscheduled trip to the hospital to see an admission. Herman Stein was a special patient. Twenty-six years before, when Jason had arrived in Hudsonville, Herman had been his first patient. The elderly man, frightened by his potential diagnosis, had needed to see a familiar face.

There had always been the possibility that Herman's Paget's disease would mutate, and the new symptoms he experienced pointed to a dire diagnosis. The increased skin temperature over a developing bony mass plus a significant weight loss had forced Jason to order his friend into the hospital.

Jason stabbed his ball-point pen against the blotter with enough force to break the point. He tossed the pen in the wastebasket. In medical school and during his internship and residency, he had been warned about becoming overly involved with his patients. The warnings hadn't taken.

Herman hadn't been the only cause of his lateness. Jason smiled. If the near collision with Margaret Carr hadn't produced a series of time-consuming, vivid fantasies, he would have been home an hour ago. One step, or maybe two, and she would have been in his arms. With a groan he grabbed his black medical bag and headed for the door. Action might be the only way to cure the developing obsession. The next time he encountered her, he would invite

40

her to dinner. Maybe then he would remember whom from his past she resembled.

As he walked to his sleek silver-gray sports car, he noticed a gathering of dark clouds. The moisture-laden air smelled stale. By the time he reached his car, he felt as though he had spent the last few minutes in a sauna. He tossed his jacket and medical bag on the passenger seat, started the car, and, wanting instant coolness, flipped on the air conditioner. The initial blast of searing air made him regret his impatience. Why was he acting as though time sped while he stood still?

When Jason reached the development, he parked beside a bright blue sedan. Idly he studied the license plate. Hadn't he seen the car in the employees' lot at the hospital? The three-letter combination, TUT, had caught his eye. No one from the hospital lived in cluster A. He knew everyone except the new neighbors. Did this sedan belong to Margaret Carr?

If so, she was married. Several weeks ago, gossip at the pool had centered on the new couple who was buying the end unit. "They had no children. . . . They had one. . . . She had toured the unit alone. . . . He traveled in his job." Jason closed his eyes. Margaret Carr looked like a woman who would drive a comfortable sedan. Had she worn a wedding ring? He couldn't remember.

Some subtleness in her posture and her attitude spoke of long years in a comfortable relationship. He had seen the same look in the eyes of the wives of his friends. Knowing her marital status didn't dull the desire she had stirred. He groaned. She was married and he hated the thought.

Jason pulled the key from the ignition. He slung his jacket over his shoulder and grasped the medical bag in his other hand. His shoes hit the concrete walk with heavy slaps. Margaret Carr was married.

When he reached the commons, a figure huddled on a bench beneath a full-leafed maple tree caught his eye. A girl, he decided. Was she a runaway? Should he offer help? As he reached the bench, he slowed.

"Daddy?"

The low, hesitant cry startled Jason. It couldn't be, not after all the years of futile searching. He turned and stared.

"Daddy." She lifted her head.

"Beth?" His voice cracked. Her features were softened versions of his own, but she bore no resemblance to the image of his daughter he carried in his memories. In these, she had remained a two-year-old.

42

"Beth." The question vanished from his voice. His throat ached and tears rose in his eyes. He held out his arms the way he had when she was two and waited for her to fling herself into them. She didn't move. His shoulder muscles tightened.

"Come with me. It's too hot to sit out here and talk. How long have you been waiting? I wish you had called my office to let me know you were here. I would have come home sooner." He hardly recognized the babbling voice as his own.

"I . . ." She shook her head and reached for the duffel propped against the bench.

So did Jason. Their hands touched. She flinched. An iron band gripped his chest. What had made her so wary? What kind of life had she led? Fingers of guilt rushed to fill every fragment of his thoughts. Could there have been other ways he could have used to find her? Why hadn't he suspected Janine's plan to leave and found a way to keep her from vanishing with his child? These same questions had haunted him for fifteen years. Would he ever find the answers?

"Let me carry that. You take my bag." He studied her face. Dark smudges beneath her eyes told a story of deep exhaustion. Her pale skin had an unhealthy tone. He noted puffiness

43

around her eyes. Was she ill? He shook his head. This was his daughter, not a patient. "You look tired."

"It was a long bus ride. I couldn't sleep."

Hoping to ease the self-consciousness from her voice, he smiled. "When you were small, I used to put you in the car and drive you around the block until you fell asleep. Never took more than five minutes."

Her lips curved into a tentative smile. He saw questions in her eyes and knew he didn't have the answers. What had Janine told her? Where had they been? How had they lived? As he opened the condo door and started up the steps, these questions tumbled in his thoughts.

In the foyer he hung his jacket on the cherry coat tree and carried the duffel into the hall. Beth's gasp made him turn. She stared at the portrait hanging above the gateleg table that had belonged to his mother.

"Is that me?"

"I had it copied from the last snapshot I took of you." The picture had been a talisman for weaving fantasies in which he found his daughter. He had never dreamed she would come to him.

"She looks happy . . . free. . . ."

He reached for her. His fingers brushed her arm. She retreated until her back pressed

44

against the wall. A lump grew in his throat. "Has it been that bad for you?"

She shrugged. "We never stayed anywhere long enough for me to know what was good or bad. Mom's into her own things, like parties, men, music. . . ." Her voice trailed away.

He swallowed. "How did you find me?"

"The divorce papers . . . I never knew I had a father. I thought one of her friends, well, you know." Her blue eyes, full of too much knowledge, studied him. "You're not that old. Mom said you were an old man."

Jason tensed. How like Janine, he thought. Had she taken Beth out of love or for spite? He might never know the answer. "I looked for you. I still do. Every summer I go to California, hoping to find you."

"I think she knew you would. That's why she changed our name a dozen times. She said you clung to everything, even your patients, that you suffocated her and wanted to make her old."

"I'm sorry."

She shrugged again. "It's not your fault. I'm sure you have your views of her."

"Sometimes I wish I could talk to her and learn what went wrong."

Beth's smile unfolded. "That would be great. She's kind of wild these days since my stepfather died. He left her enough money, but there's this creep. She has no sense. I think she's going to marry him."

"Isn't that her choice?"

Her body slumped. "I told her he was a user. We fought about him . . . about me . . . about you. . . ."

"Me? Why?"

"I wanted to call you. I wanted her to come with me. She told me not to be a fool, that you had forgotten we ever existed. I had to know the truth."

"I'm glad you came." Tears glistened in her blue eyes. He was afraid of reaching for physical contact again. She reminded him of a deer that ate eagerly from a feeder but fled when a human approached. "How long do you plan to stay?"

"I don't know."

"You can stay forever if you want. Do you want to call your mother and let her know you've arrived safely?"

She shook her head. "She's on a trip with her friend. Do you think I could take a shower? It's been four days of buses and bus stations."

Jason lifted her duffel. "I'll show you the guest room. Has its own bath."

"Thanks."

He took towels and soap from the linen

46

closet in the hall and dropped the duffel inside the guest room. "See you soon."

In the yellow and white kitchen he leaned against the counter separating the eating area from the cooking space. He pushed away from the counter and walked to the refrigerator. With a glass of iced tea in his hand, he stood at the window and looked at the sky, where gray twilight had been deepened by dark clouds. Could he and Beth cross the years of separation? Memories of her childish laughter made him smile. Trust wouldn't come overnight. Before they became more than strangers linked by genetic strands, he had to learn why she had come.

His stomach rumbled. Remembering that nearly eight hours had passed since lunch, he returned to the refrigerator. What do teenagers eat beside junk food, he wondered as he rummaged in the freezer. He took out two hamburgers, two buns, and a package of fries.

While the burgers sizzled in the broiler and the fries baked in the oven, he sat at the table and made a tossed salad. Beth appeared in the doorway. She wore a blue T-shirt large enough for two over a pair of calf-length black pants. Her chestnut hair had been pulled from her face and tied at the nape of her neck with a flowered scarf. Her cheeks now had some color.

"Dinner in ten minutes," he said. "I bet you're starved."

"A little bit."

"It's hamburgers. I wasn't sure what you'd like."

"Burgers are fine." She sat across the table from him and rested her hands on the table.

Jason sighed. She looked exhausted, near tears, and lost. "Is iced tea all right? I don't have any soda."

"Milk?"

He poured a glass of milk and put the food on plates. Then he sat across from his daughter and waited for her to speak. After the first few bites, she began toying with the fries.

"Are you all right?" He put his fork on the plate.

She nodded. "I'm not as hungry as I thought."

Guilt rose and slapped him. Had his reception disappointed her? Was she regretting her decision to leave a familiar place for the unknown? "Why did you come to me?" he asked. Surely more than a quarrel with her mother had triggered her flight.

She stared at the table. "Because . . . because . . . do you want me to leave?" She slid from her chair. "If I'm going to be a bother, I can go."

He saw a dozen clashing emotions in her eyes and on her face. In his haste to go to her, he knocked his chair over. The crashing noise startled him. Beth backed away, easily evading his arms. His hands dropped to his sides. "That's not what I meant. I want you here. I'm glad you came. I just want to know what's wrong so I can help you."

"I'll tell you, but not now." Tears slid down her cheeks. "I'm really tired. I only cry when I am. Do you mind if I go to bed?"

"Go ahead. We'll talk tomorrow at dinner. I leave the house around seven A.M. My office number and money for lunch will be on the refrigerator. There's a deli on Horton, two blocks from here."

She paused in the doorway. "Daddy. Thanks." Her voice rang with weariness.

He watched her walk away. Shoulders slumped, head bent, her posture spoke of sorrow. He felt helpless. How could he help her if he didn't know about her problems? He ate the food on his plate without tasting it. Beth seemed more like a stranger than his child. She had changed so much from the image he held in his memories. Give it time, he told himself.

Restlessness drove him to the living room. He strode across the deep-piled maroon carpet and turned the television on and off without checking the listings. Downstairs in his den he flipped through the pages of a medical journal, not finding an article interesting enough to catch his attention.

How could he reach his daughter? Should he attempt to get in touch with Janine? If Beth refused to tell him, how could he learn where his ex-wife lived? He left the condo, strode across the commons and down the hill to the tennis courts and the swimming pool.

A gibbous moon slid in and out of the dark clouds. He stood at the chain-link fence, watching the wind-roughened water in the swimming pool. A jagged streak of lightning flashed in the distance. Another and another followed. Thunder, deep and sonorous, rolled in the lightning's wake.

The deep rumble of thunder caused Maggie to sit up. She flipped off the television and padded across the pewter-gray carpet to the sliding doors leading to the balcony. Flashes of lightning ripped across the sky, leaving trails of light. She opened a door and heard a wind chime clang in a wild melody.

She moved to the edge of the balcony and watched the storm arrive.

Raindrops splattered on the roof, beating in

a steady rhythm. As she inhaled, she caught the blended scents of wet concrete and earth. Holding her hands out to catch the rain, she leaned against the railing.

Raindrops splattered on and around him. Jason turned and sprinted down the path. Giant strides carried him across the commons. A flash of lightning illuminated the row of condos where he lived. He stopped and stared at the woman standing on the balcony of the unit next to his.

Like a priestess of some long-vanished religion, Margaret Carr stood with her hands held out to catch the rain. Light from the room behind her defined her body. Jason laughed. The bright blue sedan belonged to her.

Rain washed his face. He licked the moisture from his lips and tasted freshness and renewal. He pretended the rain was her fingers lightly caressing his skin.

The rising wind billowed Maggie's silk caftan around her legs and hips. She sighed. The movement of the fabric against her skin felt like a caress. Lightning flashed. She stared at the man on the commons. He stood with one foot forward. The triumphant pose reminded her of a medicine man whose rain dance had succeeded.

Lightning flashed again. Jason Knight, she thought. For a brief instant she closed her eyes. When she opened them again, the commons was deserted. Had he been there, or had he been an illusion created by her vivid imagination?

She grasped the balcony railing. Since their first meeting a week before, he had taken a major role in her fantasies. Did he live here, and what would she do if he did? How often could they meet before he remembered Maggie Morgan, West Shore Hospital, and George? She imagined his deep voice asking questions, demanding answers. Beyond a few basic facts, no one in Hudsonville knew anything about her dead husband.

A gust of wind carried a spray of rain across her face and soaked her caftan. She backed away from the railing and stood just inside the sliding doors, watching the storm.

Don't anticipate trouble, she thought. Worrying about what might happen only added to her inner turmoil. The mantel clock struck ten times. Time for bed, she decided, and slid the door closed.

As Jason slid the balcony door open, he heard a clock chime. He tightened the tie at the waist of his muted green beach pants. Rain beat on the balcony roof. He looked toward the unit where a short time ago he had seen Margaret. She had vanished. Had he dreamed her presence, or had he superimposed her face on some other woman's body? He shook his head. Why was he so fascinated by this woman?

Rain driven on the wind lashed his bare chest. He retreated to the living room and slid the door closed. Who was Margaret Carr? He couldn't rest until he solved the puzzle of why he thought he knew her.

He turned and crossed the living room and stood outside the partially open door of the guest room. Beth had come to him, seeking help for a problem she hadn't disclosed. He could think of a dozen reasons, and most of them predicted a disaster. He pushed the door fully open. In sleep his daughter resembled the child he remembered. The blue sheet tangled around her curled body. He crossed to the bed, brushed her hair from her face, and kissed her cheek. She sighed. He backed from the room and went to the kitchen.

Margaret Carr had worn the same wary look as Beth. Had he, sometime in the past, given her a reason for the caution? The edge of the counter pressed against his hip as he drank a glass of milk. Moments later he headed for bed.

Three

On Tuesday morning Maggie sat at the desk in the nurses' station and listened to the night nurse's report on Mr. Patton. She jotted several bits of information on a flow sheet. The elderly man's temperature and white blood count were elevated. Maggie looked at April. Her preceptor's expression answered Maggie's unasked question. Mr. Patton had probably developed an infection. Another question arose. Was the infection confined to the soft tissue or had it invaded the bone?

As soon as the night nurse turned the page in the district care plan book, Maggie left the station. Ten steps beyond the door, she halted abruptly. The blood pressure machine she dragged bumped into her heel. With his jacket slung over one shoulder, Jason Knight strode toward her. His blue shirt enhanced the color of his eyes. He waved. "Good morning, Margaret."

Pretending she hadn't heard, she ducked into Mr. Patton's room and closed the door. Why did Jason Knight make her feel such a rush of conflicting emotions? Stop acting like a teenager, she told herself. If she continued bolting every time she saw him, his curiosity about her identity would be honed. Would she ever be able to talk to him about George?

Her breathing slowed as the jolt of adrenaline faded. She crossed the room and pulled the curtains around the window bed. "Good morning, Mr. Patton." She wrapped the blood pressure cuff around his thin arm.

"Mornin'. When's breakfast?"

"In forty-five minutes. You'll have time to wash and for me to shave you."

His broad grin revealed toothless gums. "Girlie, that's the best news I've had in days. Feel more like a grizzle bear than a man these days."

Maggie noted his blood pressure on the flow sheet and put the electronic thermometer probe under his tongue. The numbers on the digital readout changed so rapidly, they blurred. When the beeper sounded, his temperature registered at one hundred one point six.

Five minutes later Maggie headed to the station to record Mr. Patton's vital signs on the board for the unit secretary to chart. She glanced through the window. Jason Knight sat at the desk, reading a chart. She remained entranced. An urge to run her fingers through his thick chestnut hair gripped her. Realizing the foolishness of her thoughts, she shook her head and retreated to the utility room.

As she gathered supplies, she silently lectured herself. If Jason didn't notice the way she ducked and ran every time he came to the unit, her coworkers would. Speculation would become gossip, sweeping through the hospital like the wind. She had to find a way to remain calm in his presence. While trying to find a solution, she returned to Mr. Patton.

The blue curtains drawn around the first bed let her know someone was with Mr. Stein. She heard Jason's deep voice. Though she couldn't discern the words, the tone held caring and comfort. Maggie stood outside the curtains at the foot of the bed and tried to stifle a wish that the gentle words and the soothing voice spoke to her. So often in the past week she had wished for a sympathetic ear. Laura would listen, but she lived two hours away, and because of her hectic schedule as an obstetrician, most of Maggie's attempts to reach her friend had failed. Maggie sighed and slipped behind the curtains surrounding Mr. Patton's bed.

"Girlie, you all right?"

Maggie looked at the elderly man. "Just daydreaming."

He snorted. "Fool thing to do. That's what kept me from getting anyplace in this life. Got to act."

"I'll remember that."

"Looks like you already know. Got no wedding band. Got sad eyes. Speaks of hurtin', but you ain't sittin' on your duff, twiddlin' your thumbs."

Maggie tried to smile. She had always worn her feelings on her face.

"Could you wash my feet? Cain't rightly reach them."

Glad for something to divert her thoughts from another journey along pity road, she nodded. "And your back. I'll even use lotion and powder."

He cackled. "Then I'll be smellin' like a . . . one of them ladies at the bar. How's about I take you for a drink when I get on my feet? Know a place where there's a hot country band."

Maggie smiled and reached for the washcloth. After completing the bath, she refilled the basin and shaved the elderly man. Then she changed the dressing covering the incision on his hip. The skin around the staple line glowed red and felt hot. She noted her observations on the flow sheet.

Breakfast trays arrived just as she applied the last piece of tape to hold the dressing in place. Congratulating herself on the efficient use of time, she went to the station and pulled Mr. Patton's chart from the rack.

Several minutes later the station door opened. Dr. Giancardi entered. His O.R. greens looked as though they had been tailored to fit. He walked to the rack and pulled out several charts. "Has anyone seen Mr. Patton's chart?" he asked.

"I have it," said Maggie.

He sauntered over and flashed a shark's smile. "Well, hello, Margaret Carr. You're look-ing"—his dark eyes focused on her breasts and Maggie fought the urge to cover them—"lovely today." He rested a hand on the back of her chair. "I hope Hudson General is living up to your expectations."

"I have none."

"Then I'd better try harder." One of his fingers touched her back and moved in lazy circles. The skin between her shoulder blades itched. He leaned over and put his mouth beside her ear. The sweet, cloying odor of his aftershave assaulted her. "Have you been divorced long enough to need a sympathetic ear and a bit of action?"

Maggie considered how to handle this man. Even if he had been her age and unmarried instead of ten years younger, she wouldn't have been interested. She put her hands on the desk. "I'd like to talk to you about Mr. Patton. The skin around his incision is red and hot to the touch. His temp and white count are elevated."

The Barber's finger continued moving on her back. Fighting the urge to slam the chair into his gut, she edged the chair backward. Using the chart as a shield, she rose and faced him.

He cleared his throat. "I'll order something for the temp and remove the staples. He's leaving for the county home in a day or two."

"Even if there's an infection?"

"Don't worry about that. What you're seeing is a reaction to the metal staples." He reached for her hand.

Before he touched her again, Maggie shoved the chart into his hands and walked to the door. "I'll get a staple remover and meet you in his room."

For five minutes she stood in the utility room and fought the need to scream and bash the Barber. She inhaled deep breaths until she felt light-headed. When the string of names she whispered sputtered to an end, she picked up the equipment she had come for and left the room. Two weeks and three days, she thought.

Dr. Giancardi waited at the bedside. "At last, my prayers have been answered. Did you have to go to central?"

"I'm still learning where things are stored." Maggie stood across the bed from the doctor and smiled at Mr. Patton. "You're going to have the staples removed."

" 'Bout time. Hip feels like a too-full tire and ready to burst." The elderly man winced and grabbed Maggie's hand as Giancardi ripped the dressing off.

Dr. Giancardi removed the last staple and dropped the remover on the bed. "Carry on, Nurse." At the door he turned. "Oh, Margaret, call me tomorrow so we can plan our meeting."

Fearing he would see the revulsion in her eyes, Maggie stared at the sheet. His teasing had gone beyond the joke stage. There had to be a way to let him know she didn't like or want his attentions.

"Man's a jackass," said Mr. Patton.

Maggie mentally echoed the patient's comment. She rebandaged the incision, gathered the discarded staples and dressings, and pulled her gloves over the material. Before returning to the nurses' station, she walked to the utility room and threw the glove-covered material in the container for contaminated material.

In the station April looked up from the chart she held. "How's it going?"

"I'm done. Can I help you?"

April shook her head. "I have a terrific idea. Why don't you check the crash cart?"

"Again?" Maggie couldn't keep her dislike of the tedious task from her voice. Since her first day on the unit, she had spent at least thirty minutes every afternoon with the cart.

"And again until you know the location of every drug and every piece of equipment."

"You're right. A thorough knowledge of the cart will be vital in an emergency, but I don't have to like it." Maggie wheeled her chair to the cart and reached for the clipboard.

At ten minutes to eleven the next morning Maggie stood beside Mrs. Schultz's bed with her hand on the side rail. "I want to get you up so I can make the bed."

"Later," said the elderly woman. "I'm feverish and weak. What was my temperature this morning?"

"Ninety-eight point two." A hint of exasperation crept into Maggie's voice. The same question had been asked eight times.

"That's not even normal. I have to have a fever. I have osteomyelitis. That's a bone infection, you know." She patted the white hair Maggie had just brushed. "How can you trust that machine?"

"Digital thermometers are very accurate." Maggie's hands tightened around the side rail. How had her morning become a shambles? With two patients, she should have completed morning care and been in the nurses' station, charting. She still had to change Mr. Patton's dressing and make both beds.

Earlier, when breakfast trays had arrived, Maggie hadn't been in the room to set up Mrs. Schultz. The elderly woman had started complaining. Demand had followed demand, eating into Maggie's carefully planned schedule. She barely managed to leave the room long enough to give out the nine o'clock medications.

"I'm leaving." Maggie glanced at the second bed and saw the top covers had been turned down in preparation for an admission. She

63

hoped the new patient had a sense of humor. Being able to laugh at Mrs. Schultz couldn't hurt.

"Why are you leaving me?" asked Mrs. Schultz. "There are several other things I need. You girls never have time to spend with a sick, lonely old woman."

Maggie inhaled. "I'll be back in fifteen minutes." The old woman's shrill whine pursued Maggie into the hall.

"You look whipped," said April. "Problems?"

Startled by the younger nurse's voice, Maggie whirled. "I'll handle her somehow."

"Don't feel bad. She gets to everyone. Try thinking of her as a two-year-old and you'll have the key to control."

"Mine or hers?" She laughed softly. April's advice reminded Maggie of the things her daughter had said. "If only it were that simple. I feel sorry for her. She's very needy."

"Greedy's more like it. She sucks attention like a syringe. I can understand why her children seldom come to visit."

Maggie matched her pace to April's. "If I ever act like that, I hope someone shoots me." She shook her head. "I'm wasting time. I told her fifteen minutes and you can be sure she's watching the clock."

April opened the station door. "Take a break. Do another check of the crash cart. I'll settle Mrs. Schultz."

"Not the crash cart," said Maggie. "I'll change Mr. Patton's dressing and get him out of bed." She walked down the hall to the elderly man's room, where the material for the dressing change had been waiting at the bedside since seven-thirty.

As soon as she pulled the dressing free, a fetid odor nauseated her. A yellow exudate stained the gauze pad. The same thick matter oozed from several areas along the incision line. Recalling her two-hour session with the infection control nurse, Maggie turned to leave the room.

"Where ya goin', girlie?"

"I forgot something I need for the dressing. Be right back."

"I'll be here. Not going anyplace but the poorhouse."

The fear in his voice halted her. "You'll find it's not a bad place."

"Sure hope you're right, 'cause I'm a-thinkin' it's a life sentence."

She hurried to the utility room and picked up a test tube and a packet of sterile swabs. After culturing the exudate, she redressed the wound. In the nurses' station she filled out a lab requisition.

The middle-aged unit clerk took the vial from the basket. "I'm on my way to a meeting. I'll deliver this."

"Thanks. When you get back, put in a call to Dr. Giancardi."

The heavyset woman glanced at the slip and shook her head hard enough to make her dark curls bounce. "You've got guts. Guess you like learning the hard way."

Maggie pulled two charts from the rack. What did Helen mean? Hospital policy had dictated her actions. With a shrug she opened Mr. Patton's chart and began writing.

At two o'clock the fifth call to the orthopedic surgeon's office reached him. "Dr. Giancardi, it's Ms. Carr from four ortho."

"Hello, Margaret," he drawled. "I've been waiting for your call. When?"

His voice, laced with suggestion, made her feel soiled. "I'm calling to let you know Mr. Patton's incision is draining a purulent exudate and I've sent a culture to the lab."

"You did what?" His voice crackled with anger.

"I sent a culture to the lab. The drainage plus the elevated temp and white count point to an infection."

"Just who do you think you are? Call the lab and cancel the test. I didn't order it."

"Miss Fixx said hospital policy requires cultures of all draining wounds."

"You heard me. Cancel it."

Though he hadn't shouted, Maggie's body tensed. "I can't do that." He slammed the phone hard enough to hurt her ear.

Five minutes later the nurse manager opened the station door. "Ms. Carr, to my office at once."

Maggie left her pen in Mr. Patton's chart to mark her place. As she followed Lorraine Phillips, Maggie marveled at the perfection of the woman's bleached, teased, and sprayed blond hair. Had she entered a time tunnel and ended in the fifties? The nurse manager sat behind her desk, where untidy piles of papers spilled from several wire baskets. Lorraine rested her hands on the green blotter. Her red nails looked like bloody claws.

Maggie sat in one of the chairs facing the desk. In the week and a half that she had been at Hudson General, she had seen the nurse manager three times. "Is there something wrong?" she asked.

The nurse manager pointed a finger. "There's plenty wrong. You've managed to infuriate one of our most important orthopedic surgeons. Do you have any idea how angry Leon is about the unauthorized culture you sent to the lab? Who gave you permission?"

"Hospital policy."

"On this unit I make the policy. Our doctors are always allowed the privilege of writing their own orders. From now on, before you act impulsively, check with me."

Would Giancardi have ordered the test? Maggie doubted it. Her impression of the surgeon showed her a man who cut every corner he could as long as he didn't get caught. She held her anger as close as a poker hand. "Is that all?"

The bleached blond smiled. "I'm sure you can understand my position. I believe you were a head nurse once."

"That was in the dark ages of nursing." Maggie rose and left the room, closing the door softly behind her. As soon as she ducked around the corner, she slumped against the wall.

"I gather the Queen Bee just reminded you that you're only a drone." Charlene Rodgers patted Maggie's arm. "What bad thing did you do?"

"Sent a wound culture on one of Dr. Gian-

68

cardi's patients to the lab."

The black nurse chuckled. "Fools and angels rush, you know. Don't you know the Queen and the Barber are playmates. He doesn't follow the same rules as the other doctors."

Like George, who delighted in flaunting the rules and regaling her with stories of his clever evasions, Maggie thought. "I know now, and I won't forget."

"Never thought you were dumb." Charlene walked away. "Hang in there. Tomorrow's another day."

And so it was. By Thursday Maggie wished she had turned off the alarm and pulled the covers over her head. At ten A.M. she stood outside the room shared by Mrs. Schultz and Caroline Douglass, convinced she had reached her level of incompetence. The sound of two high-pitched, whining voices filled the air.

"Selfish old witch," cried Miss Douglass. "If you want a private duty nurse, hire one. That dear Margaret is not your personal maid."

"You should talk," shouted Mrs. Schultz. "Fluff my pillows. There's a wrinkle in my sheets and you know how sensitive my skin is. Lotion my feet."

"You wouldn't recognize sarcasm if it was

shouted in your good ear. My requests only echoed yours."

Maggie inhaled and wondered if another appearance would quiet the pair. Would they be happy if someone sliced her in two, half for each? Except today, she had three patients.

"Hey, Maggie." April bounced down the hall. "You were right on target. The culture's back on Mr. Patton. Staph aureus. Sensitivities to follow. Want to be the one to tell the Barber? He's in the station."

"Why not? He can't be any angrier than he was yesterday." She squared her shoulders and entered the station. After she pulled the lab slip from the district's basket, she approached the surgeon. "Dr. Giancardi, the culture's back on Mr. Patton."

An angry glare from a pair of dark eyes strafed her face. "I've already had a call from the lab and from Miss Fixx. I'm ordering a medical consult." His smile chilled her. "Do you like Hudson General?"

Maggie stepped back. "Yes."

"Then in the future, I suggest you tend to nursing and leave the doctoring to those who have medical degrees." His voice contained a brittle edge. "If you weren't new here and out of practice, I'd take action, but I'm willing to give you another chance."

One of the two doctors who had just entered the station stepped toward them. Helen turned in her chair.

Maggie met Giancardi's stare. "I'd still follow hospital policy." She turned and just missed colliding with Lorraine Phillips. "Sorry."

"Ms. Carr, what are you trying to prove?" asked the nurse manager. "Do you have something against doctors?"

Maggie shook her head. "I believe in following hospital policy."

"I suggest you tend to your patients instead of harassing the doctors. I've spent twenty minutes soothing two of the patients you've neglected."

Maggie swallowed defensive words. She bolted from the station and sought refuge in Mr. Patton's room. As she assisted the elderly man to the chair and made his bed, she considered her actions and decided she had done nothing wrong. She wouldn't give in to threats from a doctor, or from Lorraine. Maggie Morgan Carr wasn't a quitter.

Jason tapped his fingers on the oak desk as he listened to Leon Giancardi's smooth voice.

Distrust of the other doctor rose in his thoughts. ". . . so could you see him and order any antibiotics you think necessary?"

Was Leon trying to share the blame for the infection, a tactic he had used successfully in the past? "I'll meet you at the hospital at one-thirty so we can go over the case together," Jason said.

Leon laughed. "You don't need me. It's my afternoon off and I have hot plans."

"It's my afternoon off too. Look, Leon, if you're not there, I'll leave my recommendations and you can come in this evening and write the orders."

An exasperated groan vibrated against Jason's eardrum. "I'll be there."

Ten minutes later Jason completed his dictation. He grabbed his medical bag and several of his own consultation forms. How many wound infections did this make for Leon this year? The orthopedic surgeon carefully spread his requests for consults among the medical staff, making tracking difficult. The knowledge that something had to be done made Jason uneasy. He couldn't act alone, and none of the other doctors seemed to care. Four years ago the practice committee had shelved a study of Leon's patients and practices.

Money had been the reason. A hundred-thousand-dollar contribution to the hospital's building fund and a generous donation by Leon's wealthy parents every year had altered the committee's viewpoint.

The bright afternoon sun made Jason regret his decision to accept the consultation. He could be at the pool. A frown wrinkled his brow. That morning, he had offered to introduce Beth to some of the teenagers who lived in the complex.

"I'd rather wait," she said. "It's too hot and I'm still feeling tired from the trip."

Jason was no closer to learning why she had run to him than the day she had arrived. He entered the hospital and walked to the elevator.

As he turned the corner to four orthopedics, he saw Margaret Carr. As he watched her swaying hips, his body reacted with a hot surge of desire. He followed her to the nurses' station. If he talked to her, would she acknowledge his interest?

He entered the station. Where was she? Had it been another hallucination? Then he looked into the med room and saw her. He crossed to the window and stood, watching her graceful movements. She looked up. He waved and she nearly dropped the medicine cup she held.

When she turned her back to the window, Jason frowned. Why was she so wary? Just yesterday he had learned that the marriage rumors were false. Was she widowed or divorced, and how badly had she been hurt?

A hand clapped his shoulder. "Jason, what . . . oh, yes. Isn't she marvelous? How I'd like to get my hands on her superstructure. Have you ever seen the like?"

Jason stepped away from the window. Leon's comments brought a rush of shame and made him feel like a voyeur. He walked to the chart rack and pulled Mr. Patton's chart. "Tell me about the patient." He flipped the chart to the vital-sign sheet and noted the patient's temperature had been elevated for almost a week. "Didn't the temp elevation make you wonder?"

"I didn't know about it until this morning." Leon sat at the desk beside Jason. "You know how the nurses around here are."

Jason frowned. Most of the nurses on this unit were conscientious to the point of nagging. He studied the order sheet. "I see where you ordered something for an elevated temp on Tuesday."

"Routine orders. Forgot to do that after surgery. You know how it is. The pace in the O.R. is hectic."

"I'm afraid I don't know. I haven't seen the inside of an O.R. since my intern days. What are you trying to hide?"

Leon smiled. "Caught me. I'll level with you. I had wondered if something was brewing, but I didn't want to get the delectable Margaret in trouble. She has enough going against her, age, a return to nursing after many years away, and being dumped by some jerk."

"What are you hinting at?" In his peripheral vision Jason saw Margaret Carr leave the med room.

"She's been out of nursing a long time, and I figured she forgot about using aseptic technique and contaminated the wound. A few antibiotics and we're home free. He's a social service case, so there's no threat of trouble."

"Just a minute, Dr. Giancardi."

Jason saw the surprised look on Leon's face and heard controlled anger in Margaret Carr's voice. She stood with her hands on her hips. Her green eyes flashed.

"I'm not going to play games with you, and I'm not going to cover for you either." She turned to Jason. "Read the nurses' notes, Dr. Knight, and you'll see what he's found so convenient to forget. When I make a mistake, I'm not afraid to admit it."

The station door hit the edge of the desk with a bang. "Maggie, I need you right now," cried April Grayson.

Margaret Carr wheeled and hurried to join the other nurse. Jason remembered to breathe. Though he admired her stand, he wished she had kept quiet. She could lose her job by challenging Leon. Was there any way to protect her from the surgeon's anger?

"I wonder what it would be like to turn that anger into passion?"

Jason stared at the other doctor. "Don't even think about it." His voice rang with his desire to protect Margaret. The strength of these feelings surprised him.

"So that's the way it is." Leon's sly smile irritated Jason. "I wouldn't dream of intruding, but please let me know when you're tired of her lush assets." He waved and walked to the door.

Jason reached for the phone, and while waiting for the results of the sensitivity studies, he impatiently tapped his fingers on the desk. Then he wrote a series of orders for intravenous antibiotics. On the consultation sheet he carefully documented the early signs of the infection and the attempts of the nurses to reach the surgeon. He put the original in the chart

76

and kept the copy for his records. As he left the unit, he looked for Margaret.

Maggie stood in the center of the lounge and groped for a calm center. Charlene Rodgers sat at the rectangular table in front of the window. "Rescue mission completed. I'm sure glad I saw the standoff. Successful?"

"Almost," said April. She turned to Maggie. "What did you accuse the Barber of doing?"

"Trying to shift the blame. He tried to pass Mr. Patton's infection off as my mistake."

"I warned you to ignore him." April and Charlene spoke in unison.

"Warnings be dammed," said Maggie. "I'll take the responsibility for my own mistakes, but not his. I told Jason Knight to read the nurses' notes and see what the real story is."

"Fools and angels," said Charlene. "Honey, you're neither. Don't none of us peasants cross the Barber 'less we have us another job."

Maggie shook her head. "What if a patient sues? You'd be stuck with the malpractice label while he dances free. Are you crazy?"

"Might be, but it's called job preservation," said April. "Lorraine's very protective of her doctor."

"Good thing the Queen's taking a bit of comp time this afternoon," said Charlene. "You could be holding a pink slip, 'cause he's her man and you know the rest." The black nurse undulated from the chair.

"Does he get away with anything he wants? Malpractice, sexual harassment?"

"And more," said April.

Maggie shook her head. "There are laws that require us to report bad medical practice."

"Not us and not here. Let the doctors police their own." Charlene waved from the doorway.

April handed Maggie a cup of coffee. "Leon Giancardi's family gives a lot of money to the hospital. The board and administration are grateful."

Maggie inhaled the rich aroma of the coffee. "So if payment's demanded for one of his errors, one of us will be sacrificed. That kind of thinking stinks. I'll be glad when I'm on nights and out of this."

"Will you be? You'll have time on nights to read charts and see a lot more." April walked to the door. "Let's go chart."

At three Maggie joined April at the desk and gave a report to the evening nurse on her three patients. When she finished, she closed her eyes. There had to be a way to protect herself.

While April completed report, Maggie considered her options.

"Schedules are in," announced Helen. "Who wants copies?"

A chorus of voices responded. The unit clerk used the fax machine to make copies. Maggie straightened. She had the answer.

April rose. "Are you coming?"

"I want to look at Mr. Patton's chart," said Maggie.

"Why?"

"I'm not sure."

"See you in the A.M. How would you like to have the district?"

Maggie laughed. "You're joking." She waited until the evening nurses left the station to make rounds. Carrying Mr. Patton's chart, she stopped beside Helen's desk. The heavyset woman looked up. "Yes."

"Can you show me how to adjust the fax machine? I might need to know how when I'm on nights."

Ten minutes later Maggie had mastered the process. When Helen left the desk, Maggie opened Mr. Patton's chart. She copied the entire manuscript and folded the papers. Then she found an envelope and addressed it to herself.

As she walked to the elevator, Dr. Giancardi strode toward her. He glared as he passed her. Though she recognized his fury, she knew she could deal with anger easier than with lust.

In the parking lot she slid behind the wheel of her car and drove to the post office. She sent the letter to herself via registered mail. When she got home, instead of yoga and a hot bath, she carried a glass of wine to the balcony.

Four

Jason slid the silver-gray sports car between two sedans and turned off the ignition. In hope of easing the ache that had begun during the confrontation between Giancardi and Margaret, he massaged his temples with his fingertips. Why hadn't someone warned her about the orthopedic surgeon's vindictive nature? Would Leon heed the warning to leave her alone? For ten years the suave doctor had been used to having the nurses accept his smiles, innuendos, and arrogant demands.

A groan rumbled through Jason's chest. What was he going to do about the situation? Decision time approached. The beat in Jason's head thundered. Would he continue to play the monkey game with the rest of the doctors on the hospital staff and not hear, see, or speak?

He closed his eyes. Who was Margaret Carr, and why did he have a growing feeling that he knew her? During the scene in the nurses' station, he had visualized a younger woman with a mane of red hair caught in a ponytail, standing, hands on hips, facing down a doctor. The arrival of April and Margaret's hasty departure had erased the name he had nearly spoken. Who is she? He shook his head.

Enough, he thought, and reached for his jacket and the black medical bag. Surely April would warn Margaret that continuing the battle would lead to her defeat. Giancardi, convinced of his own perfect nature as a surgeon and a lover, would systematically destroy anyone who quarreled with his ego-centered view.

His shoes slapped the asphalt walk. Joanna Evans's career at Hudson General had been ruined because she had decided to fight for one of the nurses. Somehow, the proof she had gathered documenting Giancardi's careless mistakes had vanished. Days later her effectiveness as a nurse manager had been destroyed by a vicious whisper campaign citing an incident from her past that had never occurred. Even written proof of her innocence hadn't saved her job.

Then there was the stormy night last summer when he and the nurses in the emergency room had fought to save the life of a young nurse. When the young woman had learned she meant nothing to Leon, she had attempted suicide. Though she had recovered physically, she had left Hudsonville carrying a large distrust of men.

Pushing thoughts of Leon aside, he walked upstairs. The sound of music and voices produced a smile. Who's with her, he wondered. He reached the living room and learned the only guests Beth entertained were those on the television screen. He rested a hand on the pale green wall and watched the changing expressions on his daughter's face. Would he ever grow tired of studying his child? Regret for all the missing years brought a deluge of sadness. He swallowed. Beth was here and his. His until she decided to leave . . .

Beth leaned forward. With avid intensity she stared at the television screen. A commercial flashed into view. She turned and smiled. "It's about time you got home. I thought you were coming to have lunch with me."

He hadn't thought to call. For too many years, his time had been his own. "So did I, but there was a patient at the hospital I needed to see."

She made a face. "I know. Business first. When Mom finally told me about you, she said one of the reasons she left was that your patients always came first."

He sat on the arm of the dark green sofa. "She was wrong, though I'm sure there were times when it seemed that way. Do you remember anything from those years, our walks in the park, the Sunday mornings when I took you to the hospital while I made rounds so your mother could sleep late?"

She shook her head. "I used to dream about a man's voice, deep and soothing. It made me feel safe. That's all I remembered."

Jason inhaled. Had she come to him because she needed protection? Was this the right time to ask? Before he framed the question, she rose from the couch. "Are you ready for lunch? I'll get it."

"You don't have to wait on me. Have you changed your mind about coming to the pool?"

She shook her head. "Another day."

Jason followed her to the kitchen. "A friend

of mine has a son and daughter about your age. You used to play with Pete and Karen. I'd like to see you make some friends."

She put a plate and glass on the table. "I'm fine."

"Aren't you bored, sitting in the house all day?" He studied her face. Janine had hated staying at home and had taken every chance she could to escape the house and Hudsonville.

"I'm used to amusing myself. Until Mom married Ted, we moved at least once a year. I had few chances to make friends."

Jason filled his glass with iced tea. What could he say? Nothing could change her past or his. "I'm sorry."

"Don't be. After Mom married Ted, I made a couple of friends. . . ." She stopped talking and walked to the door.

"Get your suit and come with me."

"I didn't bring one."

He laughed. "Now, that's a problem. What if we go shopping this afternoon and then eat out?"

"You don't have to buy me anything."

"I want to. There are fifteen birthdays, Christmases, and assorted holidays to make up for."

85

Her laughter sounded like moments from his memories. "That could cost a fortune."

"And be worth every cent."

"Then you're on." As she left the kitchen, she turned. "Eat your lunch and go swim. I have to make a list of the things I need."

Jason sat at the table. Sunlight warmed his back. He ate pita bread stuffed with fresh vegetables mixed with a creamy dressing Beth assured him was low in calories and in saturated fat. What a mixture she was, alternating between teenager and adult. He drank sun tea and laughed over her insistence on the difference in taste that he didn't discern.

After putting the dishes in the sink, he changed into swimming trunks and pulled on a pair of bright blue beach pants. He grasped the ends of the long towel draped around his neck and headed for the door. "I'll see you in an hour."

"Take your time. We can't leave until after four. My soaps, you know."

"Fantasy and nonsense."

"Have you ever watched one?"

"There's never been time." Or the inclination, he thought.

She laughed. "Some rainy Thursday I'll educate you."

"You're on."

Jason jogged across the commons and down the path to the pool. Children's voices rode the air currents. He stopped to peer through the mesh fence at the wading pool, and for once felt no sense of loss or longing.

A pair of teenagers waved. He returned the greeting. Would Beth like Pete and Karen? If Beth would just move away from her self-imposed isolation, her life would be less lonely. Was she afraid her mother would find her and drag her back to a life she didn't want?

There was no reason for her to be afraid. At seventeen, she could emancipate herself and he would back her. An involuntary shudder shook his body. Was she hiding from the police? He shook his head, signed the book, and walked to the pool. Two women waved.

Jason dropped his towel on the grass and stepped out of his beach pants. Robyn Grant clapped. "More, more," she called.

"Smart mouth." He dove into the cool water. After completing five laps, he pulled himself onto the edge of the pool.

"Showoff," said Robyn. "You're late today. Don't you know Joanna and I time our Thursdays by your regular appearances? I'm hurt that you forget our rendezvous?"

"What will Sam think when he hears rumors about this meeting?" asked Joanna Evans.

Jason sat on the grass between the women. "That she's a dreamer."

"It's a good dream." Robyn winked. "Who's the sweet young thing you're hiding in your condo, and don't you think you should have consulted with your friends first?"

"Or at least warned them," said Joanna. "We've been fighting questions."

Jason flicked water on them. "I refuse to be grist for your gossip mill. She's my daughter."

Robyn gasped. "Beth! You're kidding. How did you find her? When? Why didn't you let us know? We'd have thrown the biggest party cluster A has ever seen."

Idly, Jason pulled blades of grass from the ground. Why hadn't he called the Grants? Their friendship had seen him through the rough weeks and months after Janine and Beth vanished. He rested his hands on his knees. Even now it seemed too soon to share his daughter with others. "She found me . . . on Monday."

"You mean Janine told her about you?"

"Beth found a copy of the divorce papers

and pulled the truth from Janine. Technically Beth's a runaway."

Joanna looked at him. "Have you let your ex-wife know she's here?"

"I don't know where Janine lives."

Robyn shook her head. "Is this Jason Knight, straight as an arrow, card-carrying, rule-following Jason talking? I can't believe you're abetting a minor's delinquency. What's she like?"

"Quiet, composed, and holding a lot inside."

"Nothing like Janine," said Robyn. "Do you think she's afraid of something?"

Tension settled around his shoulders. "I don't know."

"Does she baby-sit?" asked Joanna. "I could use help with my twin terrors."

"I'll ask her." Jason studied the face of the slender blonde, glad to see she looked content and happy. When she had first arrived in Hudsonville, they had dated, but she had quickly realized there was no room in his life for more than friendship. He rose. "Time for another swim."

"Hey, there's a teen party at the clubhouse tomorrow evening," said Robyn. "Sam and I are chaperoning. Bring Beth. I'm sure Pete and Karen will be happy to show her around.

They still think of her as a lost princess."

Jason groaned. "Their imagination parallels yours."

Robyn picked up her towel. "Bring her to the commons' party next Saturday. I want to ask our new neighbor, but I never see her."

"She's a nurse at the hospital."

"Then you ask her."

Jason shook his head. How could he admit to Robyn that Margaret avoided him as though he carried some dread disease? "If I see her. She works on orthopedics. That's not my usual beat."

"You do consults there," said Joanna.

"What's she like?" Robyn slipped her feet into a pair of thongs.

"Quiet, composed."

Joanna laughed. "And holding a lot inside. She sounds like a clone of your daughter. Do you know something you're not telling?"

He knew Margaret, yet he couldn't remember her. As for secrets, if he could remember where or when, he might be able to answer Joanna's question. Without responding, he dove into the water and swam several laps. When he left the pool, Joanna and Robyn were gone. Just as well, he thought. He rubbed his hair with a towel and dried himself.

When he reached the condo, he stopped in the living room doorway. Beth perched on the arm of the couch. The sight of the shapeless dress she had worn on her arrival made him frown. Why hadn't he noticed her skimpy wardrobe? Carte blanche, he thought. He would buy all the things she admired. "Be with you in a few." Ten minutes later he met her in the foyer. "Ready?"

"I set."

"We go." Jason smiled. Beth giggled. A feeling of warmth spread through his body. From some hidden corner she had pulled the ritual they had developed years ago. That he had touched and remained a part of her life pleased him.

In the car she ran her hand over the gray leather seat. "How fast will this go?"

"Way beyond the speed limit, but you'll have to take my word. Do you drive?"

She shook her head. "I've never had the chance to learn."

"I'll arrange for lessons. What kind of car would you like?"

Her smile faded. "You don't have to buy me."

Jason groaned. "That's not what I meant. It's just . . . I'm excited about having you here. I'm not trying to do more than give you the things I've missed giving you over the years."

She sighed. "It's only . . . I'm not used to being more than a bother. I've never forgotten how upset Mom was when I was sick and had to stay in bed for weeks." She stared through the window. "It's not important."

Jason sucked in a breath. How could your own child be a bother? If that was how Janine had felt, why had she taken Beth when she left? "We'll make a bargain. Let me indulge myself today, and after that I'll wait for you to ask."

"It's a deal."

They found a spot in the parking lot at the crowded mall. Jason wondered if the sales or the delicious cool air had attracted the mobs of people darting about. Voices soft and loud covered the beat of rock music from the record store. People brushed past, rubbing against his arms and nudging his back. Beth looked at him.

"What a mob."

"Sure is. Where first?"

"Let's just look."

Though he would have purchased every item Beth admired, several times she stopped him with a laugh. "Those shorts are cute, but not my style. . . . The jeans are too tight. . . . Bare midriffs aren't me. . . . We've already bought two dresses. I don't need another one."

"What if some boy asks you out?"

"I'll wear jeans or shorts. Dresses are for pleasing your father, not your date."

Before Jason laughed, he caught a flash of pain in her blue eyes. He inhaled. She was too young to be in love. Anger and resentment toward the boy who had hurt her filled him. "What did he do?" The question exploded with the force of a tire punctured at high speed.

Tears glistened in her eyes. "He died."

Damn, thought Jason. He put his hand on her shoulder. "I'm sorry."

She sniffed. "I met him at school when Mom and I lived with Ted. He was alone too. When Ted died, Mom sold the house and we moved. He came to see me. On the way home some trucker forced his bike off the road."

Jason wanted to hold her close, but not there. She straightened and wiped her eyes with the back of her hand. He patted her shoulder. "It's hard now, but in time the pain

will ease. You won't ever forget him, but
there'll be room in your life for other loves."
The flash of hope in her eyes comforted him.

"Is that how it was for you? Did you think
we were dead?"

He reached for her hand. "I never believed
you were dead, but I worried about something happening to your mother leaving you
alone and your not knowing how to find me.
I never stopped looking for you."

Like sunlight, her smile blinded him. When
they returned home, he'd ask her what had
sent her running to find a voice heard in a
dream. "What next?"

"Shoes. Sneakers, sandals, and maybe a
pair of flats to go with the two dresses you
forced on me."

Jason's laughter rolled out. "My dear
daughter, those shapeless things you bought
can hardly be classified as dresses." They
passed a shop where featureless manikins displayed dresses with waists and necklines.
"Those are dresses."

Beth giggled. "For older women, not me."

Lighthearted conversation and silly observations of people passing by carried them
through dinner in the one true restaurant in
the mall.

As they drove home, sunset colored the sky in shades of red. Jason unloaded the car. They carried the packages to Beth's room. "Thanks, Daddy." She kissed his cheek.

"My pleasure." Jason put his hands on her shoulders. "Isn't it time you told me why you came?"

The color drained from her face. "I can't. Not yet. Please don't make me tell." She dropped the packages on the floor and hurried past him.

"Beth." Jason tossed his packages on the bed. Expecting to hear the front door slam, he dashed into the hall. The door to the balcony stood open. Jason crossed the living room. He stared at his weeping child. What dreadful thing had she done? Was she using drugs? What had she and Janine fought about? He inhaled and stepped outside.

Beth huddled on the redwood lounge. She looked up. "Don't send me away."

Jason walked to her. "No matter what you've done, I'm here for you. We'll face the problem together." He sat on the love seat arm. "I love you. Believe that. You can stay forever."

* * *

Words invaded Maggie's dreams and confused an already-scrambled scene. She opened her eyes. Part of her thoughts remained in the dream, sorting through impressions to find a thread of meaning.

I love you. Believe that. You can stay forever.

Now, that's no part of my dream, she decided. She pushed into a sitting position and stared at the balcony of the next unit. She blinked. The scene remained unchanged. Jason Knight sat with his arm around a woman's shoulder. She focused her eyes. Not a woman, a girl, she thought.

"He never pays attention to the under-thirty crowd." April's comment rang in her thoughts.

Maggie shook her head. So much for April's assessment. Maybe he played a game at the hospital.

Her stomach rumbled. She looked at her watch. No wonder she felt hungry. She had slept nearly four hours. Cautiously and with hope of escaping before Jason realized his passionate declaration had been overheard, she eased off the oversize chaise longue. Her bare legs stuck to the plastic strapping; her hand hit the wicker table and sent a half-full glass of wine flying to shatter on the wood deck of the balcony.

"Hello, Margaret."

Jason's recognition enhanced her embarrassment. "Hi." She stooped to pick up the largest pieces of glass.

"Be careful."

"I will." She put the broken glass on the table. She moved to the railing. Should she mention the scene with Giancardi at the hospital that afternoon? Where did he stand on the issue of the orthopedic surgeon?

"Would you like to join us? I want you —"

"Another time." Not wanting to acknowledge his young companion, she interrupted the introduction. "I fell asleep after work and it's time I had dinner."

"I'm not surprised that you collapsed. One day spent following April Grayson would exhaust me for a month."

As she turned away, Maggie caught a glimpse of the girl's expression. Was it anger, disappointment, or even jealousy? "I'll see you at the hospital."

"I'll look forward to that."

I bet, thought Maggie as she retreated to the living room. She glanced over her shoulder. Jason remained at the railing. She shook her head. He was a handsome man, and she needed to feel attractive. Somehow, he made her feel that way. A lump filled her throat. Why should she feel so disappointed? His living situation was his choice. Sighing deeply, she strode to the kitchen.

Maggie stood just inside the med room and stared at April. She had thought the younger nurse had been teasing about handing over the district. "You're kidding."

"No, I'm not. I'll be right behind you."

"Why not Monday?" Maggie clutched the clipboard where flow sheets waited to be filled with the day's data on each patient. I'm not ready, she thought. How could she set priorities when every scrap of information from report had vanished beneath a blizzard of fear?

"Insulin for Miss Douglass," said April.

Maggie nodded. "Thanks." She stepped to the door. "Helen, have the blood sugars been drawn?"

"The tech's here now."

April reached for an electronic thermometer. "I'll start vitals."

"Sounds good. Should I give you an assignment?"

"We'll play this as the reverse of your first day with patients."

After preparing the insulin, Maggie left the

station. Katherine Gordon strode down the hall. "Hello, Miss Gordon," said Maggie.

The D.O.N. smiled. "Margaret Carr, just the person I wanted to see. Do you have a few minutes?"

Maggie swallowed. Would the director add her censure to the lecture Lorraine Phillips had delivered? "As soon as I give this insulin."

"I'll meet you in the lounge."

April appeared in the doorway of the room shared by Miss Douglass and Mrs. Schultz. "I heard. Give the insulin. I'll take over until you're finished."

Maggie nodded. What would she do if the D.O.N. demanded she apologize to Dr. Giancardi? No matter what it meant to her career at Hudson General, she couldn't say she felt sorry for what she had said or done.

"Don't panic." April patted Maggie's hand. "Katherine Gordon is fair. The only error you made was in telling the truth."

"That I did." With hesitant steps Maggie walked to the lounge. She paused just inside the door and studied the D.O.N. Though she had to be close to Maggie's age, Katherine Gordon looked younger. Her brown eyes held a serenity Maggie envied.

Katherine Gordon looked up. "I'm not here

to reprimand you. April's given me excellent reports on your progress. I'd like to hear from you about yesterday's incident, but first get a cup of coffee, and please relax."

As Maggie filled a mug, she mentally edited the previous afternoon's event, deleting the personality conflicts. She sat across from the D.O.N. and began reciting the edited version.

Katherine Gordon shook her head. "Start with your first observation of Mr. Patton's problem."

Maggie inhaled and began with the day she and April had assisted Giancardi with the dressing change and ended with the copy of the chart she had sent to herself. When she finished, she looked up.

"Keep that copy you mailed to yourself." The D.O.N. pushed her chair back. "I may need it. As for the other part of the problem . . . Lorraine has no reason to question your actions. You followed hospital policy exactly. If you have any problems with either party, I want you to call me, night or day."

A nagging feeling that she had landed in the middle of a power struggle overcame Maggie as she nodded and left the lounge to find April.

The blond nurse studied Maggie. "I guess we're sharing the district. You do the gents. I've already started the ladies. How did it go?"

"Strange."

"We'll talk later."

Maggie entered room 408. Mr. Patton and Mr. Stein grinned. "Bath time," said Maggie. She filled Mr. Patton's basin.

"Guess I got you to thank for getting me these new specs. Girlie, you'd be surprised to know how different things look. You're purtier than I thought."

"And older, I bet."

"The social worker should have waited until after dinner," said Herman Stein.

"Was the food that bad?" asked Maggie.

"We had some kind of meat in white sauce."

Maggie laughed. "I believe they call it creamed beef."

"That's why I don't eat hospital food." He rubbed his bald head.

Maggie pulled the curtains between the beds. She filled Mr. Stein's basin.

Jason Knight stood outside the door. When Maggie tried to edge past, he reached out to stop her. "Would you stay while I speak to Herman?"

"Bad news?"

"The worst."

Jason's blue eyes shone with grief. Maggie wanted to offer him the comfort of a hug, but knew she couldn't perform a public act of caring without starting a flurry of gossip. "Have you known him long?"

"Since I arrived in Hudsonville greener than sour apples."

"I'm sure that makes your task doubly hard."

He nodded. Maggie returned to the room and slipped behind the curtain. She slid the overbed table to the side. Jason stood on the other side of the bed.

Herman looked from one to the other. "I should hope for good news, but your face tells me it's not. How many times have I told you to make your face a stone?"

"Too many."

The elderly man closed his eyes. "All life ends sooner or later. I've had a good one. How long?"

"That I can't say. I'll ask Carlo Raddeno to see you. Cancer is his specialty."

"Will you still be my doctor?"

"Of course." Jason stepped back from the bed. "Let me make that call."

Maggie felt torn between following Jason and staying with the elderly patient. She saw two tears on Herman's cheeks and reached for his hand.

He squeezed her fingers. "The difference between knowing and fearing is large. I should count myself lucky to have been given so long."

"Want me to take the basin away?"

His fingers tightened on hers. "Why don't you give me a backrub. Mama used to do that when I was sad."

"My pleasure." Maggie reached for the lotion.

Five

April caught Maggie's arm and pulled her into the med room. "Thank God it's Friday. This week has seemed endless. Aren't you excited to be nearly refreshed?"

Maggie wrinkled her nose at the younger woman. "There's still a week to get through."

"A piece of cake. Won't you be glad to be on your own?"

"Are you sure I'm ready?"

"As ready as any of us are." April peered through the rear window of the med room. "I'm on my way to lunch. If you need me, I'll be in the lounge." She made a face. "Just avoid you-know-who."

Maggie looked into the hall and saw Dr. Giancardi enter the nurse manager's office. "I'll try. It's been a nearly trouble-free week."

"Let's keep it that way." April pressed her face

against the window. "Sure wish her office door had a peephole. Do you suppose he's here for a quickie?"

Maggie shook her head. "Get out of here before I forget what I'm doing."

"Just don't dwell on what they might be doing."

"In her cramped office. Where? Surely not on her cluttered desk."

April paused near one of the med carts. "You're right. He wouldn't. He's as self-centered in his lovemaking as he is about everything else. He needs an atmosphere to perform."

The spite in April's voice intrigued Maggie. "You didn't?"

"Not me." April backed to the door. "He trashed a good friend of mine. She doesn't work here anymore."

The med room door opened and nearly knocked the blond nurse into Maggie. "April, are you coming?" asked Charlene. "I've zapped the hot legs in the microwave twice."

"Hot legs?" Strange visions of their lunch made Maggie smile.

"My mama's answer to buffalo wings. She thinks we need more meat to keep up our strength. I'll leave one for you."

"Thanks."

Once the pair of younger nurses left, Maggie finished preparing the noon medications. As she left the station, carrying a tray, the unit secretary waved. "You're getting an admission in 407. Patient's on the way. Want me to get April?"

Though Maggie hadn't done an admission assessment yet, she had observed April's technique several times. "She's at lunch. As soon as I finish meds, I'll see to the patient."

Ten minutes later Maggie entered 407. A gray-haired woman sat in a wheelchair staring at the window. "Mrs. Loring, I'm Maggie Carr, your nurse. Sorry I was delayed." She put an admission kit on the bedside stand.

The woman turned. Her dark eyes shone with anxiety. Pain etched lines on her face. "No problem." The low contralto voice cracked. "I've had a chance to absorb the impact of being here again. At least it's not the same room."

Maggie searched for words to lower Mrs. Loring's anxiety. "Was it a dreadful stay?"

"The first time wasn't. I was battered, bruised, broken, and happy someone was taking care of me. Reality set in two months later when I ended up in here for six weeks."

Maggie put her clipboard on the overbed

table. "Let me help you into bed. Then I'll do the admission assessment and together we'll discuss your care plan."

"Is that something new?"

"I'm not sure. I've been here only a short while."

Mrs. Loring took a deep breath. "Just lower the bed so I can catch the trapeze. I'm quite adept at self-care."

Mrs. Loring had changed into a pale green gown. Maggie took vital signs and began the assessment. "Why are you here?"

"To correct a badly treated fracture." Mrs. Loring exposed her right leg. "A compound fracture treated with a cast. I should have had surgery to put in a plate or pins to align the bones. I should have received intravenous antibiotic therapy too."

"How do you know that?" Without considering, Maggie blurted out the question.

"When I decided to sue Dr. Giancardi, you'd better believe I did plenty of research."

Maggie stared at the form. "What happened?"

The patient cleared her throat. "When he saw I didn't have insurance, he was afraid of being stiffed. He set the bone, cleaned the wound, applied a cast, handed me several prescriptions, and sent me home the next day. A great doctor, right?"

Maggie responded to the anger in Mrs. Loring's voice. She clenched her fists and tried to find a neutral response. Her feelings toward the orthopedic surgeon veered sharply away from the cool blandness nurses learned to maintain toward doctors they knew were incompetent.

Mrs. Loring made a face. "Don't answer that question. Lord knows, I'm not here to put you in an awkward spot, but please don't tell me you've fallen for his oily charms."

"He's too much like my husband was for that to happen."

"Good enough," said Mrs. Loring. "Let me tell you, as soon as Giancardi learned who I was and that I have money, he oozed charm. I forgot the pain and the feeling that my leg wasn't healing."

"How did you learn it wasn't?"

"At a month he had to change the cast. The area where the bone had penetrated the skin had healed, but was red and swollen. He patted my hand, said I was a brave woman, and that it would take time. I lapped up the flattery. At two months he went on vacation. The cast started reeking and I saw the covering doctor. An abscess had developed. I fired Giancardi, landed in here for six weeks of antibiotic therapy, and missed the first deadline of my writing career."

"What do you write?"

"Books that get published." Her dark eyes sparkled and a mischievous smile made her look like a naughty child. "Suspense, mysteries, romance. I have four aliases." She named them.

"I'm impressed," said Maggie. "I used to read your suspense and mysteries."

"What happened? Did I lose my touch?"

"I lost my position as a housewife. For the past year the only books I've read have been nursing textbooks and completely dull."

"Divorced and angry. I know the feeling."

"I wish I were. At least my anger would have a living target. It's hard to be angry with a dead man." Feeling guilty, Maggie reached for the clipboard. Betty Loring had just learned more about her past than anyone in Hudsonville. Why had she picked a patient as a confidante? "Let's get back to the form."

During the examination and information-gathering session, Maggie learned about Betty Loring's stable angina, her four normal pregnancies, and her struggle to remain a nonsmoker. After completing the initial care plan focusing on pre-op teaching, Maggie walked to the door. "I have to call in to your doctor for orders. Is there anything special you need?"

"Something for pain and a guarantee that Giancardi won't come near me."

"You have it." Wondering but not caring how much gossip Mrs. Loring's request would generate, Maggie hurried to the nurses' station. She spotted the new chart on the desk beside Helen. "Did you reach Dr. Akbar?"

"He's on his way out of town for a long weekend. Must be nice. Dr. Giancardi's covering his cases."

"Not this one. Call Dr. Akbar's office. I'll speak to his nurse."

When Helen shook her head in refusal, her curls danced. "I've already informed Dr. Giancardi that she's here."

"You heard me. Call Dr. Akbar's office."

"That won't be necessary." Dr. Giancardi rose from a seat in the corner of the station. "My dear Margaret, I can't believe you're planning to create another incident. I'll take the chart."

"You can't." Maggie's fingers tightened around the edges of the chart.

"Can't. Really, Ms. Carr."

"The patient is Mrs. Loring. She refuses to allow you near her."

"Then I'll just write routine orders."

"Since she's not your patient, I can't let you write orders without examining her. You could be letting yourself in for assault and battery charges to be added to the malpractice ones."

The suave surgeon stared down at her. "Just what are you trying to prove? Ali asked me to handle his caseload while he's away. Hospital policy states that a patient can't stay without orders."

"I'll call Dr. Akbar." Maggie kept her voice calm.

"No you won't." His dark eyes glowed with malice. "You go in there and tell her that she has the choice of seeing me or signing out against medical advice. Let her think about what that will do to her case."

"I'm sure I'll be called to testify about your demands," said Maggie. "Her wishes are clearly stated in my assessment and the nurses' notes."

"Ms. Carr, give Leon the chart and I'll see you in my office immediately."

Maggie glanced behind her. Lorraine Phillips stood just outside the partially open station door. For a moment Maggie wondered if she had been set up. She shook her head. Mrs. Loring was the intended victim. How could she prevent a real problem for the patient?

She put the chart on the desk. "Dr. Giancardi, I'd think again before I acted. Mrs. Loring is a very knowledgeable woman." She turned and marched to Lorraine's office.

The bleached blonde sat behind a desk, where stacks of papers threatened to spill on the floor. "What do you have to say for yourself?" A nasal twang colored the nurse manager's voice. "You had no right to interfere."

"As the patient's advocate, I did." Maggie closed the door and leaned against it. "If he had gone into her room, or if he had touched her, we could have been charged with abetting. If you don't believe me, check with the hospital's attorney. Mrs. Loring made her feelings about Dr. Giancardi perfectly clear."

"But . . . but . . ." sputtered the nurse manager. "Leon said . . . he thought —"

"That if he saw her, he'd be off the hook," finished Maggie. "He was wrong. Is there anything else you'd like to say?"

Lorraine's eyelids narrowed, nearly masking the anger in her pale blue eyes. "Get out. Just remember this. I'll be watching you. One complaint, one error, or one more public scene with a doctor, and you're out of here."

Maggie left the office and closed the door. Her hands shook. Her chest ached. Tears burned in her eyes. How could she continue to work here? When she reached the station, she stopped at Helen's desk. "Did you call Dr. Akbar?"

"He's on the line. I was just about to get April."

Maggie took the phone. "Dr. Akbar. Ms. Carr here. I'm calling for orders on Mrs. Loring. Did you forget her suit against Dr. Giancardi?"

"I guess I did." His nervous laughter stirred her anger. "I've arranged for Dr. Knight to see her and order pre-op tests and IV antibiotics. Let her know surgery's scheduled for Monday and I'll see her Sunday evening."

"Before you hang up, she needs something for pain." Maggie signaled to one of the nurses seated at the desk. The young woman picked up the extension.

"Tylenol number four stat. Jason will order the rest."

"Don't forget to sign the order."

"Flag the chart."

Maggie wrote the verbal order and put a red sticker on the aluminum chart jacket. She pushed the chart down the desk to her coworker.

The lanky redhead winked. "You sure know

how to stand your ground. Be careful. Her majesty hates independent thinkers."

Maggie gulped a breath of air. She turned to Helen. "Notify Dr. Knight of Mrs. Loring's admission and that she needs orders. After I give her pain med, I'll be in the lounge."

She signed for the narcotic and carried the tablet to Mrs. Loring. "This should take the edge off. Dr. Akbar said he'll see you Sunday evening. Surgery's Monday."

"Who's covering for him?"

"Giancardi."

The woman grasped Maggie's hand. "Don't let him touch me or my chart."

Her anger brought Maggie's charging to the surface. "Don't worry. Dr. Knight will be seeing you."

"Thank you." Mrs. Loring swallowed the tablet. "My lawyer suggested I have this surgery in the city, but my family and friends are here and it's such a trek. I hope I've made the right choice."

"You'll be fine." Maggie backed to the door. "I'll see you later."

As soon as she reached the hall, her smile vanished. There's no reason for a patient to be so angry or afraid, she thought. Had Dr. Akbar forgotten the malpractice suit, or had he and Giancardi dreamed up this scheme to derail it? Her heels clicked on the beige tile floor. Though she didn't want to become embroiled in hospital politics, she had to document this incident for Miss Gordon. With each step, her anger grew. She entered the lounge and slammed the door.

"Whoa," said April. "What gives?"

"You look like a hurricane ready to touch down and destroy the joint," said Charlene.

"Everything's wrong. Lorraine. Giancardi. What else?"

Charlene filled a mug with coffee. "What did the Queen Bee say this time?"

"That she's watching me. One complaint, one error, one more scene with her friend and I walk. Tonight I'll write this up for Miss Gordon."

"Lordy, chile, you're jumping right into the pot," said Charlene.

"You can't," said April. "How can you consider being a . . . a—"

"Snitch," said Maggie. "I'm not reporting Lorraine's threat, just the way she and Giancardi tried to compromise a patient."

"What are you talking about?" asked April. "Think. You can't afford to get sucked into hospital politics. Until you finish three months of

115

probation, you have no union protection."

"I don't have a choice." Maggie accepted the mug Charlene shoved into her hand. "I seem to draw the Barber's mistakes like a lightning rod."

April paused at the door. "Anything I need to know about the patients?"

"There's an admission in 407. Mrs. Loring. She's on Dr. Akbar's service. She's had her stat med, Dr. Knight's supposed to write her admission orders. Don't let Giancardi near her or her chart."

"Isn't he covering for Akbar?"

"Not for her. She's suing the Barber."

"Wonderful," said April. "You're right about the lightning-rod effect. See you." The door closed softly.

"So give," said Charlene. "Why is she suing him?"

"For malpractice. I don't think this story needs to make the rounds."

"Give me a clue. I'll make like a mouse."

"He tried to write orders on her chart. I guess he thought a jury might believe she trusts him." Maggie put the mug on the table. "Someone has to do something about that man."

"Not us chickens, honey. Let the doctors clean their own chicken coop."

"Please!" Disgust and disbelief discolored

Maggie's voice. "We all know about their buddy system." She paused in front of the window. "Doctors think other doctors can do no wrong." The lounge door snapped shut.

"Do you have something against doctors?"

Maggie turned. Jason Knight stood just inside the door.

Charlene edged past him. "See you, Mag. Ta-ta, Dr. Knight."

"I'm waiting," said Jason. "Are you setting some kind of vendetta against doctors in motion?" Sunlight streamed through the window, turning Margaret's red curls to flames. Jason groaned. Why had her words triggered anger, or was it guilt he felt?

"Nothing personal," she finally said. "I have a professional interest in the way doctors seem to condone malpractice among their peers."

"Have I?"

"In a way."

He stepped toward her. "What set you off?"

"Mrs. Loring. Dr. Akbar conveniently forgot she was suing the . . . Giancardi."

"Maybe he did forget."

"Or was bribed."

He inhaled. "Doctors can make mistakes."

"I know that. There are honest mistakes and there are ones that come from carelessness and arrogance." She slid past the table. "I haven't been at Hudson General long, but I've seen and heard about a pattern in Giancardi's way of practicing medicine that means danger. Surely there's enough material to put him under supervision."

Fingers of guilt dug deeper into Jason's conscience. He felt a need to justify himself to this woman. "I don't use him for my patients."

"You accept consults from him."

"Those people need me."

"That's covering for him, in my book."

Jason inhaled. "I know Leon's been sued several times, and the cases have been settled out of court. That doesn't make him a bad doctor. I can name a few of my colleagues who are almost as unlucky."

Maggie's hands rested on her hips. "That's a typical doctor's response. Where did all the concern you used to have for patients and the quality of their care go?" She brushed past him. "Why do doctors spend so much time covering for each other?"

Jason inhaled a subtle aroma of lavender. With great effort he forced himself to keep his hands at his sides. He wanted to grab her and shake her until she listened. "How do you know something's not being done? Keep out of this. Leon's vindictive."

"I read him clearly, but I have to do what I believe is right. I remember when—" Without finishing her statement, she left.

Jason stared at the door. I remember when, what? Once again he had nearly grasped the hidden memory that would reveal her identity. His shoulders slumped. Why had he argued with her when he completely agreed? Was it guilt? His gut reaction to her anger had crystallized his determination to act. The doctors at Hudson General had to move against Giancardi before his arrogant carelessness caused trouble for them all. To Jason, it looked as though he had been drafted to head the project.

As he left the lounge he mulled over Margaret's outburst. More than Leon's less-than-perfect behavior had stirred her anger. Had she lost a relative because of some doctor's carelessness? What had she meant when she asked where his concern for patients and the quality of their care had gone? He halted. He knew her, but where or when? Had he met her when he was in medical school or at West Shore Hospital?

Before leaving the hospital, he stopped to see Herman Stein. The elderly man clutched an emesis basin. "Other than nausea, how are you?" asked Jason.

"You're asking when your eyes can tell you? The cure is worse than Job's curse."

"Is there anything I can get you?"

"If you should see a new set of bones lying around, I could use them." A wan smile hovered on Herman's lips. "I will be fine. Your company brings me pleasure."

Jason spent a few more minutes at the bedside before heading for home and another attempt to persuade Beth to use the bathing suit he had bought her.

On Saturday morning at six, Maggie woke filled with energy. By ten she had cleaned the entire apartment. She sat at the kitchen table, drinking iced coffee and composing a grocery list. Her thoughts drifted back to the days when she had followed behind a pair of twins and an untidy husband. George had always dropped his clothes, magazines, papers, and whatever in heaps on the floor. Ellen had developed the same messy habits. She laughed softly. For the first time in a year she had thought of George without fighting nausea. One step closer to freedom, she thought. She pushed the chair from the table.

Forty-five minutes later she stood in the grocery store checkout line. The previous night she had felt too drained to face a crowded store. For the entire day Lorraine had trailed her relentlessly. Maggie released her grip on the cart handle. If Lorraine had hoped to rattle her, she had succeeded.

After unpacking the groceries, Maggie poured a glass of iced coffee and picked up the salad she had bought. A long day loomed. What now, she wondered. She carried her lunch to the balcony. Across the way she saw Jason's young friend stretched out on a redwood chaise. Maggie heard children's excited shouts. Two women and four children, all wearing bathing suits, crossed the commons. With a smile Maggie knew how she could waste a few of those endless hours.

In the bedroom she pulled on a dark green bathing suit with a blouson top, and grabbed a beach towel and a coverup. As she crossed the commons and strolled down the path to the pool, she heard children's laughter, and without regret remembered lazy days spent in the backyard pool with the twins and their friends.

For a moment she stood at the chain-link fence and watched the children play in the wading pool. She turned away, entered the clubhouse, signed the book, and looked for a spot on the grass for her towel. The tables and the deck chairs on the patio beside the clubhouse were full. She spread her towel and began to apply sunscreen.

A woman with dark hair caught in a huge barrette rose and strolled across the grass. "Hi. I'm Robyn Grant. Would you like me to smear your back?"

"Thanks. I'm Maggie Carr. Complex A, corner unit."

"Thought so. How about moving your towel over by Joanna and me? Being a stranger is the pits."

"Agreed." Maggie followed Robyn Grant.

"Maggie Carr, this is Joanna Evans, proud mother of twins."

Joanna swatted her friend. "I hope I'm more than that."

"It's a big job," said Maggie. "I have a set too."

"Do they drive you crazy?"

"Not as much as they did when they were young."

"College?" asked Robyn.

Maggie shaded her eyes from the glare of sun on the water. "Beyond that. Ellen's in her first year of residency and Morgan's launching his operatic career."

"You don't look old enough," said Joanna.

"Good genes."

Robyn leaned forward. "Did Jason tell you about the commons party tonight?" Maggie shook her head. Robyn echoed the gesture. "Figures," she continued. "Men. They never follow through. There's a barbecue at seven for everyone in cluster A. Will you come?"

"What can I bring?"

"Munchies," said Joanna. "Burgers, hot dogs, soda, wine, and beer come from the commons fund."

"There is a four-dollar donation for adults," said Robyn.

"Not bad for an evening out." Maggie rose and followed Robyn to the pool.

The slightly overweight woman stood on the edge, preparing to dive in. "Company's great. From infants to our resident octogenarian. I'll make sure you meet everyone."

"I'm looking forward to that." Maggie tested the water with her toe. As icy water from Robyn's splashing dive splattered Maggie, she gasped. She climbed down the ladder and gradually immersed herself, shivering with each new exposure to the cold water. Then she swam laps until her muscles burned. When she returned to the towel, the other women were gone. Maggie basked in the sun until her suit dried. After draping the towel over her shoulders, she slipped on her sandals.

Tonight should be fun, she thought as she headed across the commons. What to bring? Veggies and dip, she decided. She mentally reviewed the contents of the vegetable drawer and made a list of things to buy.

At a few minutes to seven she applied a touch of lipstick and slipped into her sandals. A green halter jump suit complimented her eyes. Moments later, holding the platter of vegetables and dip, she walked across the commons.

"Maggie," called Robyn. "Over here." The dark-haired woman met Maggie midway. She snatched a piece of celery and plunged it into the dip. "Delicious. Calorie-laden, no doubt."

"Actually not."

"I won't tell. Put the platter on the food table and I'll introduce you to your neighbors."

Maggie followed Robyn. As she put the plate on the table, she spotted Jason. He strolled toward her. "Margaret, good to see you."

Robyn shook her finger at him. "No thanks to you. Didn't I tell you to invite her?"

"I . . . well . . ."

Maggie laughed. "Our last conversation was

124

a bit heated. I can see why he forgot."

"So you're the one who shook him up." Robyn made a shooing gesture. "Go help Sam and Dave with the burgers. I'll make sure Maggie meets everyone."

"In whirlwind fashion." Jason winked. "Just don't let her lure you into one of her zany projects."

"They're perfectly good projects." Robyn tugged Maggie's arm. "I'll tell you about them once I know you better."

Robyn led Maggie from group to group, spouting names and occupations. Maggie filed as many as she could. She looked for Jason's young friend and finally spotted her sitting in the shadows beneath one of the maple trees. "Who's that?" Maggie asked. By the time she had Robyn's attention, the girl had vanished.

Before long Maggie's memory for names reached the saturation point. She had no idea who the last two couples were. Robyn collapsed on a blanket beside the younger woman Maggie had met at the pool. "Hi . . . uh . . ." She couldn't pull the name from the massive clump in her thoughts.

"Joanna." The fair-haired woman grinned. "Don't feel bad. Robyn has this weird memory. She can meet a hundred people and remember all their names." Two small boys pulled at her sleeve. "Meet the deadly duo. . . . Boys, I'm coming."

"Need a hand?" asked Maggie.

"I'd love to have a third."

"So would every mother and all nurses."

"I'm both," said Joanna. "Does that entitle me to a fourth?"

"You have that," said Robyn. "He's called a husband."

When the twins sat on the blanket, eating hot dogs and potato chips, Maggie, Robyn, and Joanna went to the buffet. Robyn pointed to her teenagers. "They'll spend the evening ignoring us until they want something."

"Typical," said Maggie.

A short time later Sam Grant, Dave Evans, and Jason joined them. Jason dropped to the blanket across from Maggie. She frowned. Where was his friend?

Sam Grant handed Maggie a cold beer. "I hear you're a nurse. Come to O.B. We're down several nurses."

"Though I like four orthopedics, the way things are going, I might."

Sam lifted his beer. "The hospital's buzzing about your encounters with him who would be king of the hill. You've got guts."

126

Joanna leaned forward. "Are you on the Barber's list?"

The anger in the other woman's voice surprised Maggie. "We've had our moments," she said.

Jason chuckled. "If those were moments, I'd hate to see events. If he could get away with murder, you'd be dead."

"Run, don't walk to the nearest exit," said Joanna. "I used to be nurse manager on four orthopedics and I set out to protect my staff from him. Guess who isn't and who won't be working at Hudson General in the future."

Joanna's husband squeezed her hand. "We could still sue the bastard." He looked from Sam to Jason. "What are you guys doing about the situation?"

Jason leaned back. "Nothing I can discuss."

Does he mean something's being done, wondered Maggie. She met his gaze. The interest she saw made her cheeks flush. She gulped a mouthful of icy beer. "So what are you doing now, Joanna?"

"Teaching med/surg nursing at the college. I love teaching, but I hate the way I was dumped. Be careful."

"Thanks for the warning."

Robyn stretched out with her head on her

husband's leg. "Enough hospital talk. Let's talk about my projects and you can choose one."

Sam Grant put his hand over his wife's mouth. "Don't scare her away."

Maggie looked across at Jason. Before he looked away, she caught a glimpse of yearning in his eyes. She bent her head and willed her pulse to slow. He wasn't free. And as long as her bitter anger toward George persisted, neither was she.

Six

On Monday Maggie paused outside Mr. Patton's room. The elderly man's transfer to the county home had been arranged for that morning. Though she knew his prolonged stay had cost the hospital money, she hated to see him go. He had been her first patient at Hudson General and she would miss him.

As she crossed the room, her thoughts drifted back to her first clinical experience as a naive eighteen-year-old student nurse. Sadie Brown, stroke victim, had expired while Maggie bathed her. Because she had blamed herself, the death had nearly caused her to leave nursing.

"Girlie, are you here or in another world?"

Maggie blinked. "Just tripping in the past."

"Leave that for us old folks. Social worker brung me new clothes last night, and all the things from my room at the hotel. Sure surprised me they was still there." He held out an Indian arrowhead. "Found this when I was a kid. Want you to have it."

Maggie's eyes misted. "I don't want to take something I'm sure means a lot to you."

"Who am I gonna leave it to? Got nobody." He closed her fingers over the artifact. "You've done a lot for me."

"Then thank you." She wrapped the arrowhead in a tissue and tucked it in her pocket.

He sighed. "Should feel good 'bout leavin' this place. Cain't say I do."

"I'll miss you."

He nodded. "Life's full of meetings and partings. Cain't rightly say I'm jumpin' to reach my next stop. Gonna be lonely."

"You'll make new friends. I saw Herman this morning before work. He sends his best."

"That's what I like 'bout you. You care." He put on his glasses. "Life's not gonna be the same at the home. No stops at the bar for a shot and a beer. Cain't sit in the park, watching the purty girls walk by. 'Tis a sad end to a life."

Maggie patted his hand. "I'll come visit you."

"Would you?"

The eager expectation in his voice warmed

her. "It's a promise and I'll bring you some home-baked cookies."

" 'Drather have a cake with a file in the middle." He grinned.

"Cookies or nothing."

"Chocolate chip with walnuts. Girlie, you're something else."

Maggie smiled. "Time for your last backrub." She emptied the basin, rubbed his back, and helped him dress in the trousers and sport shirt the social worker had delivered. Two battered suitcases sat on the floor near the window.

After packing his toiletries in the plastic basin, she opened the curtains surrounding the bed. "I'll be back."

"I'll be here. Ain't goin' no place on my own."

As Maggie strode down the hall to gather supplies for her next patient, her thoughts dwelled on growing old. Would all her possessions fit into two battered suitcases? Would she, like Mr. Patton, have no one who cared? She made a face. Though Morgan and Ellen had their own lives, there would always be room for her. Anger surged like an electric shock. She put her hand on the wall. He deserted me, she thought. All the dreams she had spun about traveling and having leisure to enjoy growing old whirled away on the winds of anger, leaving her with a vast empty feeling.

Shortly after breakfast trays had been collected, Maggie headed to the station for the packet of instructions concerning Mr. Patton's care. They had been prepared for the county home by the discharge planning nurse. A stretcher pushed by two men dressed in gray uniforms turned the corner from the elevator hall. She waited for them. "Can I help you?"

"We're here for Mr. Patton." Their unison delivery reminded her of a Greek chorus.

"Here are his papers. I'll go to his room with you."

"Great," said the burly, balding man at the head of the stretcher. "The nurses usually just point."

"We took the wrong patient once." The younger man winked. "Sure had a tough time explaining how Mr. Smith turned into Mrs. Jones."

"I'll bet," said Maggie.

"You got it." Once again they spoke as one.

"Just take good care of Mr. Patton. He's my favorite."

"For you I'll do anything." The younger man stroked his beard.

After the attendants transferred Mr. Patton,

his possessions, and the papers to the stretcher, Maggie kissed his cheek. "See you. Maybe next week."

"Girlie, you've made my stay here nice. Don't forget them cookies and tell Herman I'll be thinking 'bout him."

She stood in the doorway of the room and waved until the stretcher turned the corner. With her finger she wiped away the tear that slid down her cheek. She entered the room, stripped the bed, and dumped the linens in the hamper just outside the door.

Helen stepped out of the nurses' station. "There you are. The O.R.'s on the way for Mrs. Loring. Here's her chart."

Maggie flipped the chart open. Vital signs had been charted. The latest lab results were in place and the consent had been signed. In Mrs. Loring's room Maggie checked the intravenous and the identification bracelet. "O.R.'s on the way. Let me put your glasses on the stand. How are you doing?"

"Floating. The world's a blur and my anxiety ish centered shomewhere in spash. Mush remember thesh feelings and put them in a book." Her words were slurred.

"It's the medicine. Final check. Dentures out. Rings and jewelry with your family." As she spoke, Maggie sensed the presence of other people in the room. She turned. "Speaking of family, I believe yours has arrived."

"My kidsh," said Mrs. Loring. "Shue, Charlie, Ray. My tongue feelsh thick. Where's Bruth?"

"Here, Mom." The youngest of the three men grinned and winked at Maggie. "I'm Bruce. We're all present and not to be held accountable for any family secrets you might spill."

"I'll leave you for a while." Maggie backed to the door and fought a momentary wish that her children lived close enough for daily interactions. She leaned against the wall and completed her notes. When the two members of the newly established transport team arrived, she followed them into the room.

"She goes in the bed, right?" asked a slender black man.

"Is the linen pack here?" asked a muscular white woman.

"Yes to both." Maggie watched the pair disconnect the bed controls. Before tucking the chart beneath the pillow, she directed Mrs. Loring's family to the waiting room just outside the O.R. "See you this afternoon."

"Thans." Betty Loring's eyes fluttered and closed.

For the rest of the morning Maggie made beds, talked to doctors about their patients' needs, wrote notes, and gave out medications. She opted for an early lunch, ate a container of yogurt, and headed for four oncology to deliver Mr. Patton's message to Mr. Stein. "How are you holding up?" she asked.

He clasped both of her hands. "Sometimes I wonder why they should bother with such an old man as I am when there are younger people who need help."

"Perhaps you have more to give."

He sighed. "I don't know what. How's my friend Johnny?"

"He left for the county home this morning. He said he'd be thinking about you."

Herman Stein shook his head. "So many good-byes. When you reach my age, one would think it's a habit. I wish I could go see him. How I would feel if I had no family, I can't imagine."

"He has a lot of friends."

"And most are as worn and old as he is. There should be better bus service there. Who will visit him at the county home?"

"I will."

Mr. Stein kissed her fingers. "What a good person you are."

135

"Thank you."

"Herman, I've brought the borscht."

Maggie turned. Jason stood in the doorway. She rose. "I'll come back another day."

"I don't want to chase you," said Jason.

"My lunch break is over and April will be getting antsy."

Mr. Stein chuckled. "What a popular man I am. The good doctor and the pretty nurse come nearly every day. The next time you should come together and he will bring borscht for three."

"I'd like that," said Jason. "Do we have a date?"

Not knowing if he was serious or teasing, Maggie kept her answer vague. "We'll see." She hurried back to four orthopedics. She found April in the room that had been Mr. Patton's, interviewing a new admission. "Want me to take over so you can go to lunch?"

"I'm skipping lunch. Gained five pounds this month."

"Not a good idea," said Maggie. "You could give up eating the chocolates patients leave at the desk."

"So could you."

"I'd rather cut off my hand than give up chocolate. So go."

April shook her head. "It'll take an hour to clean this brat up." She rolled a T-shirt into a ball and jammed it in the bedside stand. "Chet Madigan, why weren't you wearing your leathers?"

The boy's carrot-colored hair clashed with the smears of dried blood on the hand he held across his eyes. "It's summer and it's hot."

"Leathers are safe," said Maggie.

"I'll drink to that," said April.

"You both sound like my mother."

"And this is your third accident. One day there won't be an inch of your hide left." April winked at Maggie. "He's my youngest brother's friend and I used to baby-sit him." She grinned. "If you have spare time, do the crash cart."

Maggie closed her eyes. "First med drawer." From memory she recited the contents of the compartments and drawers. "Do I pass?"

"Awesome memory. Go. Just remember to smile at the Queen and avoid the Barber."

"Is she crazy?" asked Chet Madigan.

"Just speaking in code." Maggie slipped her fingers beneath the cast on his right lower leg. The pedal pulse beat strong and steady. "You'll do. How's the bike?"

"Totally totaled."

"And so will you be if you don't start acting sensible." The motherlike tone of April's voice amused Maggie. She left the room to make rounds on the other patients in the district.

At two o'clock Mrs. Loring returned from the recovery room. Maggie checked her vital signs and the dressing over the surgical site.

Betty Loring groaned and opened her eyes. She ran her tongue over her lips. "Mouth dry."

Maggie opened a packet of lemon and glycerine swabs. "I'll get some ice chips and let your family know you're back."

"Thanks." Betty Loring closed her eyes. "I have a feeling this is going to start hurting soon."

"As soon as I check your new orders, I'll bring you an injection. Being in pain retards the healing process."

"Aren't you afraid I'll become addicted? A lot of people are."

"You're not the type, and you are the only judge of how much pain you're experiencing. I don't read minds."

"You're great."

"I'll be back soon." As Maggie filled a pitcher with ice chips, she smiled. This day would be counted as one of her best. After instructing Mrs. Loring's family not to give their mother too much ice at one time, Maggie sat at the desk and finished the day's paperwork.

By Thursday Maggie knew she wanted to keep Betty Loring as a friend. That morning, when a memory had sent Maggie's emotions on a downward spiral, the gray-haired writer had gently delivered a lecture. Just after lunch Betty presented Maggie with copies of her three latest releases. "For those times when you want to escape."

"I had planned to buy them."

"Why? I have extra copies."

Maggie took the books. "To help boost your sales the way you've boosted my confidence."

Betty used the trapeze to pull herself into a sitting position. "Remember the day I was admitted. I've heard the wildest stories of how you faced down a certain doctor and kept my suit against him from being compromised."

"I had to. Anything else would have been neglect or worse on my part. Doctors shouldn't be allowed to walk over people when they're ill."

"Or ever. I've been collecting stories about Giancardi that make me want to scream."

"Fortunately he's in the minority. I've found most of the doctors here to be good."

Betty Loring nodded. "My first husband was a doctor. He had a heart attack while trying to rescue people during a flood."

Maggie looked away. Betty's story had reminded her of the day George had ignored her plea to stop at the scene of a highway accident. I should have known then what he was like, she thought. Why was I so blind? "My husband was a doctor too," she whispered.

"I didn't mean to hit a nerve. What did your husband do to hurt you so badly?"

Maggie sighed. "Not much more than men have been doing to their wives for centuries. I've just begun to see things I refused to admit before."

"It hurts, but isn't it time you got everything out of those hidden corners?"

Maggie inhaled. "He died in an accident with a young nurse. I blamed myself. I should have seen what was going on. Late-night calls from the hospital. Weekend seminars that would have bored me."

"How long has it been?"

"A little over a year. I'll be glad when it's all part of my memories."

"You're going to have to unload the guilt first."

"How? She . . . the nurse . . . she was pregnant with his child. I found letters when I cleaned his office."

Betty Loring made a face. "So you accepted the guilt he never felt. Why? He was an adult and responsible for his own behavior. Did you demand he go out and have an affair?"

"No."

"Then why the guilt?"

"And shame. For years I heard rumors about him and the nurses at the hospital. He laughed about the stories and I chose to believe him."

"Kick him out of your life."

"How?" Betty's laughter spiced with a touch of mischief brought a smile to Maggie's lips. "He's dead."

"And gone and buried. Let me tell you what I did. My second husband was everything my first wasn't. Slime, lecher, you name it, and he was worse. I divorced him and then killed him off in my next book."

"I don't write."

"Letters, I bet. You don't have to write a novel. Just put on paper everything about him that you hated and burn it. Like an exorcism."

"I'll try."

"And if you need someone to listen, just yell. As soon as I'm out of here, we'll do lunch and compare lechers."

Maggie laughed. "That will take more than lunch."

"But it will be fun, and profitable for me. I think my next heroine will be a nurse."

Maggie walked to the door. "If I don't get back to work, I'll be an unemployed one. See you later."

On Friday at seven-thirty, Maggie stood in the nurses' station and stared at the patient board. The district was hers. All the anxiety she had felt the day she arrived at Hudson General had returned. What was she going to do? Where once she had looked forward to hiding on the night shift, today she knew she wasn't ready to accept the responsibility.

A hand waved back and forth several inches from her face. "Maggie, have you heard a thing I've said?"

"No."

"District two is yours. I'll be in three, but if you need me, whistle."

"I don't know how."

"Then yell or something." April took two steps and turned. "You'll be fine."

By eleven Maggie had completed baths on four patients and sent two home. When she finished stripping the beds, she returned to the station. Betty Loring's call light flashed. Maggie hurried to the private room. "Betty, can I help you?"

"Yes . . . no . . . I just don't feel right."

"Angina?"

"There's no pain."

"Is it a heavy feeling? A tightness?"

"Neither. I just got back to bed and I feel like I've been digging ditches."

Maggie checked Betty's pulse. Though regular, the rate was slower than usual. What's going on, wondered Maggie. She left the room and returned with the blood pressure machine. Betty's pressure was also slightly lower than usual. Maggie shook her head.

"What's wrong?" Anxiety colored Betty's voice.

"Nothing, but I'm going to call Dr. Knight and tell him about this. I've learned to trust my patients' instincts about their bodies."

"Thanks."

"I'll check back in fifteen minutes."

Maggie relayed the message to Jason's nurse. Then she reviewed the history of Betty's angina. The attacks usually followed strenuous exercise or great stress and the pain was relieved by nitroglycerine.

Maggie returned to Betty's room. The gray-haired woman slept. Her pulse was unchanged from before. Maggie slipped from the room.

April waved. "I'm going to lunch. My district's quiet. I'll be in the cafeteria."

"Brave woman," said Maggie. "Let's hope I don't need you." She strode to the med room, where she took Betty Loring's noon antibiotic from the refrigerator. She carried the intravenous pouch to the private room. "Hi, Betty."

Betty sat up. Beads of perspiration gathered on her forehead. Her skin coloring was ashen. "Maggie, help."

"What is it?" Maggie reached for the blood pressure equipment she had left in the room.

Betty pressed her fist against her chest. "Hurts." She slumped against the pillows.

Maggie felt for a pulse and found none. For an instant she froze. Four to six minutes to re-establish blood flow, she thought. Gulping a deep breath, she pulled the emergency cord above the bed. After lowering the bed to a working position, she detached the headboard and slid it beneath Betty's upper body. "Betty," she called. She repeated the assessment and began CPR.

"I know CPR."

Maggie glanced up to see the code cart

pushed into the room by two of her colleagues. A respiratory therapist, Lorraine Phillips, and Jason followed.

"Change on the count."

The respiratory therapist took over the breathing sequence. As Maggie moved to the cart, she gave a concise report of what had happened. She and the second nurse attached the cardiac monitor's leads.

"Epi, one milligram," said Jason.

Maggie opened the med drawer and pulled out a premixed syringe of epinephrine. Dopamine drip, she thought, and reached for an intravenous pouch. She filled a syringe with the medication and injected it into the pouch.

"Run a dopamine drip," said Jason.

Maggie slapped a label on the pouch and handed it to the second nurse.

"Repeat epi."

"I have a pulse."

"Blood pressure seventy over forty."

"Atropine one milligram IV push."

Maggie glanced at the monitor. "Pulse rate forty-eight."

"Pressure ninety over sixty."

"Betty," called Jason.

The patient opened her eyes. Maggie looked at the other members of the team. Their faces reflected the elation she felt. A surge of confidence made her want to crow. Today she had proved she was a nurse.

"Great job," said Jason. "Thanks, all." He turned to Lorraine. "Get a twelve lead EKG, a portable chest X ray, blood work. I'll call CCU for a bed." He reached for Maggie's hand. "Thanks for the warning. If you hadn't called, I wouldn't have come back."

With an irregular beat Lorraine tapped her foot against the tile floor. "I wish you had seen fit to tell me about the developing problem, Ms. Carr."

Maggie met the nurse manager's glare. "You were off the unit."

"Make sure your documentation is accurate and be ready to go to CCU with the patient."

"Now?" asked Maggie. "Who will take my district? April's at lunch." Her fingers tightened on Jason's hand. Would Lorraine consider this a scene?

"I'm here," said April. "When I heard the code called, I flew back. You were terrific."

"She certainly was," said Jason.

In that instant Maggie realized he still held her hand. She pulled away. "Let me complete her chart."

"I'll stay with Betty while you do," said Jason.

Lorraine strode away. Maggie shook her head and knew that no matter how often she proved her skills as a nurse, Lorraine would find fault.

As though offering support, Jason patted her shoulder. "Take your time with the chart."

"Thanks."

Aware of the undercurrent of hostility in the nurse manager's voice, Jason wondered how he could help Margaret. He would write a note, but would the commendation be placed in her record if he gave it to Lorraine?

The EKG tech arrived. Jason studied the strip and planned a course of treatment for Betty. After the lab tech drew blood, Jason stepped into the hall while a chest X ray was taken. A short time later Margaret and two members of the transport team arrived. Jason placed the EKG monitor and the portable oxygen on the bed. Five minutes later he sat in the open C.C.U. nurses' station and listened to Margaret's report.

He heard echoes of the past in her voice. West Shore Hospital, he thought. That had to be where I knew her. Which floor had she worked on, or had she been one of the droves of student nurses who had rotated from floor to floor every month?

When she finished report, he followed her into the hall. "Again, thanks."

"I'm glad you came back." She walked away from him.

"What now?"

"I start nights on Monday." She pressed the elevator button.

Nights, thought Jason. He opened the door to the stairs and started down. Why did the thought of her working nights disturb him so much?

As he headed to his office, he prayed Betty Loring's cardiac status had stabilized. Her case formed the basis of his investigation into Leon's affairs. Three other cases came to mind, but when he pulled the charts from medical records, parts were missing. O.R. reports, nurses' notes, order sheets, and progress notes had vanished.

Who had taken them? He didn't think Leon was guilty. The orthopedic surgeon's arrogant belief in his own perfection precluded this sort of admission of guilt.

Jason smiled. He owed Margaret more than the note he planned to send directly to Katherine Gordon. Maybe an invitation to dinner. For a moment he saw a candlelit table and Margaret. He shoved the fantasy aside.

When he entered his office, his nurse looked up. "You're really late."

"Did anyone leave?"

"Not a soul. They stayed for your tea and my sympathy. What happened?"

"She coded and it was a success."

"Thank heavens. Ms. Carr's a good nurse."

He nodded and picked up the charts of the first two patients of the afternoon. "An excellent nurse. I need to send a letter to Miss Gordon."

"I'll mock up a draft. . . . Your daughter called with a grocery list."

Jason accepted the long piece of paper she held out. "List. This looks like a month's worth."

"She eats healthy. That's more than I can say for my kids."

Jason nodded. Beth liked salads, chicken, and fish. He just wished she had friends to tempt her with junk food.

At three twenty-five Maggie closed the district book and sighed. April completed her report five minutes later. "Great job, Mag. I really mean it."

Maggie pulled her purse from the drawer. "Thanks."

"Where are you going? I haven't given you

your evaluation yet." April stared at the clock. "Nothing says we have to do it here. Would you like to stop at Buttons with me?"

"Buttons?"

"It's where half the day staff gathers Fridays after work."

Maggie frowned. Half the day staff were in their twenties. "I'm in uniform."

"No problem. So will the rest, unless someone stops by on their day off."

Though she felt uncomfortable about going to a bar in her whites, Maggie nodded. "I'll go."

Ten minutes later she parked beside April's aging wreck. She followed the younger nurse to a large booth at the rear of the restaurant section. A reproduction Tiffany shade hung over the oval table. Stained glass panels formed dividers between the booths.

April slid along the semicircular bench. "We won't be alone long." She thrust a folded paper into Maggie's hand. "You read. I'll order. What for you?"

"A white wine spritzer." Because the bulb beneath the shade above the table cast a dim light, Maggie squinted to read the fine print. Glasses soon, she thought. When she finished the last section, she looked up. "Thank you, but —"

"No buts. You earned every word of praise, and you've taught me a lot about observing and listening to patients and also about acting as an advocate."

"What did Lorraine say about this?"

"She has no authority over my evaluation. She'll do her own. After today's code, what can she say? If Mrs. Loring had died, the Barber would be facing a wrongful-death charge. Think about it."

Maggie nodded. "Are all her actions geared toward protecting him?"

"You'd better believe they are. He pushed her for nurse manager." April slid along the bench. "You've won a lot of friends on days, but watch the night staff. Lorraine worked nights for two years and she's still tight with them."

"Thanks." Maggie signed the evaluation form and detached a copy for herself.

"Here she is . . . the heroine of the day." Charlene slid around the curved bench to April's side. "You were terrific. I'm not even upset about missing my lunch."

"What . . ." Maggie's eyes widened. Charlene had been one of the nurses assisting with the code. "Sorry."

"No problem. I need to start a diet."

Charlene snatched a spicy wing from the huge platter of snacks. "Problem is, this woman will now stuff her face. No willpower." She winked. "What will you do for an encore?"

"Collapse. I nearly did when she opened her eyes."

"When it's over is the best time to fall apart."

By the time Maggie had finished her drink, ten nurses crowded into the booth. A young Asian nurse waved. "Good to see you again. You gave me report of Mrs. Loring. I'd like to know how you do it."

"Do what?"

"Have Jason Knight stare like he wants to take a bite."

April laughed. "You should have seen him grab her hand after the code. Thought he was going to drag her into some dark corner for some stress relief."

"I thought the Queen Bee would throw a fit," said Charlene.

"Doesn't she get enough from Giancardi?" asked a round-cheeked blonde.

"When she first came here, she had the hots for Knight," said April.

Charlene burst into laughter. "Remember the day she rubbed up and down the wall like a cat in heat while she talked to him?"

"You're kidding?"

The gossip made Maggie uncomfortable. The two smokers made her cough. She put five dollars on the table and slipped away. Moments later, she pulled out of the parking lot and headed for the grocery store.

Seven

Maggie pushed the shopping cart along the crowded aisles in the grocery store. Several times she deftly avoided collisions with other shoppers and murmured apologies. Though Friday afternoons generally found her at the grocery store, today, because of the stop at Buttons with April, she had arrived later than usual and faced a near mob scene.

As she reached the bakery section, a uniformed woman turned off the lights and left the counter. Maggie looked at the plastic-covered wares and wished she had arrived earlier. She glanced at the loaves of Italian bread and tubs of cookies. Slowly, she pushed past a rack of desserts. Why not, she thought. Since Laura's visit for her birthday, fruit had been her choice as a meal's ending. She halted the cart and, imagining the tart taste, she reached for the last lemon meringue pie. The pie moved from beneath her outstretched hand.

"Hey, that's my pie."

"Holders keepers."

She looked up. Jason Knight held the pie with both hands. His grin reminded her of a young boy pleased by a prank. "Not fair," she said. "You have a longer reach."

"Let's negotiate. Why do you want this pie?"

"It's a reward for a successful code. You owe me for that."

As though considering her statement, he cocked his head and closed his eyes. "That's a point in your favor. You were quick and efficient."

"Do I get the pie?"

"Not yet. Are you sure you want all the calories this pie represents? Aren't you watching your weight like most of the women I know?"

"Calories don't scare me. I have great metabolism and I exercise every day."

"Well . . ." He shook his head. "I'm not sure a successful code is reason enough."

"How about if I add the great evaluation April gave me?"

His laughter circled her. "I've thought of the best reason." He placed the pie in her cart.

"This is for spending a month chasing nursing's top backfield runner. . . . Chicken, fruit, fish, vegetables. You eat healthful."

"It pays off."

His appraisal brought a flush to her cheeks. "Sure does. Do you ever eat steak?"

"On occasion."

"Then how about joining me for dinner? I'll cook."

Maggie looked away. Her confusion over how to respond edged toward panic. What to do? What to say? Had his friend left? Surely he wouldn't invite her to dinner if the girl was still living with him. "Thanks, but I can't." Think of a reason quick, she told herself. Her mind refused to manufacture anything but a wish to hide.

"What about a coffee break?"

The expression on his face didn't change, but the overtones in his voice reminded her of a child afraid to beg for a special treat. She didn't want to hurt him; she had no plans for the evening. "I'd like that."

"There's a great coffee shop next door." His grin broadened and his blue eyes sparkled. "Race you to the checkout."

Maggie laughed. "Give me a ten-foot start and you're on."

"With all the running practice you've had

lately, I think you've proved our generation can keep up."

A hazy picture of the young woman who lived with Jason flashed in her thoughts. Could she really compete with youth? She made a face. Having coffee with Jason wasn't a date. They were colleagues celebrating a moment of triumph.

They arrived at adjacent checkout counters in a tie. Maggie unloaded her cart, bagged the groceries, and paid her bill. Jason waited by the door. "I won," he said.

"Not fair. I have twice as much as you."

"I end up here nearly every day. Beth likes to cook, but there's always something she forgot."

Maggie inhaled. His young friend hadn't moved out. The disappointment she felt sent her emotions plunging in a downward spiral. If that was the case, why had he invited her for coffee? The pride in his voice when he spoke of the girl puzzled her. She recalled the barbecue and how Jason's young friend had hidden in the shadows instead of being at Jason's side. Why was the young woman ashamed of the relationship when Jason definitely wasn't?

Jason followed her from the store. "See you in three minutes." Before she had a chance to say she had changed her mind, he pushed his cart away.

After the five bags of groceries lined the backseat of her blue sedan, Maggie gripped the shoulder strap of her purse. Why had she agreed to stop for coffee? What if he recalled their shared past? Would she even know how to talk or act? For so long she had shared a life and friends as half of a pair. She turned. Jason waited on the sidewalk.

"Slowpoke," he called, and waved.

Maggie exhaled a long-held breath as she surrendered to the temptation to be in the company of this man, if only for a brief time.

Jason watched Margaret. Would she change her mind? He thought of their encounters at the hospital, where she was always busy, and usually backing away. Even at the barbecue she had used Joanna and Robyn as buffers. Why was she so wary?

When she arrived on the sidewalk, he reached for her hand. Had he missed or had she made some subtle movement of rejection? He opened the coffee-shop door and allowed the aromas of chocolate, spices, and fresh-baked bread to escape. Margaret sighed.

"Is something wrong?"

"It smells like calories and heaven."

"They bake on the premises and also make their own ice cream. Vanilla, chocolate, and what ever fruit's in season. Want to pig out?"

"Yes."

He laughed. The enthusiasm in her voice and the pleasure reflected in her green eyes and her smile delighted him. How refreshing to find a woman who liked food. "My treat."

"Dutch," she said.

"Mine, please. A reward with no strings. Betty Loring would approve."

"All right." She inched past the cases of cookies, danishes, tarts, and cream-filled pastries. For several minutes she stared at the revolving display of pies and cakes. She ran her tongue along her lower lip. Jason swallowed and wished the intensity of her gaze belonged to him. She turned and smiled. "If I had known this place existed, I would have let you have the pie."

"I didn't want it. I wanted your attention." He ushered her to a booth for two.

"Why?"

Her puzzlement seemed genuine. "I've gotten the idea you're avoiding me. Any particular reason?"

She stared at her hands. "My social graces . . . I feel inept . . . It's hard being a person again."

"Practice on me."

The waitress flipped open her order book. "Hi, Dr. Knight. What today?"

"Coffee and cherry strudel with a scoop of vanilla." He nodded to Margaret. "Your choice?"

"Coffee and one of everything."

Her laughter nudged his memories. "And I thought you'd be a cheap date. I'd like to watch you eat everything that's offered."

Her cheeks flushed. "A raincheck. I'll have a piece of that sinful-looking chocolate fudge pecan pie with a scoop of chocolate ice cream."

The waitress nodded. "Want to try it with a topping of hot fudge sauce? It's scrumptious that way."

"Why not?"

The waitress grinned. "Be right back."

Jason leaned forward. "Have we met before?"

"In a past I'd rather forget."

His memories hadn't betrayed him. Why would she rather forget? Had he done something wrong? He considered how to frame a question that would bring an answer instead of a skillful evasion.

The waitress returned with their desserts. Jason stared at the plate in front of Margaret. A swirl of whipped cream topped the chocolate creation. Maggie attacked the pie with her fork. She tasted and smiled. "I feel like I've died and gone to heaven. Chocolate is my Achilles' heel."

"Is it?" His brow wrinkled and he grasped the illusive memory. He saw a young nurse with a bright auburn braid in the cafeteria at East Shore Hospital, reaching for two pieces of chocolate pie. "Chocolate is my Achilles' heel," she had said.

"Maggie Morgan. You're Maggie Morgan."

Her face looked as though a cloud had covered her inner light. Her fork clattered on the table. "You're right."

"West Shore Hospital." He shook his head. "I should have remembered."

"It's been almost thirty years." The smile slid from her face.

"But you remembered me. Why didn't you say something?"

"Because . . . Well, it's . . . Please." Her voice trailed away.

Searching for the girl beneath the mature features, Jason studied her face. Her eyes seemed less bright, less alive. None of the mischief or laughter he remembered glowed in their depths. Her slender figure was more rounded and somehow more appealing. He studied the curve of her breasts and felt an unbidden surge of desire. "You've changed a lot."

"Women always change more than men."

He had a feeling she would vanish unless he found a way to diffuse her wariness. "West

Shore Hospital. Do you remember the day the patient went into the D.T.'s and started swinging on the rods that held the curtains separating the beds in the large ward?"

Margaret chuckled. "With chest-beating and Tarzan cries at full pitch."

"And nurses, interns, and residents acting like fools, trying to capture him."

"With Miss Rayburn stamping her foot and demanding an end to the noise."

Jason shook his head. "Lord, what a witch she was."

"But a good head nurse."

Jason chewed a bite of strudel, savoring the buttery crust and the tart taste of cherries. Another memory returned. "You were the nurse who cried when John Raleigh died. How I hated losing my first patient."

Maggie nodded. "John had been a patient so often, he had become a friend. Just two years older than me. What an awful death."

"We've learned a lot about treating kidney disease. It's better now."

"Or worse if your life is tied to frequent dialysis treatments."

Jason rested his hands on the table. Did she remember how he had held her while she cried? The moment hadn't meant more to her than a friendly gesture, but he had found a dream that had been left unrealized. What would have happened if he had asked her out instead of falling for the brash charms of Bernice? "What ever happened to Bernice . . . Togan?"

"Togel." Maggie smiled. "Weren't the two of you an item? She's been married for twenty-seven years and has four grandchildren."

His thoughts drifted to the late-night suppers in the cafeteria, where interns, residents, and nurses had gathered around a large table to complain about everything. Maggie Morgan had always been there and never alone. "Didn't you marry George Carr?"

The moment Jason identified her as George's wife, a surge of nausea swept away her self-confidence and eroded the lighthearted remembrances. The aromas became sweet, cloying odors. The desserts on the revolving carousel looked repulsive. The taste of chocolate turned bitter. She pushed her chair back and half ran to the door.

"Margaret, can I help? Would you like to talk?"

How could she talk to him? Would he understand how she felt when she learned George had planned to leave her for a younger woman? Hadn't Jason chosen the same kind of life-style?

Her rubber-soled shoes made no sound on

the pavement. She reached the car, and for several minutes sat slumped in the driver's seat. She glanced at the rearview mirror. Jason hadn't followed yet. She started the car and sped out of the parking lot. When she reached the condos, she parked in her designated space.

Her heart pounded; her breath came in the short gasps of a spent runner. Carrying the groceries to the condo took three trips. She held the last bag against her chest and sprinted up the asphalt walk. Though she felt ashamed of her rude behavior, what else could she have done? When she closed the door, a sense of relief made her weak. As she carried the groceries to the kitchen, she wondered how long it would take until George no longer affected her life.

The scoop of chocolate ice cream slid from the top of the pie. His vanilla turned into a widening white pool streaked with red cherry juice. Jason stared at the coffee-shop door. What had George done to Margaret? Years ago she had been open and direct, laughing at patients' antics, offering comfort to the frightened, crying over deaths, and always challenging injustices. At least her concern for patients' rights hadn't changed.

The waitress brought the bill. She looked at the barely touched desserts and frowned. Jason left an extra tip to let her know the disaster wasn't her fault.

He walked to the door. Why was Margaret working? George Carr had been talented and political. He had caught the attention of West Shore's chief surgeon and had been offered a partnership. Though Jason had had no desire to become a surgeon, he remembered the envy he had felt so long ago.

Had George, like so many of their peers, dumped Margaret for a younger woman and found a way to keep his assets? That scenario might be responsible for her anger and caution. Though she had changed physically and her open and trusting nature had vanished, her actions since coming to Hudson General proved her integrity remained intact. He liked that about her. How could he help her regain herself? From the moment of their meeting a month ago, she had intrigued him. Over the weeks his interest had grown. There had to be a way to keep her from running every time he held out his hand.

At the condos he pulled into the spot beside her blue sedan. Holding the two bags of groceries in his arms, he strode to his unit. Her balcony stood deserted. Was she hiding inside, fighting memories and tears? Surely on Saturday or Sunday he would run into her at the pool. They would talk and he would learn.

As he entered the kitchen, he paused. Beth sat at the kitchen table. One hand held the phone. The other covered her mouth. Deep sobs sounded.

"What's wrong?" he asked, and put the bags on the counter.

Beth hiccoughed. "She . . ." Her voice rose in a fresh wail.

Jason put his hands on her shoulders. "Nothing can be that bad."

"It's . . . it's worse . . . It's too late."

"What do you mean?" His fingers tightened on her shoulders. Were her tears because of the problem that had sent her running to him? "What's too late?"

She dropped her hand from her face and hung up the phone. "I just called Mom." She sniffled. "She's married. That's why it's too late."

Jason sat next to her and took her hand. "I'm not sure I understand. Did you run away to keep her from getting married again?"

She shook her head. "That wasn't the plan. You see . . . I thought . . . I wanted . . . Never mind."

An idea began to form, but he needed confirmation. "Tell me. No matter what it is, I'll listen."

"It's . . . well . . . I thought maybe you and Mom . . . It was a dumb idea." She sighed. "Why couldn't it have worked?"

"What, Beth, what?"

She pushed her chair back and began emptying the grocery bags. "When I got here and saw you hadn't remarried and you weren't even seeing anyone, I thought . . . I hoped maybe you still loved Mom."

Jason groaned. "Oh, Beth." How could he explain so she would understand? "Your mother and I were mismatched from the beginning. She was beautiful, spoiled, and wanted life to be a continuous party."

"I know." Beth opened the refrigerator. "All I can remember from when I was a child is loud voices and music. No matter how many times we moved, she always found people like herself. Even when she got married. He was the same kind of person."

You're still a child, thought Jason until he looked into her eyes and saw the same seriousness that had colored his life. "How did you live?"

"On the money her parents left. Right after she filed for a divorce, she arranged with their lawyer to have the money transferred to some special account."

Jason remembered how the detective had tried to trace the funds that had been dispersed from the Larsons' estate. The task had proved impossible. "I'm glad you had something to live on."

She turned. "Why did she marry you if she didn't want it to work?"

"I was a doctor. She had an image of being a doctor's wife that never touched reality."

"How did you meet? Why did you marry her?"

He leaned against the counter. "She was here, visiting friends, and got sick. They brought her to my office." He shook his head. "Doctors spend too many years with books and life-and-death situations. Their social growth is retarded. I fell hard and fast for her."

She exhaled. "I'm glad you loved her once."

"Not enough to change my life-style. She hated my long hours. She was jealous of my patients and the nurses at the hospital. We had two good years, then one of going our separate ways, plus one of battles followed by silence."

"That was my fault."

He shook his head. "Never think that."

"She didn't like being a mother. Once when I was sick, she threatened to send me to my father. I wish she had."

"So do I." He put his arms around her, but

she slipped out of the embrace. For a moment he felt as though he had failed and was still failing her. "Don't hate her. Hate erodes. Hate blocks trust."

"I don't. I pity her."

As though he hadn't heard, Jason continued. "I wasted a lot of years living with anger and hate. Those days set a pattern for my life I'm not sure I'll ever break."

She studied his face. "Is that why you're alone?"

He smiled. "Was alone. I have you now, and that's good."

"You're right. It is good." She pulled a tissue from the box and blew her nose.

Jason waited for her to tell him more. She walked to the sink and splashed cold water on her face. Should he ask why she had run away? Seconds became long, silent minutes.

Beth turned. "Dinner. I forget to defrost the meat."

Knowing the sharing had ended for the day, Jason opened the refrigerator. "Let's do leftovers." He handed her a plate of chicken and a plastic bag of salad.

After dinner Beth headed to the living room and the television. Jason retreated to the den he had created using part of the basement storage area. He sat in the recliner and considered ways to gain Beth's trust. Could he enlist Margaret's—Maggie's help? Though she held her problems tight, she had a gift for reaching people. He closed his eyes and remembered the day he had held her while she cried.

Maggie's fingers rubbed furrows in the dark green velvet of the couch. She reached for the television remote and flipped from channel to channel. Had she revealed too much to Jason? Silently, she chided herself for accepting the invitation.

The doorbell rang. Her body tensed. He wouldn't, she thought. Still, he was a neighbor, and neighbors came to visit, to borrow, or to pry. Perhaps if she ignored the persistent ring, he would go away.

The peal took on a staccato rhythm. She rose, knowing if she didn't face him, her sense of cowardice would grow.

In the foyer she pressed the button to unlock the front door and turned on the hall light. She peered down the stairs. "Laura, what are you doing here?"

"I needed an escape, and no patients are due for the rest of the month. Were you sleeping or trying to avoid someone?"

"The latter, I'm afraid."

Laura lifted her left eyebrow. "Tell me. My curiosity burns like a hot coal. Is there a persistent neighbor who desires your virtue?"

Maggie reached for her friend's overnight bag. "Are you staying for the weekend?"

"If you'll have me." Humor glistened in Laura's dark eyes. "You're avoiding my question. Whom are you hiding from?"

Maggie laughed. "I'll tell all later. First let me put your bag in the guest room. How did you know I needed to talk to you?"

"ESP." Laura touched her forehead with her fingertips. "I felt the cry of loneliness in all the phone messages you didn't leave. At least a dozen hangups."

"How do you know they were all mine?"

"Simple. I know how you feel about answering machines. You're going to have to do something about that problem."

Maggie strode down the hall. "I'm working on the matter. Are you hungry?"

"Starved, but don't dash into the kitchen. Let's find a junk-food haven."

"I'll let you ignore your blood pressure tonight at a gourmet burger place. Let me comb my hair and get my purse."

Just as they reached the foyer, the phone rang. Fearing it was Jason calling for an explanation of her hasty departure from the coffee shop, she considered ignoring it.

"Phone, Maggie," said Laura.

Maggie lifted the receiver. "Carr residence."

"Hi, Bruce Loring here."

Maggie held her breath. "Is your mother . . ."

"Mom's fine. She's stable. I just wanted to say thanks from the family. Dr. Knight said you were wonderful."

Maggie smiled. Was the news about Betty or Jason's compliment responsible for the warmth spreading through her chest? "I'm glad I was there. Your mother's a great lady."

He laughed. "She wants you to visit and help her devise a scheme to spring her from CCU. They won't let her use her laptop. Messes up their machines."

"Tell her I'll stop on my way to work Sunday evening."

"I will, and thanks again. If you ever need a lawyer, my brother says it will be his treat."

"I'll remember that." Maggie's eyes misted. Her new friend would recover. Her oldest friend was here. She hung up the phone.

"A problem?"

"A happy ending for a near tragedy. I'll tell you about my first code while you eat."

Twenty minutes later they sat in a booth at the Burger Bar. Maggie drank iced coffee laced

172

with cream and cinnamon and talked while Laura devoured a giant double burger, a double order of fries, and a large milk shake. When Maggie finished her summary of the past month, Laura popped the last fry in her mouth.

"And you've survived, maybe even thrived." Laura pulled out her wallet. "You know, somewhere I've heard the name Giancardi, not recently though. What's his first name?"

"Leon."

"Leon Giancardi." Laura nodded. "I wish I could remember when or where. How old is he?"

"About forty-five."

"Any idea where he did his residency? I seem to connect the two."

Maggie shrugged. "I haven't been in his office and I sure don't intend to become his patient."

"Find out. When you have an enemy, you have to know everything you can glean. Where's your sense of self-preservation?"

"Lost."

"You'd better find it quick. Mag, you can't let things slide the way you did with George." Laura rose. "Tell me about my godchildren. Morgan sends silly postcards now and then, but silence is all I get from Ellen."

"They're fine, at least they were last week." Maggie chattered about the twins while she and Laura returned to the condo. "I really miss them."

"I know the feeling, but it's the way of life. Children fly away." She paused. "I hope I didn't trash your plans for the weekend by this surprise visit."

"I had decided on a lazy weekend. If the weather holds, we can go to the pool tomorrow and antiquing on Sunday."

On Saturday the sun rose in a cloudless sky. The humidity remained low. Maggie slept late and Laura even later. That afternoon, after a late brunch, they arranged their towels on the grass near the pool. Maggie waved at Robyn and Joanna.

"Catch you later," said Robyn.

"It's feeding time for the monsters," said Joanna.

Laura grinned. "I'm glad you've made some friends."

"Not friends yet, but we're working on it. Robyn organizes the world and Joanna teaches nursing plus raises a pair of twin boys."

"Lucky her." Laura straightened. "Who is that man staring at us?"

Maggie turned. Jason stood at the edge of the pool. A brief blue bathing suit rode low on his tanned hips. She swallowed. No man deserved to look that good. His abdomen lacked even a hint of the paunch George had developed. His back muscles rippled as he raised his arms in preparation to dive into the pool. Unable to look away, Maggie stared.

"Mag, who is he? He hasn't taken his eyes off you."

"Jason Knight." The sun felt like fire on her back. She prayed for a breeze to cool the heat stirred by his appraising look.

"As in Dr. Knight whom you challenged to do something about this Giancardi, and who ran the code, and who bought you coffee, and who knew you and George?"

"He's the one."

Laura licked her lips. "He's luscious and he likes you."

"No," snapped Maggie.

"How do you know what I'm going to suggest?"

"ESP." Jason dove into the pool. Maggie exhaled.

"Go for it," said Laura. "You deserve a long, lean lover."

Maggie laughed. "Laura, please. Besides, he has a live-in friend, and she's very young."

"Are you sure?"

"I've seen her. He's mentioned her."

"How much gossip have you heard?"

"None."

"A man who looks like that generates gossip by just breathing. It may not be what you think. Go for it." She rose and headed for the pool. "Let's get wet."

"Later," said Maggie. She studied the grass. Nights, she thought. I'll be on nights and there'll be no meetings in the hospital and no reason to tell Jason about George.

Eight

Maggie yawned and stretched. Would she make it through tonight and tomorrow night? Even after a month on the eleven-to-seven-thirty shift, her body hadn't adjusted. Minor aches had become constant irritations. Three or four hours of sleep each day left her feeling groggy.

She picked up the bag of yogurt and fruit she had packed for her three A.M. dinner and wondered if she would ever enjoy food again. Sleep deprivation poised her on the edge of constant nausea.

Maggie trudged to her car. Would a miracle occur tonight? She could live with terminal exhaustion if she could discover what she had done to alienate her coworkers. Their subtle and sometimes blatant efforts to make her feel like an outsider had battered her growing confidence in her vision of herself as a competent nurse.

Five months of her sentence remained before

she could request a transfer to another shift. The nurse recruiter's speech on the day she had interviewed for a position at Hudson General dogged her thoughts. "Choose carefully. Before you are permitted to request a change in shift or unit, you must be employed here for six months." In May Maggie had desired nights as a way of avoiding life. By July, avoidance of Jason and of further trouble with the barber and Lorraine had confirmed her choice as right.

She parked in the employees' lot. Ten minutes later she put her lunch in the lounge refrigerator and poured a cup of coffee. The aroma of the brew helped mask the acrid smell of cigarette smoke. "Hi," she said, and waved at Joyce and Mavis, the full-time night nurses' aides. A grunt and a turned head greeted her. A bud of anger blossomed in Maggie's chest. Why didn't they at least show a hint of courtesy? In a rush she left the lounge. Her shoes tapped the linoleum in rhythm with her thoughts. Why, why?

In the nurses' station, one of the evening nurses grabbed her arm. "Count?" she asked.

"Why not?" Maggie sighed. "We all know Bev will arrive five minutes late."

"And offer a lame excuse." The gray-haired nurse patted Maggie's arm. "Hang in there. Hope your night's calm, but there are five empty beds in your district."

Maggie made a face. "Great."

During report, the phone rang four times to inform Maggie of four admissions and a transfer from ICU. Maggie sent Joyce, the aide assigned to her district, to turn down the covers and put admission packs at the bedside. Quickly, she checked her notes for elevated temperatures and for patients having tests or surgery the next day.

The first patient, the transfer from ICU, arrived just as she finished the list. "Give this to Joyce," she said to Bev Johnson.

The tall, thin nurse shrugged. "If I see her." She shoved the paper in her pocket.

Maggie uncoiled her fists and followed the ICU team down the hall. Twenty minutes later, after listening to a detailed report and checking the pins, weights, and slings supporting the twenty-nine-year-old biker's broken legs, she returned to an empty station. She found her list crumpled on the floor. After smoothing the paper, she went to check and found none of the water pitchers had been removed. She did the job and took the two elevated temperatures before heading back to the station for the midnight medications and a sleeping pill.

Bev stood in the med room. "Did you give Joyce the list?" asked Maggie.

"Ya." The tall woman's stringy dark hair

179

looked greasy. Her uniform needed to be pressed. The scent of stale cigarette smoke covered her like cologne. "Don't blame me if she didn't do the work. You know these aides, they're very independent."

While Maggie hung the last of the midnight intravenous medications, Joyce sauntered into the room. "There's a real parade of patients out there. Don't you think you'd better stop loafing and help us? Bev's busy and Mavis and I can't do it all."

Maggie inhaled. The odor of cheap perfume made her sneeze. "Tell the nurses I'm on my way . . . I need to talk to you later."

"About what?"

"This." Maggie pulled the crumpled list from her pocket.

Joyce snatched the paper. "Don't go pushing the blame on me. I never seen this list. I've been helping Mavis turn her patients. You know we got the easy side."

"Did you turn our two?"

"You got a problem with work. If you wasn't so busy sittin' at the desk making lists, the work might get done."

"I have been working. There's a transfer in 410 from ICU. Multiple fractures. Pins, slings, and traction, and the things on the list are done."

Joyce's heavy hips rolled as she headed down the hall. "See you."

Maggie exhaled and headed to the nurses' station. The aide's continued defiance puzzled her. The other full-time aide, Mavis, had the same attitude.

Two nurses from the E.R. waited to give report on four patients, two twenty-two-year-old men with fractures and possible concussions, a forty-year-old woman with constant back spasms, and Herman Stein, who had suffered a pathological fracture of his right tibia. Maggie accepted the papers, helped put the patients to bed, and then checked the orders. Bev, the other R.N., sat at the desk and filed her nails. Knowing a request for help would go unheard, Maggie left the room and began the physical assessments.

Forty-five minutes later she arrived in Herman's room. Exhaustion made her want to slump in the chair at his bedside. "Why are you here?" The question sounded stilted to her ears. Had she gone on automatic pilot? She rubbed her eyes and hid a yawn in a deep sigh.

"You should ask such a foolish question. Why? Because I stepped the wrong way in the bathroom." He patted her hand. "You look tired. Where is your smile?"

"I think I left it on days." His sympathetic look

made her want to cry. Instead, she took vital signs and filled out the assessment form. He had lost at least forty pounds and the remainder of his hair since the last time she had seem him. His pain-lined face and eyes brought a rush of sadness. How many more admissions, she thought. She completed the last section of the form and capped her pen. "Do you want anything for pain?"

"They gave me a shot downstairs. When it gets too bad, I will call. And you, will you smile?"

"I'm so tired, I'm not sure I can." Maggie inhaled and let her lips curve.

"Not too bad," he said.

Maggie headed for the lounge. Because of the mound of paperwork, she decided to eat her dinner at the desk. She pushed the door open.

Like a reigning monarch, Bev sat at the head of the rectangular table. Mavis and Joyce wore rapt attention on their faces and leaned forward to listen to her low, murmuring voice. Smoke spiraled from three cigarettes.

"Who's at the desk?" Bev's nasal voice rose in pitch. "You're going to have to wait until my break's over."

"I'm eating there."

"Lorraine won't like that."

"She's not here, but I'm sure she'll hear in the

morning." Maggie took her lunch from the refrigerator.

Both aides sniggered. Bev glared. "Not from me," she said.

"Someone will, but I'm too busy right now to care. . . . Joyce, when you finish your break, could you get the admission kits for the new patients?"

Without waiting for a response, Maggie hurried to the desk. The need for a confrontation built like a summer storm. How could she challenge her coworkers without sounding like a whiner? Before tackling the stack of charts, she made medication rounds for two and three A.M. Slowly, she returned to the station.

Abby Jamison, the evening supervisor, sat at the desk. Maggie slid into the chair beside the overweight woman. Abby looked from Maggie to the stack of charts. "All yours?"

Maggie nodded. "Four admissions and a transfer from ICU. Two with hourly neuros."

"Is Bev helping?"

"What do you think?"

Abby's gray eyes showed sympathy, but her mouth firmed. "You have to confront the situation. They'll trample on you until you do."

Maggie sighed and reached for the top chart. "It's coming and I dread the aftermath. Lorraine will blame me."

"Find something on them and use it as a bargaining point. I'll back you up, but do it soon. In two weeks I'm off nights."

"Are you worried about the change?"

"Yes and no. It will give Richard and me a normal home life for a change. I've worked nights for eight years." She smiled wryly. "There are those who consider my promotion is due to his influence."

"I've heard the rumbles." For the past four years, Abby's husband had been head of administration at the hospital. "I also know you have the credentials and the experience needed."

"Which is more than some of the supervisory staff have. When Lorraine accepted the nurse manager's slot, she agreed to complete her degree. Last month she dropped out of the bachelor program. Katherine is angry." Abby paused. "Why don't you talk to her about your problem?"

Maggie shrugged. "What can she do?"

Abby rose. "Think about it. She's worried about this unit. Right after she became D.O.N., she was forced to accept a resignation she thought was unfairly sought. This time she's carefully building a case."

"I know. I've helped her."

"Good for you." Abby paused at the door. "I'll do your neuros. Charts in the rooms?" She shook her head. "You'll never get out of here on time. I'll sign your card for overtime."

"Thanks." Thinking of how much she would miss Abby, Maggie started transcribing orders on the first chart.

A half hour later and six trips to answer lights, Maggie had completed just one chart. Another light flashed. Joyce entered the station. "Get that light," said Maggie.

"I'm not your slave," said Joyce.

"But you are the aide assigned to district B."

The obese blonde put her hands on her hips. "Look, honey, I've heard about your attitude toward aides. You ain't going to push me around."

"What are you talking about?"

"As if you don't know."

"I don't."

Joyce laughed. "Are you going to deny telling Bev you'd like to have an all-R.N. staff?"

Maggie shook her head. "She quoted the wrong person."

"Well, I sure don't believe you. Do your own work. Believe me, Lorraine's going to hear about this. Now, there's a lady who knows how to treat folks. In the two years she worked nights, she never reported us for taking little naps or for taking a few minutes over on our breaks."

"Neither have I, but I'm sure there's no way you'll listen to me." Maggie rose. "Let me tell you this, starting right now, if a patient suffers

185

because you think you're punishing me, I will report you, and it won't be to Lorraine."

Joyce flounced out of the station. "I'll get the light."

Maggie sank into the seat. Had she won a point? She opened the second chart and pushed aside her desire to follow up on a minor victory. Patients and patience, she thought.

At quarter to five Maggie finished the last set of orders. Her neck ached and her eyes burned. Mr. Stein's call light came on. Maggie walked to his room.

"Where is my medicine?" he asked. "I waited and waited. For over two hours I have been in pain."

"I didn't know you wanted anything."

"The aide . . . Joyce, I told her. She said you would be right in. What is wrong with you that you should let someone suffer?"

Maggie inhaled. "I'm sorry, but I didn't get the message."

"Why? Couldn't she find you? Were you napping?"

"No. I was at the desk."

"I see. Your helper doesn't help you."

"Let me get your medicine, and, Herman, from now on, if you ask for something and wait longer than ten minutes, ring again. I'll see that you're taken care of."

"Why don't you report her?"

"It wouldn't help."

"Then maybe I should do something."

"Please don't. I'll end up being blamed." Maggie forced her lips into a smile.

She hurried to the med room. There had to be some answers to her problems with her coworkers, and it was up to her to discover them.

At six-thirty she made medication rounds and completed the neuro checks. She noticed the catheter bags hadn't been emptied. This is the last time, she thought as she emptied the bags and recorded the output. Five minutes later she repeated the statement to Joyce.

The aide smiled slyly. "We'll see."

"No, we won't," said Maggie. "I've done your work all month. Enough is enough." She retreated to the station to complete as many of the fifteen charts as she could before report. Three charts later, April sauntered in.

"Count?" asked the blond nurse.

"Ask Bev."

"Bad night?" April looked at the patient board. "Five admissions. I suppose you did them all."

"You suppose right."

"Glutton."

"No more."

"Good. I'll be glad to disturb Bev's cigarette break."

After report Maggie still had five charts to complete. She took them to a desk in the corner of the nurses' station. Lorraine strode across the room. "I don't give overtime," she said. "If you can't finish your work on time, perhaps you'd be happier elsewhere."

"There were four admissions and a transfer from ICU between eleven and one."

Lorraine's full lips curled into a sneer. "You could have asked Bev to take the transfer and one of the admits." She stabbed a bloodred-tipped finger toward Maggie's face. "Trying to prove you're super-nurse doesn't impress me a bit."

"Nothing I do will." Maggie continued writing. "You don't have to sign my card, Abby already did."

Lorraine wheeled and walked away. After Maggie signed the last chart, she slung her purse over her shoulder and left the station. Just outside the door, she froze. Leon Giancardi strode toward her.

He blocked her path. His gaze scanned her face and slid past her chin. "Margaret, you're looking . . . well, tumbled. I could provide a better time than Hudson General at night."

Holding her back rigid and her teeth clamped, Maggie walked past him. Though lashing out would ease the coils of tension gathered in her gut, the act could end her career at Hudson General. Remember Joanna, she thought.

"God, you look as great from the rear as from the front. Call me and put us both out of our misery."

"I don't think so, Dr. Giancardi."

He laughed. "I understand Jason Knight's the one these days. When you get tired of him, remember me."

I don't believe this, thought Maggie. When had that rumor started? Had someone seen them at the coffee shop? Instead of waiting for the elevator, she opened the door to the stairs. She dashed down, taking two steps at a time, and nearly lost her balance. She grasped the rail and slowed her downward plunge.

On the first floor, as she reached for the door, it opened. Jason stood in the opening. "Margaret, I've been hoping to see you. How are you?"

His eyes held an appraising gaze akin to the barber's insolent stare. The muscles between her shoulder blades tightened. "I'm fine." She slipped past him.

"Could we have dinner soon? I think you need to talk about George."

"Wrong." Maggie strode away.

"Then could you help me with a problem? Beth—"

"Sorry," interrupted Maggie. "I'm busy every

evening and on my days off." Praying he wouldn't follow, she hurried to the exit.

Ten minutes after his encounter with Maggie, Jason sat in the chair beside Herman's bed and listened to his friend talk. "So I would do something, but I think the boss lady would not listen. She has no ears for the patients or the nurses, but she will listen to the doctors."

Herman's assessment of Lorraine Phillips's attitude hit target center, but Jason wondered if she would listen to him. Two years ago, repelled by her predatory advances, he had rejected her offer of companionship. Less than a month later, rumors about her involvement with Leon had swept the hospital.

"So I ask, what will you do to help the lovely Margaret? Her fellow workers on the night shift do numbers on her every night. Will you talk to the blond lady?"

"She won't listen to me," said Jason.

"You could charm the bees from the flowers if you tried." Herman shook his head. "Margaret looks so tired and she snaps and says she is sorry. What if she treats someone who doesn't know what a wonderful woman she is."

Jason rose. "Don't worry. I'll do something." He left Herman's room. In the nurses' station he dropped the chart in the order basket.

Lorraine leaned against the med room door. "Dr. Knight, just the person I wanted to see." She crossed the room and put her hand on his arm.

"How can I help you?" he asked. Her smile made him regret the question.

"It seems there was a problem involving one of your patients last night, but he refuses to issue a complaint."

"What happened?"

"One of our night nurses deliberately delayed giving him pain medication."

"Since Herman Stein is my only patient on the floor, I'm surprised he didn't say anything. I just left his room."

Her fingers inched along his arm. "That's because he's a dear man. Maybe you could make the complaint for him."

Jason shook his head. "Why don't you have the person making the complaint document the incident and I'll look into the matter?" A scowl replaced Lorraine's smile.

Jason left the hospital and strode down the hill to his office. He'd better talk to Margaret and warn her that she had an enemy on the night shift. After dinner he decided.

As usual, Jason arrived home an hour after his expected time. Though Beth had dinner waiting, he stopped in his bedroom and changed into jeans and a knit shirt.

Beth raised an eyebrow. "I like the shirt. Matches your eyes."

He smiled. "I'll be going out after dinner for a bit."

"Too informal for a patient. Is it a medical meeting?"

He shook his head. "I'm going to see a friend."

"It's about time. What's she like?"

"How do you know it's a woman?"

"You wouldn't have taken time to look so great if you were hanging out with a buddy." She grinned. "You're really in great shape for an older man. And if your jeans were any tighter—"

"Young lady, you're being fresh." Beth's laughter and teasing pleased him. If she would let him invite Robyn, Sam, and their teens over and start making friends, he would be content. "Have you given any more thought to college?"

As though a veil covered her face, her eyes darkened. "I was in an accelerated high school program. In June, when I graduated, I was so tired of school I decided against college and I gave up my scholarship."

"You don't have to worry about money."

"There you go again. Offering before I ask. Maybe I'll take a course or two in the spring."

"Have you looked at the Hudson College catalogue?"

"I've looked."

He put his hand over hers. "I just worry about you spending so much time alone. Why not give Pete and Karen a chance?"

"Soon."

He heard a promise in her voice and smiled. The smile froze in place. Beth carried dishes from the table. Something about her gait caught his attention. What am I seeing, he wondered as he helped clear off the table. The answer eluded him. After kissing her cheek, he left the condo. For ten minutes he stood at Maggie's door. Finally, he rang the bell.

The buzzer sounded and he opened the lower door. An instant later Maggie appeared at the top of the steps. She wore the caftan she had worn the night of the storm. "Hi, Maggie," he said.

"Did you come about Herman?" Her voice shook.

"Partly. We need to talk." As he walked up the stairs toward her, a clock chimed. Nine-thirty, he thought.

She stepped back from the door. "Have I done something wrong?"

He hesitated. She hadn't done anything, yet there was a problem. Her stance was defensive, arms crossed over her chest, chin high and back straight. How could he word his answer without increasing her tension? "Are you having problems with the night staff?"

"Do eggs break when you drop them?"

"And make a mess. They do. Have you considered a shift or unit change?"

"Yes, but I can't for five long months unless there's a miracle."

"Why didn't you go back to the Island and West Shore Hospital when you finished the refresher course?" He followed her to the living room.

"Because . . ." She turned to look at him. "I couldn't face the gossip."

"And you believed there'd be none here." He shook his head. "Divorce hurts. I know. I've been there. And gossip rubs like an abrasive."

Maggie sat on one end of the couch. "Divorce. I could have handled that." Her fingers moved back and forth on the arm of the couch. "George didn't divorce me. He died in a car crash with his twenty-two-year-old mistress who was pregnant with his child."

Jason looked at his hands. The bitter edge of her voice cut the air. What besides anger did she feel? "That bastard. Oh, Maggie, I'm so sorry. I wish . . ."

Maggie looked up. She heard anger in his

voice and saw sympathy on his face. From deep within, grief welled. She inhaled to staunch the tears that had lain dormant for more than a year. She didn't want him to see her cry. "Why are you here? April says you bother with a nurse only when she's done something wrong." Her question emerged as a demand.

"To let you know that Herman and I are concerned about you. He told me what happened last night."

"And Lorraine?"

"He didn't tell her. One of your coworkers did. Lorraine cornered me and gave a twisted version of the incident and then demanded I file a complaint. Just like Herman, I turned her down."

Maggie's tears rose closer to the surface. "I'll find out who told her."

"Do you have a suspect?"

"Any or all."

"I told her to have the incident documented by the person who complained, and I'd look into the matter."

"She won't. All the other complaints about me have come from nameless sources." She looked away, but not before several tears spilled over. "Thank you and Herman, but I'll fight my own battles."

Jason rose. Instead of helping her, he had added to her pain. He turned and saw her slumped on the couch, softly crying, and he knew he couldn't leave her. In four steps he reached her side. He gathered her into his arms.

"I know . . . I understand. To be alone with the hurts others have inflicted is the loneliest thing in the world." He stroked her back. Her tears wet his shirt. He murmured in her ear, not words, but what he hoped were comforting sounds. Her curls brushed his lips. Her hair smelled of coconut and brought visions of tropical isles, sunlight, and her body glistening with oil.

"It's not fair."

"I know." She looked up. Her green eyes glistened.

"I'm sorry. I didn't mean . . ."

He continued stroking, feeling the silky material of her caftan against his palms. He bent his head. His lips found hers, and the light kiss he had meant to offer, the friendly gift of sympathy, exploded like a forest fire burning away everything except a desire to claim, to possess and to be possessed.

Her hands slid along his arms and circled his neck. Fingers softly touched the hair at the nape of his neck. Her breasts, nipples tightened, pressed against his chest. His tongue touched her lips. He shifted his position and her body caught his rhythm. He felt her heart thud and knew she was someone he had needed for long years.

The touch of Jason's mouth on hers ignited a passion that dissolved grief, anger, shame, and guilt and channeled these emotions into a molten stream. His caresses soothed and excited. She brushed her hands along his arms. The fine hair sent tiny impulses charging along her nerves.

She opened her mouth to welcome his invading tongue and counterstroked his lower lip and teeth. His hands touched the sides of her breasts, and she shivered.

"Maggie, Maggie," he murmured. He slid his hands up her arms and cupped her face. "Beautiful."

The clock chimed. Suddenly aware of the time, Maggie straightened. What had she done? A wave of embarrassment rose. The trauma of George's betrayal had shattered her belief in herself as an attractive woman. Had she clung to Jason for himself or because he was a man who seemed attracted to her? "The time. I have to go."

He stroked her cheek. "I wish you didn't."

Maggie stared at the mantel clock. "I'm sorry." She wasn't sure if her apology was for the kiss or because she had to leave.

"I'm not. What about dinner tomorrow? When are you off?"

"The next night and not until next weekend."

"I'll see you at seven-thirty."

"I have plans to meet a friend."

"Then next weekend."

"I'll let you know." She wanted to run, to hide. Why had she responded to his kiss with such abandon?

Maggie followed him to the door. She wanted to say something, but what? After the door closed behind him, she walked to the bedroom and sat on the edge of her canopied bed. What have I done?

Too restless to go home and still caught in a whirlpool of emotional overload, Jason strode across the commons and headed for the pool. The crisp air of the mid-September night did little to cool his burning body. He hadn't responded this way since the first few months with Janine, when love had been an adventure and an obsession. The thought of his ex-wife cooled him quicker than the weather. He had failed with her and locked his emotions away.

Maggie Morgan, he thought. Not Margaret Carr. Never again would he tie her to George. He wished he could obliterate the damage her husband had done and erase the effect of betrayal from Maggie's thoughts. His fingers clung to the chain-link fence. What if I blow it? He didn't think Maggie would settle for the kind of affair he had conducted since Janine left. Over the years there had been mutual pleasure with several women, but never the kind of commitment he wanted and feared to make. Knowing a resolution of the dichotomy was impossible tonight, he turned from the fence and trotted home.

Beth sat at the kitchen table, drinking a glass of milk. "Early evening," she said. "Anything wrong?"

"She had to go to work." He combed his fingers through his hair. "Happens."

"Yeah," she said. "It's awful to expect something wonderful and have it bomb."

"Is that why you came to me?"

Beth slid from her chair and carried her glass to the sink. " 'Night, Dad. See you tomorrow."

Silence gathered. Jason's thoughts clamored like a noisy crowd. He felt as though he were running amok. Was it possible to change habits developed to protect himself from hurt? Commitment came from trust. He didn't trust himself or his capacity to love. How could he expect Beth or Maggie to take the step he couldn't?

Nine

The kitchen, redolent with the aromas of butter, vanilla and chocolate, looked as though the room had been attacked by a mad baker. Streaks of white dribbled over the counter and produced an abstract painting on the dark oak floor. Maggie bent to remove the smashed egg that gave the flour picture an odd one-eyed look.

The timer buzzed. She straightened and, using a pair of bright green mitts, removed two trays from the oven and slipped in two more. She slid the cookies from the tray onto a long strip of gleaming foil, and for a moment, before yielding to temptation, stared at their golden perfection.

Heat stung her fingers. Hoping to aid the cooling process, she passed the cookie from hand to hand and remembered another too-eager tasting. Lord, she could still feel the molten, melted chocolate chips searing her tongue and throat. Deciding to resist no longer, she nibbled at the crisp edges, slowly approaching the softer center and the exquisite taste of chocolate. She sighed with pleasure.

An hour later, carrying a tin of cookies, she strode across the asphalt-covered parking lot toward the utilitarian building that housed the county home and hospital. The multiwinged building rose stark and severe in the center of the lot. She couldn't help comparing the structure to a prison. A stand of trees planted in sentry fashion separated the hospital/county home from the complex of county government buildings, graceful and colonial, surrounded by walks and gardens.

The odor of old urine assaulted her as she headed to the three-bed room where Mr. Patton waited. The room, furnished like a hospital unit, held no personal touches. Brown metal beds covered with white sheets, brown metal bedside stands and overbed tables, a television high on the wall, mounted on a brown metal rack, and brown plastic chairs completed the furnishings. Mr. Patton wore jeans, a bright red shirt, and a light blue jacket. He sat on the edge of the bed, staring at the television. He looked around. "Girlie, good to see you."

Maggie put the tin of cookies on the bedside stand. "Cookies, no file." ·

"Maybe next time." He slowly got to his feet and sat in the wheelchair Maggie had pushed into the room. With a flourish she handed him a cane. "We're going exploring today."

The elderly man laughed. "Girlie, just lookin' at you and dreamin' 'bout them cookies is more adventure than I've had in weeks."

"Maybe we'll find some pretty girls."

He raised an eyebrow. "And a beer?"

"An adventure, not a miracle."

Once outside, they left the wheelchair in the stand of poplar trees and strolled along walks, where riotous chrysanthemums in red, orange and yellow filled the flower beds. Mr. Patton chuckled. "I 'member when this used to be a farm. These government buildings is planted right in the middle of an old cow pasture and the poorhouse is in the garden. Ironic, ain't it?"

Maggie's laughter joined his. "I'd say it's pretty fitting. Tell me more."

"I used to pick apples 'crost the road and there was a pond where we used to swim. Swum in the river too."

Maggie continued to prod the elderly man with questions about the county. His entire seventy-two years, except for a four-year stint in the army, had been lived in Hudsonville. Though his stories of the history of the area varied from those she had read in books, his had the sound of tales passed down from generation to generation. His ancestors had arrived when the county was wilderness, cleared trees, planted crops, built homes, had multiplied, and then dwindled until the aging bachelor alone remained.

"Have you heard any news 'bout Herman?"

"He's back in the hospital with a broken leg."

"Guess things don't look too good for my friend." Mr. Patton leaned on his cane and stared at the empty fountain pool. "He's a good man. Educated. Has money, but he treated me real good. Gave me a radio and a 'lectric razor. Shared the food his family brought too. Cain't rightly say it was all tasty."

"I hear his family used your visitors' passes."

"Weren't many of my friends poppin' by. Hill's a bit much for old legs." He stared at the sky.

A wave of caring and concern rocked Maggie. How could she help him? There was no need for him to be in the county home where most of the patients required complete care, but the hotel where he had lived before his accident presented no viable alternative. There were so many things about the past he could share. He knew about hunting, fishing, and trapping. During his lifetime he had watched the Hudson River change from clean to a polluted waterway and seen the attempts to change the river back again.

Maggie sighed. Were there answers? "Time to go back," she said.

"I thank you kindly for your company. Girlie, you're the best. I'm rightly proud to call you my friend."

"It's mutual."

A half-hour later Maggie strode up the walk to her condo. She kicked a stone several yards at a shot. Was there some better place for Mr. Patton, or would he remain here until he became institutionalized?

"Maggie, you in a fog?"

She looked up. Robyn Grant blocked the path. "Not really. I've just come from visiting a former patient at the county nursing home."

"Drab and dreary, huh?"

"Sure is. He and I went walking in the gardens surrounding the county office buildings."

Robyn made a face. "The whole complex is a bit of twisted logic."

"The office buildings are built in a former cow pasture."

Robyn's laughter exploded. "Once manure-producing, always manure-producing. Want to talk?"

"We can." Maggie sank on a bench beneath a maple. Several scarlet leaves heralded the future. "Mr. Patton doesn't belong in a nursing home, but there's no other place for an old man existing on the edge of poverty."

Robyn pulled out a notebook. "Tell me about him. I might have a solution."

"One of your infamous projects."

"Foster homes for the elderly. Matching people who have room with those who need homes. I've a waiting list of families looking for the right person."

Maggie closed her eyes and talked about Mr. Patton, giving Robyn a list of his strengths and weaknesses. "He's a good man. A bit rough-edged. Knows a lot about Hudsonville and the county. He'd be so glad to get out of that . . . that sterile place, I bet he'd even give up dreaming about beer."

Robyn grinned. "I think . . . I hope . . . Let's just say I might have a match." She closed her notebook. I'll let you know how this turns out." She dashed down the walk. "Catch you later. I want you to come—"

Whatever Robyn had meant to say was lost as she turned the corner. Maggie pushed herself off the bench. As she entered her condo,

205

she saw Karen Grant leaving Jason's unit. Did Robyn know? She hoped this visit didn't create a problem in the Grants' friendship with Jason.

The next night, feeling energized by the past night's sleep, Maggie returned to work. Before going to the nurses' station, she stopped in Herman's room. His eyes were closed. Later, she thought, and turned to tiptoe from the room.

"Margaret, I was just resting. There's little sleep for me these days."

"I wish I had a magic pill."

"Wishes belong in dreams." He patted her hand. "Life is sometimes easy, sometimes hard. You know that."

"I saw Mr. Patton today. He sends his regards."

"How is Johnny?"

"Walking with a cane and feeling confined. He wants a cake with a file."

"Ah, no pretty girls, no beer. I wish I could lend him some family who would listen to his stories and maybe write them down."

Maggie smiled. "I told a friend about him. She's looking for a foster family."

"That's good." Herman closed his eyes.

Maggie walked to the door. "I'll see you later. Ring if you need anything."

"I go home tomorrow. My children have made a bedroom for me downstairs, and there will be an aide coming to see I don't act the klutz again."

"Good idea."

"What are you going to do about the bullies?"

"Something. I don't have a plan yet."

"I'm glad you decided to listen to my advice."

Maggie entered the station and checked the assignment board. To her surprise, instead of Joyce, Mavis had been assigned to her district. Not that the presence of the black aide would solve her problems with the staff, she thought. What's Lorraine pulling? The change had come just after she had won a minor skirmish with Joyce. "Why the switch?" she asked the gray-haired evening nurse.

"It's no favor to you," said Sue Rawlings. "Mavis's grandson was admitted last night. Bev complained that Mavis spent too much time in his room and not enough working."

"Figures Mavis would be worried. How bad?"

"Fractured femur."

Maggie reached for the medication book for

her district and checked for new orders. She made a face. Three new patients all belonging to Giancardi had been admitted to her district. After report she made rounds and returned to the station with a list of requests for sleepers and pain meds.

Mavis sat at the desk. "I took the vitals and the water out of 407. Do you mind if I spend a bit of time with my grandson?"

"Go ahead. How is he?"

"I'm right worried about him." A frown settled on her dark, round face. "Just after I got here, he threw up. Shot across the room. He don't act like himself either."

"Did you tell Bev?"

"She says I'm overreacting."

"Go see him. I'll be pushing pills for a half-hour."

At two-thirty Bev and Joyce headed for the lounge and their dinner break. Mavis walked to her grandson's room. Five minutes later she dashed into the hall and bumped into Maggie, knocking her into the wall. "What's wrong?" asked Maggie.

"Don't like this at all." Mavis's dark eyes glowed with fear. "Don't like this at all."

Maggie shook the aide. "What's wrong?"

"Don't know. He's gasping like a fish and rolling his head from side to side."

"Get Bev. I'll check him."

Maggie grabbed a portable blood pressure machine, and before she turned on the light over the second bed in the semiprivate room, pulled the curtains separating the beds. Bobby Ray Jones presented a picture of acute respiratory distress. She picked up the phone and dialed the operator. "Get the house doctor and the supervisor stat."

Bobby Ray's handsome face contorted; his mouth grimaced. "It's all right. I'm here to help you." She took his pulse and blood pressure. Both were elevated. What's going on, she wondered. The answer popped into her thoughts. Fractures of the long bone are sometimes complicated by fatty emboli. She checked his mouth and found the small pinpoint signs of hemorrhage called petechiae on his gums. The phone rang.

"Dr. Dickers here. What seems to be the problem?"

"I have a patient with acute respiratory distress. Long-bone fracture. Elevated pulse and blood pressure."

"I will be right there."

His clipped, formal tones brought relief. Maggie peered into the hall. Mavis emerged from the lounge and slammed the door. "What happened?" asked Maggie.

209

"That Bev won't get off her butt. Said super-nurse could handle the situation and she'll be out as soon as her break's over."

Maggie clenched her fists. There wasn't time for her to go after the other nurse. After swallowing the nasty comment she had been about to make, she turned. "Head for the station. Answer lights and the phone. I'll stay with Bobby Ray until Dr. Dickers arrives. Let Mrs. Jamison know what's happening."

"You'd better believe she's gonna hear plenty. . . . And Ms. Carr . . . Maggie, thank you."

Moments later Dr. Dickers entered the room. The slender doctor hurried to the bedside. "Oxygen four liters stat. Get his doctor on the line and the supervisor. We need an ICU bed."

"Supervisor's here." Abby Jamison entered the room. "I'll call ICU." She followed Maggie into the hall. "What's going on? I figured when you said stat, you meant it."

"Most likely a fatty emboli. Mavis's grandson."

Abby winked. "A rather drastic method of diffusing the situation here."

"He's not my patient."

"So where is she?"

"On break and I can handle the problem."

"Let me talk to her."

Though Maggie knew Abby's intervention would solidify Bev's attitude, she needed the other nurse. Three minutes later Abby and Bev entered the room. "Go call Dr. Abrams," said Abby. "Then quickly brief Bev."

Maggie caught Bev's glare and wondered what kind of scene would ensue as soon as the emergency ended. She entered the station. Mavis jumped up. "How is he? I called his doctor."

The phone rang. Maggie lifted the receiver. "Four ortho, Ms. Carr."

"Dr. Abrams here." The Chief of Orthopedics spoke through a yawn. "What seems to be the problem?"

"Bobby Ray Jones. Possible fatty emboli. House doctor's with him."

"Symptoms."

"Respiratory distress. Confusion. Pulse 130. Blood pressure 150 over 96. Petechiae noted along his gum line."

"Get an ICU bed stat."

"The supervisor's doing that."

"Oxygen."

"Four liters."

"Switch me to the room and thanks for being so observant."

Maggie inhaled and groped for the way to

hook-switch the call into the room. What had April said? She concentrated on the steps and prayed. When the house doctor answered, she hung up. Her knees felt weak and she felt as though she had climbed a mountain. Ellen would be proud of her machinery-shy mother, she thought. With lighter steps she hurried to the patient's room, passing a silent Joyce and a grinning Mavis. Maggie stepped into Bobby Ray's room.

Bev half pushed her into the hall. "What's the big idea?" The dark-haired nurse's pale eyes glinted. "Why didn't you tell me there was a problem? Still trying to win points with Lorraine?"

"I sent Mavis to get you."

"You know how dumb these aides are. She must have garbled the message."

Maggie stepped back. "For heaven's sake, he's her grandson. You should have listened and responded."

"Ms. Carr." Dr. Dickers's call interrupted Maggie.

"Yes."

"We can take him to ICU. Respiratory is on the way and Mrs. Jamison will go with us."

Maggie turned to Bev. "Do you want me to go with them and give report? I'll need to do the notes."

Bev shrugged. "Be my guest." She leaned closer. "Don't think this is finished. Abby Jamison won't be on nights much longer."

"Neither will I, but as long as I am, I'll make sure the patients receive good care." Maggie entered the room and then turned. "All of my patients are in stable condition."

When Maggie returned from ICU, she saw four call lights in her district flashing. Torn between answering them and getting a status report from Bev, she halted outside the first room. The light went out.

Mavis exited the room. "I'll get them. Best you see what Bev is up to."

Maggie opened the station door. Bev and Joyce sat at the desk. Bev smiled. "Here's a list of pain med requests. You don't train your patients very well. Mine are all on schedule."

"I'll take the narcotic keys. You could have medicated some of them."

"And spared super-nurse the chance to show one more time how great she is. I'm doing charts so I can get off on time. I don't have a friend who will sign my card for overtime."

Maggie took the key. Why is she my enemy? Maggie couldn't think of anything she had done to the other nurse. Bev's attitude had crystallized before Maggie had joined the night staff. What lies had Lorraine fed the other nurse? Maggie opened the narcotic cabinet.

As she delivered the last narcotic, Mavis followed her into the semiprivate room. "While we're here, could you help me turn Bertha? Joyce is tired. Bev's had her on the run."

"Sure," said Maggie.

While they worked, Mavis spoke. "I just want to tell you if anybody says anything 'bout you, I'm gonna let them know they're wrong. I'm mighty shamed of myself."

"I'm not blaming you for believing stories other people have spread."

"Said you were a spy for Miss Gordon, were lazy, hated nurses' aides and treated blacks like dirt. They were wrong and so was I. Should have made up my own mind. Anybody with eyes could see you're a good nurse."

"Thanks. Is there anything else you need help with?"

"Later, could I go see Bobby Ray?" The aide's dark eyes glistened with unshed tears. "He had to go and do this just when he was getting his life in hand."

"He was already responding to treatment when I left ICU."

Maggie returned to the station. She reached for the portable rack containing the charts for her district and saw three were missing. Bev sat at the far end of the desk, reading a chart and making notes. Maggie strolled over. "Aren't those my charts? What are you doing with them?"

"An audit. Lorraine wants it done." She shoved the charts away. "Take them. I can finish later."

Maggie carried the charts to the section of the desk where she usually sat. Odd, she thought. All the charts being audited belonged to the Barber. Was there a particular reason for selecting them?

At quarter to five, hoping a visit with her grandson would ease Mavis's fears, Maggie sent the aide to ICU. The last two hours of the shift flew. She had just signed off the last chart when Charlene arrived.

The young black nurse stared at the patient board. "All right, Bev, what did you do with Bobby Ray? Me and that man had an appointment to discuss important things."

"Ask Maggie. She's to blame," said Bev.

Maggie rose. "What's that supposed to mean?"

"You are the one who took him to ICU."

"If I had waited for you to act, you would have been walking to the morgue," said Maggie.

Charlene grabbed Maggie's arm. "ICU? Morgue? What? How? Why? Bobby Ray's some tough dude."

Maggie headed to the med room. "A fatty emboli. He's responding to treatment. Mavis was down two hours ago. Said he knew her. Let's count and then you can get the scoop from her."

"Sure." Charlene shook her head. "Wait till I talk to him. First he wrecks his car, and now this. Hope this is a final lesson."

"A friend?" asked Maggie.

"We were kind of tight in high school. Could be again, but I'm not tying myself to a loser. He blew a big time basketball scholarship and a chance at the pros in favor of the party life."

"Drugs?"

"Thank you no. Alcohol was his thing." She reached for the narcotics book. "If he doesn't get better, I'm going to haul his black . . . Let's count."

After the count was completed, Maggie followed Charlene out of the med room. Lorraine stood in the middle of the station. She smiled. "I hear you had a busy night."

"It wasn't as bad as the last one I worked," said Maggie.

"Bev told me super-nurse struck again."

Maggie turned away. "There was nothing super about what I did."

"I'm glad you realize that." Lorraine gripped Maggie's wrist. "You won't gain points with me ever. One of these days, you're going to make a big error." She moved until she faced Maggie. "Leave Leon alone. I saw you all over him the other morning."

"You're kidding." Maggie held back a laugh.

Moments after Maggie finished report, Leon Giancardi strode into the station. She bent to retrieve her purse from the drawer. A hand rubbed her buttocks. As though she had been stabbed, she straightened and turned.

"Nice glutes, Margaret." His teeth gleamed between lips swept into a predator's leer.

"Sexual harassment," she said.

"Who would believe you?"

Maggie edged away. "At least half the nursing staff."

"They have no power," he said. "When? Just tell me. No one needs to know."

"How about never?" She pushed the station door open and slipped into the hall. Charlene waved and made a circle with her thumb and forefinger. Hoping to escape another encounter with Giancardi, Maggie impatiently stabbed the elevator call button. The doors opened.

Katherine Gordon smiled. "Good morning. Why the scowl?"

"The usual."

"Do you have time for coffee?"

Though her body craved sleep, Maggie wanted to tell the D.O.N. of her decision to confront Leon Giancardi. "I'd like that."

Katherine chose a corner in the nearly deserted cafeteria. "What's been happening?"

"Giancardi and sexual harassment. Until today, innuendoes. I could handle those. This morning he stroked my rear. I'm going to sue."

"Could you document the incident and hold off?" Katherine's amber eyes narrowed. "I've been gathering complaints about him on this issue for six weeks. If we can't prove he's a danger to the patients, we can prove he is one to the nurses. Unfortunately, he's clever at finding times and places where there are no witnesses."

"There was at least one this time."

"Who?"

"Charlene Rodgers."

"A young woman who is learning how to speak her mind. I'll talk to her."

Maggie put down her cup. "Do you have any idea where he did his residency?"

"Hopewell. Why?"

Maybe Laura had heard something. "A

218

friend of mine thought she recognized his name. She did her internship and residency a few years before he would have been there."

They spent another fifteen minutes discussing the morale of the staff on four orthopedics. Maggie yawned and yawned again. She excused herself and headed for the parking lot. Jason stood beside her car.

"Hi." He smiled. "Is there a problem?"

She shook her head. "I stopped for coffee with Katherine Gordon."

He stepped toward her. "Have you thought anymore about the weekend?"

She had and she was afraid of spending time with him. He had someone and she wouldn't trespass. "Thank you, but I don't think it's a good idea."

"Why not?"

"Because . . ." She slid into the driver's seat.

"You need to talk about George."

"I need to put him in the past." She reached for the door.

Jason remained in the parking lot until her sedan vanished. What about the kiss and her response? He hadn't imagined her reaction. Damn you, George Carr, he thought. He strode across the parking lot.

After completing rounds at the hospital, he felt too restless to tackle the paperwork at the office. He drove home.

"Daddy," cried Beth when he entered the kitchen. "Thought you weren't coming home until noon." She pulled the edges of her bathrobe together and scurried from the room.

"I changed my mind. How about going out for lunch?"

"Sure."

He lounged in the doorway and studied her retreating figure. Had she gained weight since her arrival? He frowned and shook his head. Impossible.

Twenty minutes later she returned garbed in one of the shapeless costumes she habitually wore. "So where for lunch and isn't it a bit early?"

"The mall. I know you haven't asked, but I notice you don't have a winter jacket. Our winters are colder than California ones."

She wrinkled her nose. "Could you please buy me a winter coat? There, I've asked you and you didn't break your promise."

He laughed. "How about a couple of nylon jogging suits? I understand they're the rage."

"There goes your promise."

"Only if you ask."

An hour later Jason held a bulky package containing Beth's new down jacket. She pointed to a window display of men's sports fashions. "You've got to buy that one for yourself. She'll go crazy if she sees you in electric blue."

Jason tried to hide his frown. "If she even sees me."

"Oh-ho," said Beth. "Buy."

Ten minutes later Jason held two bundles. "Where for lunch?"

"How about your favorite coffee shop? I'll let you order something full of cholesterol and empty calories."

"Thought you were a member of the diet police."

"You look like you need cake and advice." She linked arms with him. "I'd say she's crazy if she doesn't grab you."

"Maybe I should let you plead my case."

Beth laughed. "Do I look like John Alden? You've got to get her attention. Could you faint, or how about an accident where you land at her feet?"

Jason laughed long and loud. "Am I taking myself too seriously?"

"Not a bit." Beth slid into the passenger seat. "You could serenade her." She made a face. "Bad idea. How about a blind date? Do any of your friends know her?"

"Robyn and Joanna do."

"Oh, I forgot. Robyn called this morning.

You're invited to dinner Saturday night. Have her invite your friend."

"What about you?"

"Karen barged in the other day. We're going to the movies."

"Great."

"She's very pushy. Wouldn't stop asking until I said yes. That's another tactic you could try."

Jason shifted gears. How could he approach Robyn without having her draw conclusions that had no basis? Suddenly, he didn't care. He wanted a chance to know Maggie better.

The phone woke Maggie. She groped for the receiver and glanced at the clock. Four-thirty. She felt like she had slept minutes instead of hours. "Hello." Robyn's excited chatter finally registered. "Back up a bit. I'm sleep-fogged."

"Boy, you're hard to get hold of. I've been trying since the day we met on the commons."

"I usually turn off the ringer for the bedroom phone so I can sleep." This morning had been an exception. She had talked to Morgan and learned he had been accepted into the Houston Opera apprentice program.

"Glad you didn't today. Found a home for Mr. Patton. He moves in next week. Are you coming to dinner tonight?"

"What?"

"I asked you the day we talked about your friend."

Had she? "I must have blocked it out. I can't."

Robyn groaned. "You've sure put me on the spot. Jason will be there, and he did everything short of asking outright if you would be here. Could you cancel the other thing?"

"It's been planned for two weeks. Talk to you later, and ask me again." Maggie sat on the edge of the bed. Why had Jason put ideas into Robyn's head? Now she would have two people to fend off.

Ten

Coffee, he smelled coffee. Jason groaned and rolled over. Olfactory hallucinations, he decided. Since Beth's arrival, there hadn't been a cup of coffee brewed in the house. Herbal teas were the norm. Had she found some new variety of tea that promised wonder and delivered something less than satisfaction? The aroma continued to tease, to cajole, until he decided he had to learn what new torment of healthy eating his daughter had invented.

He stared at the clock. How many years had it been since he had lain in bed past six A.M.? The digital read nine-fifteen. Maggie's fault, he thought. She hadn't come to Robyn's gathering. According to his friend, she had another engagement. Last night, at ten-thirty, he had left Robyn's and lingered on the commons until well past eleven, hoping for a chance to see her. Then he had come home and been unable to sleep.

After a quick shower he pulled on the bright blue jogging suit Beth had persuaded him to buy. He straightened the tangled sheets and pulled the blue tailored bedspread across the king-size bed. As he walked down the hall, the aroma of coffee grew stronger.

"Coffee?" he asked as he entered the kitchen.

Beth turned from the stove. "I've made enough for about two cups."

"You're drinking coffee?"

"It's all yours."

Jason frowned. "What do you want?" Years ago, when his ex-wife had wanted a piece of jewelry or some other luxury item not in their current budget, she had plied him with his favorite foods.

"Nothing." She turned and appraised him. "Nice." Her grin brought to mind the mischievous two-year-old he had adored.

"Your taste is impeccable." He poured a cup of coffee and rolled the first mouthful, savoring the aromatic flavors.

Beth's dark brown hair hung down her back in a single braid. Tendrils had escaped and curled around her face. An over-size red T-shirt topped a pair of jeans. Once again Jason noted the thinness of her arms and legs.

"Why don't you read the papers while I finish breakfast? The *Times* and the *Hudsonville Journal* are outside on the table."

He sat on a stool at the kitchen counter. "I'll keep you company."

"She was there when I took the papers out."

"She's probably gone to bed by now."

Beth giggled. "Poor Daddy. Another lazy woman in his life."

"Not so. She works nights at the hospital."

Beth placed pieces of French toast on the griddle. "I guess that's why you beat me home last night."

"She wasn't at Robyn's."

"Bummer."

"How was your evening?" He drained the cup, lifted the carafe, and decided to wait awhile for the second cup.

"Boring . . . Karen's okay, but she's so into boys and attracting them, I wanted to scream." She flipped the French toast. "She's so young."

"You're just a year older."

Beth shook her head. "Eons. I don't think I was ever as giddy and silly as she is. Mom, you know. Someone in the house had to have some sense."

"I'm sorry."

She turned and waved the spatula at him. "That's dumb. You weren't there. How can you

226

feel guilty for something you can't change?"

"I wish I could."

"Let's eat on the balcony. You take the tray of extras and I'll bring our plates."

Jason put the coffee carafe on the tray next to a bottle of blackberry syrup, a pitcher of orange juice, silverware, and two glasses. Outside, after refilling his cup, he stood at the railing and stared at the commons, where maple trees edged toward flaming fall foliage. How could he help Beth move out of isolation? Last night had been a step, but she seemed ready to reject the next. Though he was thankful she hadn't inherited Janine's nature, he wished — He shook his head. He just wanted his daughter to reach for friends and to set goals for her life.

Beth put the plates on the redwood table and pulled a chair out to sit down. "Isn't it great out here? Warm and cool at the same time. Dig in before the food gets cold."

He took the chair across the table from her. "I thought sausages were out." He speared a piece and ate. "Delicious."

"Fooled you. They're turkey, low in fat and calories. So were the burgers we had Friday night."

Jason shook his head. "I guess healthful can taste good." For several minutes he concentrated on the food. When he put down the fork, he stared at Maggie's balcony, wanting her to appear.

Beth giggled. Jason looked at her. "What's the joke?" he asked.

"Are you trying telepathy to lure her outside?"

"I don't think I'll answer that."

Beth pushed her chair back from the table and walked to the railing facing Maggie's balcony. "You know, an athletic man could jump from here and ninety-five times out of a hundred make it over there. About six feet, I'd judge."

He shook his head. "And what if I miss?"

"There are a lot of bushes down there to break your fall."

"I don't think today's the day I'm going to try."

"Chicken." She returned to her chair and finished her food. "If you're ever going to win her, you'll have to take risks."

"Would you?"

She nodded. "If I liked a guy, I'd find a way to spend time with him. How else are you going to know if things will work out?"

Jason considered her question. She was right, but Maggie didn't appear to want the same things he did.

Beth leaned her elbows on the table. "How

long did you and Mom date?"

"We met in February, were engaged in March, and married in June."

"Wow, talk about lightning. I met Chuck when I was twelve. It took four years for me to know he was the one. If he hadn't . . . hadn't . . ." Tears rolled down her cheeks.

Jason covered her hand with his. "Is there any way I can help?" His whole being felt her grief. Wasn't she too young to tie herself to a ghost?

She looked up and flashed a smile. "Time . . . it'll hurt less in time. Didn't you tell me that?"

He nodded. "I did. You will."

"Back to you and Mom. Would you have married her if you had known what she was like?"

But he had known and he had thought Janine was what he wanted. Pleasure-loving, sensual, ready for a good time, but he had thought once they were a family, she would grow up. "There's no way to answer that. I was different then." He poured the last of the coffee into his cup and pushed his chair back from the table. With his legs stretched out and crossed at the ankles, he considered Beth's question.

Would he have married Janine? He had been

crazy about her and the thought of her with another man had angered him. Their courtship had consisted of frantic social outings, parties where Janine had flirted outrageously, and dinners at fancy restaurants and clubs where he had tried to impress her. Their relationship had skimmed the surface without delving into needs and wants other than sex. He shook his head. How had he expected her to settle into a boring routine when he had given her a different view of himself?

He drained his cup and put it on the table. Already he knew Maggie Morgan Carr better than he had Janine. In the past, he and Maggie had worked as a team, had laughed together and had shared a moment of grief. Physically she had changed, but inside she remained the same caring person. The code, her refusal to compromise with Giancardi, had revealed more about her character than a hundred dinners or a thousand parties. Her challenge for him to do something about Leon's brand of medical practice had erased his inertia. How could he show her they could build on this knowledge?

When he opened his eyes, Beth had vanished. He carried the rest of their breakfast things into the kitchen. "What do you have planned for the rest of the day?"

"Nothing."

"After I come back from the hospital, let's look at those college catalogues Robyn sent over. If I bought you a car, they're all within commuting distance."

She stood in the kitchen doorway. "And if I told you I never want to go to college, how would you feel?"

His shoulders tensed. "Then how do you see your future."

"I don't . . ." She turned away. "Does it bother you to have a daughter who's content to be a vegetable?"

"You're hardly that. Since you arrived, I've had healthful meals, clean clothes, and a neat apartment. You need to be doing more than taking care of me."

She turned and blew him a kiss. "I like taking care of you. You need a little spoiling."

Jason shook his head. Why did he keep pushing her for answers or for action? As a two-year-old, she had been equally as stubborn. "I'm headed to the hospital. I'll be a while because I need to do some work in medical records. Need anything from the store?"

"Not today . . . Daddy, what if I invite her over? Do you think she'd come?"

"No matchmaking allowed. I've enough problems with Robyn's schemes."

Beth chuckled. "I think you need help with this one."

He shook his head. "I'll keep chipping at the edges of her resistance."

"Let me try, okay."

He shook his head. Why was Beth so interested in pairing him off? Was it because of her mother?

As he headed to the car, he whistled a random melody. He paused beside Maggie's blue sedan. A grin crossed his face. He scribbled a note and stuck it beneath the wiper blade on the driver's side. I've hammered in a wedge. How much of a chip will it remove?

Maggie fingered the note she had kept in her pocket since the night before, when she had found it on her windshield. The barely readable scrawl brought a smile that lingered through the night.

We need to talk about us. Jason.

About us, not George, she thought. How can there be an us? Jason's young friend still resided next door. How could he consider another relationship when he was still involved? She sighed. George had, but that was with a younger woman, not one his own age. She paused in the middle of the walk. In all their years of marriage, she had never found a man who tempted her. She had always felt that kind of awareness should be left at the altar. Until Jason kissed her, she had believed the rest of her life would be spent alone.

Pulling her thoughts away from the kiss, she strode up the walk. For a moment she stood on the commons and allowed the bright September sun to warm her. Finally, she went inside, showered, and slipped a dark green velvet caftan over her nightgown. She carried a cup of tea to the balcony. As she sipped the floral brew, she thought about Jason's note. Dare she respond?

"Hi."

Maggie looked up. Jason's young friend sat in a chair beside the railing of the next balcony. Maggie put her cup on the metal table. What should she do? Good manners required a response, but she had no desire to pursue an acquaintance with his girlfriend. "Hello."

"I'm Beth."

"Maggie Carr." She rose and reached for her cup. Retreat seemed the only solution. "See you around. It's time for me to hit the bed."

"Please don't go. I want to talk to you about my—" The brown-haired girl jumped to her feet and suddenly collapsed in a heap beside the chair.

Maggie moved to the edge of the balcony. "Beth, are you all right?" What had happened? A cardiac arrest? Some kind of seizure? Dreadful possibilities tumbled in her thoughts. Six minutes, she thought. Just six minutes to reach the girl and initiate action.

While these thoughts roiled, she raced through the apartment, dashed down the stairs, and flung the door wide. Ten giant steps took her to Jason's front door. She twisted the knob.

Locked, the door was locked. What now? Without a pause to consider solutions, she gulped a breath of air and retraced her steps. Her thoughts sped faster than her feet.

The police—Would there be time for them to get here? Six minutes—Maybe three left—What am I going to do?

She reached the railing of the balcony and measured the distance to Jason's. Too far to jump, she decided. Had the girl's position changed? She couldn't be sure. She stepped back and nearly fell over the chaise longue. "Fit for the tallest man. Extends to seven feet when flat." A bridge, she thought.

After lifting the lightweight plastic and metal chaise, she collapsed the head and pushed it across the gap between the balconies. A quick flip and the bar forming the legs caught over the edge of Jason's balcony.

She pulled her caftan and nightgown to her thighs and cautiously crawled across the makeshift bridge. The structure shifted with each movement of her hands or knees. Views of an imminent collapse brought a desire for speed. Trying to count elapsed seconds brought a rush of fear. She touched the rail and jumped to the balcony. Her sudden move sent the chaise tumbling to the ground. After expelling the breath she had held for an eternity, she knelt beside the girl.

A pulse fluttered beneath her searching fingers. The wave of relief she felt vanished when the pulse faltered. Then the beat resumed. "Beth, are you all right?"

The girl's eyes opened. Blue as summer skies and as blue as Jason's, thought Maggie.

"I fainted. It happens now and again. Sorry I scared you."

"Can you sit up?"

Beth raised her head several inches. "I still feel fuzzy."

Maggie pulled the cushions from the redwood chair and elevated the girl's legs. "I'd better call Jason."

"Don't," said Beth. "I don't want to upset him. Having me here has been enough shock for my father."

Maggie stared at the girl. Jason's mouth, his

chin, his nose, formed Beth's features. She glanced away and did a double-take. She's pregnant. Toxemia, low blood sugar, stringent dieting were some of the reasons she considered responsible for the collapse.

"Let me call him."

Beth grasped Maggie's arm. "Don't. Please don't."

"Then I'll call your doctor. Do you have the number handy?"

"I don't have one."

Maggie shook her head. Why hadn't Jason insisted that his daughter see a doctor? Was he ashamed of the pregnancy? Though that didn't seem true to his character, how else could she explain the neglect?

"You need to be seen by a doctor."

"If it happens again, I will." Beth slid her legs off the cushions and sat up. "See, I'm all right. I fainted. That's all." Her grin reminded Maggie of a naughty child. "I sure picked a dumb way to meet you."

"Why would you want to do that?"

Pink colored Beth's cheeks. "Dad's talked about you and I was . . . would you believe curious?"

Or jealous and protective, thought Maggie. She helped Beth to her feet. "Whatever, but I'd feel more comfortable if I called your father.

There might be a problem with your pregnancy."

Beth's cheeks flamed red. She pleated the hem of her blue T-shirt. "He doesn't know." Her words emerged in a hoarse whisper. "Not yet. It's too soon."

"How pregnant are you?"

"Four months."

"Tell your father."

"He'll want me to have an abortion." A trace of hysteria raised the pitch of Beth's voice. "I have to have this baby. I just do."

"How do you know he'll feel . . ." Maggie let the half-asked question die. Was there some physical reason that might cause Jason to insist on terminating his daughter's pregnancy? "Why is this baby so important?"

Beth's thin body slumped. "It's . . . I don't . . . I can't say. Not yet. Please . . ." Tears flowed down her face.

Maggie put her arm around the girl's shoulder. "I won't push you now, but if you want to talk about this, I'll listen. Don't you think your father will be hurt that you didn't trust him? He's not an ogre."

"He's wonderful. I wish I had known him forever."

Beth's response puzzled Maggie. Had Jason deliberately hidden the existence of his daughter? He was divorced. Why hadn't he at least been allowed visiting privileges? She yawned. Exhaustion rolled over her like a bolt of cloth unwinding. "Look, I have to get to bed before I collapse."

"I'll be all right. You can leave. You must be tired. Dad told me about your schedule."

Maggie walked to the door and stopped. How could she leave Beth alone? What if she had another episode of fainting? "I don't like the idea that you'll be here alone."

"I'm used to it."

"I'm not sure it's a good idea, unless you let me call your father and tell him about the faint. Maybe it's the mother or the nurse in me, but I don't feel right leaving you."

"I've a good idea." The impish grin returned. "You could stay here and sleep in Dad's bed. That would shake him up."

"I'm sure it would." Inwardly, Maggie groaned. Not to mention putting me in a real tight spot, she thought. "I have a better idea. Come to my place and curl up on my couch."

Beth nodded. "That's an okay idea." She brushed past Maggie. "Be with you in a minute. Have to get some snacks."

"Are chips and soda a good idea?"

"Not guilty. Fruit and my special brew. It's a

blend of citrus, apple, and papaya juice. I'll even share. Dad thinks it's great."

"Maybe later." Maggie yawned again. She waited in the foyer for Beth. As they walked to Maggie's unit, the fresh air momentarily invigorated her. "You know what? I have a friend who's an obstetrician. Maybe I can get you an appointment with her."

"Around here? No thanks."

"Her office is on Long Island, about a two-hour drive from here. If she can fit you in on Saturday, will you go?"

"Sure, but you don't have to go to all this trouble."

"I want to." Maggie smiled and knew the truth of the statement. First Mr. Patton, then Betty Loring, and now this girl had contributed to the healing process.

"Okay."

Maggie left Beth in the living room. She sat at the kitchen table and dialed Laura's office. "I'm sure she's busy," she said to the secretary. "This isn't a personal call . . . Sort of a consultation . . . I can't tell you . . . I'm sure Laura will talk to me if you just buzz her."

Three minutes later Laura's husky greeting roused Maggie from the fog settling over her. "Mag, what's up? Mrs. Greeley said you were absolutely persistent. When you have time, teach me how to get around her drill-sergeant persona."

"Just keep insisting and refuse to hang up," said Maggie. "I'm calling about my neighbor's daughter. She's four months pregnant and hasn't seen a doctor." She explained the situation. "I hate to impose, but could you fit her in on Saturday? I'm off and I'll bring her."

"Does eleven-thirty sound good? We'll do lunch."

"Great. See you then."

"Wait? One question. Is she the gorgeous man's daughter?"

"Yes."

Laura chuckled. "I told you so. See you Saturday around eleven-thirty."

Maggie returned to the living room. "It's set. We'll have to leave Saturday around nine."

"Thanks." Beth reached for the remote. "Maggie . . . are you and my dad friends?"

Maggie leaned against the wall. "Acquaintances would be a better description. I knew him years ago when he was an intern. Then I met him again in July."

"What was he like?"

"Quiet, intense, supportive. Let's shelve the talk till Saturday. If I don't get to bed, it'll be my turn to collapse. If you need me, just yell."

As Maggie drifted to sleep, a dozen scenes

from the past floated through her thoughts. She realized she had known him better than she remembered. The younger Jason had been intensely concerned with patient care. At least once his caution had caused a conflict with George over a medical clearance. George had called the senior medical resident. Jason had been overruled and the patient had died on the table. Maggie sat up. And that afternoon I wondered what kind of doctor George would become. So blind, I was so blind. Finally, sleep blurred her thoughts.

At a little past four Maggie woke. She yawned and stretched. While waiting for her head to clear, she sat on the edge of the bed and massaged the teal carpet with her toes. I ache. I'm beat. Every day, except for the times she went to bed at a normal hour, she felt as though she had aged during the night. Should she talk to the nurse recruiter about a shift change? Surely, the hospital wouldn't force someone to stay on a shift when chronic fatigue presented a danger to the patients.

A light yoga session and a shower made her feel half alive. She pulled on a green and white jogging suit and sneakers. When she entered the hall, she frowned. Had she left the television on?

Beth, she thought. Jason's daughter is here

and we forgot to leave a note for him. What if he comes home and finds her gone? He'll be frantic. She ducked back inside her bedroom and jotted a brief note.

The girl sprawled on the couch. Her hand trailed on the gray carpet. The remote lay just beyond her hand.

Maggie felt as though she were shrouded in a block of ice. She swallowed the bitter taste of bile. With steps akin to those of a sleepwalker, she crossed the room. She touched Beth's neck. The girl's skin felt warm. A steady pulse moved blood through the carotid vein. A snore removed the remnants of Maggie's anxiety. After watching the steady rise and fall of Beth's chest and counting respirations, Maggie turned and headed to the door.

The morning sunshine had vanished. A blue-gray hue colored the sky. Wind lifted fallen leaves and spun them in a slow dance. Maggie strolled across the commons. The last traces of sleep flew away on the wind. Before she reached the path to the pool, Robyn called her name. Maggie waited for her.

"Can I join you?" Robyn sounded winded.

"Sure." Maggie smiled. "Mr. Patton called yesterday. He had dinner with his family-to-be and he likes them."

"They like him too. Hey, we missed you Saturday night. Were you really otherwise engaged, or were you avoiding a certain doctor?"

Maggie frowned. Had Giancardi been there? These days, he was the only doctor she routinely shunned. "I had dinner with Betty Loring."

"I'm impressed." Robyn turned to look at Maggie. "How did you manage that? Oh, she's friendly enough, but she usually sticks to her family when she socializes. Not that I blame her. I've been at affairs with her and people are always asking her to give them copies of her books."

"She was a patient."

Robyn grabbed Maggie's arm. "Slow down. I'm too old to gallop . . . You know, Jason did everything but demand to know where you were Saturday night. Sure was fun watching him squirm. Is there anything I should know?"

"Not a thing."

"Pity. You two would look good together." Robyn stopped. "You know, I haven't seen him this interested in a woman for years. Janine's leaving the way she did crushed him. Let me tell you about those days and what a basket case he was."

"Don't." Maggie shook her head. "Isn't it Jason's place to tell?"

As though she hadn't heard Maggie's protest,

Robyn's chatter continued. "Sam and I have been his friends since residency days. We thought he was going to be Hudsonville's most eligible bachelor forever. Then he met Janine. What a whirlwind courtship that was. Five months from first meeting to marriage, and he wouldn't listen to anyone. Four years later she disappeared, taking Beth with her . . . I'm glad that child came back. Jason adored her. She was his princess."

Maggie bit her lip. *His princess is having a baby and doesn't want him to know.* Though she wanted to tell Robyn to change the subject, the words stuck in her throat.

"Who knows how many thousands he's spent on detectives who traced her as far as a commune in California. She vanished again, but he wouldn't let it rest. Every year he heads to California and searches for them. It's not fair. Janine was a bitch, a user, and spoiled."

"I wish you hadn't told me this."

"Jason won't. He's never told anyone, just bottles it inside. If there's going to be anything between you, you have to know." She sighed. "I hope Beth isn't playing her mother's game."

Maggie frowned. Beth was playing some game, but not the one Robyn had described. "Have you met her?"

"As an infant and a toddler. She's never

home when I stop during the day, and in the evening she's holed up in her room. She went to the movies with Karen. My daughter thinks she's neat."

"I like her," said Maggie. "Like most teenagers, she's confused and—" She clamped her mouth together before she revealed Beth's secret.

"And what?"

"She idolizes her father."

"That's something."

They reached the commons again. Maggie headed for home. "I'll see you around."

"How about Saturday? There a play at the Playhouse. One of my groups has a block of tickets. There are a couple left."

"Can't. I've an appointment on Long Island." Maggie broke into a half-run. Robyn had given her a lot to think about. Jason had also been betrayed by someone he had loved.

Eleven

At seven-fifteen Jason pulled into a parking space in the lot behind the hospital. Hoping to reach four orthopedics before Maggie left, he hurried toward the red brick building. As he entered through the doors next to the emergency room, the beeper he carried in his pocket sounded. He reached for the phone on the guard's desk and dialed his answering service. "Dr. Knight."

He listened to the nasal voice of the operator informing him of a patient in the E.R. "I'm there," he said. So much for plans, he thought.

He entered the E.R. and stopped at the desk. "What and who?"

"Thomas Devlin," said the unit secretary. "He's in cubicle two. G.I. bleed."

Jason struggled to compose his features. He and Thomas Devlin were due for another session about the man's drinking problem, but first this new crisis had to be handled.

He pushed the curtains aside. A young Asian-American nurse turned. "Dr. Knight. That was fast."

"I was already here. What gives?"

"Mr. Devlin arrived twenty minutes ago," said Mai Chung. "He vomited a large amount of bright red blood containing clots. Pressure is 80 over 62, pulse 126, and respiration's 30."

Jason noted she had elevated Thomas's feet and positioned him with his head to the side. "Oxygen nasal canula at five liters. Hook him up to the monitor. We'll run a Ringer's lactate at a hundred an hour. Start a second line with saline at KVO rate. Type and crossmatch for four units, CBC, lytes, and a twelve, ABGs stat, and coagulation studies. Flat and upright plates of the abdomen. I'll insert an NG tube."

While Mai Chung called the lab, X ray, and the blood bank, Jason reached for the chart and scrawled the orders. She returned with the nasogastric tube. Jason threaded it through Thomas's nose. "Get me some normal saline so I can irrigate."

For the next half-hour Jason drew saline into an irrigation syringe, gently instilling the solution and waiting several minutes before withdrawing the fluid. Finally, the fluid remained free of clots.

"Thomas, you're going to be a guest for a while. I'm going to start treatment; looks like you're going to need several units of blood. I've called in a gastroenterologist to do an endoscopic exam. Have you been going to AA?"

The patient looked away. "Not yet."

"If you're trying to kill yourself, there are a lot of easier ways. What's happening at home?"

"She tossed me out. Said if I didn't stop drinking, I couldn't come back."

"Do you want to?"

Thomas nodded. "Of course I want to. What's the big deal with a man taking a drink now and then?"

"Nothing, but you know once you start, you don't know when to stop. Your body's telling you something. It's about time you listened."

The dark-haired man nodded. "Would you call Kathleen and let her know? This is the last time. I promise."

For a moment Jason considered offering transportation to the next meeting. Instead, he walked to the desk and wrote admission orders. Then he called the patient's wife. He stuck his head behind the curtain. "I called. She'll be over as soon as her mother arrives to watch the kids. I'll check on you later." Jason left the E.R. and went to make rounds on his other patients in the hospital.

Though he had planned to be at his office by ten, he ran overtime. When he saw the time, he shrugged and stopped to see Thomas Devlin. Kathleen sat at the bedside. Before Jason had time to do more than examine Thomas, he was being paged over the loudspeaker. "Dr. Knight, report to the E.R."

"I'll see you later," he said to the couple.

When he reached the E.R. desk, the secretary looked up. "It's going to be one of those days. Mr. Chung, cubicle three."

Jason entered. Mai stood at the bedside. "Dr. Knight, I am going to yell at him," she said, looking at her grandfather.

"Mr. Chung," said Jason. "What have you done to upset Mai?"

"He didn't refill his blood pressure medicine, that's what." The young nurse looked as though she might cry.

Jason patted her shoulder. "Send one of the other nurses in. I'll let you know what we're going to do as soon as I finish the examination." He turned to the patient. "Why?" A shrug was Jason's only answer. "Do you have a headache?"

"Yes. My eyes are blurred too."

Jason wrapped a blood pressure cuff around the elderly man's arm. The blood pressure registered at 226 over 148. Pulse rate was 112. Without waiting for the nurse, he connected the monitor leads and studied the screen on the wall. Perspiration covered the patient's face and chest.

Rae Grace, an overweight blond nurse, entered the cubicle. "I sent Mai to the lounge. What do you need?"

"IV diazoxide now and I'll repeat every fifteen minutes. Blood gases stat, CBC, lytes, cardiac enzymes. Stat chest X ray. I'll call C.C.U. for a bed and for a surgical and cardiac consult."

When he finished assessing the data as it arrived, Jason wrote admission orders and talked to the surgeon about placing an arterial line and arranged for Ken Blanda, a cardiologist, to see Mr. Chung. Then he went to look for Mai.

The young nurse sat in the lounge. She jumped up when Jason entered. "It's my fault. I was there yesterday for dinner and I didn't remind him to reorder his medicine."

Jason shook his head. "It's not your fault. Have your parents thought more about having him move in with them?"

"He's so stubborn. They ask. He refuses.

They yell. He closes down. If I wasn't getting married next month, I'd move in with him."

Jason nodded. "Talk to them again and I'll see about getting home health aides in several times a week when he goes home."

"Thank you, Dr. Knight."

Jason walked to the door and headed to the office. What a day this had turned out to be. At the office he plunged into work immediately and spent most of the afternoon playing catch-up. At quarter to six he saw his last patient.

Mrs. Simms took the chart from him. "Hate to be the bearer, but Abby Jamison's on the phone. She's in the E.R. with her daughter."

Jason groaned. "Tell her I'm on my way. Would you call Beth and let her know I'll be late?"

Ten minutes later he strode into the E.R. waiting room. Abby Jamison jumped to her feet. The obese, gray-haired woman looked exhausted. "What's the problem?" he asked.

"It's Pam. She collapsed at cheerleading practice this afternoon. Richard is away at some conference. I'll be so glad when I get on days."

"What do you think is wrong?"

"All summer, she's been overly concerned about her weight. I think she's anorexic. She's lost at least twenty pounds. I feel so guilty."

"Let me examine her."

The pretty black-haired girl's sallow skin and extreme thinness made her mother's concern a possibility. Jason studied the lab results and then completed a thorough examination. Dry skin covered her prominent bones. There were no fatty deposits. Jason sat beside the examining table. "Pam, your mother's worried about you, and so am I. You're underweight—"

"I'm not. I can't afford to gain an ounce or my clothes won't fit. Doesn't anyone understand how important it is to be thin?"

Jason shook his head. "Let me show you these lab results. You're anemic." He explained the results to her. "This test shows your blood chemistry is out of line and in fact, it's dangerous to your health. Have you ever passed out before?"

"Last month, but that was because I was at the beach and got too much sun. What are you going to do?"

"I can send you home with a special diet and have you try it for a week, or I can admit you to the hospital and start special intravenous feedings called hyperalimentation. The choice is yours."

She looked at the floor. "I'll try the diet, please, and I promise I'll be good."

"Being good has nothing to do with this. There's a nurse I'd like you to make an appointment with. She deals in eating disorders."

"Don't tell my father."

"I won't, but I think you'd better talk to him and to your mother."

She looked away. "Maybe another day."

"Get dressed and I'll talk to your mother." Jason left the cubicle and walked to the waiting room.

Abby looked up. "Was I right?"

"Yes. I'll give you a copy of the diet I'd like her to follow, and call my office in the morning to make an appointment for next week. She asked me not to tell her father."

Abby sighed. "They used to be so close, but lately she hardly talks to him. I can't understand why she's doing this. She's always been the perfect child, social, active, straight-A student."

Jason patted her hand. "Don't push her for answers. Do you remember Leslie Boucher?" Abby nodded. "She's set up an office and she's counseling people with eating disorders. I'd like Pam to see her."

"I'll call her as soon as we get home." She looked at him. "You look beat."

"It's been one of those days."

Jason left the hospital. Dark clouds gathered in the sky. Maybe it's the weather that's making me feel a hundred years old, he thought. He started the car and headed home. In some ways Pam Jamison reminded him of Beth. Was his daughter anorexic? Was she skipping meals when he wasn't home? These questions bothered him as he strode up the walk to the commons. A piece of paper taped to the dark wood of the front door caught his attention. He pulled it free.

Jason, Beth is with me. Will explain when I see you. Maggie.

How had his daughter managed this, he wondered. He was certain the explanation was part of some convoluted matchmaking scheme she had designed. I'll ground her, he thought, until the ridiculousness of the idea struck him. She had done that to herself.

Large raindrops splattered on the walk. He crossed to Maggie's unit and rang the bell. Just as he reached out to ring again, she opened the door. His awareness of her and the knowledge that he wanted more than a friendship drove all thoughts of his daughter away. "Hi," he said. "We need to talk." Maggie's smile removed a few pounds of the weight he carried.

"Yes, we do. She's fine."

Her statement momentarily confused him. "Who? Beth?" I'm sure she is."

"She's sleeping. We could go upstairs, but we might wake her. I think she's exhausted."

Or a good actress, thought Jason. He wondered how much energy Beth had expanded dreaming up a scheme. "I'm sure you're right."

"We could walk and talk."

He stepped aside. "In this?" Rain poured in a steady stream. "If you don't mind a quick dash, we can talk at my place."

"I've an umbrella." Maggie stepped outside and opened her umbrella. "Lead on."

They reached the door of his unit. Jason let her enter first. "I'll start a pot of coffee and change. It'll be good to talk to someone who understands."

"Bad day?" she asked.

"One I'd rather not repeat, beginning with a massive G.I. bleed, followed by a hypertensive crisis and capped by an anorexic teenager."

Maggie followed Jason upstairs and down the hall to the kitchen. His unit, though larger, mirrored her layout. Jason stood at the counter and filled the coffeemaker, using the last bit of coffee he had stored in the freezer.

Maggie sat at the table and looked around. The kitchen had a dining area separated from

255

the cooking area by a counter. Moments later Jason returned wearing a pair of blue jogging pants and a blue T-shirt.

The aroma of brewing coffee filled the air. He inhaled deeply. "God, that smells good. Beth's a tyrant. Has me eating healthy and coffee has become a treat. As of today, I'm taking back my right to drink what I please."

"You mean you don't like her special brew."

"It's not bad and decaffeinated sun tea quenches thirst, but coffee does a lot more." He took two mugs from the cabinet. "Milk? Sugar?"

"Black."

"A woman after my own taste. Black and strong."

She laughed. "A woman who has to fight to stay awake for the night shift."

"Those are brutal hours. Why don't you ask for a change?"

"I can't for a little less than three months unless a miracle occurs."

He filled the mugs and sat across from her. "So what happened with Beth?"

Maggie looked at the table. Was he treating this as a joke? "She fainted."

He groaned. "Sorry you had to get involved with one of her schemes. She has this notion

. . ." He put down his mug. "How can I explain without looking like a fool?"

Maggie sipped coffee and looked at him over the rim of the mug. "She said it was a dumb way to meet me, but she really fainted."

"And conveniently left the front door unlocked so you could reach her quickly."

"Wrong."

"Oh, you yelled at her and she languidly roused."

Maggie shook her head. "Actually, I used my chaise longue as a bridge and crawled over to your balcony. She really fainted. What do you know about her health history?"

His shoulders slumped. "Until she arrived, I hadn't seen her for fifteen years. She's told me so little."

The pain in his blue eyes drew Maggie's attention. "I'm sorry." She rose and walked to the counter for the carafe. After refilling both cups, she put it back. Jason's shoulders looked as though a ton of worries had settled there. She stood behind him and kneaded the knotted muscles.

"Ah." He sighed. "You have great hands."

"You're as tight as spandex pants. Talk."

"About Beth? About my patients? Do you think she might be anorexic?"

257

Maggie bit her lower lip and hoped her tension didn't communicate through her massaging fingers. "I don't think it's that."

"Maybe I'd better set up an appointment for her with one of my colleagues."

"I've made an appointment for her with my own doctor. We'll see her Saturday."

He turned. "You don't have to do this."

"I want to. When I suggested calling you or calling a doctor here in town, she freaked out."

"What's she afraid of?"

Though she knew the answer, she remembered her promise. "I'm not sure of the entire story."

"Will you tell me what the doctor says?"

Maggie inhaled. Trapped, she thought. "I will if Beth doesn't."

He rubbed his forehead with his hand. "I feel guilty about her. The little things she's let slip tells me her life hasn't been wonderful. I wish I had known what Janine planned. I should have started searching immediately."

Maggie's hands rested on his shoulders. "You can't change what happened. I know that. Some days I feel the same way, but all that does is tie my emotions into knots." She thought of the day he had held her and of the explosive kiss. That meeting had begun the

258

healing process. She wanted to give him the same gift.

Her fingers stroked his neck. Jason turned. The guilt she expected to see changed into desire.

"Maggie."

The whisper, full of yearning and need, vibrated through her and brought an answering response. He rose, stepped around the chair, and pulled her into his arms.

"Maggie?"

The question in his voice forced her to raise her head so he could read the answer in her eyes and on her face. His lips touched hers and she responded with an eagerness reminiscent of the day she had first learned what a kiss did to her body. His hands inched down her back, pulling her closer and closer. As the kiss deepened and tongues explored and tasted, her body moved against his in a primal dance. She wanted to give him comfort, to show him love, and to let him possess her completely if only for this moment.

Jason felt the subtle changes in Maggie's body. Desire shot through him with enough power to throw his neurons into overdrive. His hands reached her buttocks and pulled her tight. He fit his body to her mating dance. For an instant or an eternity they swayed against each other. Then he drew back and sucked in a ragged breath.

"Maggie," he whispered.

"Yes." Her voice held a promise.

With her hand in his he led her down the hall and opened his bedroom door. On the threshold he paused, giving her a chance to change her mind. She looked up at him. Trust, desire, and even love shone in their green depths. She moved ahead of him. He closed the door. She turned and walked the two steps separating them.

What if I blow this? His frantic thoughts were buried beneath a storm of sensation. As though they had done this before, their actions moved in harmony. Her hands slid beneath his shirt and moved along his skin. He touched her chin with his fingertips and raised her face until his lips captured hers. His hands slid down her back and moved beneath her sweatshirt until his fingers found the hooks of her bra.

When he broke the kiss, she stepped back. She pulled her shirt over her head and let her bra fall to the floor. For several seconds his eyes devoured her full breasts rimmed with the dark areola of a woman who had given birth. He pulled off his T-shirt. Her hand touched his chest; her fingers stroked small circles.

"Maggie, are you sure?"

Her slow smile sent messages along nerve endings and pronounced a wordless acceptance. With quick movements he stripped off the remainder of his clothes. He turned and found she had done the same. The intensity of his desire for her had been building since the moment he had met her again. He hesitated. Would the consummation leave him with nothing? She stepped toward him and all his doubts and fears vanished beneath a storm of need.

"Maggie, I want you. I need you."

She sensed his hesitation, and though the same doubts stirred in her, she continued walking to him. "I want you. I need you." Her words echoed his. The truth of her words filled her, and she knew that for today, only this moment had a meaning.

Jason caught her outstretched hand and led her to the bed. His hands teased and caressed her body. His mouth touched her throat, kissing, tasting, moving downward, and leaving electrified sensations in their path.

She felt alive; she felt beautiful. She felt all the things George's betrayal had destroyed. "Thank you," she murmured.

"You're the giving one," he said.

Kisses and caresses built to a fevered pitch. Jason pulled away and fumbled in the bedside stand.

"There's no need," she whispered. "I'm beyond the days when I have to worry."

"There are other reasons than pregnancy to use protection. How can we preach safe sex if we don't practice it?"

She kissed his fingers, knowing he was right. Once the condom was in place, Maggie kissed his fingers. Then their lips touched and tongues tangled and tasted. She raised her hips to meet his thrusting pelvis. Their dance became a frantic flurry of movement. Maggie convulsed in a lightning moment and felt Jason's echoing climax.

Tears, unbidden and yet necessary, wet her face. Jason kissed them away. "I know. I understand. I'd like to cry too."

For a time Maggie snuggled against Jason while the sensations their lovemaking had raised slowly subsided. Lovemaking, she decided. Though she wasn't ready to admit she wanted more than this moment, there had been more to the encounter than the physical reactions.

Jason brushed her curls from her face. "Lady, you are supersensational. I don't want to let you go."

Maggie turned to face him. Her fingers traced the muscle lines on his chest. "I have to go to work tonight." For an instant she felt the desire to cling, but she had done that once and her sense of independence had been shredded. What lay between Jason and her had to be played lightly.

"It's not that late."

"I know, but Beth will wake and come charging over. I'm not ready to let her know her misfired scheme worked."

Jason laughed and pulled her against his chest. "You're right. We'll have to let her wonder for a while. Are you good at hiding secrets?"

"Unfortunately not. Keeping secrets makes me feel guilty."

Jason released her, knowing if he grasped for more than she was willing to give, the fragile web they had woven together would break. He sat on the edge of the bed and watched her dress. "Would you like to go out to dinner Saturday night?"

"I would, but Beth and I are headed to Long Island and my doctor. I'm not sure when we'll get back. Laura's also my best friend, and we're planning on lunch."

"I forgot." He tried to think of something else

to say, something that would keep her there. "I'll have something ready when you get home. Sunday there's a craft fair in town. We can make a day of it."

"I'd like that."

He rose and quickly dressed. "Don't run."

"I can't stay."

"I don't mean today. I mean run from what's happening between us."

"I won't, but let's take this day by day."

How many days do we have left, Jason wanted to ask. He put his hands on her shoulders. "Maggie Morgan, years ago I held you for a brief time. I wanted to kiss you that day, but I didn't. Since seeing you again, I've wondered what would have happened if—"

"No ifs," she said. "We can't change the past."

"I know. I'll give you time, but not forever."

She nodded. "Sounds fair."

He kissed her cheek and then her lips. Maggie felt her desire to run from this man ebbing. With an effort she pulled away. "Go fetch your daughter."

"Is your chaise still in the bushes?"

"I hope so."

They walked down the steps together. Before opening the door, Maggie hugged Jason. "See you Saturday evening." She stepped outside.

The rain had stopped. Instead of going home, where Jason's daughter waited, Maggie headed across the commons. She felt excited, exhilarated, and self-conscious about what had happened.

Jason watched Maggie run across the commons. He understood how she felt. This evening would be part of his memories forever. He also knew the awkwardness Maggie had felt about confronting Beth. Would his daughter suspect what had happened? Had she really fainted, or had it been a ploy? He wasn't sure he accepted Maggie's assessment.

He stopped and searched in the bushes between the two balconies and pulled the plastic and aluminum chaise free. He looked up and calculated the distance. Why had she taken such a risk for a stranger? She could have been injured. His lips compressed. If this had been a trick, Beth would feel the edge of his tongue.

The door of Maggie's unit was unlocked. Water dripped from the plastic webbing of the chaise. He propped it against the wall. "Beth," he called. "Are you awake?"

She appeared at the top of the stairs. "Daddy, what are you doing here?"

"I met Maggie. She told me you were here. Did you really faint?"

"Honestly and truly. Sure felt like a dummy when I woke up. Where is she?"

"Jogging."

"Really, Dad. Where are your social skills? You should have invited her to dinner as a reward for taking care of me."

"I did. She turned me down."

"Brother, I should have been there." She followed him downstairs.

He thought of the magic shared with Maggie. No, you shouldn't have been, he thought. "She told me she'd made an appointment with her doctor for you." He hesitated before asking the question that had bothered him since this afternoon. "Have you been skipping meals when I'm not here?"

"Never." She brushed past him and ran upstairs. "Coffee. I smell coffee." She dashed down the hall to the kitchen. "Two cups. I guess you did more than meet her."

"We talked."

"About?"

"You. My miserable day."

"Was it really bad?"

"The worst for years."

"I'm glad you have someone to listen who understands the pressures of being a doctor.

Wouldn't you like to have her around all the time?"

"Don't push. I enjoy Maggie's company."

"How are you going to have it if you don't do something?"

"She and I are going to the craft fair on Sunday."

"All right," Beth shouted. "Sure makes my fainting spell worthwhile."

He looked at her. "And if it was a fake, you'd better be prepared for a scolding." He walked to the door. "Have you ever fainted before?"

"A couple of times."

"Why don't you ask your mother to send your medical records and we'll find a doctor here in town? You shouldn't impose."

"Maggie said I'm not. She wants to take me. You know, she acts more like my mother than Mom ever did." She opened the refrigerator. "What are we going to do about dinner?"

"We're going out. I'm starved."

"Why don't you call Maggie?"

"Don't push. Grab an umbrella and let's go." As they headed to the car, Jason looked at Maggie's unit. Was she home, or was she still avoiding his daughter?

* * *

Maggie stood on the path on the far side of the commons and watched Jason and Beth until they disappeared. Rain misted on her face and hands. She wished she had agreed to go to dinner with them and she wished she could convince Beth to be open with her father. If she had accepted the invitation, she would have pushed and lost the girl's trust.

She hurried inside. The chaise, propped against the wall, made her smile. Memories of the evening's lovemaking made her cheeks feel hot. She felt like an adolescent after a first date. How was she going to spend an entire day with the girl without giving her feelings away?

She stopped at the top of the stairs. How did she feel? Jason was a sensual man. He had brought a sense of wonder to their encounter, and though at that moment she believed in herself as a woman, she wasn't ready to think of a lengthy affair.

She reached the kitchen, opened the refrigerator, and planned a dinner of leftovers. Why wouldn't Beth tell her father about her pregnancy? Jason was an understanding man. Maybe on Saturday she would learn the answer.

After dinner she took a long bath. The hot water relaxed her. She closed her eyes and imagined Jason's hands held the soap and the washcloth. Fool, she thought. But for the rest of the evening, and for hours after she arrived at the hospital, she found herself thinking about Jason and grinning like an idiot.

Twelve

On Wednesday night Maggie put her lunch in the lounge refrigerator. Mavis waved and Joyce nodded. As Maggie headed to the station, she wondered if the thaw would continue. Since Monday night even Joyce had been, if not cordial, at least polite. Bev was off tonight and Peggy Land shared the duty. Maggie opened the station door in time to see the buxom night nurse and one of the evening nurses enter the med room.

Before Maggie opened the district book to check for admissions, Mavis entered the station. "Maggie, have you heard the news?" Dark eyes in a full moon face sparkled. "Bobby Ray's back. I made sure he was put in your district, but you've got to work with Joyce. The queen bee's been listening to Bev again. Guess they think they're gonna make you give up."

Maggie purposely ignored the reference to Bev and Lorraine. She refused to be drawn into the battle. "How's he doing?"

"Much better. Doctor said he's right lucky. . . . Now, you let me know if Joyce doesn't do her share. I had a talk with her this morning on the way home."

Maggie smiled. "Thanks." She opened the district book and quickly turned the pages. Bobby Ray was the only new patient. After report, she left the station to make rounds. The patients in the first five rooms slept. The promise of a quiet night hovered within her grasp.

In the sixth room lights burned bright. Kevin Blake and Bobby Ray stared at the television. The handsome, muscular black man turned and squinted at Maggie. "Don't I know you?" asked Bobby Ray.

"You might not remember."

"Sure do. You were here the night I went sour."

"You look much better than you did that night."

"Grandma and Charlene said you saved my life. Thanks." His gaze strayed to the television. A commercial flashed on the screen.

"Just make good use of that life of yours."

271

He groaned. "Are you going to nag me too? Grandma's been giving orders. Charlene's been candy-talking. What's your style?"

"I expect action." Maggie laughed. "What are you going to do when you get out of here?"

"Get myself back to school. Leave alcohol in the bottle and call Charlene to see if we can work things out this time."

"She's a beautiful woman who deserves the best."

"I'm gonna try."

"That's all anyone can expect." Maggie checked his cast, crossed to his roommate's bed, and set out the equipment for pin care.

The hours of the night flew. At seven thirty-five Maggie and Peggy Land walked to the parking lot. Jason strode across the asphalt. He waved. Peggy grinned. "I bet he's not hurrying to see me."

"Maggie, do you have a minute?" asked Jason.

His deep voice vibrated through her. "Sure."

Peggy grinned. "See you." She walked away.

"How's Beth?" asked Maggie.

"Back to normal. Are you sure she fainted?"

"She had all the signs. Thready pulse, cold, clammy skin, loss of consciousness."

"I wish I didn't think she had orchestrated

the event." His blue eyes twinkled. "Still going with me on Sunday?"

"Of course. I've even allocated a special knickknack fund."

His smile warmed her. "Do we have to wait until then to get together?"

Remembering his kiss, his touch, and the excitement of his lovemaking, she felt her body respond. "Our schedules tend to conflict."

"Not always. This is my afternoon off. How would you like to join me for a walk after lunch?"

"Evening would be better. It takes me all day to get three or four hours sleep."

"Six-thirty?"

"See you, then." Maggie watched him walk away. The temptation to forget the walk and make love with him instead spun a web around her tangled emotions. She shook her head. Until she knew if she had responded to the man or to the need to feel attractive, she had to slow the headlong rush into his arms.

Peggy waited beside her car. "Lucky you. He's every nurse's dream." She grinned. "Wish I could see the Queen Bee's face when she hears. She'll turn purple. You should have seen the way she chased him. Took the Barber on the rebound. She'd drop him in an instant if Jason Knight smiled at her like that."

"You've got the wrong idea. We're neighbors. The other day his daughter fainted and I just happened to be there to give first aid."

Peggy's eyes widened. "I thought his daughter died and his wife left because he blamed her."

Maggie walked away. Because she had been a victim, she hated gossip sessions. Were she and Jason going to be the subject of idle speculation? Determined to stop any stories, she inhaled. "Beth's been living with her mother in California and came to stay with Jason this summer. Guess you can't believe everything you hear."

That evening Jason left his unit just as Maggie stepped outside. He paused and savored a moment of watching the way she moved. Her rust-colored jogging suit made her hair glow like molten copper. "Hi," he called. "I was just on my way over."

"That makes my timing perfect, then," she said.

Jason frowned. Had she been hesitant about having him come to her door? Was she so eager to see him, she had rushed? The dichotomy between fear and hope held him motionless. Instead of joining him, Maggie headed across the commons. His fears tripled. He trotted across the grass until he caught up to her. "What's the hurry?"

"You invited me for exercise." Her smile chased negative thoughts away.

"You're right." He had, but the desire for indoor exercise hit like a shock. All he could remember was the taste of her lips, the feel of her skin, and the way her body had responded to his rhythms. He shoved his hands into his jacket pockets. A light breeze stirred her copper curls. They strode down the path past the swimming pool and skirted the tennis courts. Shouts and teasing yells reached his ears. He paused near the basketball court and watched a mixed group of teenagers at play.

Maggie jogged back to where he stood. "Is there a problem?" she asked.

He shook his head. "I'd like to see Beth out here with them."

"Give her time. She's confused right now."

Was Beth confused, and about what? His daughter seemed content with her chosen isolation. Now and then Karen Grant stopped by, and instead of going out, the girls vanished into Beth's room. He held Maggie's hand as they crossed the commons. "Do you have to go in now?" he asked.

"Would you like to come in for coffee and cake?"

275

"What kind of cake?"

"Chocolate with mocha fudge icing."

He laughed. "I should have guessed it would be chocolate."

"That's my weakness."

Jason stopped walking and pulled her closer. "What if I were chocolate covered?"

Maggie laughed. "That might be an interesting development," she whispered.

Her sensuous whisper acted like the wind on glowing embers, turning Jason's desire into fire. "Let's do it," he said.

"Another time." She pulled free and ran.

Had he frightened her? He remained in the middle of the commons, wanting to run, to capture and to possess her. A deep sigh shuddered through his lungs. More than her body, he wanted her love. Was that fair, when he was afraid to return that love? Janine had shown him how easily he could fail.

Maggie turned. "Slowpoke. You're in need of a caffeine infusion."

"Lead me to it." He ran toward her.

Jason followed Maggie upstairs and down the hall to the kitchen. The bright abstract wallpaper and the gleaming wood floor held a warmth his kitchen lacked. Maggie poured two cups of coffee and cut slices from a large cake.

Jason lifted the fork and tasted the chocolate

cake. "Delicious. Did you make it?"

"This afternoon." She cradled her cup. "The hardest thing about being on my own is cooking for one. I was used to healthy appetites and an uninvited guest or two." The phone rang. Maggie lifted the receiver. "Ellen, what's happening? . . . I see. . . . That's great. . . . It's going okay. . . . I'll call you back. . . . I have company. . . . Will do."

She turned to Jason. "My daughter. She's a first-year resident." Her hand remained on the receiver. When it rang, she smiled. "This will be Morgan."

Jason studied Maggie's face as she talked. He saw love and pleasure. Who was this man?

"I'm great. . . . You are. I'll do my best to be there. . . . When? . . . I'll be waiting. . . . Let me go. . . . I have company. . . . No. . . . 'Bye."

Jason held his hands in his lap. He wanted to take the phone from her. What was happening to him?

She looked at Jason. Her green eyes glowed. "It's amazing how the two of them seem to know when one calls home. They're fraternal twins and opposites in everything except this."

Her identification of the caller as her son erased his growing concern. "What does your son do?"

"He sings. He's in an apprentice program in Houston."

"I wish Beth knew what she wanted to do."

"She's young. Ellen always wanted to be a doctor, but for his first two years of college, Morgan was determined to be a meteorologist. I used to think of his golden voice going to waste, and cry. Thank heaven calculus defeated him."

Jason leaned his elbows on the table. "Beth doesn't even have the *wrong* plan for her life. She doesn't want to go to college. Getting a job doesn't interest her."

"Give her time to find her way." She poured more coffee into her cup.

He shook his head. What did Maggie know about his daughter that he didn't? He frowned. Why didn't she trust him? He had given her every chance to confide in him. He finished the last bite of cake. "I'd better go. I gathered a lot of material on Sunday that I need to review. I don't like what I've seen of Leon's records so far." He waited for her to remind him that she had seen the problem first. When she didn't, he smiled.

Her green eyes narrowed and her expressive face announced her interest. "Have you called the National Practitioners Data Bank?"

"I don't have the authority to request information from them. Besides, they list only disciplinary actions and malpractice suits, not cases that never got that far."

"Have you talked to Katherine Gordon?"

He frowned. "I keep putting it off."

"She might have the authority to get the data. Aren't hospitals supposed to query the bank every two years?"

"You're right. I'll talk to her." He headed to the door. Maggie followed. He turned. "I'm glad I suggested the walk. It's been fun."

"Yes, it has."

Though he hadn't meant to kiss her, and had meant to keep things light, something in her eyes drew him. He pulled her into a light embrace and gently touched his lips to hers. Before she could feel the lightning responses of his body, he stepped back. He brushed the back of his hand along her cheek. "I'll see you Saturday evening after your expedition with Beth." He opened the door and stepped outside.

Maggie stared at the door. She was glad he had left; she wished he had stayed. With a sigh she walked upstairs, where she straightened the kitchen. Until Saturday evening, she thought. How would he react when he learned she knew about Beth's pregnancy . . . and had kept his daughter's secret from him?

* * *

On Saturday morning Maggie hurried home. She made a large pot of coffee and took a cold shower. After drinking two cups of the strong brew, she felt almost alive. When the mantel clock chimed to signal eight-thirty, she sat at the kitchen table, drinking a third cup. The doorbell rang. She walked to the foyer and unlocked the door.

"Hi." Beth stepped into the lower hall.

"You're early," said Maggie. Beth wore a loose denim jumper. If Maggie hadn't known about the pregnancy, she would never have guessed.

"Dad left to make rounds at the hospital and I decided to come over."

"Would you like toast or orange juice? I won't offer you coffee."

"Dad said you gave him a fabulous piece of empty calories last night."

The look of yearning on Beth's face and in her voice made Maggie chuckle. "Would you like a piece of cake?"

"Yes, but don't tell Dad. I have to set a good example. He's at the age where he has to watch his diet, you know."

"I'd say he's pretty fit."

"It's very important for him to stay that way."

Maggie frowned. A note of desperation had crept into the girl's voice. Why was it so important? In the kitchen she cut a piece of cake and poured a glass of milk.

Beth took a bite. She sighed and rolled her eyes. "It's everything Dad said it was."

Maggie refilled her coffee cup and sat across the table from the girl. "Are you nervous about today?"

"Kind of."

"Don't be. Laura's low-key. She'll give you good advice. We've been friends for twenty-seven years."

"That's longer than I've been alive." Beth finished the cake and drained the glass of milk. "The longest I was ever friends with anyone was five and a half years."

Maggie glanced at the clock. "Why don't we leave now in case traffic is heavy? I'll nap in Laura's office while you do your thing."

The drive out was smooth and uneventful, and the worst part centered around finding a parking place near Laura's office. They found a meter five blocks away and mingled with crowds of shoppers. Beth hesitated at the door of the office. Maggie tugged on her arm. "You'll be fine."

"Will you be here if I need you?"

"Of course." She opened the door and pushed

Beth ahead of her.

Laura's office nurse looked up. "Maggie Carr. It's been ages. How are you?"

"Fine, Bernice. This is Beth. She's scheduled for eleven-thirty."

"Hi, honey. Let me get you started on the paperwork." The nurse led Beth down the hall. Five minutes later she returned. "Again, how are you?"

Maggie studied her former classmate. Jason had dated Bernice for months. What would he think of her now? Bernice's iron-gray hair aged her. She had lost most of the sultry prettiness of her youth. The twinge of jealousy Maggie felt faded. "I'm exhausted. Worked last night."

"How is orthopedics? I nearly choked when Laura told me that's where you were working. All that lifting would kill my back."

"There's not much on nights. I enjoy the challenge of being back to work."

"How much challenge can bones, casts, pins, and wires be?"

Maggie grinned. "There's a lot more than that. I've run a code, prevented a fatty emboli from doing permanent damage to a young man, made some interesting friends, and guess who I ran into?"

"I won't even try."

"Jason Knight."

Bernice's hand flew to her mouth. "Jason Knight. Really. What's he like nowadays?"

"He's aged wonderfully."

Bernice stared at Maggie. "You know, I always thought he was kind of interested in you."

"But he dated you."

"There was George."

Maggie sighed. There had been George. Bernice touched her hand. "I'm all right," said Maggie.

"You'd better be. Tell Jason hello. I bet he doesn't remember me."

"He did."

Bernice sighed. "Those were the days." She turned away. "I'd better get back to work."

"And I'm for the couch in Laura's office."

"You know the way. Catch you later."

As Maggie drifted to sleep, she pushed away thoughts of Jason and Bernice holding hands, kissing, and making love. That was years ago, she decided. Does it matter?

"Mag, wake up. You've had an hour."

Maggie rolled over and nearly fell off the narrow couch. She stretched; she groaned; she rubbed her eyes. Finally, she sat up.

Laura shoved a cup of coffee into her hands. "You sure bring me interesting cases. Unwed mother hiding her pregnancy, rheumatic heart disease."

The gulp of coffee burned Maggie's tongue. Laura's words jolted her awake. "Rheumatic heart disease?"

"You've got it."

"I never considered heart disease. How bad? Should you have told me?"

"I thought you knew. She said you took care of her when she fainted."

"She never told me anything about her health history." *That's why she doesn't want Jason to know.* "What are her chances of surviving?"

"With the proper care and a carefully monitored delivery, they're good."

Maggie looked up at Laura. "This is going to make her father frantic, but he has to know. Help me convince her to tell him."

"I've tried. She said she will, but only when it's too late for an abortion. She's one determined young woman. What gives?"

Maggie stared at the floor. "Years ago her mother vanished with her. For years Jason's been searching for them. In July she appeared on his doorstep. What am I going to tell him?"

Laura sat beside Maggie. "Sounds like you care a lot for him."

"I'm not sure what I feel. He makes me feel attractive and . . . I don't know."

"This is what you get for trying to mother everyone. I wish I could tell you what to say.

Isn't it her place to tell him?" A knock on the door interrupted their discussion. "Come in," called Laura.

When Beth entered, Maggie rose. "I'll wait outside."

Beth grasped Maggie's hand. "Don't go. Please." Fear shone in her blue eyes.

"Are you sure you want me here?"

"Stay in case I don't understand everything." Beth joined Maggie on the couch. "Besides, someone has to know."

Your father, thought Maggie, but she left the words unspoken.

Laura walked to her desk. "According to the sonogram, you're nearly six months pregnant." Laura talked about the changes in Beth's body, about labor and delivery, and about the potential problems her cardiac status could cause. "Right now things look good, but I'd like to have some tests done. Could you stay and be admitted to the hospital for a few days?"

"No." Beth turned to Maggie. "Dad would let out all the gears on his car, and five minutes after he got here I'd be in the operating room."

Laura leaned forward. "I can't force you to have the tests, and perhaps it would be best if the doctor you choose in Hudsonville ordered them. I'm sure he'll want to see the same things I do."

"I don't know any doctors there. Could I call when I choose one?"

"What about Dr. Grant?" asked Maggie.

"He's Daddy's friend. He'd tell."

Maggie inhaled. "Your father has to be told."

"I'll tell him. I promise."

When, wondered Maggie. When you collapse? When you're on the way to the delivery room? How could she convince Beth to seek medical care on Monday? "I hope you do."

"When I make promises, I keep them." Beth rose. "Thank you, Dr. Richards. I really want this baby. Just give me time to make plans."

"Monday," said Laura. "I'll expect a call from another doctor."

Maggie patted Beth's hand. "I said I'd help you. We all will."

Beth closed her eyes. Several tears trickled down her cheeks.

"Are we still on for lunch?" asked Laura.

Maggie looked at Beth. "It's your choice."

"Sure. I'd be a real creep if I said no."

"Let's go." Laura grabbed her shoulder bag by the strap. The phone rang. She made a face and picked up the receiver. "Mary . . . calm down. How far apart? . . . I'll meet you at the hospital." Laura shrugged. "There goes lunch."

"Just another day in the life of a busy obstetrician. I understand," said Maggie.

286

"You always do. Oh, I'm having dinner with one of your nemesis's fellow residents. I'll let you know what I learn." She turned to Beth. "I want to hear from a doctor by Monday, or I'll do it for you."

"How about coming for Thanksgiving dinner?" asked Maggie. "The twins will be there."

Laura laughed. "You know I can't plan that far ahead." She walked to the door and waved. "See you."

Maggie looked at Beth. "She was late for her wedding because of a delivery. We'll grab a bite to eat here before we go home, but first we'd better check the meter."

After lunch they headed for Hudsonville. Beth leaned her seat back and dozed until they reached the Tappan Zee Bridge. She sat up and rubbed her eyes. "Sorry. I really crashed."

"Rest is a good idea these days."

"That's what Dr. Richards said. She's very nice. I wish she lived here."

"So do I. It's hard not being able to see her every week."

"Do you ever think about moving back?"

Maggie shook her head. "I like Hudsonville."

"And Dad?"

"We're friends."

"Is that all?"

Beth sounded disappointed. Maggie hid a

smile. "That's enough for now." She turned into the complex. "Are you going to call a doctor Monday?"

"I promised. Would Dr. Richards really call?"

Maggie parked the car and turned off the engine. "You'd better believe she would. She's serious about your needing care."

Beth sighed. "I'll tell Daddy too, but not yet."

Maggie unfastened her seat belt. "I don't understand why you won't tell him tonight. At least about the pregnancy."

Beth's shoulders hunched. "You don't understand. He'll force me to have an abortion. My mother tried to do that. That's why I came here. I have to have this baby. He's all I have of Chuck."

"You can't be sure what your father will do."

"Since I've been here, he's been wonderful about some things, but he's also tried to push me into college, to have friends. To control my life."

Maggie closed her eyes. "If something happens to you because he doesn't know what's going on, it will destroy him."

Beth looked up. Tears glistened in her eyes. "I'm going to die. Mom told me I would. She said no kids, no sports, no fun. You know about my heart."

Maggie nodded. "I do now, but couldn't she

288

be wrong? Laura believes you'll be fine with the right care."

"Maybe, but there are other reasons."

"Like?"

"You see . . . well . . . I thought . . . I wanted the baby to bring them together again. She needs a man like my father. Except for Ted, all the men in her life have been creeps who live off her. It's too late. She married this guy who'll take everything she has and then dump her."

Maggie tried to sort through the threads of Beth's story. "What if the worst happens? What about the baby?"

"Daddy can have him . . . her. He needs someone to love."

Maggie looked at her hands. Beth was right about Jason's needs. How easily I could love him, she thought, if only I could trust myself and my feelings. "Your father loves you. Having you here has fulfilled one of his dreams." She closed her lips before she shouted the question foremost in her thoughts. How could Jason love a child who was responsible for Beth's death?

"What am I going to do?" Beth's soft sobs changed into body-racking wails.

Maggie got out of the car and opened Beth's door. She pulled the girl into her arms. "Try to trust him."

"I've never relied on anyone but myself. How can I depend on him?"

Maggie inhaled. "I've promised to keep your secret, but not forever. Make the appointment and then tell him."

"I will. I promise."

Maggie kept her arm around Beth's shoulders. "Let's get inside and do some damage-control before your father sees you in tears."

Beth nodded. "What am I going to tell him about today?"

What about the truth, thought Maggie. "You'll think of something." She unlocked her front door. "Go wash your face with cold water. I'll cut some cake for dessert."

"That's mean," said Beth. She wiped her eyes. "While you and Dad pig out, I'll have to drool."

"Make an exception and eat a piece tonight."

When Jason saw traces of tears in his daughter's eyes, he froze inside. Every dire diagnosis he knew goose-stepped through his thoughts. What had the doctor found? He looked at Maggie. Even her smile seemed less than encouraging. He waited for one of them to speak.

"How soon is dinner?" asked Beth. "We brought cake from Maggie's for dessert."

Jason's hands tightened. "Why the tears?"

Beth looked away. "I was telling Maggie about my friend who died."

He put his hands on her shoulders. "What did the doctor say?"

"I'm healthy." Beth made a face. "She insisted I find a doctor here to have some tests done and send for my medical records. Do you have any recommendations?"

"I'll give you a couple of names later. Let's eat. It's steak, salad and baked potatoes with sour cream and butter."

"Steak, sour cream, butter, Maggie's cake. Wow, it's overdose-on-cholesterol time."

Maggie laughed. "Guess it will be bread and water for the rest of the week."

"Fruit and vegetables," said Beth.

As soon as she cleared the table, Beth headed to the living room and the television. Jason and Maggie lingered at the table. "Is she really all right?"

"She'll be fine."

Why had she hesitated for a moment before answering? He rose. "Let's take a walk." Maggie followed him down the hall. Jason grabbed a light jacket from the coat tree in the foyer. "What did the doctor say?"

"That Beth is healthy and there is a potential problem she'd like checked out. Beth wants to tell you everything herself. I gave her a week to find a doctor and put things straight before I tell you."

"Is it precancerous?"

"Heavens no." She inhaled. "I wish . . . I hate being in the middle."

Jason put his arm around her waist. "Relax. I'll be patient, but it's going to seem like forever."

Maggie turned to look at him. "Want to stop at my place? There's a movie I'd like to see." She inhaled. "For a whole year I cracked books and crammed facts. It was a year without friends, movies, or novels."

"Are you still angry?"

She shook her head. "About George and returning to work?"

"Yes."

"I'm putting the hurt aside and I think I'm glad to be learning how to be independent again."

Jason gave her a quick hug. He liked her and he thought she liked him, but he also knew he wanted her love. "What movie?" He held her hand as they entered her unit.

Thirteen

Maggie stood in front of the full-length mirror in the bedroom and studied her outfit. Because the forecast for the day predicted temperatures in the low seventies, sunny skies, and a cool breeze, she had chosen a light-weight forest-green wool skirt. The loose, light-green cotton sweater made her eyes seem huge and brilliant. Her curls, freshly colored to hide the gray, shone like the copper bottoms of the pans hanging on her kitchen wall.

"And it's heigh-ho, we're off to the fair." Softly, she sang the words of an old song. For an instant the notes froze on her lips. Thoughts of a summer Saturday, years ago, when George and the twins had shouted the same song with gusto, brought a flash of sadness.

Summer's gone, she thought. Autumn now

filled her life. A smile chased shadowy thoughts away. Her life had changed, and though the changes had brought pain, she had grown. She grabbed her purse and tucked a string shopping bag in the outer pocket. Healing had begun and the prognosis was hopeful. Even a month ago she would have felt as though she were drowning in sorrow and anger.

The doorbell rang. He's here. She held her breath and willed her heart to beat in a steady fashion. He's early, she thought. So was she. As she dashed down the stairs, she wondered if the same impatience drove him.

She opened the door. "Good morning." Aware of the song in her voice, she felt her face flush.

Jason stepped inside. "It's a beautiful day and so are you."

The glow in his blue eyes drew a sigh from her lips. Need, hope, desire, flitted quickly across his face. Black jeans topped by a pale blue sweatshirt hugged his body. She reached up and brushed an errant lock of warm brown hair from his forehead.

"Hi," she whispered, knowing her voice betrayed her inner yearnings.

Jason pulled her into his arms. His fingers

brushed her curls and touched her lips. Maggie fitted her body to his. As his lips touched hers in gentle exploration, he took slow steps, edging her toward the stairs. Her arms circled his neck. The kiss became an adventure and drove away all thoughts except the man and the moment. With a great effort she broke the kiss. "The fair?" she whispered.

"No fair." He laughed. "You're right. Anticipation becomes you." His hand slid down her back, and for a moment he held her hips tightly against his. "Later."

"Later," she promised.

"Yeah."

His eyes reflected regret. A wry smile brought the hint of a dimple to his right cheek. The smile faded, and for an instant she saw a picture of a child deprived of a treat. She pursed her lips. Her affair with Jason was moving too fast. How could she slow the progress?

Once before she had rushed into a relationship. Less than a year after her first date with George, they had been married. She remembered the smug pride she felt the day she flashed the diamond engagement ring. Had any of the smiles and congratulations from the other nurses concealed knowledge of her future husband's other loves? She had been so caught up in arrogant preening, she hadn't cared to explore her doubts. Hadn't the engagement proved she was the better woman?

As she followed Jason into the sunlight, the irony of the two situations struck her. Like George, Jason was the subject of the nurses' fantasies. Was she falling into the same trap? Years before, knowing how the other nurses envied her had brought pride and arrogance. With Jason she wanted to hold her feelings close, to understand what and why she felt attracted to him. She didn't want to be envied by her peers; she wanted only to be loved by this man.

"Have a good time."

Maggie turned. Beth leaned against the balcony railing. She waved. "Go change your clothes and come with us."

"We'll wait," said Jason.

"I have things to do," said Beth. "I'm going to look at the Hudson College catalogue. Maybe I'll take a couple of courses this spring."

"Good idea." Maggie smiled. If Beth was thinking about college, perhaps she had chosen not to believe her mother's warnings about dying during childbirth. Would Beth

296

tell her father this evening about the pregnancy and release Maggie from the secret that made her feel guilty? "You can tell us later what you've decided." She turned to look at Jason. His smile changed into a frown. Had he noticed the way the T-shirt molded to Beth's rounded abdomen? Maggie couldn't decide if the pregnancy had become more obvious overnight, or if the guilt she felt made her see something that wasn't there.

Jason took Maggie's hand. "I like that better than the other idea," he called. "This morning she was planning to read the want ads and find a job."

"Maybe she wants to do both so she can pay her way."

"She knows I'll support her." He turned toward the walk leading to the street.

Maggie sought an answer. Though she hadn't known Beth for long, she recognized the girl's independent nature. Yet, Beth also needed to be loved and accepted for herself. "I think she knows that, but she also doesn't like to be smothered."

"I hope that's the reason and not that she's trying to keep me off balance the way Janine did." He shook his head. "My ex-wife took and took. The only time she gave was when she wanted something I couldn't afford."

Maggie shook her head. "Beth's not like that. How often has she even asked you for things you *can* afford?"

He nodded. "You're right, but still . . ."

"Give her a chance to sort out her life."

"I don't have much choice, do I?"

"Do any of us when we have kids?" She stopped and looked down the hill toward the river sparkling in the sunlight. "I'm glad mine are grown, but that doesn't mean they've solved all their problems."

Jason tugged on her hand. "According to my friends, as kids grow older, problems get bigger."

"And fortunately fewer."

As they started down Horton Street to the level part of town, Maggie was amazed at the number of parked cars filling every available space and a few that weren't suitable as parking places. As they neared the wooden horses blocking off the area for the fair, the stream of people became a flood. "Where do they all come from?" she asked.

"Everywhere," said Jason. "It's a beautiful day, but even on a dreary day there are at least ten thousand browsers. We're here early. Wait until this afternoon."

"Let's hope we're done before the mob arrives."

"We will be even if I have to throw you over my shoulder." Jason pulled her close. "Where do you want to start?" he asked.

"With the first booth." She grinned. "I'd like to see everything."

He groaned. "Was this my idea?"

"Yes." Maggie led the way around the barrier, deftly avoiding elbows, swinging purses, and a dozen pushing people. Voices, some shrill, some booming, but all carrying excitement, raised her expectations.

The first booth exhibited custom-made jewelry. Maggie paused to watch the jeweler bend silver wire into an abstract design.

"See anything you like?" asked Jason.

"A lot, but not enough to buy." She quickly passed a display of paintings, paused to admire some rocks painted as cats, ran her fingers over some pottery mugs, and oohed about some cunning animal hand puppets. Jason's hands rested on her waist as a constant reminder of his promise.

"Girlie, how the heck are you? Should have known I'd see you here. Got any of them cookies for sale?"

Maggie turned. Mr. Patton sat in a wheelchair in the middle of the street, forcing lines of people to move past him like a stream around a rock. Two towheaded boys tied bright balloons to the arms of the wheelchair.

"Mr. Patton, how are you? You look terrific."

"Cain't say I'm doing poorly. Want you to meet the boys. Chet and Rob. Ain't they something else?"

"They sure are. I guess you're enjoying your new home."

"Make me feel like part of the family." He beamed at the boys. "Their folks are around someplace. Left me to keep order here. . . . This is the lady who made the cookies."

"They were good," said one of the boys.

"He let us eat most of them," said the other.

"Do you remember Dr. Knight?" asked Maggie.

Mr. Patton extended his hand. "I do. Cain't rightly say I was partial to the things you done to me."

"You got better, didn't you," said Jason.

Mr. Patton slapped his thigh. "Got me there, but if it weren't for girlie here, I'd still be in that prison." The boys began pushing the wheelchair. "Take care of her, and if I hear 'bout you hurtin' her, you'll answer to

300

me. Good seein' you."

"And you," said Maggie.

"What was that all about?" asked Jason.

"After he was transferred to the county home, I visited him. He was out of place and miserable. Then I told Robyn about him, and he has a home."

"Ah, yes, Robyn's projects." He took her head. "And the warning?"

Maggie smiled. "I think he was teasing."

She and Jason strolled past several booths where the clusters of people hid the displays. Maggie hoped Jason would forget what the elderly man had said. She needed no protection from Jason, only from herself.

Maggie spotted a display of adorned crystal boxes. She pulled Jason through the crowd. "Music boxes," she said. "My friend Laura collects them." She turned crystals and held several wooden boxes to her ear before choosing a rosewood box bearing a large rose quartz crystal. "Guess what she's getting for Christmas?"

Jason examined several of the boxes. "Maybe I should do some shopping too. Do you think Beth would like one of these?"

Maggie lifted the one that played Brahms "Lullaby." "This one, I think."

"Isn't that one for a baby?"

Or a baby's mother, she thought. She hoped Beth would tell her father soon. Maggie knew she would enjoy sharing the excitement of planning for a baby. "She'll love it."

Jason paid for the music box. Maggie tucked the package in the string bag with the one she had bought.

"What else do you think she'd like? I'd like to buy her everything she's missed, but she gets upset when I try."

You can't buy back a lost childhood, thought Maggie. "Christmas is different."

"I hope so. In so many ways she's too independent."

"Isn't that good?"

"I'm not sure."

They passed several more booths before Maggie stopped again, this time at a booth where ornaments hung from strings of artificial evergreen. She chose a sassy angel for Ellen and a gaunt Santa for Morgan. "For my kids. I've given each of them an ornament every year since they were born."

Jason envied the pleasure he saw in her eyes. He sighed. She had so many traditions born of living with a family. He had been cheated of that experience. "Maybe I should

302

do something like that for Beth. We've never had time to develop our own holiday customs."

Maggie's hand slipped into his. "You can start new traditions."

How, he wondered. He brought her hand to his lips and kissed her fingers. "Will you help me learn?"

She turned her head. Jason pursed his lips. He hadn't meant to become so serious. The whys of the invitation to become more a part of his life eluded him. The feeling that time flew, sweeping life away too fast for him to chase, frightened him. There's no need to rush, he thought. He had done that once. An uncomfortable silence separated Maggie and him. Though she stopped to browse, though he bought several gifts, he felt isolated from her.

They reached the small park on Main Street where a horseshoe of food booths surrounded a large yellow tent. "Are you hungry?"

"Yes."

He laughed. "That's what I like about you. Most women go all coy when food's mentioned."

"I like food."

They strolled along the horseshoe. Jason savored the variety of aromas. "What would you like?"

"A taste of everything." She pointed to the various names above the booths. "Mexican, Chinese, Greek, Italian, Middle Eastern."

Jason put his hand on her arm. The last time she had said the same words, she had run away. "Everything?"

She nodded. "Let's make sample plates and share."

"Sounds good."

He began at one end of the horseshoe and selected something from each booth. Fried rice, moussaka, fajitas, crisp pizza, curry, barbecued beef. He carried two plates to a table. Moments later Maggie arrived with her selections. She looked at his choices. "What, no dessert? That's about all I chose. Does Beth's influence follow you?"

Jason laughed. "She does head the diet police. I was thinking about buying ice cream on the way home. Will you be too full for a hot fudge sundae?"

"Don't worry. By the time we walk the rest of the fair, I'll have an appetite."

Jason grinned. "I like that about you . . . soda or beer?"

"Lemonade."

When he returned, they began to eat, sharing everything, talking of inconsequential things, and laughing. Had he ever felt this carefree, he wondered.

With her fingers Maggie lifted a piece of baklava dripping with honey from her plate. "Would you like a taste, though I'm not sure how well it will go with beer."

"I'll risk it." He opened his mouth. Maggie fed him the pastry. He caught her wrist and sucked honey from her fingers. The green of her eyes intensified. He wanted to grab her and carry her back to the condo.

"I can't believe my eyes. Did the pair of you meet here, or is this a planned expedition?"

Jason turned and saw Robyn standing beside the table, holding a partly eaten hot dog in her hand. "Sort of," he said.

"Which?" She waved her hand. "Joanna, hurry up. You're not going to believe this."

"Sit down," said Maggie. "It's like this . . ." She lifted the string bag bulging with purchases. "I needed someone to carry my things."

"Is that all you've bought? I had to send Sam home." Robyn grabbed a cup of soda from Joanna. "Do you believe this? After all the times I've tried to arrange a meeting between them."

Joanna smiled. "Stick to your projects. There's a better chance of success." She perched on the edge of the bench. "Have you seen Dave? He and the twins were supposed to meet us here a half hour ago."

"We've neither seen nor heard them," said Jason.

"Wretch. Are you saying the men in my life are loud?"

Maggie reached across the table. "When there's a pair of twins, they always sound like four."

"Don't I know." Joanna swigged her soda. "I hope this time it's a quiet little girl."

"Congratulations," said Jason. "Are the two of you going to hang around forever?"

"I'm insulted." Robyn rose. She winked at Maggie. "Don't believe half of what he says."

When the two women strolled away, Jason covered Maggie's hand with his. "Sorry about that."

"It was fun. Made me feel like a kid again."

Jason nodded. He wondered if she also felt young and unsure of herself. She had brought laughter back into his life. He frowned. The

306

opposite of laughter was tears. Could he have one without the other? He couldn't make a commitment without taking risks. Knowing he wasn't ready yet, he sighed.

Maggie wondered what the changing expressions on Jason's face meant. She could ask, but the answers might be ones she didn't want to hear. She gathered the empty plates and rose.

As she dropped them in the trash barrel, Jason reached for her hand. Her string bag dangled from his fingers. "You forgot this. Good thing you brought me along. What now?"

"This way," said Maggie. "There are still a lot of things to see."

"And a lot to buy," he said.

He put his hands on her shoulders as they edged around a cluster of chattering people. A pair of children running wild crashed into Maggie, knocking her against Jason. "Sorry."

"I was right about the mobs." They stopped at a display of hand-painted T-shirts. Jason picked up one showing a princess hanging from a castle tower. "I'll take this."

"For Beth?"

"This seems to be her current uniform."

At the next booth Maggie paused to exam-inc some earrings. "Do you think your daughter will like these?" Cloisonné butterflies dangled on a chain from a cluster of bright flowers.

Jason nodded. "I'll take them."

"No, you won't. Christmas, remember?" She bit her lower lip. She hadn't meant to hint that their relationship might endure.

"Maggie," called a rich contralto voice. "And Dr. Knight. How are you?"

"Fine," said Maggie. Jason echoed her response. "Betty, what are you doing here?"

"Autographing books for our local literacy fund, but we ran out of copies of mine."

"I didn't know you had a new one."

"Last week."

"What's happening with your suit?" asked Jason.

Betty Loring shrugged. "My lawyer said his insurance company has made a new offer."

"How do you feel about that?" asked Maggie.

"It's not for public exposure."

Maggie noticed Jason had returned to the T-shirt booth. "Why don't you come to lunch and we can talk?" she said.

Betty stared after Jason. "Do you have time, or is your social calendar full?"

"I'm taking one step a day."

"Good idea. I must say you and he look good together. How did this come about?"

"His daughter fainted and I took care of her."

"Good plot material. Can I use it?" Betty stiffened. "Let me vanish. Here comes my biggest fan, and she never wants to buy a book."

Maggie strolled past several booths and stopped at one where exquisite baby things were displayed. Beth, she thought. She has nothing for the baby yet. She began with a delicate pale green woven blanket and added smocked nightgowns with ties on the bottom, a sweater, booties and a bonnet. Just as she selected several embroidered creepers, Jason appeared at her side.

He grinned. "How does it feel to know you're going to be a grandma?"

"I'm —" She stopped before she told him the baby clothes were for Beth.

"So how does it feel?"

Maggie straightened. Why had she agreed to keep Beth's secrets? What can I say? I can't lie. I'm already guilty of that. She tucked the package in her string bag and turned away. "Let's not talk about it now."

Maggie's response to his question puzzled Jason. If he was due to be a grandfather, he would walk with pride. Maggie acted ashamed. Inwardly, he groaned. He hadn't meant to make her think about her age. How could he tell her that she was the perfect age, the perfect everything for him?

Though they looked at the rest of the displayed crafts, something had vanished from the afternoon. Jason struggled to devise a plan to restore laughter to their day. He couldn't allow her to close him out. When they reached the ice cream parlor, he hesitated and then continued past. His offer of a treat belonged to a different time and two other people.

At nearly four P.M., they reached the door of Maggie's condo unit. She turned and smiled. "Thank you for the wonderful day."

"Does it have to end?" Her desire to leave him standing outside her door troubled him. Had his teasing ruined the rapport they had found? He enjoyed her company. She made him laugh. There had been few lighthearted moments in his life since he had lost his child. Though Beth's coming had filled a corner of his life with sunlight, there were other dark corners to be lit. "Coffee? Do you have any?"

310

"Don't you?"

He shook his head. "Beth has removed temptation from the kitchen."

Maggie chuckled. "Poor victim. I'll have to make a fresh pot. Can you wait ten minutes?"

"If I must."

He followed her upstairs and into the kitchen. There, he placed the string bag on the counter. "Maggie . . ."

"Jason . . ."

They spoke at the same time, and then were silent. Her green eyes, huge and shining, seemed filled with questions he wondered if he could answer. Without speaking he strode across the kitchen and took her into his arms.

For a long time he just held her. Though he feared commitment, he was afraid to let her go. As he buried his face against her hair, his body responded and so did hers.

"Maggie," he whispered.

She looked up. "I'm here."

His mouth touched hers; he ran his tongue over her lips. Instantly, she parted them. His tongue explored her mouth. He ended the kiss slowly. "Can coffee wait?"

She smiled. "Since it hasn't been started . . ."

Together they walked to the bedroom. Jason

slowly undressed her, taking time to kiss and caress each bit of flesh he uncovered. The scent of lavender on her skin enveloped him. When she stood nude, he smiled. "You're beautiful and exactly right for me. I like the laugh lines on your face and the things we share. I'd even like the few gray hairs I've found."

Maggie slid her hands beneath his sweatshirt. "Aren't you hot?"

"Incredibly."

As she undressed him, her hands teased and explored. "I think you're exactly right for me too."

They walked to the four-poster draped with sheer aqua material, and lay on the flowered spread. Jason kissed her gently. "The thing about being older is that one can take all the time they want."

"I know. When you're young, it's frantic and exciting and let's hurry to connect."

He laughed. "Let's connect slowly."

Kisses and slow explorations sent fever through Jason's body. Each nerve ending seemed to be alive. When he entered her, they moved as a unit bonded by passion. As he climaxed, he felt her body convulse. His lips found hers. Had she cried his name? He held her close. Words of love formed in his thoughts, but he left them unsaid.

He stroked her hip. "Mmm," she murmured, and snuggled against him. Her breathing slowed. He held her while she slept. Soon he drifted with her.

An hour later he roused. Maggie still slept. He brushed her curls with his hand and breathed a kiss on her cheek. Then he eased his arm from beneath her and covered her with the spread. Though he wanted to stay, he couldn't. He might say words he would regret. He wasn't ready to say he loved her or that she would forever be a part of his life.

After he dressed he returned to the bed and touched her cheek. One day soon he would tell her how he felt.

In the twilight between sleep and wakefulness, Maggie heard a clock chime. She yawned and stretched. As she rolled on her side, she inhaled. The aroma of Jason's aftershave and of their lovemaking scented the spread. The place beside her where he had lain was empty and cold. Hoping to recapture a moment of the magic, she pulled the spread to her face. An aching sadness rose. He had left, and there had been no promise of a future between them. Could she make one? Could he?

She slipped from the bed and pulled her velveteen caftan over her head. In the kitchen she brewed the pot of coffee she and Jason wouldn't share. As she sipped the brew, she wondered if he regretted their day. Was he as afraid of making promises as she was?

She put the string bag on the table. Each item brought a memory of the almost perfect day. Jason had forgotten to take the things he had bought. The subtle promise of his return brought a smile to her face.

Fourteen

On Tuesday morning at six-thirty Maggie completed final rounds on her patients and hurried to the station to finish her notes. As she neared the corner of the hall leading to the nurse manager's office, the sound of voices, low yet angry, caused her to stop.

"I said I want you to look at the chart and do the usual."

Maggie frowned. Who was Lorraine talking to, and what chart did she mean?

"This is getting old," said Bev.

"You heard me." The nurse manager's voice held a threat.

"Haven't I paid enough for one mistake?"

"You know what I know and what I can do."

"I think I'll leave Hudsonville," said Bev.

"No, you won't. I need you where you are, and don't even consider asking for a transfer to another unit."

Maggie leaned against the wall. What's going on, she wondered. She pursed her lips. Did the threat have anything to do with Bev's frequent audits of Giancardi's charts?

"I'll do it, but not this morning. It'll have to wait until tonight. The patient isn't in my district."

"You'd better pray no one reads that chart before then."

Maggie heard a door slam. Bev scurried around the corner and headed to the station. Hoping the other nurse hadn't seen her, Maggie followed. Which chart? Six of the fifteen patients in her district were Giancardi's. Was Bev the person who was removing damaging notes from his charts?

As she wrote her final observations, she left the barber's charts for last. She managed to check four of his before Charlene dragged her into the med room for narcotics count.

"Bad night?" Charlene asked.

"No more than usual."

"Bev sure looks like it was."

Maggie unlocked the outer and then the inner door of the narcotics cabinet. "Lorraine and she had an argument ten minutes or so ago. The Queen was dreadfully upset."

"Boy, that's a switch." Charlene pushed beaded braids over her shoulder. "Thought they were best pals."

Maggie decided to change the subject. No sense starting a rumor when she didn't know what she wanted to discover. "How's Bobby Ray?"

Charlene sputtered, "He's . . . well . . . good."

"I didn't mean to pry. Mavis said he's healing rapidly."

"He's going to school, but Hudson College this time. Accounting and business."

"Give him my best." She opened the narcotics book. "Let's get this done so I can go home and sleep. Demerol fifty."

"Four and a full."

"Check."

That evening Maggie strolled into the nurses' station at ten. The evening nurse raised an eyebrow. "What's the occasion?"

"I need to check some charts. I was in a rush this morning, and I think I wrote the wrong notes on some of the charts."

"Don't I know how that can happen when you're pushed to get out of here on time," said Sue Rawlings. "Lorraine's such a witch about overtime. Even if there were three codes at ten forty-five, I bet she'd have a fit about signing the cards."

"You might be right, but she does have a budget."

The gray-haired woman leaned one hand on the desk. "I don't know how you can be so charitable. She hates your guts and would take any chance to trash you."

Maggie inhaled. Did everyone in the hospital know about Lorraine's animosity? "Let me get the charts and take them to the lounge." To avoid arousing suspicion, she lifted the two charts she hadn't checked the night before along with two others. "I'll be back to count in a half-hour or so."

"Good enough."

In the lounge Maggie poured a cup of coffee and opened the first of the charts. Nothing, she thought after a quick examination. The second chart provided the answer in the nurses' notes.

"Patient screaming and grimacing. Repeatedly grabbing at the dressing over her incision and calling 'Mama.' Unable to verbalize answers to questions about pain levels. Call placed to Dr.

318

Giancardi at ten-thirty. Call placed to Dr. Giancardi at eleven-thirty."

The record reported seven calls before a response. There's nothing unusual about the time lag, thought Maggie. He's always slow to respond. As she turned the pages to locate the doctor's progress report, Mavis bustled into the lounge.

"What are you doing here so early?" asked Maggie.

Mavis beamed a smile. "My niece just had a baby, so I snuck in to see her."

Maggie chuckled. "That's a side benefit to working nights."

" 'Specially since they won't let me come down after I've been here. They always say I'm contaminated. And you?"

"Some auditing work."

"You too. Hope you don't get as caught up in busywork like that Bev. She's always reading charts and shirking her real work."

"You know me better than that."

"Sure do. How come you're doing things for Lorraine? Seems to me she'd rather see you out of here."

"It's not for her," said Maggie.

Mavis's broad grin revealed large white teeth. "I know you're friends with Miss Gordon.

Guess she's finally seen there's plenty of odd things happening here. What's up?"

Maggie shrugged. Though she and Katherine Gordon shared a mutual concern about the barber's way of practicing surgery, they were hardly friends. "When I can say something, I will."

"Guess that means I keep my butt out." Mavis lit a cigarette and sat at the table.

"How's Bobby Ray?"

"He's healing real well. Sure hope he remembers his promises and straightens up. He talks a good story, but I'm waiting for some action."

Maggie recalled the determination she had seen in the young man's eyes. "I think he'll be fine. Just don't nag him too much."

Mavis put her hand on one hip. "Now, that's gonna be hard. Nagging's what I do best."

Maggie chuckled. She gathered the charts in her arms and headed to the door. As she stepped into the hall, Bev turned the corner from the elevators. Maggie hurried to the station, slid the charts into the rack, and signaled Sue to begin the count. When Bev arrived in the station, Maggie stood in the med room.

When she left the med room for report, Bev nodded. "Looks like a quiet night."

"Let's hope so. At least all the beds are full."

Maggie reached for a clipboard and attached several sheets of paper. One of the three evening nurses sat beside her. "Boy, is Anna Jackson's family upset. I think they're out of line." She lowered her voice. "I'm not one for defending you know who, but . . . How can they think she's in pain when she's totally confused?"

Out of the corner of her eye Maggie saw Bev push her chair closer. Maggie nearly mentioned April's nurses' notes but held back. "There are ways. Restlessness, increased confusion."

"This morning he wrote an order to medicate her with Demerol when she becomes agitated. I would think a tranquilizer would. be a better choice." The woman laughed. "Rumor says he reamed April for causing trouble."

Maggie made a face. Didn't anyone read the nurses' notes? Before she could mention the careful charting done by the day nurse, two recovery room nurses arrived at the station, pushing a stretcher. "We're here with Mr. Fletcher. Where does he go?"

After turning to scan the patient board, Maggie spoke. "Four-oh-nine." She turned to the evening nurse. "Did you know about this?"

A nervous laugh prefaced the answer. "Guess I forgot."

321

Maggie rose. "Let's get the patient settled so we can finish report."

Ten minutes later Maggie listened to the report from the recovery room nurses. "He came directly from the E.R. to us. Pressure cooker exploded and the gauge sliced his thigh and fractured his femur. A high price to pay for homemade grape jelly."

Sue Rawlings nodded. "I refuse to use pressure cookers. When I was a kid, my mother's went up like a rocket and brought down half the kitchen ceiling."

As soon as report ended, Maggie headed to 409 to check the patient. The Chief of Orthopedics entered the room. "Ms. Carr, good to see you." He turned to the patient. "Nick, I'm leaving you in good hands. Ms. Carr is one of our best nurses."

Maggie felt her face flush. "Thank you."

"What I'd really like is to know why you're buried on the night shift? We could use someone like you on days."

"Hospital policy states that new employees begin on the evening or night shift and must remain there for six months."

"Maybe that policy should be changed."

For the next few hours Maggie fitted rounds around frequent checks on the new patient, who was still groggy from the anesthesia. By morning her feet hurt and she wasn't sure she wanted to take another step. I'm off tonight, she thought.

On Thursday night when Maggie returned to work, Sue Rawlings bustled up to her. "Have you heard the latest? The Barber's done it again."

"I've been off."

The gray-haired woman perched on the edge of the desk. "April's on probation because of Mrs. Jackson. I told you how upset the family was."

"Why is April taking the blame?"

"As usual, he's sliding through on a technicality."

"How?"

"He states that she never called him."

"But the nurses' notes clearly documented her attempts to reach him."

The nurse frowned. "What notes? Besides April, you may be the only one who's seen them. The ones for that day are gone. April's been accused of taking them to protect herself."

"I don't believe that." Maggie's hand flew to her mouth to cover a gasp. The meaning of the conversation between Bev and Lorraine became clear. Though Maggie hadn't heard a name, she knew what must have happened. How could she prove Bev had taken the notes? Whom could she tell? Definitely not Lorraine.

She sat at the desk and wished she had shown someone else the notes before the arrival of a patient from the recovery room had driven the matter into hiding. There had to be something she could do, but what?

Maggie glanced at Bev. The thin nurse stared at the floor. Did she feel guilty? Maggie hoped so. "Everyone knows that April's a conscientious nurse. There's something going on and I'd like to know who has it in for her." She noted the flush that crept from Bev's neck to her face.

"Maybe it wouldn't have mattered who the nurse was," said the evening nurse.

Maggie shrugged. "Report. Don't you want to get out of here?"

Sue began report. Maggie's mind drifted to April and her problem. Why had Bev been pushed into doing Lorraine's dirty work? Learning the answer was the first step in proving April's innocence.

All night the district demanded a steady pace, leaving Maggie little time to sit at the desk. She wanted to talk to Bev, but the dark-haired woman seemed to be leaving the station when Maggie entered or the reverse. The situation continued for the rest of the night.

At six-fifteen, knowing the younger nurse always arrived early, Maggie stationed herself at the lounge door and waited for April. When she strode down the hall, Maggie walked toward her. "I heard. Do you want to talk?"

"I don't have time," said April. "I have to check all the charts in my district to make sure none of the notes are missing."

"Not all," said Maggie. "Just the Barber's patients."

April nodded. "I think you're right, but one never knows. What do you know that I don't?"

"I think I know how it happened, but I have no proof."

The blond nurse's shoulders slumped. "It doesn't matter. I'm looking for another job. I can't stay here and have something like this happen again."

Maggie opened the lounge door. "I saw your note. In fact, I read it. I'll document that I did."

"What good would that do? You won't be believed. I can hear the Queen pointing out that we're friends, and friends will do anything for each other. Remember her warning to fire you.

She'll accuse you of making trouble for the barber and do just that."

"You can't let yourself be pushed around like this," said Maggie. "What about the B.S. program at Hudson College? If you leave, you'll end up with a long commute and probably a different shift."

April backed into the hall. "Thanks for trying, but don't put your job on the line. I just can't imagine who took those notes. Lorraine never goes near the charts."

"Bev." Maggie repeated the conversation she had overheard. "I wish I knew what Lorraine had on her."

"Drugs."

"Drugs? What are you talking about?"

"I heard rumors that one night several years ago there were several tubexes of Demerol missing. This was when Lorraine worked nights, just before I started here. The old nurse manager couldn't prove anything."

Maggie smiled. Joanna had been the nurse manager and might be able to tell her what had happened. If she was lucky, she might learn something to clear this mess. Several nurses strode around the corner from the elevators. "Let's count," said Maggie. "Just don't quit yet."

"I have to find a job first and then give a month's notice." April opened the station door.

"Don't give up without a fight." Maggie crossed the station and entered the med room. She handed April the narcotics keys. "What do you plan to do about him until then?"

"Have a witness when I place calls to him and have whoever cosign the nurses' notes."

"That's a good idea. Keep a copy of those notes for yourself as well."

April unlocked the narcotic cabinet. "Now, that's another good one."

When Maggie left the hospital, she felt restless. The need to learn more about the rumor April had heard blew traces of tiredness away. As soon as she started a pot of coffee, she dialed Joanna's number. When the other woman answered, she invited her for coffee.

Five minutes later Joanna rang the doorbell. "What's up?"

"Some questions about four ortho."

Joanna walked upstairs. "If you hadn't rescued me from housework, which I loathe, I'd go home. What do you want to know?"

"Coffee first. I've doughnuts too."

Joanna patted her stomach. "Do you have juice? I'm being a good girl. One cup of coffee a day, and that's when my nerves are jangling."

Maggie poured coffee for herself and juice for Joanna. "Here's what happened the other day." She sketched April's situation. "I'm sure Bev's taking the missing chart material for Lorraine, and I want to know what Lorraine knows. April mentioned a rumor about drugs."

"I don't want to talk about this."

"Why?"

"That was the beginning of my problems at Hudson General. Though I followed up on the rumors, I learned nothing."

"Are you willing to see another nurse trashed because you want to hide from unpleasantness?"

Joanna shook her head. "When you put it that way, it sounds bad. Here's what I know. When I came on duty one morning, there was a panic in the nurses' station. Two tubexes of Demerol one hundred were missing. Both Bev and Lorraine swore they had been dropped and smashed. The cardboard box was wet, but no broken glass. Lorraine said they'd put the material in the Sharps container, and you know we can't open them."

"Did you go any further with this?"

Joanna shook her head. "Don't ask me why I didn't. I sure heard about that from Katherine Gordon. She had heard the rumors and said I had used poor judgment."

"Were there rumors about either of them using drugs?" Maggie picked up a cream-filled doughnut and bit into it. Chocolate-flavored whipped cream oozed out. She sighed with pleasure.

Joanna reached for one. "The only thing I can think of is that Bev's husband died of cancer three months later. I always wondered."

Maggie licked powdered sugar from her fingers. "I think I'll talk to Bev. April's a good nurse."

"Don't. In a month or two the matter will be buried." Joanna put the doughnut on the plate. "Anything involving Giancardi tends to do that."

Maggie felt a surge of frustration. Everyone complained about the man, but no one did a thing. "It doesn't seem right." She knew she couldn't let the matter rest, but she also knew any further discussion wouldn't help.

So, evidently, did Joanna. Her next question nearly made Maggie choke.

"What's with you and Jason? Robyn and I both think that you're the best thing that could happen to him."

"We're friends. There's nothing more to tell." She rose and went to the refrigerator and took a package of veal from the freezer. "How are your boys?"

"In kindergarten, a full day session. Thank heavens I don't have to find sitters. They used to run through one a month." Joanna finished her juice. "I tried to get Jason's daughter for the evenings when I teach and Dave's busy. She's not in school. She doesn't have a job. What's with her?"

Maggie knew she couldn't confide in Joanna. What Joanna knew, Robyn always learned. The story of Beth's pregnancy would reach Jason, and he would react. "She's confused and trying to cope with learning the father she thought had deserted her really loves her."

Joanna nodded. "Robyn's told me things about her mother that made me scream."

After Joanna left, Maggie started spaghetti sauce simmering in the Crock-Pot. Then she went to bed. Had Beth made a doctor's appointment yet? Had she told her father? Tonight Jason and Beth were coming to dinner. She would corner the girl and demand answers.

The aroma of garlic and blended spices filtered down the hall. Veal parmigiana heated in the oven, water for pasta boiled furiously. Maggie hoped the meal wouldn't give Beth indigestion. She remembered that during her own pregnancy one day spicy food had been fine and the next day the same dish had made her want to die. She set the table in the dining room and waited for the doorbell.

Though Beth picked at her food, she ate. Jason made up for his daughter by taking seconds of everything. After dinner he offered to do the dishes.

"You're banished to the living room," said Maggie. "Take the coffee carafe with you and enjoy."

Beth giggled. "Overdose on caffeine, you mean."

"Since there's none at home, or at the office, I've become a coffee sneak at the hospital."

Maggie laughed. "I've heard the day shift complaining about how they brew a pot and suddenly it vanishes. Are you saying it happens on every unit?"

"Daddy!" said Beth.

Jason laughed. "No more than two or maybe three cups a day." He carried his cup and the carafe to the living room.

Beth carried the plates to the kitchen. Maggie stored the leftovers in the refrigerator. "Did you call the doctor?"

The girl pushed her chestnut hair back from

her face. "I tried, really, I did. A dozen busy signals every day. Twice I was put on hold and cut off."

Maggie inhaled. "Tell your father. Doctors have a way of cutting through this nonsense."

Beth blanched. "Please, not yet. Next week, I promise."

"That's not good enough. I said a week. Laura said the same thing. You have to tell him now."

"I can't."

"What can't you tell me?" asked Jason.

"Nothing. It's nothing."

"Beth," said Maggie.

The girl slumped on one of the kitchen chairs. She stared at her hands. "Daddy, I'm pregnant."

Jason moved quicker than Maggie believed possible, and she couldn't tell from the look on his face what he meant to do. She prepared to defend Beth.

"Pregnant," he said. "Who? When? Why didn't you tell me."

"Since before I left home. Mom and I argued about it. She didn't want me loving anyone but her."

Jason put his hands on Beth's shoulders. "I'm not your mother. I wish you had told me."

Beth rose and hugged her father. "I'm sorry, but I was afraid you wouldn't understand."

Maggie felt happy about Jason's acceptance. His deep caring for his daughter showed.

"Honey, I'll be here and we'll do what you want. An abortion, an adoption, or keep the baby. I'll support your decision."

Beth stared at him. "Abortion. You sound like Mom. It's too late. Next week I'll be six months." She shook her head. "Not adoption either. I want this baby."

The rising panic in Beth's voice made Maggie step toward her. "Beth . . . Jason . . ."

Jason stroked his daughter's hair. "Then we'll keep the baby. I'll sacrifice my study and we'll finish the other room in the basement for the two of you."

"Really?" Hope shone in Beth's eyes.

Maggie swallowed. There was more to tell. Though she was happy for both of them, Jason had to know the whole story. The time for him to face the possibility of losing his daughter was now. She cleared her throat. "Beth, there's more to tell."

"I will, soon," said the girl.

Maggie shook her head. "He has to know everything so he can help you. If you don't tell him, I will."

Beth pulled free from her father's arms. "I thought you were my friend. How can you do this when things are so wonderful?"

"Because they might not stay that way."

Jason stared at them. What hadn't Beth told him? Nothing would make him withdraw his support. "Beth, you can tell me. I promised I'd take care of you, and I won't go back on my word."

Beth pressed her face against his shirt. "I have rheumatic heart disease."

Her mumbled words didn't clearly register. "What?" he asked louder than he had planned.

Beth stepped back. "I had rheumatic fever when I was ten."

Jason placed his hand on the table to steady himself. A rheumatic heart, pregnancy, swollen feet and hands. She was probably pre-eclamptic. "I'll call Sam Grant. He'll arrange an immediate abortion."

"No!" Beth's scream jolted him.

"Yes," said Jason.

Maggie touched Beth's shoulder. "Calm down."

"You see. I told you what he'd do." Beth put her hands to her ears. "I won't listen to another word either of you says. Why did you have to spoil things?" She turned to her father. "I won't

334

have an abortion. I'll leave here and live on the streets if I have to."

Anger roiled inside Jason. Maggie had known. Why hadn't she told him instead of letting the news emerge in this fashion?

Maggie caught Beth's arm. "There's no reason for dramatics. Until you have the tests Laura suggested, no one knows what care needs to be taken."

A stubborn look appeared on his daughter's face. "It doesn't matter what the tests say. I'm going to have my baby."

Maggie's eyes pleaded with him, but Jason couldn't listen. "No. I refuse to take that risk with you. We're just beginning to be a family. If I lose you . . ." He turned to Maggie. "Would you accept this if she were yours?"

"Before I decided on such a drastic solution, I'd find out why this baby is so important." Maggie faced Beth. "No one can force you to have an abortion."

Jason clamped his teeth together. Why had she said that? "You have no right to advise my daughter."

Her green eyes flashed. "I can't stand here and watch you push her away. Ask her why she wants the baby."

"The baby doesn't matter. Do you think I

335

want to lose my daughter when I've just found her?"

"Stop it," screamed Beth. "I won't have an abortion. I won't."

She pushed past him and evaded his attempt to grab her arm. He turned to Maggie. "Stay out of things that don't concern you. She's my daughter."

"And you're acting like a dictator. Isn't all this excitement bad for her heart? Jason, please listen to me and to her."

"I thought we were friends. How could you hide this from me?"

"She promised to call a doctor here and asked me to let her tell you."

A door slammed. "No more. You've done enough." He spun on his heel and rushed away.

Maggie stared after Jason. Tears spilled down her cheeks. What's wrong with me, she thought. We had no commitment. After George's death I didn't cry. Why today? Tears spilled faster. She sank on one of the chairs. He had told her to stay away. How could she? Since the day Beth had fainted, Maggie had felt protective.

She gulped and tried to stem her tears. What was she going to do about Jason? She knew his fears for his daughter were justified. Doctors knew every complication, so did nurses. Didn't he know his behavior would strengthen Beth's determination? He had been cheated out of her years of childhood. If he didn't listen to her, he would lose her again.

Maggie wiped her eyes with the bottom of her blouse. Reality smashed barriers. She loved him and she had lost him.

Stay out of things that don't concern you. His harsh command rose in her thoughts.

How could she? She cared about Beth. Three shaky steps took her to the sink, where she splashed cold water on her face. She would find a way to help Beth and maybe Jason as well.

Fifteen

Bright morning sunlight streamed through the bedroom window, causing Maggie's eyes to water. She turned on her side and yawned. For a moment, memories of the previous night threatened to make the tears real. She held her breath and pressed her fingers against her tear ducts. A new spate would only make her headache worse.

Trapped, she still felt trapped. If she hadn't helped Beth . . . If she hadn't made the appointment . . . If she hadn't promised to keep the pregnancy secret . . . If Jason hadn't asked her to let him know . . . Being caught between Jason and Beth had put her into a position where she couldn't win.

With a moan she slid out of bed, pulled on an ancient sweat suit spotted by bleach and stained by paint. After a breakfast of coffee and toast she attacked the apartment, discharging her frustrations in scouring, polishing, and vacuuming.

As she began the bathroom, the phone rang. Her body tensed. Who, she wondered. Jason? She didn't want to talk to him. Why hadn't she invested in an answering machine? She sat on the edge of the bed. On the eighth ring she lifted the receiver. "Hello."

"Mag, what's wrong? You sound dreadful."

Laura's assumption brought a smile. "You can tell that from one word?"

"You'd better believe I can. You been getting prank calls?"

"No. I just don't want to talk to a certain person."

"You and the hunk have a fight?"

"I'd hardly call it that. More like he issued an ultimatum." Maggie rubbed her toes along the teal carpet.

"What then?"

"He made some unjustified accusations, and it's the last time I'm going to be the filling in a sandwich."

"Mmm. I take it he learned about the pregnancy and he's not supportive."

Maggie leaned against the mound of pillows on the bed. "Yes and no."

"Has Beth called a doctor yet?"

"No, but I'm sure he has."

"When did she tell him?

"Last night, and only because I pushed her. When he heard about her heart, he immediately cried abortion. She called me a traitor and stormed out. He blamed me for interfering, and followed." She sighed.

"I'm sorry."

"Why? I got myself into this, and like I did with George, I read Jason wrong. How did Beth know he'd react this way? And don't tell me heredity."

"She said he was overprotective. Doesn't his reaction prove that?"

"I guess so." Maggie rubbed her forehead.

"Speaking of doctors. I should have gotten back to you last week, but it's been nonstop babies. I've delivered nine and assisted with four C-sections."

"What are you talking about?"

"Giancardi, Leon, former resident in orthopedics at my old hospital. Remember I had dinner with an old acquaintance of his?"

Maggie sat up. "What's the scoop?"

"Two months before his residency ended, your Dr. Giancardi abruptly left the program. My dinner date wouldn't or couldn't tell me the reason. He closed down and said there had been rumors but he wouldn't repeat them. Let me tell you, I went all out to learn. Even offered my gorgeous body."

Maggie laughed. "Now, that's being a true friend. What does it mean?"

"He can't ever be board certified."

"A lot of doctors aren't."

"You're right. I'm not sure how you can use this information, but it's all I learned."

"I can at least let . . ." Maggie groaned. How could she tell Jason when they weren't speaking? "Are you going to see this man again?"

"This weekend, unless the babies keep dropping."

"Tell me about him."

As Laura talked, Maggie thought about the information her friend had produced. If not Jason, could Katherine Gordon do anything with the information? Still, what had she learned other than a rumor with no support?

"Mag, got to go. My beeper's going frantic. Talk to you soon."

"Maybe I'll get down again."

"When? Just name the day. You can go on the delivery wagon with me."

"See you."

As she slid from the bed, the phone rang

again. Betty Loring's husky voice dissolved any idea that Jason had decided to apologize. "Betty, how are you?"

"Totally livid."

"The suit. What happened?"

"Come for lunch. I don't want to short out the phone lines."

"Give me a half hour. I'm in the middle of cleaning house."

"Come as you are."

"I'd be arrested as a vagrant. See you."

After a quick shower Maggie dressed in brown slacks and a tan sweater. As she left her unit, she glanced toward Jason's balcony, and for a moment considered knocking at his door. Reluctantly, she turned and headed to the parking area. His silver sports car wasn't in its usual spot. I could have called Beth, she thought. Was the girl still there, or had she fulfilled her threat to run away?

At a few minutes past noon she pulled into the wide driveway beside Betty's house. Her heels clicked against the flagstones of the walk. The first few notes of Beethoven's Fifth sounded when she rang the bell.

Betty opened the door. "Lord, you make me feel underdressed. Look at me."

The jeans Betty wore had patches over

342

patches, all gaily embroidered with astrological symbols. "They're definitely ornate," said Maggie.

"My lucky jeans." Betty's dark eyes held simmering anger. "I should have kept them on until the suit was settled."

"I take it that it was."

"Worse luck. No trial."

"Was it a good settlement?"

"My lawyer is ecstatic. He never believed I really wanted to go to trial and see that man's face plastered on the front page of the newspaper."

Maggie followed Betty through the foyer and into the hall overlooking a sunken family room. "I guess some people have different priorities."

Betty made a face. "Money. How can anyone believe money is compensation for pain and suffering?"

"To lawyers, money is love. Some lawyer convinced the parents of the young woman who died with George to sue his estate."

Betty shook her head. "You're kidding."

Maggie shook her head. "They dropped the case after my attorney countersued. It was her car and she was driving."

"I've heard of greed, but that's too much."

"What are you going to do now?"

"I'd like to write a book about doctors who get away with malpractice."

Maggie frowned. "Nonfiction? The research might be tricky."

"I've folders of cases, but I think I'll stick to fiction. There's a better chance of success."

"Let me know if I can help. At least run your idea past me. Some of the cases I've read about aren't malpractice, just human error."

"Did you know he never completed his residency?" Betty pulled a loaf of bread from the oven.

"Where did you learn that?"

"While researching for the suit, I talked to a nurse who worked at Hopewell Hospital when he was a resident. One day he strutted the halls and the next day he vanished." The gray-haired woman opened the cabinet. "Something about a patient's death. She wasn't very clear. What do you think might have happened?"

"Any number of things." Maggie sat at the table in the alcove separated from the main part of the kitchen by low cabinets.

"Such as?"

"Not too long ago I read of how a resident operated on a private patient for the attending doctor and was caught."

344

"Sounds kind of like ghostwriting." Betty leaned on the counter. "Do you like clam chowder?"

"Love it."

"Back to Giancardi. Could the family of the case you read about have been able to sue if they had known?"

"They might have."

Betty grinned. "I like that. Now, how do I plot this so he doesn't sue me?"

"Don't ask me. You're the writer. Does your surgeon have to be orthopedic?"

"I guess not. I'd better let this simmer and mix with some other ideas."

Maggie took a taste of the chowder thick with chunks of potato, celery, and minced clams. The creamy texture and the heat of the soup soothed her. She tore a piece of bread from the crusty loaf on the table. "I want the recipe."

"I'm not sure I can duplicate it. Next time I make some, I'll call you. It's never the same twice."

"I'll come running with notebook and pen."

By the time Maggie left Betty's house, she felt relaxed and ready to tackle life again. She thought about calling Beth, but decided to wait until her emotions were less raw.

* * *

A week later Maggie stood outside her condo door and stared across the commons. September had become October and the bright leaves had fallen from the maple trees to form quiltlike patterns on the browned grass. As she searched for her key, she shifted the box containing a coffee ring she had bought at the bakery on the way home.

The door of Jason's unit opened and Beth stepped outside. "Maggie, are you still mad at me?"

"I wasn't mad."

"Really? Could I talk to you?"

Maggie inhaled. "As long as you don't put me in the middle again." She shifted her package and unlocked the door. In the kitchen she started a fresh pot of coffee and plugged in the iron. A basket of clean uniforms sat on the table.

The girl slumped on a chair. "I'm sorry about what happened. Dad's angry at you, and it's all my fault for not having the guts to level with him. I didn't mean the things I said to you. I should have told him instead of letting you force the issue."

Maggie nodded. "Yes, you should have."

"Is there any way I can make up for what I did?" Beth grinned. "I know. How about blindfolding him and leading him over here?"

Maggie rested the iron on its end. "Silly idea. Your father and I are adults. We'll have to solve our own problems."

Beth rested her elbows on the table. "I'd sure feel better if you guys were friends."

Though Maggie agreed with Beth, she wasn't sure she wanted to risk herself again. Something special had been sidetracked and she was afraid the laughter she and Jason had shared could never be recaptured. "Tell me what's been happening with you."

"I've seen Dr. Grant and Dr. Blanda. I've had the tests and they say I'm fine. I'm going to be admitted to the hospital for observation two weeks before delivery day."

"I'm glad." Maggie lifted the white trousers she had just ironed and fastened them to a hanger.

Beth smiled. "I can't believe it. In two months I'm going to have a baby."

"Have you given up the idea that you're going to die?" As she asked the question, Maggie knew the answer was important.

"I guess so." Beth stared at a point beyond

Maggie. "It's hard to accept. For months Mom wept and screamed that I wanted to die and leave her alone. She read me articles from nursing magazines and medical journals. She handed me reports from five doctors she had called. They all read like doom and gloom." A deep sigh escaped. "You know, she acted like she owned me."

"That's a rough idea to deal with."

Tears glistened in Beth's eyes. "I'll never treat my child like that."

"I know you won't."

"Would you like to go shopping for baby things with me? I can't ask Daddy. He's already bought more maternity clothes than I'll ever wear."

Maggie remembered the things she had bought at the craft store. "Just a minute." She ran down the hall to her bedroom and picked up the bag. "I almost forgot I had these," she said when she returned to the kitchen.

Beth opened the bag and lifted out the pale green blanket. She oohed and aahed over each new thing. "They're beautiful." She jumped up and hugged Maggie. "I love you."

Tears formed in Maggie's eyes. "I love you too. Now, about your shopping expedition. I have a better idea."

"Good. You, me, and Dad. I like that. He needs you. I know he does."

Maggie sighed. "No matchmaking, please. I know you care, but what ever you're dreaming up, don't."

Beth made a face. "I guess you're right, but I wish . . ."

So do I, thought Maggie. She pulled her thoughts away from dreams. "What you and I need to do is make a list of the things you'll need. Then you can tell him and he can buy the things on the list and no more."

"Okay."

"Is that it?"

Beth inhaled. "Can I move in with you?"

"Why?"

"He's going to drive me loony, up the wall, bananas, and every kind of crazy there is. His latest idea is that I shouldn't cook, clean, or do anything but stay in bed. We have a cleaning lady. He comes home at lunchtime to check on me. He'd feed me if I didn't threaten to bite. You'd think I was the two-year-old he lost."

"In some ways you are." Maggie held up a hand. "Isn't it better for him to fuss than be indifferent?"

Beth shrugged. "A week ago he was angry

and then pleased. Now he's being ridiculous."

"He loves you."

"I know, but I'm used to being busy. I was cooking for Mom and me when I was nine. By ten I was doing everything but writing the checks to pay the bills. Please let me come. I'll pretend it's a vacation."

Maggie shook her head. "Think about how your father would react. I won't be put in the middle again."

Beth made a face. "He'd come over and talk to you. Sure he'd be angry at first . . ." She grinned. "You could invite him to move in too."

Maggie turned off the iron. "You're going to get both of us in trouble. You can't move in. You can't dream up schemes. I mean it."

Maggie lifted the freshly ironed clothes from the back of the chair. "I'm sure he's worried about how you can go to school and take care of the baby."

"I'm going to college only to please him."

"What do you want to do?"

"I'm not sure. Maybe something with food." She followed Maggie down the hall. "You know, at first I wanted this baby to bring my parents together, and that was a dumb idea. But now . . ." Her smile radiated joy. "When I feel the baby move, I want to hold it and I wonder if it will be a boy or a girl and who it will look like. No one understands how much I want this baby."

Maggie hung the clothes in the large double closet. "Then you'll have to show him that you can handle being a mother and make plans for your future. Talk to him. Don't just demand to have your way about this."

"We have been talking." Beth leaned against the door. "He keeps saying he doesn't want my baby to live the way I did. I'll never let that happen."

Maggie nodded. "I believe you. Give your father a chance to understand you're not the child he lost."

"You're right, as usual." The clock chimed. "Let me scoot. The cleaning lady's due. Make that list and I'll come and get it tomorrow."

After Beth left, Maggie returned to the kitchen. One down and one to go, she thought. Would Jason ever get past the anger and the hurt that resulted from his daughter's confiding in a stranger?

By the middle of October Jason found himself thinking about Maggie with increasing frequency. He regretted the scene he had caused the night he had learned about Beth's pregnancy. In trying to hide his fear of losing his daughter, he had lashed out at Maggie. Why had Beth failed to come to him?

He sat in his car behind the condos and realized how hard it was to be a father to someone who was nearly an adult when he had missed all the steps in between. Hurting Maggie had been unfair. He needed to tell her that. But how? He started the car and sped to the hospital. Maybe if he saw her, he would know what to say.

Inside the hospital he took the steps two at a time and headed to the fourth floor. Breathing like a marathon runner at the end of the race, he arrived on four orthopedics. Maggie left one of the patients' rooms. She stopped short.

Jason stared. Though her uniform looked rumpled and her auburn curls tousled, she looked beautiful. Would she speak if he approached her? He decided to find out.

Abruptly, she turned and dashed back into the room. His shoulders slumped. That answered his question. When she left the room, carrying a clipboard, hope rose. Maybe she hadn't seen him. He took a step and stopped.

Maybe she had. Unable to decide, he turned and walked to four med/surg, where he had three patients to see.

On Friday evening Maggie drove to the grocery store. Though she generally shopped in the morning on her way home from work, today she had been too tired. Groceries for the week and the ingredients for Halloween cookies for the neighborhood children were on her list. Yesterday she had opened the box of cookie cutters and pulled out the cats, witches, pumpkins, and ghosts that she had used every year since the twins had started school.

She pushed the cart to the produce section and stopped to put a head of lettuce, a bunch of celery, and other salad vegetables into the cart. Then she saw Jason. She recalled another time they had met in the grocery store. His blue eyes had glowed with mischief. She had wanted to brush the lock of hair from his forehead. Remembering the days following that chance encounter, she wished she had run away that day as she had to do today. Quickly, she pushed the cart to the soda aisle. She waited at the end like a child playing hide-and-seek.

While she lingered at the meat display, trying to plan menus for the week, she glanced around. Jason stood at the fish counter, engaged in a conversation with the butcher. She stared at his broad shoulders and narrow hips. Willing her body to stop reacting, she grabbed several packages of chicken.

There's nothing for us now. What there had been was ruined the evening he had learned about Beth's pregnancy.

She arrived at the checkout counter and saw that Jason stood two customers ahead in the same line she had chosen. What was she going to do?

He unloaded his cart and began bagging groceries. Though she thought about moving to another line, she watched the way his body moved and how his hands lifted items from the cart. He turned and stared at her. For a moment she thought he would speak. Instead, he nodded. Her greeting died on her lips; her shoulder muscles tensed. When would she be able to see him and not react? "Never," cried some part of herself.

On Halloween evening Beth dashed down the steps, holding a high-peaked witch's hat in her hand. "Have fun with the trick-or-treaters," she called.

Jason carried a box filled with bags of candy to the lower hall. "Don't scare the kids."

"They'll love me." She opened the door and waved.

Jason set the box on a table and settled in a chair. Beth was headed for the community center, where the teenagers had created a haunted house. He smiled. Something had happened recently to his daughter, and he liked whatever it was. She had begun to socialize, and though reluctantly, she had completed an application for the spring semester at Hudson College.

He waited for the doorbell. One problem on the way to being settled, he thought. Now there's only Maggie.

The doorbell rang. He opened the door. Identical Peter Pans held out pillow cases. "Trick or treat."

"Do I know you?"

The twins giggled. "We're Peter Pan."

Jason dropped treats in their bags and waved at Joanna. The twins ran across the lawn. He watched them and saw Maggie. He took a step and then stopped. The twins hugged her. Unlike the small boys, he had no reason to run across the lawn and sweep her into his arms. Would she ever smile at him again?

He groaned. The distance between them was of his own making. "Maggie," he whispered.

Another group of children arrived. He handed out treats. For the next hour, children arrived and left. He watched Maggie and searched for a way to express an apology or an invitation. All too soon the last child left. Maggie closed her door. Jason stood on the walk with the words of apology still unformed.

October slid into November. Maggie felt as though life had become as gray as the skies. Work had settled into a routine and for a week the patients had slept most of every night. Slowly, Maggie chipped away at Bev's unfriendliness until she discovered an underlying sadness flavored the other nurse's personality. As yet, she hadn't asked Bev about the missing notes. April seemed to have forgotten the incident with Mrs. Jackson, and had made no further comment about resigning.

On the first Saturday of November, Maggie sat at the desk and smothered a yawn. A call light came on. She pushed away from the desk and hurried down the hall to the patient. Mavis headed in the same direction. Maggie reached the room first. "Mrs. Miller, can I help you?"

The middle-aged woman sat up in bed. Her hands grasped the side rails. "Can't breathe. Help me." Her brown eyes shone with the same panic as Maggie heard in her breathy voice.

"I'm here." Maggie pulled the overbed table in front of the patient. "Lean on this. Pursed-mouth breathing, please."

"I'm going to die. I can't breathe."

"Let me get help. I'll have someone call your doctor." Maggie stepped into the hall and called to Mavis. The black aide turned. "Have Bev call the house doctor and Dr. Knight. Mrs. Miller is having an asthma attack."

"What's she doing here?" asked Mavis.

"Overflow. The medical floors are full."

"It's the weather. I'm on my way."

Maggie opened the oxygen and attacked the nasal tubing. "Mrs. Miller, here's some oxygen."

"Don't leave me."

"I won't until the doctor comes. Remember your breathing." Maggie took vital signs and listened to Mrs. Miller's chest. She heard a few wheezes and areas of diminished sounds.

Bev entered the room. "Doctor's on the way. Wants an IV started. Respiratory's been called for a treatment."

When the therapist arrived, Maggie left to make rounds on her other patients. She had just returned to Mrs. Miller's room when she sensed the presence of another person. She turned. Jason stood in the doorway. She inhaled and pulled her professional persona like a cloak around her emotions.

"Dr. Knight, would you like a report?"

"Let me examine Mrs. Miller first." His voice held the same icy formality as her own. He crossed the room and put his hand on the middle-aged woman's wrist.

Wishing his hand enclosed hers, Maggie slipped into the hall. She leaned against the wall. Would he ever understand that she had been caught between a promise and desire?

When Maggie left the room, Jason gathered his thoughts and concentrated on Mrs. Miller. Ten minutes later he smiled. "You'll be fine. Do you believe me?"

She nodded. "I get so scared. The nurse was wonderful. She has such a soothing touch."

He looked away. Her statement reminded him that Maggie's touch was anything but soothing. Stimulating, sensuous, exciting, he thought. And lost. Was there hope of regaining and rebuilding the friendship? "She's a special person. Now, I want you to relax and concentrate on letting the treatment work. Will you be all right if I leave and talk to Ms. Carr."

Mrs. Miller's nod released him. Jason stepped into the hall. Maggie leaned against the wall. "Maggie," he said.

She turned. "Yes, Dr. Knight."

The smile he had wished for didn't appear. She remained a nurse, calm, cool and professional, not the woman he had held in his arms, had kissed, had almost allowed himself to love.

"I'd like the respiratory treatment repeated hourly times three. If there's no improvement, call me."

Maggie nodded. He thought he saw a flicker of interest in her green eyes, but he couldn't find a way of changing their encounter from patient-centered to personal.

"I'll have the aide sit with her for the rest of the night. Thank you for coming."

"I was in the E.R."

She pushed away from the wall. "Let me get Joyce and make rounds."

Jason turned. The house doctor could have handled the situation, but he had wanted to see Maggie and talk to her. Here wasn't the place or now the time to tell her why he had come. He had wanted to see her and to find a way to step across the gulf separating them. Too late, he thought. He hated the knowledge and himself for making it the truth.

Sixteen

The steady sweep of the wiper blades cleared the misting rain from the front window of her sedan. Maggie backed out of her space in the lot behind her condo unit. A dreary November day had become a drizzly night. Her thoughts mocked the action on the windshield, switching from Beth and Jason to the hospital. Why couldn't problems be cleared away as easily as the rain?

Six weeks had passed since she and Jason had collided over Beth's decision to have the baby. His warning to keep out of his daughter's life had been impossible to heed. Did he know that Beth had apologized and that she popped in several times a week for advice or to complain about being smothered.

Maggie sighed. A week ago she and Jason had faced each other at a patient's bedside.

Had she seen regret in his eyes? After leaving the patient, she had waited for him to speak about something other than Mrs. Miller's asthma attack. The moment had stretched to an awkward silence.

She pulled into a spot in the hospital parking lot and hurried through the misting rain. When she reached four ortho, to her surprise Bev had arrived early. The skinny, dark-haired nurse stood in the med room with one of the evening nurses. Maggie reached for the unit book and several flow sheets.

After report she set out to make rounds. Before entering 403, a private room, she checked the flow sheet. "Andy Palmero, work-related injury, fractured tibia and fibula. Cast applied at seven P.M. by Dr. Giancardi. Admitted for observation. Possible concussion. Contusions of chest. Medicated at ten-thirty for pain."

"Hi, Mr. Palmero. I'm Maggie Carr, your night nurse."

Perspiration covered his forehead. Though his skin was deeply tanned, his pallor suggested shock.

"Get my doctor." He spoke through clenched teeth.

"What's wrong?"

"Pain. Leg."

Maggie walked to the foot of the bed and began a neuro assessment. Though there was good capillary filling, his foot was swollen so much, she couldn't locate the pedal pulse. "Describe your pain."

"Beyond belief. Had kidney stones. This worse."

Maggie checked her notes again. An hour ago he had been medicated with Demerol 100 one and Vistaril 50. "Did the pain medication have any effect?"

He shook his head. "I'm tough, but if I had a saw, I'd cut the damn thing off."

"Let's not go for anything that drastic. When did the pain begin?"

"Nine. Nine-thirty. Forever."

"I'll call your doctor."

"Do that. I want him here. Nurse had to call him before. Bastard didn't want pain stuff. Concussion."

Maggie nodded. "That's standard treatment. With head injuries, narcotics can mask serious symptoms." She shone a penlight in his eyes and watched the pupils react in a normal fashion. "Can you tell me where the pain is centered?"

He pointed to his calf. "Toes feel funny too."

She returned to the foot of the bed and unfastened the safety pin she kept in her pocket. "Tell me which is the strongest. Now or now."

"Second."

She continued checking the toes of both feet, noting the decreased sensations of his left foot as compared to the right. "I'll be back soon."

"With my doctor?"

"I can't promise that, but hopefully with some answers." As she stepped into the hall, Joyce ambled toward her. "Did you get Mr. Palmero's vitals yet?" asked Maggie. "I have to call his doctor."

"What's this? Another crisis?" asked the obese aide. "Do you go looking for them?"

"Not particularly."

"I'll have to say nights aren't boring since you started here." She thrust a clipboard at Maggie. "They're all here and water's been removed in four and six."

"Thanks." Maggie continued to the station. Though Mavis had become her friend, Joyce remained distant, but the overweight woman was no longer disruptive.

Maggie considered Mr. Palmero's symptoms and didn't like the conclusion she reached. Probable compartment syndrome, she thought. If that was the case, excess swelling had caused the tissues within the fascia to become compressed, constricting nerve and blood supply. Within five hours damage could become permanent, and in twelve an amputation might be necessary. Nearly three hours had passed since the onset of symptoms. She glanced at the clipboard and groaned. Giancardi strikes again.

In the station, she placed a call to his service. "This is the nurse on four orthopedics. I want to speak to Dr. Giancardi immediately regarding Mr. Palmero."

"He called you back an hour ago."

Maggie gripped the phone. "I need to talk to him. It's an emergency. Tell him Ms. Carr needs an immediate call back."

"I just hope you're ready to hear a tirade."

"Whatever it takes." Maggie hung up. There had to be something she could do for Mr. Palmero while she waited for the call.

Bev left her chair in a corner of the station. "What's wrong?" she asked.

"Mr. Palmero. Cast applied this evening. He's experiencing excruciating pain in the calf area. Sounds like a compartment syndrome."

"I saw one of those once a couple of years ago when Lorraine and I worked nights. They had to do a fasciotomy and remove part of the muscle. Was a messy situation but Lorraine earned points with the Barber by—never mind."

Maggie wondered who had been the goat. "Something not nice, I'm sure."

Bev's thin shoulders hunched. "Who's the doctor?"

"Giancardi."

The dark-haired woman made a face. "I don't envy you."

Maggie looked up. "I'll go down fighting for the patient."

Bev sighed. "I'm in. Want me to check your assessment?"

Maggie dropped her pen on the desk. Why had Bev offered to help? Had she become tired of being pushed around by Lorraine? "That would be great. He's in 403. Mr. Palmero."

"Leave the chart out and I'll add my observations."

Maggie swallowed. Could she trust the other nurse not to write a contradictory note? Bev had to be the one removing pages from selected charts. Maggie completed charting her observations and rose. In the med room she prepared the medications due for twelve and one A.M. The phone rang. She grabbed the extension on the wall beside the refrigerator.

"Dr. Giancardi here. What's the big idea? Don't you realize all the calls to doctors after midnight must be made by the supervisor."

"I called at eleven-forty."

"Cute. About Mr. Palermo, he's a wimp. I ordered a hefty dose of Demerol an hour and a half ago."

"Just a minute." Maggie described the patient's symptoms. "I think there's a bigger problem than low pain tolerance."

"You're not paid to think."

"Have you considered compartment syndrome?"

She heard low music in the background. "Leon honey, don't leave me hanging like this," crooned a husky voice.

Lorraine, thought Maggie. Would the nurse manager call Bev and order her to remove parts of the record? Would Bev comply, or had she become tired of her role?

"I've considered that you like making trouble for me and I think this will be the last time."

"Are you coming in to see him?"

"No. I've got better things to do tonight." The phone slammed in Maggie's ear.

For a moment she sat and stared. What now, she wondered, and searched her memory for the treatment of compartment syndrome. "Split the cast. Elevate the leg. Ice packs." Without a doctor's order she couldn't take the first step. Would the others work?

Quickly, she completed medication rounds. Then she stopped in the kitchen and filled rubber gloves with ice. She entered 403. "Mr. Palmero, any change?"

"Worse. Other nurse elevated leg. No help."

Maggie heard his effort to control the pain.

Anger coiled tighter inside her. How dare Giancardi refuse to come in! "I'm going to pack ice around the cast to see if that will reduce the swelling."

"Call . . . my . . . doctor."

"Let's try this before I make a second call." He bit his lower lip. "Will you?"

"Call? You'd better believe I will."

"Thanks."

Maggie returned to the station. Janice Petty, the supervisor, stood at the desk. The petite redhead turned. "How are things? No problems, I hope."

"There is one," said Maggie.

"Really. Do you look for disasters?"

Though the supervisor's low voice dripped sweetness, Maggie had learned that Janice Petty hated problems. "No," she said. "I have a patient who had a cast applied to a fracture this evening. I think he's developed a compartment syndrome."

"Oh, dear, who's the doctor, and what did he say?"

"It's Giancardi, and he refused to come in."

"Really, Margaret. I've heard about your personality clash with him. Lorraine warned me that you were a troublemaker."

Maggie shook her head. "Come with me and see the patient."

"I don't have time." Janice smiled. "If you're so concerned, call the house doctor. Let me know what he says."

Maggie stood at the door until Janice reached the corner. "How did she become supervisor?" she muttered.

"By being sweet and having a master's degree," said Bev. "She's worse than useless."

"Agreed." Maggie called the house doctor. Ten minutes later, Dr. Davis arrived. She walked to Mr. Palmero's room with him. After he completed the examination, Maggie followed him into the hall. "Compartment syndrome?" she asked.

"I concur. Get the cutter and I'll give his doctor a call. Who?'

"Giancardi."

"I won't give his doctor a call."

"Why not?"

"House doctors are forbidden to see or to treat his patients. Though he's the one who made the request, we were kind of relieved. One of ours caught a big suit and nearly lost his job here."

"So the patient loses his leg." Anger bubbled to the surface. She felt an eruption building. "So what do I do?"

"Call your supervisor. Call Giancardi. Call the Chief of Orthopedics."

Aware of the rapidly vanishing minutes, Maggie stood in the hall. What now? She inhaled and returned to Mr. Palmero. "Has the ice helped?"

"No. Dammit. Get my doctor."

Maggie returned to the station. She called the supervisor. "Mrs. Petty, the house doctor saw the patient and though he agrees with my assessment, he can't do anything for the patient. Why did you have me call him when you knew the house doctors weren't allowed to treat Giancardi's patients?"

"We have to protect the hospital in case of trouble."

"What about the patient? There's going to be trouble if you don't call Giancardi and demand he come in."

"Really, Ms. Carr. Don't tell me my job. Everyone knows you have it in for Leon. I won't call him."

"Mr. Palmero insists we reach his doctor now."

"You do it. I can't."

"Then what good are you?" Maggie returned the receiver to the cradle. To call or not to call? Did she have a choice? Though the Barber would rant, she wasn't going to find herself being blamed for his mistakes. She reached for the phone and dialed the doctor's service.

"Would you have him call four orthopedics?"

"He already did that. He's going to be angry."

"He'll be furious if he's sued because you didn't pass the message along. The patient demands he call."

Bev stood in the doorway. "You're crazy. Why not let the bastard be sued?"

Maggie shook her head. "We're here to protect the patient. Besides, he'd try to shift the blame." Twenty minutes later the phone rang. "Four orthopedics."

"Be prepared to be fired tomorrow. I will not tolerate your continued harassment."

"Just a minute." Maggie inhaled. "The patient demanded I call you. The house doctor checked Mr. Palmero and he agrees with my assessment. It's been four hours since the pain began. The injection hasn't helped. Sounds like there's a problem."

"You're not paid to make diagnoses."

"And you can't assess a problem over the phone."

"I don't care to have some stupid nurse who's been out of practice for years telling me my business. Repeat the Demerol and Vistaril stat."

"Fine," said Maggie. The light in 403 flashed on.

Joyce ran into the station. "You'd better get

371

to Mr. Palmero. He's gone crazy. He threw the water pitcher at the wall. Want me to call security?"

"Let me see him first." Maggie reached for the door. "Bev, keep an eye on my patients, please."

"Sure."

Maggie entered 403. "Mr. Palmero."

"Get my doctor. Do something. Dammit. I want him here."

"I've called him twice."

"Is he coming?"

"I don't know."

"Give me his number. Joyce wouldn't. He's the boss's nephew. Don't care. Time to fire him. Give me the phone."

"I'll do better." Maggie lifted the receiver and dialed. "The next voice you hear will be his answering service. I'll be back in ten minutes."

As she ran down the hall, Maggie made a decision. Katherine Gordon had told her to call if she had trouble with Giancardi or Lorraine. This situation fit the criteria. She found the D.O.N.'s number in the unit directory. A sleepy voice answered.

"It's Maggie Carr. Sorry to bother you, but I have a problem." She gave a brief history of the events to date.

"How sure are you?"

372

"Better than ninety percent."

"Give me ten minutes. How long has the problem existed?"

"Since around nine this evening."

"You've talked to Giancardi and to Mrs. Petty twice. I'll settle this, and I'll want to see you tomorrow afternoon around three."

"Thanks."

Maggie pulled Mr. Palmero's chart. Before adding the new material, she read Bev's note. She turned to the dark-haired nurse. "I thank you."

Bev studied her hands. "I had to do it. You're not afraid to put yourself on the line. I wish I had your guts."

"I'm not sure guts have anything to do with it." Maggie smiled. "Charlene Rodgers is always saying 'Fools and angels.' I'm probably the first."

Bev sighed. "I wish—"

The phone rang. Expecting to hear a raging Giancardi, Maggie held the phone a few inches from her ear.

"Ms. Carr. Dr. Abrams here. I understand you have a problem. I'm on my way in. Do what you think is necessary."

"Do you mean that?"

"I do."

Maggie walked to the treatment room and took the cast cutter from the shelf. Though she could wait, the sooner the cast was loosened, the better for the patient. As she carried the equipment to 412, she reviewed the demonstration of how to use the machine she had witnessed during orientation.

Bev walked toward her. "What are you doing?"

"I'm going to cut the cast."

"Have you gone crazy?"

"I don't think so."

"Do you want to lose your job and maybe your license?"

"The patient's leg is more important."

Bev shook her head. "I have to say you're a fool, but I admire your determination. You're going to be ruined."

"You're wrong. Dr. Abrams is on the way in. He told me to do what's necessary."

"You really do have guts."

Maggie entered Mr. Palmero's room. He slammed the phone down. "I suppose you're here to put me in a wheelchair and send me home."

"I'm here to cut the cast and relieve the pressure."

"You're going to cut the cast. Should you?"

"It has to be done."

"I'm a nonpatient. Fired Giancardi. Said I couldn't stay."

Maggie shrugged. The cast cutter whined shrilly. She scored the cast from the thigh to the toes. Then she cut the cotton batting covering his leg.

"Ah." Mr. Palmero's sigh hinted of contentment. "Maybe you shouldn't have, but I'm glad you did."

"Do you still have pain??" asked a deep voice.

"Some, but a lot less."

The Chief of Orthopedics approached the bed. He winked at Maggie. "Ms. Carr, once again I'd say you were right on target . . . Mr. Palmero, I'm Dr. Abrams, head of orthopedics. I'm taking over your treatment for tonight."

Mr. Palmero ran his fingers through his dark hair. "It's going to be longer than that, I hope. Fired the other one. He said I have to check out."

The tall, elegantly dressed man turned to Maggie. "Call the supervisor. There's a form I want her to bring down. Request for a Change of Doctor. I want it in five minutes. Then bring me the setup for an infusion measure of compartment pressure. It's in the treatment room. I'll be with Mr. Palmero. You probably have a dozen things to do."

After locating and delivering the setup, Maggie headed to the nurses' station and called

Janice Petty. Joyce handed her a list of requests for pain medication. Maggie prepared them and took out her two and three A.M. antibiotics. Shortly after three she returned to the station.

Dr. Abrams sat at the desk. He looked up. "Pressure readings confirmed your suspicions. I'll come in later this morning and do another." He signed his name on the chart with a flourish. "I'm sure you'll hear about this, but don't worry. I'm taking over the case and I've documented that you acted on my orders."

Maggie smiled. "I'll make copies of my notes and yours just in case."

"Good enough. As I've said before, we need more nurses like you." He strode from the station.

As the clock moved toward the time when the day shift arrived, Maggie's stomach tightened. Her hands shook as she made copies of her notes and Dr. Abrams's progress report. Bev frowned. For a moment Maggie thought the other nurse might protest. Bev's reaction convinced her that the dark-haired nurse was responsible for the pages missing from a number of charts. As a precaution she addressed the material to Katherine Gordon and asked Mavis to deliver the envelope on her way home.

At six-thirty Maggie glanced through the med room window and saw Lorraine enter her office. Maggie gave a pre-op med and returned to the station. Mr. Palmero's chart was missing from the rack. She inhaled and fought rising nausea. Though she believed she had made the right choice, she knew being right wouldn't protect her.

Charlene and April walked in and herded Maggie to the med room. Charlene closed the door. "Are you sitting on your brains?" she asked. "Honey, I don't know if you've got guts or a self-destructive syndrome."

"Why did you do it?" asked April.

"What?"

"Don't play dumb. Joyce is in the lounge, regaling everyone with a story of how you cut a cast on the Barber's patient and how he's going to get you." The blond nurse shook her head.

"Please tell us Joyce is spinning dreams."

Maggie raised an eyebrow. "She has the facts, but maybe her interpretation is wrong."

"Lordy, why are you acting so dumb?" Charlene's braids writhed as she shook her head.

"Compartment syndrome," said Maggie.

"And the Barber?"

"Refused to come in."

"It's been nice knowing you." Charlene

reached for the narcotics book. "While you're still employed, let's count."

After report Maggie grabbed her purse. Mr. Palmero's light flashed. "I'll get that," she said.

"Thanks," said April. "Tell him I'll be there in ten minutes or less."

Maggie glanced toward Lorraine's office. Could she escape without being pulled in for questioning? The Barber strode down the hall. Though she had no reason to feel guilty, she prayed he wouldn't see her. When he entered the nurse manager's office, she slipped down the hall to 403. "Mr. Palmero, what do you need?"

"Aren't you supposed to be off duty?"

"I'm on my way. Your nurse is sending a patient to the O.R. What do you need?"

"Do you have any idea when my doctor will be in?"

"I'm here." The door closed.

Maggie turned. Dr. Giancardi and Lorraine stood at the foot of the bed. "But . . ."

Giancardi glared at Maggie. "Ms. Carr, what are you doing in here?" He looked at Lorraine. "I thought you were taking care of her."

"There wasn't time before report." The bleached blonde smiled. "I had a very long night, so I was late getting here this morning."

Mr. Palmero elevated the head of his bed. "I

378

think I should ask you what you're doing here, Doctor. Didn't we settle this last night?"

"I understand you were in pain and the nurses weren't helping you. I was sure you didn't mean what you said."

"I meant every word."

The smile slid from Giancardi's face. "Then I'm afraid you'll have to sign out against medical advice. Lorraine, do you have the form?"

"Right here, but . . ."

"Have him sign."

Mr. Palmero shook his head. "Not until I read and understand every word. You can come back later."

"You have no reason to sign that," said Maggie.

"I know." Mr. Palmero nodded. "Not long ago, another doctor advised me never to sign anything I didn't understand. It's called informed consent."

Maggie nodded. Dr. Abrams must have been the adviser. Because she didn't understand all the levels of the situation, she turned and left. As she stepped into the hall, a hand clamped on her arm. "I'm not finished with you," said the Barber.

"I've nothing to say other than I acted in the patient's interest."

Rather than cause a scene, Maggie walked

379

down the hall beside the Barber. He opened the door of Lorraine's office. "After you. I believe you've interfered for the last time."

"Once again I have nothing to say."

Lorraine entered and closed the door. She crossed to the desk and lifted a glass paperweight. For a moment Maggie thought she was going to throw the object. Lorraine cleared her throat. "You're fired."

"Fired," said Giancardi. "That's only the beginning. I'll see you lose your license for practicing medicine. What right did you have to split my patient's cast?"

"Is he your patient?" Maggie measured the distance to the door.

"He was until you interfered."

"Wrong. He was until you refused to come in."

"You never informed me of the severity of the problem."

Maggie shook her head. Why had she come here, where she was trapped between the pair? "I spoke to you twice. It's documented. The house doctor saw Mr. Palmero and agreed with my assessment."

The Barber turned to Lorraine. "The house doctor sees none of my patients, and you know that. Is this another thing you've neglected to tell your staff?"

"Leon, she knew. You know how she loves to make trouble for you."

Maggie smiled. "You don't have to worry. The house doctor refused to do anything."

"This isn't a joke," said Lorraine. "Get out of here and don't bother to come in tonight."

The barber reached the door. "Thank you, my dear. And, Ms. Carr, you'll find yourself facing a suit for interfering between a doctor and his patient. No nurse who's been on the shelf for years is going to tell me what to do. If this is an example of your behavior, I don't blame your husband for dumping you."

Though she knew she should keep quiet, his words jarred a response from Maggie. "You should talk. You never finished your residency."

He left the room and slammed the door. Maggie turned to leave.

"Once again, Ms. Carr, you're fired."

"I don't think so."

"Don't go running to Jason Knight or Katherine Gordon either. You'll find they have little to say around here."

Maggie opened the door. Though it was only eight A.M., she felt as if she had spent the entire morning in that room. Home, she thought. Sleep. Then I'll decide what to do.

* * *

Jason lingered over the single cup of coffee Beth had allowed him that morning. She sat across the table from him and leaned her chin against her hands. "So when are you going to talk to her?"

He put the cup down. "She doesn't want to talk to me, and frankly, I don't blame her."

Beth stretched. "You haven't even tried. I went to see her and apologized. She knows it was my fault. You saw the list she made and you saw the beautiful things she bought for the baby."

Jason pushed his chair back from the table. He had been with Maggie when she had bought the baby clothes. Why hadn't he guessed from her reaction when he had teased that she had been hiding something? Moments from that day moved through his thoughts. Maggie's laughter. Mr. Patton's warning. Robyn's and Joanna's teasing. The exciting pleasure of making love. He rose. "Beth, let it be. I'll see you this evening. Don't do too much."

"What's there to do? Maybe I'll make a neighborly call."

"No matchmaking schemes."

"Gee, you sound just like her."

"I mean it. Let us work things out for ourselves."

Beth blew him a kiss. "Boy, the pair of you sound like clones. See you."

When Jason arrived at the hospital, he headed to four orthopedics to clear a patient for surgery that afternoon. April Grayson waved to him. "Have you heard about Maggie?"

He shook his head and tried to banish horrid thoughts. "No."

April tugged on his arm. "Come to the lounge. I don't want to talk about it out here. Charlene and I have been taking turns looking for you."

Jason followed her to the lounge. Had Maggie been in an accident? Had she hurt herself lifting one of the patients? The door clicked closed. "All right. What's wrong?"

April checked the locker room and then the lounge. "Last night, one of Giancardi's patients . . ."

Jason listened to April's recital and assessed the facts. Did the blond nurse know the whole story? Surely Maggie wouldn't do anything wrong.

"So she split the cast and the patient's pain lessened immediately. Giancardi was in this morning and he was livid. Lorraine fired her."

"Can she do that? Isn't Maggie a hospital employee?"

383

"I don't know what she can do, but if Maggie believes her and doesn't call in, she can be fired. Lorraine told her not to come in tonight. Charlene and I have been trying to get her, and three times there's been no answer."

"Wouldn't Lorraine's telling her not to come in cover her?"

April made a face. "We wouldn't have heard, except the office door was open. Lorraine will lie." April grinned. "When Lorraine learned Dr. Abrams had come in to see the patient, I thought she'd have a stroke."

"How did Maggie handle this?"

"When she left she looked like she'd been bled hourly for a week. I hope she's all right. Maybe I should call again."

Jason touched her hand. "She'll be all right. Let me see what I can do. We're neighbors."

Though he wanted to run to his car, he forced himself to remain calm. She'll be fine. She's a fighter. But he remembered the look on her face when he had told her to leave Beth alone. She hadn't fought that night. He reached the car. Maggie needed his support.

Seventeen

When Jason reached the parking lot behind the condos, he saw Maggie's blue sedan. Relief swept through him. His pulse rate slowed; his ragged breathing calmed. Why had he been so worried? He closed his eyes and waited for the vapors of fear to disappear. For the first time in his life someone's problems rose larger than his patients' or his own. Did he care enough about her to burrow beneath the shifting sands of sexual attraction to reach the solid rock of love?

As he strode up the walk, he considered the things April had told him. The young nurse's tale of Maggie's latest problem had been disjointed. Could he help Maggie by presenting Dr. Abrams with the data he had collected? He hated the thought that Maggie's career at Hudson General could be destroyed the way Joanna's had been.

He paused at the end of the walk. Leafless trees reminded him of the barren days since he and Maggie had quarreled over Beth. Six weeks without Maggie had seemed longer than the fifteen years without Janine. He had been unfair to Maggie. A dozen times a day in as many different ways, Beth had hammered in nails of guilt. He groaned. Maggie nurtured her patients, his daughter, and, if he would accept, him.

Would she speak to him? Last week when they had met at Mrs. Miller's bedside she had looked so expectant. He hadn't acted; he had hesitated until the moment for action had passed.

He rang her doorbell once, twice, and a third time, pausing between rings while he counted slowly to a hundred. Where is she? Embers of fear fanned by winds of anxiety glowed brighter. April's description of Maggie as someone who had been bled hourly haunted him. He shook his head. She was fine. Maggie was a survivor.

After a fourth ring he crossed the narrow strip of grass between the units and dashed upstairs. Beth appeared in the living room doorway. "Daddy, what's wrong?"

"Maggie had a problem at work last night and was trashed by her nurse manager. She's not answering her phone or her door."

Beth frowned. "I saw her a while ago. She waved and said she was beat. She didn't look upset. So what happened?"

"From what I heard, a patient ran into trouble. The doctor refused to come in and she took an action nurses aren't supposed to take."

"I think that's brave."

"But foolish."

"Is the patient all right?"

Jason leaned against the wall. "I never asked, but I'm not sure that would matter. The nurse manager and the surgeon aren't her friends. That pair of vultures could rip apart the strongest person in the world."

"So you're going to jump in and be Maggie's defender." Beth grinned. "That's great. Does it mean you and she are . . . are . . . well, you know."

"Probably not. After the way I acted, I figure she'll slam the door in my face."

"You mean you haven't apologized yet." Her hands moved to her waist, pulling her T-shirt tight over her bulging abdomen. "How many times have I told you to go see her? It's not as if she lives miles away."

Jason sat on a chair at the kitchen table. "I guess I was afraid."

"Tell her that. I bet you were trying to control her too."

"Beth." Jason tapped Maggie's phone number. He counted the rings and after twenty replaced the receiver. "What now?"

"You'll think of something."

All his thoughts dwelled on Maggie and what she must have felt when Leon and Lorraine cornered her. April said there was door-slamming and yelling. "What if—" He clamped his lips together.

"What if what?" Beth stood at the stove. "You could always go see her."

"How? I can't teleport through her front door or break down walls. I don't even know who has the key to her unit."

"I bet Laura does."

"Do you still have her phone number?"

"Daddy, she lives two hours away." She put a cup of coffee in front of him. "It's instant that I have for emergencies. I think this is one."

"Thanks."

Beth sat next to him. "Remember how she came to me?"

Jason shook his head. "You've lost me."

"The day I fainted and she used her chaise to get from her balcony over here."

"Our chaise is too short."

She tilted her head to one side. "I still think an athletic man could jump across."

"I'm willing to take a risk, but leaping from one balcony to the next is a bit much."

She put her hands on the table. "Boy, you sure give up easily. If Maggie thought someone needed her, she'd find a way."

Believing this to be the truth, Jason leaned his elbows on the table and sipped the coffee. There had to be a way to reach the balcony of her unit without risking multiple fractures and a lengthy stay on the orthopedic unit. Though that notion has possibilities, he decided. What about a ladder? There was one in the basement laundry room. He rose and headed to the door.

"Where are you going?" asked Beth.

"To get a ladder."

Beth giggled. "Are you planning to play Romeo?"

"Yes."

Her giggle became a laugh. "This is so romantic."

Jason rolled his eyes upward. Did Beth know something she wasn't telling? He bounded down the steps and entered the laundry room. As he dragged the stepladder to the door, he wondered if it was long enough.

Beth pulled on a jacket. "Are you sure you're up to this?"

Jason looked at her. "We'll soon know." He crossed the strip of grass and positioned the ladder below Maggie's balcony, where the clump of rhododendrons narrowed. As he started the climb, the ladder wobbled.

"I'll hold it," said Beth. "Looks a bit short. Don't you have a longer ladder?"

"No." He took another step. "You'd better back off. If this thing topples, I don't want to land on you."

"Maybe Mrs. Grant or Mrs. Evans has a longer ladder. I don't think they'd mind helping out. I have the means to call them." She held up the portable phone.

"Don't you dare." Her laughter told him she had been teasing. He reached the narrow top step and waited for the ladder to stop rocking before he stepped onto the top, where words burned in the wood proclaimed it was not a step. He inhaled and stepped up. His hands grasped the upright bars of the railing.

"Be careful," said Beth.

He lifted his right foot and placed it on the edge of the balcony. Perspiration collected on his forehead and a drop ran down his face. After taking a deep breath, he lifted his left foot. The ladder crashed to the ground.

"Daddy," called Beth.

He swung his left leg forward and over the railing. For a short time he lay on the narrow horizontal piece of metal. Then he dropped to the floor of the balcony. Beth had disappeared. He sat on the chaise longue and caught his breath.

"Daddy, are you all right?"

He looked up. Beth stood across the six feet she had suggested he jump. "I think so. This isn't something I plan to do often."

"Good. I have a question. What are you going to do if she isn't home?"

"Her car's in the lot."

"Sometimes she takes walks in the morning."

"Then I guess I'll sit here until she returns."

"Good luck. Kiss her for me."

"Go away." Suddenly, he felt foolish. How was he going to explain his presence? What if she were angry? He rose and pushed against the sliding door. "Maggie," he shouted as he stepped into her living room. "Are you all right?"

Giancardi's face, dark with fury, loomed above her. Though Maggie knew she was asleep, she couldn't wake up. She heard Jason call to her. Huge ropes twisted around her body. She struggled to free herself, but they clung as though they had been coated with glue. She screamed and the sound echoed in her head.

"Maggie, are you all right?"

Her eyes opened. For a moment she wondered if the nightmare had ended. Slowly, she became aware that the ropes were sheets that had wrapped around her legs and torso during her restless search for sleep. She untangled herself and used her elbows to push herself into a sitting position.

"Maggie."

Jason stood in the doorway. Maggie blinked. Was she still asleep? "What are you doing here?"

"April cornered me and gave me a garbled version of your night's adventure. She and Charlene have tried to call you, but you didn't answer. They're worried."

"And you caught their fear." She pulled the covers over her legs. "I turn my phone off in here. If I don't, every salesman in the world calls."

He walked toward the bed. "Call your friends so they can stop worrying."

"Later," she said. "How did you get in?"

"I used your trick. Sort of."

"The balcony?"

He nodded. "I used a ladder."

"That was a good idea." She yawned. "Now that you know I'm all right, let me go back to sleep."

As though he hadn't heard, he continued speaking. "What happened? April said Lorraine fired you. Doesn't that worry you?"

"She tried, but she can't. As to what happened . . ." She inhaled and told him the story. "So, I'm not worried. Dr. Abrams will back me up. Of course, Giancardi threatened to sue me for interfering in a doctor/patient relationship."

"That could be serious."

"It could, except the patient fired him, and I didn't make the suggestion."

"Are you going to work tonight?"

"Why not? At three o'clock I'm meeting Katherine Gordon. Lorraine will be there and she'll have to back down."

"I wish I had your confidence." He sat on the edge of the bed. "Don't dismiss the pair lightly."

"I don't. There's a lot I haven't figured how to handle. Lorraine's been blackmailing one of the nurses and Giancardi never finished his residency."

"What? How do you figure that?"

393

Maggie drew her knees up and wrapped her arms around her legs. "Laura had dinner with someone who knew him back when. He told her. Betty Loring discovered the same thing when she was researching her case against him."

"You could have told me."

Had he forgotten how long it had been since they had talked? "We weren't speaking, remember." Jason shifted and moved closer. He reached out his fingers and touched hers. His thumb stroked circles on the back of her hand. She felt warmth radiate up her arms. Wishing she weren't so responsive to his touch, she took a deep breath.

"You're right, and that's my fault. I'm sorry about the way I reacted, but sorry doesn't win awards. It's just that I hate surprises."

Maggie edged away. Before allowing herself to be seduced into forgiveness, she had to set boundaries. "I know you were hurt because Beth didn't tell you and because you were frightened for her, but you should have seen I was trying my best to help. I can't let that happen again."

Jason looked away. "You're right to feel that way." He sucked in a breath. "I care about you, more than I realized. That's why I came."

Maggie pleated the sheet with her fingers.

She wanted more than sex and caring. Her feelings for him had moved beyond surface emotions.

He caught her hand and kissed her fingers. "We need to work together."

"On this, I agree."

"I've missed you."

Maggie yielded to the emotion in his voice. "I've missed you too."

"Can we start over?"

She raised an eyebrow. "As in, hi, I'm Maggie Morgan Carr, your new neighbor. I knew you years ago."

Jason laughed. "Maybe not that far." He rose. "Though I'd like to explore this new friendship, can we wait until this evening? I left the hospital without making rounds and my office hours begin at ten."

"You'll never make them."

"I'm always late." He kissed her forehead. "Until this evening."

"What am I going to tell Beth when she comes prying? She's sure to have reached some faulty conclusion."

"Or the right one. Leave it to her imagination."

"You've got to be kidding."

"Probably." He strode to the door, turned,

and blew her a kiss.

Maggie leaned back against the pillows. What now, she wondered. He cared, but did he love her? She couldn't afford a deeper involvement until she knew. One-sided love always led to pain. She had learned that lesson well.

At ten minutes to three Maggie arrived at the nursing office. Early, tense, and worried, she thought. Could Katherine's intervention keep Lorraine from further tactics designed to make my work situation less perfect than it already is? She paused just inside the door of the large room where the secretaries and supervisors had their desks.

The receptionist looked up. "Ms. Carr, go on back. They're waiting for you."

They, wondered Maggie. Her stomach coiled into a knot. She knocked on the door. Abby Jamison answered. "Maggie, good to see you again. Come in."

"I'm early."

"Early is good. Lorraine was supposed to be here at two-thirty but she's late. Want coffee?"

"Though I've had four cups already, I think I will." She followed Abby into the room.

Katherine Gordon sat at her desk. "Margaret, I'm glad you came early. I received the copy of the documentation this morning and I've talked to Dr. Abrams. He said you did a perfect job."

Maggie took the cup of coffee Abby handed her and sat in one of the chairs facing the desk. "I hope he's right."

The door opened and Lorraine sauntered into the room. Her sour expression brought a frown to Maggie's face. Lorraine crossed the room and stood in front of Katherine's desk, blocking Maggie's view of the D.O.N. "What's she doing here?" Her red-tipped finger stabbed toward Maggie. "I requested a private meeting."

Katherine straightened the papers on her desk. "I had planned this meeting before your call. Perhaps if you had arrived on time, you could have stated your case without witnesses. As soon as Janice Petty arrives, we'll begin."

Abby looked at Maggie and winked. Then she rolled her eyes. Maggie wondered what message the former supervisor had meant to convey. The door opened a second time and Janice Petty hovered in the doorway.

"Come in," said Katherine. "Now that everyone's here, let's begin. First I want to say that I have received a full report of last night's incident from the patient, the house doctor, and

Dr. Abrams, in addition to reading the nurses' notes."

"How did you get them?" asked Lorraine. "You haven't been to the unit to review the chart."

"I was," said Abby. She walked to the window. "I discovered the chart was locked in your office and you were off the unit at some meeting. Funny thing. There were none scheduled."

Lorraine turned to Maggie. Her lips curled into a sneer. "This was a private meeting with Dr. Giancardi's lawyer. He intends to take legal action. What do you think about that, Ms. Super-Nurse?"

Maggie inhaled. "He may be in for a surprise."

Katherine tapped her pen on the table. "At this moment I'm concerned with the nursing part of this problem. Mrs. Petty, why did you refuse to step in to address the problem?"

"I didn't think there was one." The redhead smiled. "You see, Lorraine had warned me about Ms. Carr's other attempts to cause trouble for Dr. Giancardi."

"Did you examine the patient?"

"Why should I have bothered? I knew . . ."

Abby turned from the window. "You knew nothing and chose to do the same. Isn't that your usual style?"

"Are you jealous? Just think, I'll soon be on days too."

Maggie wondered what the interchange between the pair meant. What did it have to do with her?

"Let's get back to the problem at hand," said Katherine. "Maggie, did you inform Mrs. Petty about the problem?"

"Twice," said Maggie. "The first time was when she was on rounds and the second by phone."

"But . . . but . . ." Janice protested. "How was I to know you knew what you were doing? After all, you've been out of nursing for ages and chose the night shift because it was easier."

Maggie bit her lip to keep from attacking the supervisor verbally. What right had she to make that kind of judgment?

"Then there was all the more reason for you to check," said Abby.

Lorraine leaned forward. "Ms. Carr called Leon after midnight. I know she wiggled out of another problem by pointing to hospital policy. This time she can't. Staff nurses are forbidden to call doctors after midnight."

Maggie straightened in her chair. "Mrs. Petty refused to call and told me if I thought it was important to make the call myself. There's documented proof that a compartment syndrome existed. I made copies of certain pages of the chart so they wouldn't come up missing, the way others have."

"Are you accusing me?" asked Lorraine.

"I wouldn't dream of it." Maggie leaned back. Watch your mouth, she cautioned herself.

Katherine picked up a piece of paper. "I've studied this carefully and I find Ms. Carr showed excellent nursing judgment and tried to solve a problem before it became a disaster for the patient and for the hospital. She will remain as a staff nurse on your unit unless she requests a transfer. Nurses at Hudson General are here to protect the patients, not the doctors. Since I was personally involved, I know she followed protocol."

"What do you mean, you were involved?" asked Lorraine. She turned to Janice Petty. "Why didn't you tell me?"

"I didn't know."

Katherine rose. "Ms. Carr, I'd like to thank you for your quick actions last night. I only wish you had received the cooperation you deserved. You can go. Janice, Lorraine, we'll continue this discussion."

Abby left her position at the window and

walked to the door with Maggie. "What a relief."

"It's much more, as you'll soon learn. Hold off on asking for a transfer."

"I still have to work with them."

"You can do it."

"You're right." Maggie smiled. She would ignore any tricks Lorraine tried by not giving the woman a clue as to how she felt. She waved to Abby and headed to the elevator.

At four-fifteen, two cancellations allowed Jason a breather. He tried Maggie's number. No answer. Was she still meeting with Katherine Gordon? What had been decided? Had the results fulfilled his fears? How could he help?

Marvin Abrams, he thought. He dialed the orthopedic surgeon's number and was put on hold. Three minutes later a deep voice spoke. "Jason, what can I do for you?"

"It's about Leon. I've been gathering evidence about cases that should have resulted in malpractice charges but didn't. Some because parts of the charts were missing, and others because the patients had no legal advice."

"I'll be glad to see what you have."

Jason cleared his throat. "It's been brought to

my attention that he never finished his residency."

"So, that's why . . ."

"What?"

"He's always maintained he's too busy to study for and take his boards. Without a completed residency he's not eligible. Could you drop your data off, say around six? Looks like the orthopedic surgeons have some housecleaning to do."

"I don't have documentation about the lack of a completed residency."

"No problem. Within a week or two I will. Don't worry. Something will be done about the situation. Last night I experienced firsthand an example of the way he practices medicine."

"I'm also worried about Ms. Carr. This isn't the first time she's stood up to him."

"Don't worry. I've taken care of that end. She's one of the best nurses we have at Hudson General, and there are a lot of good ones." He chuckled. "I take it the rumors are true."

"Maybe." Jason hung up and stared at the diplomas on his office walls. How could there be rumors when he and Maggie had been at odds long enough for a hundred other people's stories to take their place? He strode to the door. Four more patients to see. Then a stop to drop off the material on Leon and home for a shower and to change clothes. He smiled. Not long until he saw Maggie. Could he convince her, and himself, that they could be friends?

At quarter to seven he arrived at Maggie's door. "I smell coffee."

"What no fee fie fo fum?" She laughed. "I guess the way to a man's heart is through his olfactory nerve."

Jason paused. Though this morning he had been fully prepared to make a commitment, the feeling had dissipated. "Could this be considered sexual harassment?"

"Coffee. Hardly, more like pandering to an addiction."

"How did your meeting go?"

"I'm still a night nurse on four ortho. I'm not sure what went on after I left. I'll probably hear a dozen variations of the truth tonight."

Jason followed her to the kitchen. "I handed all my materials to Dr. Abrams and told him what you had heard about Leon's residency."

"Was that a good idea?" Maggie filled two cups with coffee. "Cake?"

"Yes and yes. Some action had to be taken. I've sat on my information long enough. Dr. Abrams can use it better than I could have. The results may not be everything we'd like to see, but it's a start."

Maggie sat across from him. They ate in silence. Jason wasn't sure what he wanted to say. He finished the cake. "Delicious . . . Maggie . . ."

"Jason . . ."

He laughed. "You first."

She toyed with her fork. "I appreciate your being worried about me. It's been a long time since that's happened." She put the fork down. "I like you a lot, but sometimes I feel like we're in a runaway train speeding downhill."

"And nearly leaving the tracks because of rocks in the way. Like that?" She nodded. He reached across the table. "I know the feeling. How about just being friends until we're sure there can be more?"

"Trust," she said softly. "We have to find that. I've been hurt and so have you. I think we've both lost the ability to depend on someone else."

He inhaled. "For me, it's being in control and always making the decisions. This is going to be rough."

"You can do it." She reached for his hand. "Want to go for a walk?"

"Sounds good."

When they returned from the walk, Jason

kissed her lightly. He stepped back before he grabbed her and carried her upstairs. She was right about runaway feelings and building trust.

That evening Maggie sat at the desk listening to report when Bev arrived. Bev looked drawn and as though she had been crying. She paused beside Maggie's chair. "I'm glad she failed."

"So am I. We'll talk later."

After report Maggie made rounds. When she returned to the station, Bev was alone. The dark-haired woman shook her head. "She was so sure she would win."

"Maybe she's not as powerful as she thought."

"She raked me good because I agreed with you and did an evaluation of Mr. Palmero."

"Are you going to continue letting her bully you?"

"You don't understand."

"Maybe I do. There was some missing Demerol and you had a dying husband."

Bev slumped on a chair. "Who told you? Lorraine said no one would learn the truth. Did she—"

"No one told me. I put together a number of stories. Talk to Miss Gordon."

"I can't. Lorraine would . . . she'd call me a liar." She put her hands to her face. "It was

405

such a dreadful time. He had so much pain and his doctor wouldn't increase his dosage because he was afraid he'd become an addict. As if that mattered. One night a patient requested an injection and then changed his mind. I took the tubex home. Then I started taking and charging them to the patients. Lorraine caught me."

Maggie put her hand on Bev's shoulder. "And since then she's been using her knowledge for blackmail. Don't let it continue. Talk to Katherine."

"I'll think about it."

Maggie rose. "My district's quiet tonight. Is there any way I can help you?"

"Pin care in 420. I've five of them." Bev wiped her eyes on a tissue. "Thanks."

The hours of the night sped. Maggie had just finished preparing a patient for surgery. She stood in the hall to finish the chart.

Lorraine strode toward her. "Ms. Carr, give me a minute of your time."

"Yes."

The bleached blond grabbed Maggie's arm. "You may think you've won, but we'll see. You've an evaluation due next month, and dear, sweet, gullible April won't be doing it."

"Is that all?" Maggie turned to leave.

"Didn't you hear me?"

"Yes, but I'll continue to be the patients' advocate and I won't compromise myself." Maggie entered the patient's room and handed the chart to the transport team.

Eighteen

A week after the meeting in Katherine Gordon's office, Maggie sat at the desk in the nurses' station finishing her charts. The day nurses clustered at the door of the med room. Their low buzzing voices reminded her of swarming insects.

"Well, I heard . . . That's not the way it was. This is how . . . Wrong. I can't believe . . ."

Charlene detached herself from the group. "If we really want the scoop on what went on, here's someone who was there." Her beaded braids switched like a predator's tail. "Maggie, tell us what really went on."

Maggie continued writing and hoped her silence would express her views on gossip. What had happened in Katherine's office belonged there, not sweeping through the hospital.

"Give," said Charlene. "You've no reason to protect them. They're not your friends. We are. What kind of ultimatum were you given?"

Maggie closed the chart. "Don't push." She took her purse from the drawer.

"Don't look now, but here comes trouble." The black nurse patted Maggie's shoulder. "Need a convoy."

Leon Giancardi paused outside the station door. Maggie shook her head. "I'm not afraid of him. Don't you have meds to give?"

"It's your choice, but if I saw him coming, I'd want all the witnesses in the world." Charlene sighed. "I like you, but I don't understand your suicidal impulses. That's one mean S.O.B."

Maggie opened the door. "Dr. Giancardi."

"Ms. Carr. One battle doesn't win a war." He smiled. "I'd be glad to change the battlefield. How about one on one on satin sheets?"

"Excuse me, please."

"Be my guest." He stepped aside.

Maggie held her shoulders back and marched down the hall. She frowned. Last evening Jason had been strangely silent when she had asked what action the doctors planned to take against Giancardi. The rumors covered every possible scenario. She grabbed her coat from the locker room and hurried to her car. Maybe she could coax some facts from Jason tonight.

At quarter to six Jason stood at the door of his office. For the first time ever, he was ready to leave the office early. The phone rang. "Marvin, how are you? . . . I'm fine. . . . You have . . . I see . . ." He laughed. "You know what I'd really like . . . You're right. It's a start? . . . Can I tell her? . . . How serious? I'm not sure . . . I'm sure there are. Hospitals are like stagnant pools for breeding rumors. Thanks for calling."

An urge to cheer made him laugh. Maggie had won at least one of her battles. He grabbed his coat and his black leather medical bag. As he left the office, he switched out the lights.

At home he whistled as he showered and changed into jeans and a sweater. A note from Beth fastened to the refrigerator door informed him that she was having dinner at Robyn's. The note continued. "She's invited us to spend Thanksgiving with them at their lodge in Vermont. I told her we'd love to. She said to ask Maggie and don't blow it this time."

Jason chuckled and poured a glass of juice.

410

He stood at the kitchen window while he drank. Though he and Maggie had spent every evening together, Beth had been their shadow, acting as a buffer and a diversion. Even the presence of his daughter hadn't lessened his desire to carry Maggie to the bedroom.

The timer on the oven buzzed. He opened the door and took out a steaming, savory casserole. The doorbell rang. He hurried to answer. Maggie walked upstairs. She carried a foil-covered dish. "Dessert," she said.

"Your timing is perfect. Just took dinner from the oven."

"Great. I'm starved. I spent all day finishing my Christmas shopping."

He made a face. "Bah, humbug."

"This year will be different. Where's Beth?"

"At Robyn's." His fingers brushed her hand. "Do you mind her not being here?"

"Of course not."

He studied her face and thought he saw hesitation. Trust, he thought. We're building trust. "What's for dessert?"

"Chocolate fudge pecan pie."

"Good thing Beth isn't here. We'd have to listen to her moans of envy and those self-righteous lectures on the advantages of healthful eating. There's coffee."

"Your weekly allowance."

He shook his head. "I stopped and bought some on my way home. I'm keeping it in my medical bag."

Her laughter acted like an aphrodisiac. He took the pie from her hands, set it on the table, and drew her into his arms. He meant to keep the kiss light, but his hunger for her burst from the tight restraints. His tongue slid between her lips and tasted the minty flavor of her mouth. Growling low, he pulled her hard against his chest.

Maggie caught the fire of his kiss. Before she surrendered to the promise of a blazing confrontation, she put her hands on his chest. He looked down at her. "Sorry. It happens every time."

"I know."

He stepped away. "We're good together. I wish you could trust me not to hurt you. I'm not George."

"I know you're not." She sat on one of the kitchen chairs. She wished he would say something to let her know that what they had would last beyond a week, a month, a year. She couldn't be content to go from day to day, wondering if there would be another.

She dished Brunswick stew onto her plate

and took a taste. "Delicious. You or our missing chaperon?"

"Beth. She really likes to cook."

"Did you ever think of the Culinary Institute instead of college for her?"

"No, but it's an idea." He ate for a few minutes and put down his fork. "I have some news for you about the barber."

"Yes."

"As of tomorrow, he'll be allowed to practice surgery only under Dr. Abrams's supervision."

"Will he accept the decision?"

Jason shrugged. "It's the only way he'll be able to continue at Hudson General. Of course, he can always go back and finish the residency. Can you see him doing that?" He reached for her hand. "Be wary around him for a while."

"Forever," said Maggie.

"Good thought. Are you up for a movie tonight?"

"I'd like that."

On Thanksgiving morning Maggie hurried home from work. The twins were due; Laura had given a three-quarter promise to drive up with them. She had hoped Beth and Jason would join the party, but they were having dinner with the Grants at their lodge in Vermont.

She pulled into her parking place. A gray coupe slid into the next space. Morgan and Ellen got out and caught her in a hug.

"You look terrific. . . . I've missed you. . . . What's going on in your life?" Questions and statements flew between them.

Maggie took a deep breath. "Not out here. It's cold. We have all day and tomorrow to talk."

Ellen linked arms with her mother. "Bring the bags," she called over her shoulder to her brother.

"So much for liberated women," he said.

"Where's Laura?" asked Maggie. "Didn't you stay at her place last night?"

"She's in the delivery room," said Ellen. "She said this is the very last one and she'll arrive around noon."

"She'll miss most of the parade," said Maggie.

Morgan laughed. "We heard her plaints at five o'clock this morning and I'm sure she'll repeat them this afternoon. She's such a kid about parades."

"Everyone has their childish moments," said Ellen. "Aren't you into baseball cards?"

"What's for breakfast?" asked Morgan. "Since Laura woke us at five with her news, my dear

414

sister rushed us out with nothing to eat but a stale doughnut and a cup of reheated coffee."

Maggie opened the door and led the way upstairs. "Come to the kitchen. I think there might be a snack to carry you over until dinner."

"It's great to be here." Ellen and Morgan spoke in unison.

"It's great to have you." Maggie opened the refrigerator and handed things to Ellen, who passed them to Morgan. "Orange juice, assorted rolls. Wait till you taste the chocolate croissants."

"Are you still overdosing on chocolate?" asked Morgan.

"Every chance I get."

Ellen pulled the string from the box. "Chocolate croissants, chocolate cream-filled doughnuts. Mom, I love you."

Maggie laughed. Though Morgan had her temperament, it was Ellen who shared her love of chocolate. "Heat the croissants and rolls. I'll scramble some eggs, and there's ham and cheese. Someone start coffee. Hope you don't mind sharing a room. Twin beds in the guest room."

"What, no bunk beds?" asked Morgan. "Remember the summer cottage."

"Not that story again," said Ellen. "You'll never let me forget the long step down."

"Or the fights over who slept on top." He hefted the twin bags. "While you ladies do kitchen things I'll put these in the bedroom." He paused. "Mom, do you have to work tonight?"

"Not until tomorrow night. I work Christmas."

"So do I," said Ellen.

"Me too," said Morgan. "I have solos at three churches. Good thing they're all in a cluster."

Maggie cracked eggs into a bowl. "I hope they're paying well."

By the time the eggs were done, Morgan had set the table and poured coffee. Ellen heaped the heated rolls on one plate and the doughnuts on another. Maggie dished out eggs. "Now, tell me everything that's been happening."

"That would take a month," said Ellen. She looked at her brother. "Who goes first?"

"You before you burst."

Ellen exhaled. "I'm enjoying the residency program, but I'd rather be closer to home. Do you think in about two years there might be an opening around here for a pair of family practitioners?"

Maggie dropped her fork. "A pair."

"Yeah." Ellen's smile radiated joy. "One of my fellow residents is also a displaced New Yorker. We're friends. Someday when we get time to concentrate on each other, there might be more. You know I never jump into things."

"A lesson I'm learning," said Maggie. "I'll ask around. I wish you could have met my neighbor. He's a G.P. here."

Morgan winked. "Just a neighbor?"

"We're friends." Maggie shook her head. "Don't push."

Morgan grinned and made a face at his sister. "Back to you. Is one of this pair of physicians domestic?"

"We manage. You could share space with us. It's not that far to the city."

"Who knows where I'll be. As soon as this year in Houston is over, I'm heading to Europe."

"How are you fixed financially?" asked Maggie.

Morgan grinned. "Are you offering to bankroll me?"

"I wish I could."

"I'll be all right. I've been eating light and accepting every offer of a meal I get. Lean and hungry pulls the invites in."

Ellen's laughter rolled out. "It's called flirting

with old ladies."

"And young. I can't help I'm a hunk."

"Of cheese," said Ellen.

Maggie looked from one to the other and wished her life and goals were as settled as theirs. She finished the last bite of croissant and emptied her coffee cup. "If you're finished, there are potatoes to peel and a bird to stuff."

"Let's get moving," said Morgan. "Stuffing first and then potatoes with the parade."

"If you promise not to make a mess," said Maggie.

"Who, me?" Morgan lifted his hands and shrugged.

Ellen opened the refrigerator to put the juice away and get the bowl of stuffing. "Um-um. Pumpkin pies and kirsch cake."

Morgan loaded the dishwasher. "Just think, Mom, next year I can compare yours to the real Black Forest cake. Any cookies?"

"In the jar. You're as bad as John Patton."

"A man," said Ellen. "Tell us more."

"Is he nice?" asked Morgan.

Maggie laughed. "He's seventy-two and a walking history lesson."

While Morgan packed stuffing into the turkey and Ellen washed potatoes, Maggie prepared candied yams. She told them the story of

Mr. Patton and how she had sprung him from the county home. Ellen told several tales about her patients and her experiences. Morgan talked about the opera stars he had met.

As they sat in the living room, peeling potatoes and watching the parade, Maggie thought of other Thanksgivings and decided this was the best one for years.

"Mom, could I ask you something?" Morgan's voice sounded tentative.

"Sure."

"Do you still hate Dad?"

"What an awful question," said Ellen.

"It's not," said Maggie. "For a while, maybe I did. I was hurt, disappointed, and angry with him and ashamed and upset with myself. I felt guilty."

"Whatever for?" asked Ellen.

"I blamed myself for not being the proper wife for him."

Morgan cleared his throat. "Why? He chose to get involved with another woman. I hated him."

Maggie shook her head. "Don't say that. Your father was searching for something I couldn't give him. At least he had the courage to look." She waved away their protests. "He should have had enough courage to speak out though."

"Do you mean that?" Their question echoed

"Yes." Maggie picked up the bowl of pota
toes. "Let me put these in water."

The doorbell rang. Morgan darted down the
hall. He returned with his arm around Laura's
shoulders. "The gang's all here."

Laura handed Maggie two bottles of wine.
"Smells good in here. When do we eat?"

"Not until two," said Maggie.

"I'll fix you a plate of goodies," said Ellen.
"Do you want coffee or tea?"

"Either. I'm beat." Laura peered into the living room. "Where's the hunk? I thought you'd
surely have him here."

Morgan and Ellen stared at Maggie. "Hunk?
What hunk? Is there something you're not telling us?"

"He's my neighbor." She shook her head.
"Auntie Laura has been too long without food.
She's inventing stories."

"Mother, you're blushing," said Ellen.

"You can tell us," said Morgan. "We won't
tease you."

"His name is Jason Knight. He and his
daughter live next door. They're with friends in
Vermont."

"How is Beth?" asked Laura.

"Thriving."

Morgan kissed Laura's cheek. "Looks like you're next."

"I'll pass," said Laura.

Laughter and teasing continued for the rest of the day. Laura left at seven. Maggie walked her to the car. "They look great, don't they? I didn't think about how much I missed them until they got here."

"You look great too. This Jason has been good for you. Is it serious?"

"We're trying to become friends."

"After going to bed together. That's weird."

Maggie shrugged. "I know. We're going about this backward." She kissed Laura's cheek and watched while the dark sedan drove away. Jason's unit was dark. He'll be home sometime tomorrow, she thought.

On Friday evening Maggie left Morgan and Ellen watching television and eating popcorn. She glanced at Jason's unit. Several lights told her he and Beth had returned. Why hadn't he called?

During report she was saddened to learn Herman Stein had been admitted the day before. Because there hadn't been a private room on oncology, he had been placed in 409.

Sue Rawlings sighed. "He's not going to make it this time."

After report Maggie began her rounds in Herman's room. He opened his eyes. "Margaret, I've been hoping you would be working."

Maggie reached for his hand. "Are you in a lot of pain?"

"It has passed beyond pain. I feel like I am floating."

"Is there anything I can do for you?"

"Find out if my friend Jason has come home from his trip. I want to see him for a bit."

"What about your family?"

"We have said our good-byes. I sent them home. Tomorrow they will have much to do."

"I'll call Jason." She squeezed his fingers. "I wish there were more."

"Your being here brings me joy. You are a good person." He closed his eyes. "Johnny's new family brought him to my house. He is happy and you made it so." He opened his eyes. "I would like a smile."

Maggie forced herself to smile. "It's hard to lose a friend."

"Tell me what you did yesterday."

"My children were here, and my best friend. We shared a lot of stories and laughter." She told him bits about what Ellen and Morgan were doing.

"That is good." He patted her hand. "You should tell Jason what your daughter wants to do. He could use the help." He closed his eyes again.

Maggie returned to the station and placed a call to Jason. "Jason, it's Maggie."

"What's wrong?"

"It's Herman. He was admitted yesterday afternoon and has been slipping in and out of consciousness all day. He wants to see you."

"Give me twenty minutes. Is his family there?"

"He sent them home."

"I'll sit with him. He shouldn't be alone."

Maggie returned to Herman's room. His respiration had grown slow and irregular. She hurried to complete rounds and to give out medications. When she returned to the room, Jason stood beside the bed. Grief darkened his eyes.

"Herman," he said. "I'll stay with you awhile."

The elderly man opened his eyes. "Jason, my friend."

Maggie backed to the door. "Call me if you need me."

"I will."

For the next three hours she opened charts, did treatments, and gave medications. After Peggy, Mavis, and Joyce returned from their break, she walked back down the hall to Herman's room. Jason turned. "It's over. I need to call his family."

"I'll let the supervisor know. Is there anything I can do for you?" Though she wanted to reach out to him, she was afraid of the chemistry that usually flared between them. "There's fresh coffee in the lounge. The others have finished with their dinner breaks."

"Thanks. I'll use the phone in there. I'll need his chart too."

"No problem."

Jason returned to the bedside. Tonight an era in his life had ended. He remembered the day he opened his office and found Herman at his door. "I have come to see the new doctor."

"Are you sick?"

"Not today, but there will come a day. Like you, we have just moved here from the city so we will begin our lives here together."

Jason sighed. He reached out and touched Herman's hand. Flesh that remained warm belied death. "Good-bye, old friend." Jason turned and left the room.

In the lounge he poured a cup of coffee. The

ache inside grew. Would the pain leave? Other patients had died without leaving him with this need to be held. He sucked in a deep breath and dialed the phone. Herman's son answered on the first ring. "This is Dr. Knight . . . Five minutes ago . . . Will you be coming in? . . . I'll let the nurses know. . . . I'll miss him too."

Jason walked to the window and stared at the moonless sky. Grief built, but his tears were blocked. The lounge door opened. Maggie walked toward him. He held out his hands.

She took them. "Are you all right?"

He shook his head. "No."

"I remember how you told me he was your first patient."

"And a good friend. After Janine left, he fed me borscht, chicken soup, and advice."

"It must be hard to lose a good friend." She moved closer and touched his face. "It was an easy death."

Jason looked at her, read the caring on her face and heard the sympathy in her voice. Nothing lasts forever, he told himself, and if there is no beginning, there can be no end. A part of him rejected the reasoning.

"Maggie, I need you." Her sigh renewed his doubts, but he had to push them aside or retreat back into the sterile life he had been living for fifteen years. "Could I come over in the morning when you get home from work?"

"I'd like that. My kids are leaving right after I get home. Do you want to meet them, or should I call when they leave?"

"Call. And thank you."

"Is Herman's family coming in?"

"No. They've said their good-byes."

Maggie nodded. "I'll let Joyce know and we'll get him ready." She brushed his cheek with a kiss. "Will you be all right?"

He nodded. "I'll be waiting for your call."

At seven-thirty Maggie left the hospital. In her thoughts she relived the moments in the lounge. Jason needed her, but need wasn't the same as love. What was she going to tell him?

She pulled into her parking space and hurried up the walk. Morgan and Ellen were in the kitchen. Morgan grinned. "We're having turkey and cheese omelets. Want one?"

"Just juice and toast," she said. "Eating too much before I go to bed gives me dreadful dreams."

"Good thing you're not a resident," said Ellen. "Usually the snack I grab as I'm climbing into bed is my only meal of the day."

Morgan nodded. "Since my day begins at noon, a midnight snack is dinner for me."

"Wait till you get older."

Morgan · hooted. "You may be gray, but you're not old."

"What?" she said in mock horror. "Never gray. I'll go to my grave as a redhead."

As soon as they finished eating, Morgan looked at his watch. "If I'm going to make that plane, we'd better boogie."

"Grab the bags and we'll fly low," said Ellen.

Maggie walked to the car with them. She hugged them both and waved until the car was out of sight. With a sigh she turned. Jason stood at the end of the walk. "I see your company has left."

Maggie shook her head. "Were you lurking in the bushes?"

"As a matter of fact, I was."

"You should have introduced yourself. Ellen and a friend are interested in settling in the area when they finish their residency."

"Next time. Can we talk?"

Maggie unlocked the door. Inside, Jason turned her to face him. "I meant what I said last night. I need you in my life."

"For how long?"

"Today, tomorrow, forever. . . . I can't promise. All I know is that we're good together."

She stepped back. "I need more than that."

He groaned. "I want to make promises. It's been so long, I've forgotten how."

She reached for his hand. "There's time to learn. I'm not going to vanish. How are you feeling about Herman's death?"

Jason walked beside her up the stairs. "I wasn't surprised. I knew how little time he had, and yet . . ."

"I know the feeling. Expectation never equals the event."

"I thought about how much I'll miss him and then I thought of Beth. What am I going to do if she . . . ?"

"She won't. Aren't the doctors pleased with her condition? That's what she tells me every time she pops in." She poured two cups of coffee and handed one to him. "You can't dictate her life the way you can your patients'."

He lifted the cup. "Patients don't always listen either. . . . Why am I making such a hash out of life these days? I upset Beth. I upset you. I overreact and then feel sorry."

Maggie leaned against the counter and sipped the coffee. "I think I understand. That's how I felt last year."

Jason slumped in a chair. "I should have remembered you're not Janine and you aren't trying to steal Beth. She probably found it easier to tell you about the baby because you're a woman."

Maggie inhaled. "She's looking for a mother. I seem to fit her picture of one."

He pushed the coffee cup away. His gaze swept from her head to toe. "That's not the picture I see. Beautiful, sensuous, and a hundred other things." He rose and took the coffee cup from her. As he put it on the counter behind her, he bracketed her with his arms. "I don't need words. I need you."

Maggie rested her forehead against his chest. "I need more than sex."

"I care about you. I like being with you. I crave your touch. Can we build on that?"

Can we, she wondered. And what happens the next time we disagree? His hands massaged her shoulders. She understood the craving. Her need for him had invaded every cell of her body. His fingers touched her neck and tilted her face upward. The kiss swept her doubts away like a forest fire. Maggie knew she was lost. Though sex wasn't enough, if that was all he could offer, she would accept. She leaned into the embrace. Her fingers massaged the muscles of his back.

"Jason," she whispered.

"Not here," he said.

With hands tightly clasped they walked to her bedroom, stopping for frequent kisses and lingering caresses. In the bedroom they undressed, tossing clothes into heaps. Then, clinging to each other, they walked to the bed.

"You're magic," he whispered. "You give so much."

She covered his mouth with her lips and pulled him down on the bed with her.

Later, in the lingering glow of their spent passion, Maggie's hands stroked his chest, his abdomen, sweeping lower with each touch. If this is all, so be it, she thought. A part of her yearned for words of love and promises of endurance.

"You're too much," he said. "I feel sixteen." His caresses and kisses sent sparks to renew the dying embers of their recent explosive joining. He knelt between her legs and claimed her again.

Replete, thought Maggie. She pulled Jason close. Soon his ragged breathing subsided into the steady sounds of sleep. She drifted toward dreams.

The doorbell sounded in staccato rings. Who, what? Remembering another rude awakening, Maggie slid out of bed and pulled on the sweat suit she had worn the day before. As she ran to the door, Jason sat up. "Maggie, what's wrong?"

"I don't know," she said.

Nineteen

As she ran to the door, Maggie pulled a dark green sweatshirt over her head. Her first fears that something had happened to Ellen and Morgan subsided. That kind of news would come by phone, not with a knock at the door. She pressed the buzzer and dashed down the stairs. Beth opened the door. "What's wrong?" asked Maggie.

Beth's chestnut hair was pulled back into an untidy braid. Her blue eyes glistened with unshed tears. "My water broke. This wasn't supposed to happen."

Maggie pulled her inside and put an arm around the girl's shoulders. "Are you having contractions?"

Beth nodded. "I think so. I don't feel well. My heart's racing. They wanted to put me in the hospital next week to monitor me." Tears

432

ran down her cheeks. "Maggie, I can't find Daddy."

Maggie reached for Beth's wrist. A rapid, thready pulse beat against her fingers. Knowing she couldn't let Beth see how the accelerated heart rate worried her, she looked away. "Calm down. Your father's here. Come upstairs and I'll tell him you're here."

A pool of clear fluid puddled on the slate floor of the lower foyer. "Oh, please," moaned Beth. "I'm so afraid."

Maggie put her hand on Beth's abdomen and felt a moderately strong contraction. "When was the last one?"

"I don't know. I can't think. Maybe right after my water broke. It's been about fifteen or twenty minutes."

"Come on upstairs."

"I can't. I'll make a mess." Beth covered her face with her hands. "I don't want to be a bother. All I ever do is make trouble for people."

Maggie opened the folding chair she had used on Halloween and had never put away. "Sit here. You're not a bother and you're not making trouble. I'll get some towels for you to sit on." She ran upstairs and opened the linen closet.

Jason appeared in the bedroom doorway. He

433

zipped his jeans. "What's happening? Is that Beth I hear?"

Maggie nodded. "She's in labor."

He grabbed her arm. "Are you sure? Sam didn't want this to happen. It's too soon. What are we going to do?" Maggie watched the usually calm man fall apart. "I've got to get her to the hospital. Don't just stand there. Move."

"Your shoes," said Maggie. "Get your shoes and shirt."

He turned and then whirled back to face her. "There isn't time. This shouldn't be happening. Next week they were going to admit her. How will they know what her baseline values are?"

"Calm down. There's time." Maggie pulled several thick white towels from the shelf. She pushed Jason into the bedroom. "Get dressed. I'll drive." She pulled on her sneakers. "Jason, move."

"Daddy." Beth stood at the end of the hall. "I think I had another one. Daddy, don't let me die."

Jason pushed past Maggie. "I won't. That's a promise. Let's go."

"Your shirt, your shoes." Maggie handed Beth the towels. "You're not going to die. You're going to have a baby right here if your father doesn't move."

"It's going to be a girl," said Beth. "That's

what Dr. Grant said the sonogram showed. Daddy, will you love her like you wanted to love me?"

Jason groaned. "How can you ask that?"

"I have to know that you'll take care of her."

Maggie wanted to scream. Instead, she grabbed Beth's shoulders and turned her around. "Go sit down."

"I think I need to walk," said Beth. "Sitting makes me nervous."

"Then walk to the chair in the lower foyer." Maggie turned to Jason. He held his shirt and stared after his daughter. "Get dressed right now." Maggie plucked the shirt from his hands and slipped the sleeve on his right arm. "You're not helping her by falling apart." She dropped his shoes at his feet.

Jason tied his shoes and buttoned his shirt so one side hung longer than the other. Maggie shook her head. "Let's go." She grabbed her purse and keys from the hall table.

Jason inhaled. "Maggie, you worked last night. You're tired. I can drive her."

Though his voice sounded calm, there was still a wild look in his eyes. Maggie shook her head. "You'll drive as fast as that car of yours can go, and both of you will end up in the hospital. I'll drive. Someone has to remain calm."

Beth screamed. Jason's pupils dilated. "We've got to hurry." He dashed down the stairs, scooped up Beth, and opened the door. Maggie trotted down the walk beside him.

"The towels. I'm going to mess your car," said Beth. "Oh, I think it's another one."

Maggie looked at her watch. "That's twelve minutes."

Jason settled in the backseat. Maggie started the car and pulled out of the parking lot. He barked orders. "Can't you go faster? It's shorter if you cut across Raymond and head up Broadway to Stanton."

That's the way we're going, she thought. She wanted to order him into silence, but she refrained. "Keep your cool. We'll be there in plenty of time. . . . Beth, did you call Dr. Grant?"

"I forgot."

Jason's hands were clenched so tightly, the skin over his knuckles looked jaundiced. Every whimper, every moan, every sound Beth made, jabbed with the force of a thrown knife. He should have been at home instead of at Maggie's. His need for her seemed selfish. How could he have let his daughter face the onset of labor alone? What effect would this have on her heart condition? "Honey, I'm sorry you couldn't find me."

"Daddy, it's all right. I knew Maggie was home and that she'd know what to do."

Her words illuminated his failure. Didn't she think *he* knew what to do? Did she trust Maggie more? Stop it, stop it, he thought. Beth needed a woman to be with her. Of course Maggie understood the things Beth felt. He never could.

"What is Beth going to do when I'm not around to provide a home and financial support? How can she raise a child alone?"

"It's more like you'll be raising her," said Beth.

He hadn't realized he had spoken aloud. How could he take back the words expressing his fears?

"Stop being so negative, both of you," snapped Maggie.

Jason slumped in the seat and grappled with his guilt. What kind of father was he that he couldn't give his child hope?

Maggie swung the car into a spot in the emergency room lot. "When we get inside, stop and call Dr. Grant and Dr. Blanda. Then go to admitting and complete the paperwork. I'll take Beth up to labor and delivery."

A small corner of his thoughts bubbled with resentment. He should be the one in control. He had never felt so dependent, so lost in his life. "I want to be with Beth."

"I can't fill out the forms." The double doors opened. Maggie pulled a wheelchair from the line in the entry. "Sit," she said to Beth. She turned to Jason. "We'll see you upstairs." She pushed Beth down the hall.

" 'Bye, Daddy," called Beth.

Unable to move, Jason stared after them. Papers, phone calls, Beth's in labor. Anxiety rocketed. He gulped a deep breath and reached for the phone on the security guard's desk.

"Sam, Jason here. Beth's in labor. Yes I'm sure. Her water broke. I'll call him."

He hung up. Papers, admitting, Ken Blanda. What's wrong with me? His thoughts darted in a dozen directions. He hadn't been this nervous when Beth was born. He had been calm, in charge, and had patiently listened to Janine's pleas to be put to sleep. Not today, he thought. Through the fog of fear he heard Ken Blanda's voice.

"It's Jason. Beth's in labor. She's here. Sam's on his way in."

The soothing tone of Ken's voice irritated Jason. Of course he was upset. Beth wasn't a patient; she was his daughter. The dial tone registered. He looked around. Beth. He should be with his daughter instead of standing in the hall, acting like an idiot. After hanging up, he charged to admitting. While he filled out papers and wrote a check, he kept one eye on the clock and watched the minutes rapidly disappear.

Maggie pushed Beth down the third floor hall past the patient rooms and through the double doors marked LABOR AND DELIVERY. Her active involvement in this event would soon be over. Jason had attended the birthing classes with Beth. She shook her head. Unless he calmed down, he would be little use in the delivery room.

"Maggie, oooh."

With one hand on Beth's abdomen, Maggie studied her watch. Beth's labor progressed faster than most primiparas usually did. When the contraction ended, she stopped at the desk. "I'm here with Beth Knight. Dr. Grant and Dr. Blanda are on their way."

A nurse hung up the phone. "That was him. Take her to room three. Are you going to stay?"

"Can I?" asked Maggie.

"Please, please," said Beth.

"Until your father comes," said Maggie.

"Good enough." The nurse laid a scrap of paper on the counter. "Don't want her alone. Short staff today," the note read.

Maggie nodded. In room three she helped Beth undress. When Beth was in bed, Maggie applied the monitor leads. The nurse bustled into the room. "Bless you. You must be a nurse."

"Four ortho, nights," said Maggie.

"And you know how to set these things up. They usually play dumb on the regular floors."

"I had to take a C.C.U. course on my way to a B.S."

The nurse stuck a thermometer under Beth's tongue. She reached for the girl's wrist. "What are you doing on the orthopedic unit?"

"I'm a recent refresher."

"That's great. Contractions?"

"Ten minutes apart, moderate strength, lasting about thirty seconds. Her water broke about an hour ago."

The digital thermometer beeped. The nurse fitted a fetoscope on her head and leaned over Beth's abdomen. She held her watch so she could see the second hand. Maggie watched the woman's lips move as she counted. "Strong heartbeat. Looks like this little one is raring to go. Ring me when the next contraction starts."

"Will do," said Maggie.

Beth grasped Maggie's hand. "Will you stay until . . . until . . . Daddy's going to need you."

Maggie inhaled. "Don't even think about leaving us. You're going to be fine."

Beth drew her legs up. She grimaced. "Stop it, please."

Maggie hit the call button. Beth's scream filled the room. The nurse hurried in and timed the contraction. "Now, that was a good one. Ring for the next."

Tears flowed down Beth's face. "I'm scared. It's much too soon for the baby to come."

"Almost eight and a half months," said Maggie.

"But the cleaning lady told me eight-month babies die. Promise me you'll stay with Daddy. He's been alone so long."

The pulse beneath Maggie's fingers raced, skipped several beats, and began again. "Enough hysterics."

"Promise me you'll take care of them."

"Beth, enough. I'll help you with the baby. Your father can take care of himself."

"Are you mad at him again?"

Maggie thought of the morning and of love. "Not one bit, though I must admit he irritated me with his backseat driving this morning."

"Then I can die happy."

Maggie grasped Beth's shoulders. "One more remark about dying and I might slap you. You're not going to die."

441

"She's absolutely right." Sam Grant and Dr. Blanda approached the bed. "She'll slap you and I'll spank you," said Sam.

"You don't understand. My mother had all these reports from doctors. They said my heart will stop."

"Beth!" shouted three voices.

Maggie kissed the girl's cheek. "Rather than slap you, I'll leave. See you later."

"Don't go."

"I'll be in the waiting room." She waved at the nurse as she passed the desk.

Just outside the double doors, she met Jason. "How is she?" he asked.

"Progressing rapidly. Both doctors are with her."

Jason hugged her. "Why don't you go home? I'll call you."

She touched his cheek. "I'll be in the waiting room. I couldn't sleep, so there's no reason for me to leave."

Like a caged animal, Jason paced from the bed to the door of the labor room. Each time Beth cried out, he rushed back to the bed. A half hour after he reached the room, he grabbed Sam's arm. "Do something. How long are you going to let her suffer?"

The burly man shook his head. "She's in labor. Try to think like a doctor. You know we can't rush this."

"I can't."

"Then leave. You're making everyone nervous."

"How dare you say that!" Jason stared at the monitor screen. Beth yelled. Her heart rate accelerated. "Dammit, do something."

Sam grabbed his arm and pulled him to the door. Though half a dozen inches shorter, the obstetrician's beefy body supported more muscle than fat. "Go to the waiting room. Go buy some cigars. Calm yourself down. You're not helping her with all this roaming around. She's doing fine."

"She's tachycardic."

"And being monitored by the best cardiologist on the staff. Do I have to call security?"

Jason shook his head. Sam was right. His presence in the labor room enhanced Beth's fear. Though he strove for calmness, his anxiety rode close to the surface and slipped out too easily. He strode down the hall and paused in the waiting room doorway.

Maggie had curled up on a low orange-plastic-covered couch. He slumped in the chair beside the couch. She opened her eyes. "How's Beth?"

Jason shrugged. "According to Sam, she's doing fine. They threw me out. I couldn't just stand there. Sam said my pacing made them nervous." He grimaced. "What if something happens and I'm not there?"

"Why are you so worried? They're good doctors. She'll be fine."

He rose. "She's not fine. I saw the EKG strip. There was a short period of fibrillation. If she dies, it will be my fault."

"How can you say that?" Maggie touched his arm. "Her heart condition stems from an improperly treated childhood illness. You weren't there."

He walked away from her. "I should have been. I should have realized what Janine had planned."

"Do you read minds? Should I have known what George was doing?"

"That's different." A deep sigh escaped. "I didn't try to please her. I should have kept her from running away."

"Short of making her a prisoner, I don't see how you could have."

Though her words made sense, he couldn't accept the logic. "Go home. Don't you have to work tonight?"

"I'm staying. I love Beth and I love you."

He stopped short. "Don't say that. How can

444

you love me? I'll never be able to make the kind of commitment love demands." He turned away and slouched in a chair.

Jason's withdrawal hurt more than his rejection. How could he close her out? Why did he believe he couldn't love? He had cared about Herman. He loved Beth. Would he continue punishing himself forever?

A nurse wearing white scrubs appeared in the doorway. "Dr. Knight, you have a granddaughter. Six pounds six ounces. Eighteen inches long. Apgar of ten. She has lungs you wouldn't believe."

"How's my daughter? Can I see her?"

Maggie frowned. Had he heard what the nurse said about the baby?

"The doctors are working to stabilize her. I'll let you know when you can see her. In the meantime, why don't you pop by the nursery?"

Maggie reached for his hand. "I'll go along with you."

"You go. I'll wait here."

"Code 99. Code 99, delivery room one."

"That's Beth." Jason pushed Maggie aside. "If I had been with her instead of in bed with you, I could have gotten her here in time."

His eyes looked as though he had passed beyond sanity. "Her labor went too fast for twenty minutes to make a difference."

Jason turned. "Go home, Maggie. I don't need you."

Maggie stared at the closing door. Last night, you did. This morning too. She held back the words. I won't let him push me out of his life. She rubbed her arms with her hands and felt cold and alone.

Reaching Beth became Jason's only goal. He brushed past the nurse who stood at the delivery room door. When he let Janine steal Beth, he had failed her. He wouldn't do that today.

"Dr. Knight, you can't go in there."

"She's my daughter." What right had they to shut him out? What right had Janine to keep Beth from him? His thoughts whipped from the past to the present until he couldn't separate remembered emotions from the ones now shocking his system.

"Beth," he whispered.

The doctors, dressed in white gowns over green scrub suits, cast grotesque shadows on the pale green walls. He watched their lips but couldn't hear what they said. Frantically, he tried to remember what they should do to save his child. If he couldn't remember, how could they succeed?

He crept across the room and stared at the

446

monitor on the crash cart. Ventricular tachycardia. That one lucid thought brought forth nightmarish knowledge. From tachycardia to fibrillation to death in minutes.

He held his breath. The screen showed no positive change. She's not converting. She's going to die. My fault, all mine. I should have insisted—

He heard Beth's voice. "I'll run away and live on the streets."

His eyes widened in horror. Ken Blanda lifted the paddles from the cart. Beth's body jerked in an artificially induced convulsion. Jason turned and fled.

"Dr. Knight, what do you think of your granddaughter?"

"She killed her mother."

He pushed through the double doors and dashed down the hall. His eyes focused on the pay phone and he knew what he had to do.

"Joanna, let me talk to Dave. It's an emergency. . . . Dave, you know the couple who wanted a baby. They can have Beth's. She killed her mother."

In the midst of his friend's protest, Jason slammed down the phone. His head hurt. He needed air. The elevator was too slow. He opened the stairwell door and dashed down the steps as though he were being pursued. As he entered the lobby on the first floor, his name blared from the loudspeaker.

"No," he said. "I can't deal with a patient right now."

The page pursued him as he headed for the door. "Dr. Knight," called the receptionist. "It's Dr. Grant." Jason shook his head. "He says it's urgent."

Jason took the receiver from the woman. "I can't deal with anything right now," he said. "Do whatever has to be done."

"Where the hell are you?"

"Sam, I can't cope."

"With what? Being a grandfather doesn't make you old."

"And that should make me forget Beth's death."

"Are you crazy? Ken and I just took her to C.C.U."

For several seconds Jason mulled over Sam's statement. "She's alive?"

"Get up here and see for yourself."

The weight of guilt lifted. Jason handed the phone to the receptionist. He took the steps to the second floor two at a time. In C.C.U. he saw Sam and Ken. "What room?"

"Eight," said Ken.

Jason crossed the hall and stood just inside the door of the room. Beth looked pale and fragile. Her hair lay in limp, matted strands. Jason walked to the bed. Though he wanted to scoop her up and hold her close, he bent and kissed her cheek. "Oh, baby, you gave me quite a scare. How are you?"

"Tired." Her smile came within a degree of burning him. "Did you see her? She's so pretty. She cried so loud. They said that was good. I wish—"

"What?"

"That I could have her here. I'll worry about her being alone."

"I'm sure the nurses will spoil her. They'll let you know how she's doing."

"It's not the same as holding her. I wanted to breastfeed, but I can't."

"Of course you can't. You'll need all your energy for getting better."

Tears filled her eyes. "I don't want to be an invalid. That won't be fair to her. What do you think of Megan Elizabeth?"

"Who?"

"For her name." She closed her eyes. "I'm so tired."

Jason glanced at the monitor for reassurance. A regular beat showed on the screen. "I bet you are." He kissed her forehead. "I'll be back later."

"Daddy, where's Maggie? She promised she

would stay. I want to see her."

"I sent her home. She has to work tonight."

"Tell her to come and visit." Beth smiled. "I really like her."

"And she likes you." Jason frowned. He heard Maggie confessing love for Beth and for him. What had he said to her? He returned to the open nurses' station, where a line of monitors showed the status of the patients in the rooms.

Ken Blanda smiled. "You look wiped."

"I feel that way. What now?"

"She's doing very well."

"How much damage has this incident caused her heart?"

Ken shrugged. "I can't say without running a number of tests, and I can't schedule them until she's recovered. Maybe a valve replacement is needed. Her collapse today came from the sudden release of all the pressure."

"Do you think she'll be able to take care of a baby?"

"Why not? She'll need help at first, but I don't see any problem."

Sam perched on the edge of the desk. "You're going to need someone soon. The baby will be coming home before Beth. Probably Monday. What sent you running?"

Jason shook his head. "I think I went crazy.

I don't remember . . ." He closed his eyes, but no memories surfaced.

"Shock can cause amnesia." Ken clasped Jason's hand. "Now you know why we don't let families in the room during a code."

Jason nodded. All he remembered was fear and being helpless. He reached for the phone and dialed Maggie's number. Why had she left? She had seemed determined to stay. What had he said? Her phone rang and rang. That's right, he thought. She turns it off so she can sleep.

Maggie sat in the cafeteria, nursing a cup of coffee. Her head ached. How was Beth? Had Jason meant what he had said? He had been frantic. Beth's cardiac status had been shaky. He blamed himself. She understood the stress he had felt, but his words had hurt. Intending to call obstetrics, she put the cup down. As she rose, April and Charlene put trays on the table.

"What are you doing here?" asked April.

"Are you deaf and blind?" Charlene slid onto the chair across from Maggie. "We waved. We called. I even did a bit of soft shoe to get your attention. You been tripping in space-cadet land?"

Maggie smiled. "Beth Knight just had her baby. I drove them here."

"What did she have?" asked April. "We're probably the last to hear."

"A girl, six pounds six ounces."

"Then why so glum?" Charlene's dark eyes widened. "The code. Was that her?"

Maggie nodded. "I haven't found the courage to call."

April put her sandwich on the plate and strode across the large room. Moments later she returned. "She's in C.C.U. and stable."

Maggie sighed. Thank heaven Jason didn't have another death to face.

April frowned. "What death?"

"Herman Stein."

"That's right, they were friends," said April.

Charlene grinned. "So give. What's between you and Jason Knight?"

Where before she would have said they were friends and neighbors, since she had confessed her love and been rejected, she didn't know what to say. "I don't know."

"When you do, make sure we're the first to know." Charlene made a face. "We're always last on the gossip line."

"Speaking of gossip, have you heard about the barber?" asked April. "He's leaving Hudson General."

"Some hospital in Connecticut accepted him on staff. Can you believe that?" asked Charlene.

"I can believe anything," said Maggie.

"Someone said Lorraine's job hunting," said April.

Charlene laughed. "We're thinking about having a bash."

Maggie shook her head. "I won't believe that one until her office is empty."

"You're right," said Charlene. "Queens don't abdicate without a fight. Lordy, look at the time. We're going to get our butts kicked."

Maggie watched April and Charlene scurry out the door. She rose. Home, she thought. Sleep, but first a baby. She rode the elevator to three and walked to the nursery. A masked nurse responded to her tap on the window. "The Knight baby," she said.

The nurse pushed a clear plastic bassinet to the window. Maggie studied the sleeping infant. A lock of hair had been combed into a curl. A Kewpie doll, she thought. She smiled. Beth will need my help with the baby. If Jason lets me. She shook her head. She wouldn't let him push her away again.

Twenty

Jason stood in the emergency room parking lot. The town fire whistles, a Saturday noon event, blared and hooted. Maggie's blue sedan had vanished from the spot where several hours ago she had parked. Had she forgotten she had brought Beth and him to the hospital?

Wave after wave of relief washed away the remains of his fear for his daughter. Ken Blanda had pronounced her out of danger. She was weak. Her condition was fragile. A second shock might send her heart into another round of tachycardia. She might need surgery to replace her mitral valve, but she was alive.

For a moment he thought about the tiny infant he had seen in the nursery. Arms and legs moving, her face red from crying, had brought him memories of Beth as a newborn.

As he started down the hill toward home, exhaustion struck. Herman's death, Beth's cardiac emergency, and his loss of control of the situation added to the physical tiredness he felt. He groaned. What had he said to Maggie during that short period when chaos had completely shattered his sanity? He must have hurt her badly to make her walk away. Her laughter and caring had revitalized his life as much as Beth's arrival had.

He reached the condominiums. For a moment he stood in the lot behind the units. His shoulders slumped. She wasn't there. Where had she gone? A memory slid from behind the shroud of amnesia. He had sent her away; he had said he didn't need her. What else had he said and done during those vanished thirty minutes?

Go home. I don't need you.

I'm staying. I love Beth and I love you.

What had happened to make her leave? He pressed his hands against his temples. The answer refused to come.

He plodded up the walk and unlocked the door of his apartment. He trudged upstairs. The blinker on the answering machine in the living room flashed. He slumped on the couch and listened to the messages. Robyn shouted congratulations. His answering service informed him that a patient had been admitted to the hospital and he should call with orders. He interrupted the machine to call and issue orders. Then he called his nurse and asked her to clear his schedule for the next week. Her excitement over the baby rang in his thoughts until he heard the next message. Frowning, he pressed the replay button.

"Jason, we need to talk about the matter you mentioned this morning. Were you serious?"

What had he said to Dave Evans? He reached for the phone and changed his mind. Right now he felt too battered emotionally and physically to discuss legal matters. He kicked off his sneakers and stretched out on the couch.

With her body aching for sleep and her emotions screaming for comfort, Maggie pulled into the driveway of Laura's ranch house. She slumped in the seat and relived Jason's rejection. Though part of her wanted to make excuses for his behavior, another part was filled with anger at his inability to reach out and share.

The car door opened. A blast of chill air hit her face. "Maggie, what's wrong?"

"Everything."

"Well, don't sit out there. Come in the house."

Moments later she sat on the flowered couch in Laura's living room and held a cup of coffee in her hands. "Thanks."

"So tell me why you look like death."

"Beth had her baby." Maggie sighed. "She coded."

"Died?" asked Laura.

"She's in C.C.U. and stable at present."

Laura shook her head. She took the coffee cup from Maggie's hand. "That's good news. What are you running from?"

"Maybe myself. Jason told me to leave and that he didn't need me." The words gushed out. "We were together when Beth went into labor. She came to me because she couldn't find him. He blames me. He told me to go away. Even when I told him I loved him, he said he didn't need me." The tears she had bottled inside spewed free. "What am I going to do?"

"You're going to go to bed and sleep."

"I have to work tonight."

"You're going to call in sick."

"I'm not and it's the weekend."

"Don't argue. Do you think I'm going to let you drive back and put yourself and every driver on the road in danger?" Laura handed Maggie the phone. "Call now. That will give them time to find a sub."

Though she reluctantly dialed the phone,

Maggie knew Laura was right. Exhaustion had ruined her reflexes and dulled her mind. When she hung up the phone, she looked at her friend. "I feel like a coward."

Laura made a face. "You're a fighter. You always were. Go to bed. When you wake up, you'll see things clearer."

That evening when he left for the hospital to see Beth and at regular intervals on Sunday Jason tried to reach Maggie. Her phone went unanswered; her car was missing from the parking lot. Where was she? He blamed himself for her disappearance. What a mess he had created during that blank period when his usual calm control had been melted by volcanic fear. Would she understand and accept that he had been another person for that time? If not, he had lost again. At least he still had Beth and little Megan.

Late Saturday afternoon, feeling refreshed and ready for any challenge, Maggie kissed Laura's cheek. "Thanks."

"What are friends for if not to add starch when the spine starts wilting. Confront him. Slug it out."

"That's your way."

Laura laughed. "I'm sure you'll find a way that's uniquely yours."

Maggie arrived in Hudsonville at eight. Jason's silver sports car wasn't in the lot behind cluster A. She got ready and left early for the hospital. Before going to see Beth, she stopped at the nursery.

The evening nurse, a short, dark-haired woman came to the anteroom door. "Hi, you're Dr. Knight's friend, aren't you?"

"Neighbor," said Maggie.

"If that's how you want it, but I've heard different. Want to put on a gown and hold her? She's a doll."

A glance at the clock showed Maggie there was time. She pulled on a gown and accepted the infant. She felt a smile lighten her sadness. "She is a beauty." Was this the way Beth had looked when Jason first saw her, she wondered.

"It's a pity she's up for adoption," said the nurse. "I had a hard time believing Dr. Knight would do a thing like that."

"What?" The nurse's statement startled Maggie. The baby cried. Maggie lifted her to her shoulder and rubbed her back. "Where did you hear that?"

"One of the day nurses heard him telling someone that over the phone just minutes after she was born. He said she killed her mother."

"That doesn't make sense," said Maggie. Beth was in C.C.U. Why had she left in such a rush when Jason dashed into the delivery room after the code had been called? "His daughter coded and she's a patient in C.C.U. I'm headed there to see her."

"My friend didn't make this up."

"Maybe she misunderstood, or maybe he wasn't thinking straight. Maybe he was frantic and thought she had died."

"Who, Jason Knight? He's Mr. Cool during codes. Takes control and keeps things running smoothly."

"But he wasn't in control of the code," protested Maggie. She handed the baby back to the nurse. "Just how widespread is this story?"

The nurse shrugged. "Try containing anything around here."

"You're right." Maggie hurried away from the nursery and downstairs to C.C.U. The instant she stepped into Beth's cubicle, she knew the girl had heard the story. Her eyes were bloodshot and red-rimmed, her face swollen. Maggie crossed to the bed and put her arm around Beth's shoulders. "It'll be all right," she crooned.

"How could he do a thing like that?"

"I don't know. Did you ask him?"

"He was in this evening before I heard." Beth sniffed. "Some nurse came in ten minutes ago and told me."

"Just what did you hear?"

"She wasn't a nurse in this place. She said she knew a couple who were desperate for a baby and they would give me enough money to get on with my life. I told her to get out." Beth yawned. "The nurses just brought me something to calm me and it's making me sleepy." She yawned again. "When I said my baby wasn't for sale, she said, 'That's what your father said.' How could he?"

Maggie watched the line on the monitor change. "I don't know, but we're going to find out. Not tonight. I'm due upstairs in twenty minutes and it's too late to call in sick."

Beth clung to Maggie's hand. "How can I protect her? Dr. Grant and Dr. Jensen, the pediatrician, came by today. They said Megan Elizabeth will be discharged tomorrow and that Daddy could make the arrangements. I can't let him take her."

Maggie sat on the chair beside the bed. "Then find out if I can take her until we get this straightened out."

"I don't want to put you in the middle again and give Daddy a chance to be mad at you."

"That won't matter."

"Not again. What's wrong with him? You seem so right together."

"I think he flipped out and went crazy yesterday. When they called the code, he went to pieces. Oh, he acted calm enough, but his eyes . . . He looked like a cornered animal. He pushed me away."

"Why?"

"Something happens to him when someone wants to share his problems. He closes down. I thought that when Herman died and he came . . ." She sighed. "Let's try to solve your problem."

Beth nodded. "Could I come to you when I leave here? Just till I can find a place to live and some kind of job or something."

Maggie nodded. This time she willingly decided to step between Jason and Beth. She needed time to discover the truth before he drove his daughter away.

Beth groped in the bedside stand. "My key. You'll need her clothes and the car seat. You can't take her without it."

"You're right." She took Beth's hand.

Tears trickled down the girl's face. She wiped them with her hand. "If only Daddy loved us the way we do him . . . You know, three people could give one little girl a good home."

Maggie felt hot tears on her cheeks. Why

had Jason made such a dreadful decision, one that wasn't his to make? Why did he want to put his daughter into the same kind of agony he had endured? She reached for the tissue box, and before taking one for herself, offered the box to Beth. "Two people will give her a home full of love."

"Are you sure?"

"Absolutely."

"Maggie, I love you."

"And I love you." She looked away. She loved Jason as well, and instead of a dream, loving him had become a nightmare. "I'll pick up the baby tomorrow morning."

"Megan Elizabeth," said Beth. "Have you seen her?"

"The nurse let me hold her."

Beth sighed. "I wish I could."

"You will. I'll find a way to smuggle her in."

Before Maggie hung up her coat in the locker room, Sue Rawlings grabbed her arm. "This has been some weekend. Is Dr. Knight's daughter really putting her baby up for adoption?"

Maggie slammed the locker door. "Don't believe everything you hear around here. That's all I'm going to say."

"You're no fun. I figured you'd have the inside story." The gray-haired woman followed

Maggie into the lounge. "Well, I do have something for you. Lorraine was in this afternoon. She never comes in on the weekend."

"Maybe she had paperwork she couldn't do at home."

"Maybe she was clearing out her office."

Maggie turned. Bev stood behind Sue. "What?" asked Sue.

"She's had an offer she can't refuse," said Bev.

"As tight as the two of you were, you should know," said Sue.

"Were we friends?" Bev walked to the door. "Let's go count."

Maggie watched the thin nurse walk away. Bev looked different. She moved with more confidence and the beaten look had vanished from her face. Maggie fixed a cup of coffee. Mavis and Joyce wandered into the lounge.

"Did you hear?" asked Joyce.

"I've heard too much gossip today," said Maggie. "See you for report in ten minutes."

At odd and infrequent intervals during a busy night Maggie thought about Jason. Had he really put Beth's baby up for adoption? Could he have done something so hurtful? Had Dr. Blanda told him something about Beth's cardiac status that meant she would never be able to physically care for an infant? Adoption seemed drastic. There were nannies for hire and as the child got older, day care programs available. If he found a partner, he could cut back on his hours at the office. She could—She shook her head. Evidently her involvement with Jason belonged in the past. He hadn't called her or stopped by to talk. His denial of his need for her must be true.

As she left to go home, these thoughts occupied every corner of her mind. Why couldn't he admit he needed someone, if not her, then Beth and the baby? Was being in control so essential to him?

"Maggie . . . Margaret Carr." Katherine Gordon's voice shocked her into awareness.

"Katherine, hi."

"You could get killed walking around in a fog. Do you have time for coffee?"

"A rain check, please. I have a busy day planned."

"No problem." Katherine smiled. "How would you like to be the nurse manager on four ortho?"

Like a bowling ball scattering the pins at the end of the alley, Katherine's question sent Maggie's thoughts flying. "Me? Then the rumors about Lorraine are true?"

Katherine shook her head. "Can't anything

happen around here without the word spreading before it's official? I got her resignation a half hour ago."

"She cleared out her office yesterday."

"Of course. Would you think about taking the job?"

"Aren't there others with more seniority?"

"Perhaps, but four ortho is a troubled unit. We need someone who has your qualities. I'm not asking for an immediate answer. Think about it and come in on Friday at two-thirty and we'll talk."

"I'll do that. Thanks." Maggie turned to leave. Jason stood at the door to the stairs. "Ja—" Before she reached the stairs, he vanished. Maggie walked to the exit. The rumors must be true. Why else would he avoid me?

When Jason saw Maggie engaged in conversation with Katherine Gordon, he decided not to interrupt. The things he had to tell Maggie would take longer than a few minutes. He smiled. At her place or his, they would have the privacy he needed when he told her what she meant to him.

He headed to the fifth floor, where two patients waited to be discharged. As he walked down the hall, he caught several nurses staring with what he considered hostile looks. If he had

466

been on four orthopedics, he would have believed the nurses were expressing their views about his treatment of Maggie. But here?

Twenty minutes later he stopped on four med/surg to see the last of his hospitalized patients. A cluster of nurses became silent as he approached. Several of the women walked away without replying to his greeting.

What else did I do during that half-hour when my actions and my emotions were ruled by chaos? Though he could have cornered someone and demanded an answer, would the person on the spot tell the truth?

With a sigh he headed to C.C.U. He entered Beth's cubicle. "Hi, honey, how are you feeling? Has Ken Blanda been in?"

"Daddy, how could you!"

"How could I what?"

"You know." She turned her head toward the wall. "I don't want to talk about it because my heart pounds and the nurses get excited."

But he didn't know what she meant. Her stony expression told him nothing. She had closed herself behind glass walls and her eyes demanded an answer to a question he didn't know.

"Maggie's going to pick up Megan Elizabeth."

"She doesn't have to. I've cleared my schedule."

467

"No."

"Just no? No explanation?"

"You know why. Please, let's not talk about this anymore. Dr. Blanda said I have to learn how to remain calm."

Jason shifted his weight from foot to foot, not knowing what to say. "I'll come back later. Is there anything you need from home?"

"Nothing. I can't wear my own things here."

Jason stood with his back to her and fought to keep his voice calm. "Don't close me out. You did before. I love you. I went crazy when I thought you were dead. There's a half hour I don't remember."

"You . . . you . . . Daddy, I love you."

Jason looked at the monitor screen and watched Beth's heart rate accelerate to near-dangerous levels. He turned. "I'll go, but we have to talk."

She didn't answer. Jason walked to the door. What had he done? Why couldn't he remember? Maggie, he thought. Even if I've hurt her, she'll tell me.

When Maggie arrived home, Robyn and Joanna waited at her door. Joanna danced from foot to foot. "What took you so long? When I worked at Hudson General, the night nurses hot-footed it out of there five minutes early."

Maggie turned the key in the lock. "Katherine Gordon cornered me."

"About?" asked Joanna.

"She's offered me the nurse manager's job on four ortho."

Robyn stopped at the top of the stairs. "How will you handle Leon Giancardi?"

"If you choose to believe the rumors, he's leaving."

"Good riddance," said Joanna. "Start the coffee. I think I'll binge today."

Maggie filled the coffeemaker, got out cups, spoons, milk, and the remains of a coffee ring from the weekend. "So what brings you here?"

"Jason," said Joanna.

"What happened to him?" asked Robyn. "Sam just shakes his head when I ask."

"Saturday morning he called Dave and said Beth was dead and the baby was up for adoption." Joanna reached for the sugar.

"She called me," said Robyn. "When Sam came home, he said Beth was stable."

Maggie poured coffee into the cups. "I'd say he went crazy." She sat at the table.

"But why?" asked Robyn. "Why would he want Beth to give up her baby after what Janine did to him?"

"I really don't know," said Maggie.

"Probably because he likes everything neat and orderly," said Joanna. "Always on time, always following the rules. Patients are the only people who got more of his time than he scheduled for them. I hope his daughter never learns."

"She has. She's hurt, angry, and fighting to stay calm so she can leave the hospital."

"What is she going to do?" asked Robyn.

"Move in with me."

The pair of women gasped. Joanna nearly dropped her coffee cup. "Are you crazy?" she asked.

"He'll never forgive you," said Robyn.

"He told me to get lost. I'll haunt him. He said he didn't need me. I'll prove that he does."

Joanna laughed. "I love it. Are you going out and buy duplicates of everything?"

Maggie pulled a key from her pocket. "There's no need. Beth gave me her key."

"Are you going to take the baby to the hospital when you work?" asked Joanna.

"Auntie Robyn hereby volunteers." Robyn jumped up. "Let's get moving before he comes home."

"He has office hours," said Joanna. "They're sacred."

By nine-fifteen Maggie, Robyn and Joanna had finished removing baby things from Beth's room. Maggie paused in the kitchen and fastened a note written in bold letters to the refrigerator.

"That should make him think," she said.

"Or confuse him completely," said Joanna.

"Do I get the baby tonight?" asked Robyn.

Maggie shook her head. "Megan Elizabeth is mine tonight and tomorrow night. See you when I get home."

"Wouldn't miss it for the world," said Robyn.

Maggie let them out. As she hurried to take a shower, she wondered how Jason would react to the note.

At quarter to ten Jason spotted Maggie's car in the condominium parking lot. His nurse had managed to cancel all his appointments except for one and he had left the office a half hour after arriving there. As he entered the commons, he wavered between going to see Maggie or getting the baby things. Deciding to ask Maggie to go to the hospital with him for the baby, he unlocked his door and ran up the stairs and sprinted down the hall to Beth's room.

He halted in the doorway and braced his hands on the frame. The bassinet, the car seat, the stacks of clothes that had covered Beth's dresser, had vanished. Who? Why? Beth had insisted Maggie was taking the baby, but he hadn't believed her. He turned and headed to the kitchen, where he put water in the teakettle and set it to boil. As he opened the refrigerator to get milk for the coffee he intended to retrieve from his medical bag, he found Maggie's note.

How could you do to Beth what Janine did to you?

He frowned and sat at the kitchen table. After pulling the instant coffee jar from his medical bag, he poured the water. The aromatic steam rose from the cup as he read the note again.

The shroud of amnesia tore. He entered chaos again, but this time as a viewer rather than a participant. I didn't, he thought, but he knew he had. He groaned. How could he make it right? He had ruined Beth's image of him and hurt Maggie.

Maggie, he thought. He needed her smile, her laughter, and her kind of concern for others. Leaving the untouched cup of coffee on the table, he hurried to her unit. Though he rang the doorbell a dozen times, she didn't answer. He sucked in a deep breath. If he couldn't see her, he had to talk to Beth, and though it hurt, he had to tell her he accepted her decision to leave his house.

The chill air stung his face. Grief burned in

his chest. Though he had wished he could keep Beth forever, forever had ended today.

At the hospital he walked up the stairs and entered C.C.U. He stood in the doorway of Beth's cubicle. She looked up. "Hello."

"I love you. When I thought you were dead, I shattered into a thousand pieces. I came to tell you I'm backing off. Will you at least come to see me and bring Megan Elizabeth?"

"Oh, Daddy, we'll be just next door." She smiled. "You might consider asking Maggie if she'll let you come to see us."

"I'd like to ask her more than that." His shoulders slumped. "I don't even know where she is."

"In the nursery, getting my daughter and trying to find a way to smuggle her in to see me. You could help her with that."

Jason crossed the room in three steps. He pulled Beth into his arms. "I love you. I love the baby. I love Maggie."

"Why don't you go tell her that?"

"I'm on my way." Jason bolted from the cubicle, pushed through the C.C.U. double doors, and dashed up the stairs. He laughed. Control had been lost on the day he had first seen Maggie and again the day Beth had come into his life. He had just been grasping at the rigid armor he had worn for years while it rusted and fell apart. He paused in the doorway of the nursery and watched Maggie and his granddaughter.

Maggie grabbed one of the baby's moving legs and slipped it into the sleeper leg. She brushed the curls from her forehead. "Stay still. It's been ages since I've done this." She captured the other leg and then snapped the one-piece garment.

As she put on the baby's sweater, she bit her lip. "Little clothes mean little buttons." A man's chuckle caused her to turn her head.

Jason grinned. "Don't you wish you'd opted for a nursery assignment?"

Maggie picked up the baby. "Hardly. I can't imagine anyone choosing to confine herself with fifteen or more screaming babies."

He moved closer. She couldn't read the meaning of his facial expression. "Yet, you've chosen to live with one."

"It's temporary until someone whose name is unmentionable comes to his senses. Jason, how could you!"

He put his arm around her waist. "Would you believe until I read your note, the only thing I remember about Saturday was telling you I didn't need you? I lied."

"That's the story I've been spreading."

He ran a finger along the baby's arm. "She

looks like Beth."

A tiny hand grasped his finger. Maggie watched his gaze soften. He looked like a man besotted. "What are you going to do?" she asked.

He looked up. For an instant, desire flashed in his blue eyes. She sighed. "Try to share as much of her life as you and Beth will allow . . . Who's going to stay with my Meggie when you're at work?"

"Robyn volunteered."

He lifted the car seat to the dressing table. "Do you think she'd mind being bumped by a grandfather?"

"I think she'll dance around the commons."

"Will Beth let me?"

"We'll have to ask her."

"We can pretend the carrier's my medical bag."

Maggie laughed and put the baby in the infant seat.

Jason lifted the carrier. He reached for Maggie's hand and hurried her out the door. He pushed open the stairwell door. Carefully, he put the car seat on the floor and pulled Maggie into his arms. "I've wanted to do this since I saw you dressing the baby."

Maggie slid her arms around his neck. "Why didn't you?"

"A bit public, don't you think." His tongue slid along her lips. She leaned into the kiss.

"April, close your eyes. There's an X-rated scene ahead," said Charlene.

Maggie tried to wiggle from Jason's arms, but he held her close. "I guess we're undone."

April paused on the step just before the landing. "We have an exclusive, my friend."

"That we do." Charlene winked. "Mag, how we gonna respect you when you're the boss?"

"I promise not to have a messy desk," said Maggie.

April hooted. "You're all right, boss lady." She moved past them and joined Charlene.

The black nurse waved. "See you guys."

When the pair of young nurses disappeared, Jason released Maggie. "What was that all about?"

"This morning Katherine offered me Lorraine's job." She shook her head. "I can't believe the way news travels around here."

"Let's go tell Beth about us before she hears a rumor. I figure we have three minutes." Jason lifted the baby. He reached for Maggie's hand. "I love the way you care about others. I love the way you care about me. I love you, Maggie Morgan Carr. You're a mood elevator, a cardiac stabilizer, and an aphrodisiac."

Maggie laughed. "I love you. Let's introduce

Megan Elizabeth to her mother and let Beth know her matchmaking schemes have finally succeeded."

She stood on tiptoe and kissed his cheek.

Taylor—made Romance From Zebra Books

LET ARCHER AND CLEARY
AWAKEN AND CAPTURE YOUR HEART!

CAPTIVE DESIRE   (2612, $3.75)
by Jane Archer

Victoria Malone fancied herself a great adventuress and student of life, but being kidnapped by handsome Cord Cordova was too much excitement for even her! Convincing her kidnapper that she had been an innocent bystander when the stagecoach was robbed was futile when he was kissing her until she was senseless!

REBEL SEDUCTION   (3249, $4.25)
by Jane Archer

"Stop that train!" came Lacey Whitmore's terrified warning as she rushed toward the locomotive that carried wounded Confederates and her own beloved father. But no one paid heed, least of all the Union spy Clint McCullough, who pinned her to the ground as the train suddenly exploded into flames.

DREAM'S DESIRE   (3093, $4.50)
by Gwen Cleary

Desperate to escape an arranged marriage, Antonia Winston y Ortega fled her father's hacienda to the arms of the arrogant Captain Domino. She would spend the night with him and would be free for no gentleman wants a ruined bride. And ruined she would be, for Tonia would never forget his searing kisses!

VICTORIA'S ECSTASY   (2906, $4.25)
by Gwen Cleary

Proud Victoria Torrington was short of cash to run her shipping empire, so she traveled to America to meet her partner for the first time. Expecting a withered, ancient cowhand, Victoria didn't know what to do when she met virile, muscular Judge Colston and her body budded with desire.

Available wherever paperbacks are sold, or order direct from the Publisher. Send cover price plus 50¢ per copy for mailing and handling to Zebra Books, Dept. 4220, 475 Park Avenue South, New York, N.Y. 10016. Residents of New York and Tennessee must include sales tax. DO NOT SEND CASH. For a free Zebra/ Pinnacle catalog please write to the above address.

CATCH A RISING STAR!

ROBIN ST. THOMAS